**Dear Reader,**

After three decades, w

Here in Australia and New Zealand, Harlequin Mills &
Boon is nearly thirty years old and our range of books
has kept on growing with us. So much so that it's now
hard to bring you all our new titles at the start of each
month - there just isn't enough room on the shelves!

So, starting next month some of your favourite series
will be available at the beginning of the month and others two weeks later. You will find full details about this
change - from June - on the inside front and back covers
of this book. There, you will see which Harlequin Mills &
Boon series will be available from the 1st of every
month, and which series will be in-store from the 16th
of every month.

This means that there'll now be exciting new books
coming out every two weeks rather than every four
weeks. And you will still have at least four weeks, sometimes longer, in which to buy your favourite Harlequin
Mills & Boon series. And if you're one of our many readers who visits the Harlequin Mills & Boon section two
or more times a month, you can now count on seeing
new books there *every second week*!

Happy reading!

**The Team**
**Harlequin Enterprises (Australia) Pty Ltd**

# Down to the Wire

# LYN STONE

Harlequin
Mills & Boon

*Intimate*

First Published 2004
First Australian Paperback Edition 2004
ISBN 0 733 55277 3

Published by
Harlequin Mills & Boon
3 Gibbes Street
CHATSWOOD NSW 2067
AUSTRALIA

Printed and bound in Australia by
McPherson's Printing Group

**LYN STONE**

is a former artist who developed an avid interest in criminology while helping her husband study for his degree. His subsequent career in counter-intelligence and contacts in the field provide a built-in source for research when writing suspense. Their long and happy marriage provides firsthand knowledge of happily-ever-afters.

This book is dedicated to the retired
Special Agent Ray Mixon and his family,
Molly, Joyce, Donna, Debbie, Eddie and Billy.
Thanks for being such good friends all these years.

# Prologue

"Corda never should have gone to Colombia in the first place, considering his past three assignments. He hasn't had more than five consecutive days off in the last three years. DEA's using him up." Holly Amberson tossed the classified folder she was holding onto the table, shook her head and clicked her tongue. "You'll have a dead body or a burned-out shell if you don't extract him now."

"Thank you, Holly," Jack Mercier said, appreciating her concern for a fellow agent she had yet to meet. If she had a fault, it was the fact that she wanted to mother them all, even though at twenty-eight Holly was the second youngest person in the room. But profiling was her main trick, so her take was very credible.

He looked around the circular conference table at the new team he was forging, a conglomeration of exceptional talent gleaned from major government agencies in an attempt to pool those contacts and resources for Homeland Security, its Terrorist Threat Integration Center in particular.

The concept was not unique, but the personnel present were. The team, named Sextant, Latin for the six segments of a circle, would have carte blanche to combat terrorist threats any way they saw fit, hopefully before any acts were implemented. Almost six months old, Sextant was a civilian special ops prototype meant to erode the rivalry that currently existed among the agencies of the government. Its success was essential.

He had given them Corda's file and they'd had overnight to consider what they thought should be done. Now he was addressing them in order of hire. Though Jack was the leader by virtue of appointment from his position at the National Security Agency, and had the final say, their ranks were equal and their opinions crucial in forming this and any other decision affecting the team. "Will, your input?"

"I say let Corda finish up or all he's done so far down there will be for nothing and he'll be mad as hell. Probably with *you* for pulling him out."

Jack gave only cursory notice to the playful, nearly concealed kick under the table Holly issued Will for disagreeing with her.

Camaraderie had formed already, amazing Jack with how well they all got along considering their diversity. And how accustomed they were to calling the shots in their former jobs.

Holly, his first recruit, had been Special Agent in Charge of an FBI counter-terrorism team based right here in McLean, VA. Will Griffin had distinguished himself with the ATF in Houston, rising to a supervisory position very quickly.

But there were the others to hear from on the issue of Joseph Corda and his final mission for the Drug Enforcement Agency. Clay Senate was formerly with the CIA in covert ops and would know more about Corda's actual situation than any of them. "Your assessment, Clay?"

"Make contact. Give him the choice. I agree with Will. Corda will turn his resentment this way if we yank him now."

"Clay's right," Eric Vinland said before being asked. "Besides, if Corda's to be a member of this outfit, he's supposed to get a vote, too. Right?"

Eric's boyish smile flashed. Clay couldn't get over how young Vinland looked compared to the others, even Holly. And how deceptively naive he could seem. Yet he was a master player when it came to infiltration, blending with the enemy, as he had done for the Defense Intelligence Agency during the past six years.

"I'll go," Eric said, as if it were a done deal, the decision already made. He was good at reading faces and Jack suspected his own had just been read.

"No, not you. We'll contract this one out," Jack told him, watching for any sign of resentment or surprise. He purposely didn't give Vinland his reasons. Maybe it was unnecessary to keep testing them the way he did, but the overall mission of the team was vital. He needed to examine every nuance.

Instead of arguing, Eric shrugged, as if he had fully expected that answer. "Then I've got just the person."

Eric casually slid a file past the one empty chair at the table, the vacant place waiting for Joseph Corda to complete the circle and make Sextant complete.

# Chapter 1

By all rights, he should be dead as a doornail.

Joe Corda lay where he had fallen during the attack, his 9mm as empty as his soul, the last round spent. He surveyed the clearing full of bodies. Five, by his count, maybe another one over in the bushes.

They were new recruits, all of them, little or no training, couldn't shoot worth spit. Half of them probably shot one another. Some death squad. He had heard them coming for a quarter of a mile.

Joe felt the sting then. A ricochet must have caught him, or maybe a graze. The nick on his forehead oozed blood, already drawing flies. The whole blamed country was filled with flies. And damned mosquitoes the size of bats. He slapped at his neck, swatted the insects away and wiped the blood off on his sleeve.

Close call, he thought. Close, but certainly acceptable when this was practically a suicide mission to begin with. The chief hadn't called it that, but Joe had known going in that it would be worse than dicey. This was the fourth such assignment he had survived within the last couple of years. The third one to end on a similar note. This script was definitely getting old.

"Just ain't my time right now," he muttered. His own words, even spoken that quietly, rang clear in the silence around him. God, he had sounded almost disappointed.

Hearing what he'd said and how he said it suddenly tripped some trigger within him, alerting him to the fact that death no longer bothered him all that much. Even the flashes of precognition he'd had the night before hadn't upped his pulse rate. They came as he had hovered on the edge of sleep, two brief still shots. One, of the business end of an automatic staring at him like a big round eye about to wink out his life. The other, a quick glimpse of Humberto's woman looking scared to death.

He usually didn't waste time dwelling on death, especially his own, but for some reason, now it was hard not to. He had been teasing it, maybe even courting it this time. Probably on the other missions, too, now that he thought about it.

"The big sin," he grunted.

He was no stranger to sin, of course, even big ones. In his thirty-two years, he had broken just about every commandment sent down from the mountain and a few he was sure God forgot to tell Moses to write down. Not that Joe claimed to be all that religious. Not even close to a good Catholic anymore. But early lessons stuck and he did recall that suicide was the one biggie that kept you out of the churchyard.

Joe shook his head, realizing he was a little out of it right now. The adrenaline still pumped through him like a shot of pure horse.

"Good thing I'm quitting," he muttered aloud. He'd gotten reckless. Cocky. It was time to get out of the business. And he was going to. This was his last gig with DEA. His papers had gone in. It would be official now that this mission was over. He would go home, do his report and be done with it all. He wondered if the new job would be something where he wasn't so tempted to dare the devil the way he'd been doing. If not, he'd decline it.

The shine had rubbed off his enthusiasm pretty early in the game, but he liked to think the core of it was still in there somewhere. He just couldn't find it anymore.

Dad sure would want it to be there. Giving up on any thing was not an option for him. His native Cuba had at least one refugee who'd become American all the way to the bone before he reached puberty. José Corda was a Yank for sure, and he had bred his son to value freedom, to fight for right and be a stand-up guy. Two voluntary stints in 'Nam and a chest full of medals said a lot about what the old man believed. Joe had spent most of his life just trying to measure up.

The mission here was straightforward enough: get inside the cartel, pinpoint the fields for destruction, wreak all the havoc he could at the compound and destroy Carlos Humberto.

Drugs were now the main export here. A damned shame as Colombia was a beautiful country rich with emeralds, gold and even platinum. Paramilitary groups were everywhere, all financed by the drug trade, all unstable as a crate of Mason jars filled with nitro.

Three months were enough. Joe was off the clock as of today. He'd cut it very close, satisfied everything would hit the fan in less than a half hour after he left. He glanced at his watch. Yeah, the truck would have blown by now. The sheds had gone up. He'd heard the explosions not long before these shooters showed up. The crop dust would happen tomorrow or the next day.

Joe had effectively cut off the head of one snake, for all the good it would do in a country writhing with them. Humberto's current shipment of heroin had blown sky-high before it reached the plane. He'd take the heat from higher up when his coca and opium poppy crops fell to the aerial eradication.

Joe only wished he had been able to make the payroll in Humberto's fireproof safe disappear, too. But what he had accomplished should do the trick.

He wiped his face again and reached in his pocket to find his extra clip.

"Ah, amigo, do not trouble yourself to reload," came the silky dark voice of Humberto.

The rascal spoke English, which he had never done before within Joe's hearing. Joe was supposed to be Cuban, highly recommended to Humberto by one of his main contacts in the States who had turned helpful after he had been apprehended with a suitcase full of uncut heroin.

Joe's vision from last night had just become reality. He had known it would.

Humberto held the automatic loosely, but his finger was twitching on the trigger. The deadly eye of the barrel stared at Joe.

He looked away, nodding in the direction of the bodies of Humberto's men. "You got here a little late for the fireworks, Slick."

Humberto's black eyes were menacing, his teeth gritted. "You have destroyed my life, Corda. I shall enjoy killing you. It is the one pleasure left to me now."

"Found out my name, huh? Somebody been telling tales out of school?"

Humberto nodded slowly. "Oh yes. Someone you trust."

"Well, that really narrows it down. Humor me. Curiosity might kill me before you get the chance. Who was it?"

"Very well, why not? The final word you hear, Corda, will be the name of your Judas." Humberto stepped closer, firmed the grip on his weapon, pointed it directly at Joe's chest and opened his mouth to speak.

Joe instinctively ducked to one side just as a single round barked. Strange, he should have felt the impact before he heard the sound. And there should have been more than one.

"God, don't tell me you missed at that range," he said, laughing, waiting for the burst of fire that would finish him off. This was it. He braced.

"I never miss," came the soft, calm, unaccented voice of a woman.

Joe jerked upright again. Humberto was gone. Instead, cool as the proverbial cucumber, there stood the goddess. She kicked at Humberto's dropped automatic with the toe of her boot and strode over to peer down into the ravine where Humberto lay. "Chest shot. Dead center."

That's what they all called her at the compound, *The Goddess.* She was a knockout. Long wheat-colored hair, sea-blue eyes, perfect build—not skinny, certainly not fat. Perfection. Humberto's houseguest or hostage or mistress. No one was quite sure. Maybe even Humberto hadn't quite made up his mind about that yet.

Joe blew out the breath he'd been holding, then laughed again, more rationally this time. "You be sure to tell me what old Hummy did or didn't do that pissed you off that much. I'll make a note."

She almost smiled, but seemed to think better of it. Considering what she'd just done and since her Beretta now rested beside one well-shaped thigh, Joe didn't believe she intended to carry out Humberto's plan for him.

Instead, she gave him her free hand. "Get up. It would be a good idea to leave now. Morales will send someone else out if the men do not return soon. He will probably do that anyway. For Humberto. The place was an inferno when I left. No one even noticed me leaving."

Joe struggled to his feet, weaving a little once he was standing.

The hand she had offered him felt cold to the touch, even in this heat. And it had trembled just a little. Ms. Sure-shot obviously wasn't quite as unaffected by all this as she would like him to think she was.

"You coming with me?" he asked as politely as he knew how. She was holding a pistol, after all.

"I can hardly go back," she retorted, but her voice remained pleasant. Almost too deliberately calm. She looked over at the ravine again. "I got rid of the money. He'll be blamed since only he and Morales had access to it. Supposedly."

"My my. I wonder how you managed that." He smiled for real. "And why you did it."

She gave a half shrug. "I figured it was time someone made a move. It seemed you were planning to retire there."

"Not hardly." There was no sound in the ravine, but it wouldn't hurt to make sure Humberto was dead. He started to go check.

She grasped his elbow, halting him. "Forget it. We don't have the time. Grab another weapon and let's move out."

"You're not Spanish," he observed as he scooped one of the automatics off the ground and checked the magazine. In the week since she had arrived at Humberto's stronghold, he had never heard her use anything other than Spanish, pure and accent free. Now she spoke English like a Vassar graduate.

"Brilliant deduction," she replied, plowing through the undergrowth ahead of him.

"Are you somebody's little agent, by any chance?" he asked.

She scoffed. "I am no one's *little* anything, Mr. Corda."

He brushed aside a prickly frond and turned sideways to slip between two trees. She *was* little and cut a narrow path. "A freelance...what, then? Mercenary?"

She stopped for a second to adjust her boot. The woman had a wicked, dimpled smile that turned a man inside out and left his guts exposed. Anyway, that's just what it felt like when she turned it on him now, and she wasn't even applying it full force. However, her eyes weren't playing the same game as those lips of hers.

"Think of me as a student of human nature." She had pocketed her pistol after shooting Humberto, and picked up one of the AK-47s. It now rested in the crook of one arm, the barrel pointed too close to his foot.

Joe backed up a step, pursed his lips and fitted the automatic he had chosen into a more comfortable position to carry. "You picked some strange specimens to study," he observed with a heavy sigh.

She brushed aside the bushes with her forearm. "I'm not quite finished yet," she informed him. "I have one left to dissect."

"You talking about me?" he asked. She was having to work at being clever. Working damned hard and pretty much succeeding, he had to give her that. But he sensed something in her that she wasn't about to reveal to him. Her movements were a little too studied. But there was no point in provoking her right now by calling her on it. "You can't be talking about me."

Her low, sultry laugh sent chills down his spine despite the intense heat of the jungle at midday. He got the feeling she was already taking him apart, piece by piece. Trouble was, he didn't mind it. Not at all.

She pushed past him to take point. He didn't mind that either since it sure improved the scenery up ahead. She looked pretty damned good in those jungle fatigues Humberto had provided for her. *Hot* was the word and it had nothing to do with the weather.

"Would hanging out with you count as a death wish?" he asked just to make conversation.

She stopped and turned all the way around to face him again, her eyes narrowed as if she really were studying him. "What makes you ask such a thing?"

"I'm drawing the line at suicide," he told her. "I just decided that a few minutes before you showed up."

He watched her prop a hand on her hip and incline her head as she shook it. "One of a kind, aren't you?"

Joe grinned at her assessment. "I devoutly hope you believe that. You have a real name, or should I just keep calling you Goddess like all the other *bastardos* around here?"

"Martine," she admitted after a few seconds of dead silence.

"Great, can I call you Marty?" he asked as she turned to take the lead again.

"Not while I'm holding a weapon," she replied wryly. "Last warning."

"Martine it is." He could be agreeable when necessary. "Do you have a last name, or are you so well known you only need one, like Cher or Sting?"

"Just Martine for now. We'd better go find Vargas."

She said nothing else until they reached the outskirts of Paloma Blanca. Neither did he. Joe knew she was psyching herself up to deal with what might happen next, just as he was.

Things were about to get even more interesting.

Miguel Vargas, whom the natives knew as Father Miguel, was Joe's only contact in the area, though he hadn't had the chance—or even a good reason—to meet with him yet. He had received a spiel about Vargas's background and mission before coming down here since they were supposed to be coordinating their efforts. It had been as brief as the one Vargas probably received on him, Joe was sure. There was that old thing with the agencies di-

vulging as little info as humanly possible to each other,.
even when lives were at stake.

Martine obviously knew that was where Joe was headed
and why and who Vargas really was. It was time she
explained a little more fully how she had found that out.

"Hold up a minute," he demanded before they left the
shelter of the forest and entered the village.

She stopped until he reached her side. She was no
longer smiling, which didn't surprise him much. There
wasn't a helluva lot to be tickled about in their situation.
"Let me see Vargas alone first," she said.

"Why? Confession?"

"Trust me."

Joe snorted. "Yeah, right."

She said nothing.

Vargas was no more a priest than Joe was. He was with
the Company, the CIA. Joe figured he probably did some
good for the natives just to kill time. You had to walk the
walk in a situation like this.

"Why don't you tell me exactly what you *are* doing
here, Martine. If it's classified, just say so and I'll shut
up."

She blew out a sigh, then tightened her lips.

"C'mon," he urged. "What's the deal?"

With a quick glance toward the village, she then looked
back at him. "I need to ask Vargas something." She
moved on as she spoke, walking a few steps ahead of
him. There was this little hitch in her voice. Just a quiver
like women sometimes got just before they let loose with
the tears.

Joe didn't believe she was going to cry, not for a hot
second. A woman who could shoot a man and not blink
would hardly be the weepy kind. He'd give Martine the
benefit of the doubt. After all, she could have blown him
away just as easily as she had Humberto.

The trail widened, so Joe moved up to walk beside her.

"So, how'd you hook up with Humberto?" he asked, trying his level best not to sound judgmental, even though he was.

"He found *me,*" she told him as she looked him straight in the eye. "I was on my way to find Vargas. The jeep I hired in Bogotá hadn't quite made it to Paloma Blanco when Humberto intercepted us. He obviously knew the driver who must have alerted him I was coming. I had no choice about going with him to the compound." She hesitated, just a beat. "So I complied."

"Played along, huh? You must have had a good reason to leave Bogotá when you know it's so dangerous outside the cities."

"Yes."

"Want to tell me what it was?" he asked.

"Not yet."

Joe clicked his tongue and pursed his lips. "O-kay. You haven't seen Vargas at all, then?"

"No," she said. "That squad you took care of back there—" she said, nodding the way they had come "—they knew this is where you were headed."

"So you followed…and armed. How resourceful of you," Joe said without sarcasm.

"I listen a lot," she admitted. "And I'm very good with locks."

"That how you got to the money?"

"Precisely," she confessed. "I figured Humberto would have a hard time explaining what happened to it. That the rebels were likely to take him out of commission permanently. It was slated for the purchase of weapons. But you knew that."

"Yeah. What did you do with it?"

"I hid it under the seat in the truck that was leaving."

*The truck he had set to blow sky high.* Joe laughed out loud. She had a mind on her, this girl.

"You don't believe me?"

He just smiled. Hell, he wanted to kiss her senseless. She was his new best friend. She had wrapped up his assignment as if they'd planned it out together in detail.

"All right," she said with an air of nonchalance that made him see red. "Believe what you will. I only have to see Vargas and then get us out of here."

"Then let's do it," he suggested, stepping into the clearing ahead of her. Maybe he was taking a chance, having her at his back with a loaded weapon, but her leaving the country within the next twenty-four hours probably depended on his staying alive to help make it happen. *Probably* being the key word, of course. She could have other plans.

"I called for a pickup. In code, of course," she said in a low voice as they wound around through the ramshackle huts to Vargas's temporary home.

"You simply phoned home, I suppose?"

"Exactly. I called my contact in Bogotá from the compound and gave a prearranged signal."

"So where's the rendezvous?" he demanded.

"We'll discuss it later." Her tone did not invite a debate, so Joe let it be. Anyway, Vargas would have something arranged in the way of transportation.

The villagers they encountered seemed very careful not to notice them. Joe could hardly blame them when both he and Martine were wearing the green camouflage uniforms worn by the paramilitary ELN faction. *National Liberation movement, indeed.*

Though she'd been nervous before, Joe noticed she had suddenly stopped trying to hide it from him. "Does it seem unnaturally quiet here to you?" she whispered.

"Wouldn't *you* cut the conversation if two armed strangers were prowling your streets? There was a massacre in La Gaberra not long ago. A few of General Silva's guys strolled in and wiped out every living soul, right down to the old folks and the kids. I'm just surprised these people aren't already running for the hills.''

Joe saw no reaction of horror from her. Either she didn't believe him, she'd already known about the event or atrocities didn't bother her. She was hard to figure.

''Where are you from?'' she asked, forgetting her suggestion that they not exchange biographies at the moment. She didn't sound all that interested anyway. She was too busy checking doorways and rooftops for threats. It didn't look like she was a novice at that, either.

''California,'' he lied. Turnabout was fair play. She'd know he was lying, of course. He was about as south-in-the-mouth as Andy of Mayberry when he wasn't speaking Dad's Espanole.

She halted, her gaze fastened on the largest of the shacks, and threw out an arm to stop him before they left the alley. ''That must be it.''

He smiled down at her. ''Yeah, well, there's a cross on top so it's safe to say it's not the grocery store.''

She looked up, biting her lip for a minute as if she had something she wanted to say. Then she sighed and tucked the Beretta in the back of her belt. ''Wait here for me.''

He figured the worst that could happen was that she would turn over her information to Vargas and Joe wouldn't get to hear what it was. That was okay by him. She had her own agenda, he had his.

Joe just couldn't imagine any agency he knew sending a woman like her down here to take care of business. *Any* business at all, but especially this kind of thing. Her beauty would make her too vulnerable, no matter how well trained she was.

''Sure, go ahead.'' He looked at his watch. ''Five minutes?''

''Five's good,'' she said, sounding distracted. ''Thank you.''

He nodded and watched her cross the road and disappear into the open doorway of the ramshackle church.

Had someone sent her here to check his progress? Or maybe Vargas's? Was she with the Company? She had obviously known what Joe's job was all along.

*Five minutes, hell.* He wanted to know what was going on here. Cursing under his breath, he readied his weapon and headed for the chapel.

When he ducked to enter, a bullet thunked into the door frame just beside his ear. Two more rounds echoed the instant he dropped and rolled. Damn, it was so dark in here after the bright outdoors, he couldn't see.

"Hold your fire," she shouted. "He's dead."

Joe's eyes adjusted rapidly. The agent cum priest lay sprawled across the floor in front of his rough-hewn pulpit, pistol still gripped in his hand. Another man lay across the room, also dead.

Question was, who had fired first? And why?

# Chapter 2

Joe lowered his own weapon. Maybe not a smart move. She could do him next, but he figured if that was her intention, she would have done it before now. "What the hell happened?"

She shrugged and pursed those tempting lips. Like that was supposed to shift his attention? He had to admit, it did just a little and that made him mad.

"The other man shot Vargas when he leaped to protect me. And I just…reacted."

"Oh, what a relief it wasn't planned," Joe said sarcastically. "Never mind that Vargas was the one who was supposed to get us a ride out of this drug den."

"I told you we have a way out." There was the slightest hitch in her voice again. "You still believe Vargas was one of the good guys?" she asked. "I think he might have turned."

"Might have?" Joe looked at the dead man again.

That sort of brought up the question of whose guys *she* might be one of, Joe thought with a grimace. He'd hate

to kill her. Never had killed a woman. But then again,
he'd never had real reason to. He sure hoped he didn't
have one now.

It was then Joe recalled again the vision he'd had of
her face. Probably only a dream. He'd been half asleep at
the time, had even had a drink with Humberto before he
went to bed. It was impossible to know if it had been an
actual flash, one of his blinks of the future like the one
of Humberto's gun staring him in the face. But he could
see the one of her even now in all its detail. The face of
the goddess, frozen with terror.

He almost laughed. What a crock. This woman would
never wear an expression like that even if he held the gun
to her head and meant business. He shook off the memory.

"You want to tell me what's going on or are you waiting for me to guess?" he asked.

She ignored his question as she removed the weapons
from Vargas and the unknown corpse. When she gave
them to Joe, he noticed her hands. The long fingers were
graceful, yet not delicate. Her nails were beautifully
shaped, yet not overly long, the smooth ovals devoid of
anything, even a coat of clear polish. The outer edges of
her palms, like his, were ridged, a result of intensive,
long-term martial arts training. Trouble was, hers were
shaking. Just a little bit, but the tremor was there.

He thought about turning one palm side up and checking her life line, then decided he didn't want to know if
the crease had a sudden break in it. His own fate seemed
directly related to hers at the moment. Living was looking
better and better.

"Vargas could be the one who gave you up. I was
present when Humberto received a message from someone here today that gave him a heads-up on what you
were doing. But whoever sent it didn't know your face,
couldn't describe you. When you left the compound and
headed for Paloma Blanco, Humberto figured it must be

you. He decided to terminate you in private, just in case there was another operative within the compound he didn't know about.'' She shrugged. ''Then after you left, all hell broke loose, and Humberto knew for certain you were the one.''

''If that's true and you already have a chopper coming for us, why did we come here? To get rid of Vargas?''

''No. I needed to talk to him. Ask him some questions. Too late for that now.'' She shook her head.

''Well, one of them would have killed me if you had let me walk in here with you. So you saved me again,'' Joe said. ''Jim Dandy to the rescue.''

''What?''

''Old song. I'm into golden oldies. What do you like? Classics? Salsa, maybe?''

She frowned. ''Jazz. What does that have to do with anything?''

Joe sighed and stood up. ''Nothing, I guess. Just seems a shame to be dodging bullets in the company of a total stranger. They'll be coming after us, Martine. Now would be a good time for us to get acquainted. Who are you with?''

''I'm with an independent contractor. Your boss hired us to see that you made it home.''

''Which boss?''

She shrugged. ''Mercier.'' When Joe didn't reply, she added, ''With Sextant.''

''Wrong answer. Mercier already sent someone to give me a hand and extract me early. I declined.'' Too much info to part with, maybe, but Joe wanted some answers.

''He actually made it here? Contacted you?'' Her blue eyes flew wide with what looked like hope. ''When?''

''Two nights before you showed up, I think. It was dark as pitch. I never saw him. No one did. In and out like a shadow.''

''Thank God,'' she murmured, crossing herself. ''That

was Matt Duquesne. My brother.'' She shrugged. ''We were to meet back in Bogotá but he was gone too long. I figured he must have run into trouble. He must have opted for a route out without involving Vargas. He might have sent a message I didn't receive. Or sent it after I left the hotel.''

''That's what you were going to ask Vargas? About Duquesne?''

She sighed. ''Yes. Unfortunately. When Humberto brought me to the compound, there was no indication Matt had ever been there. And of course, you still were. So I thought Matt might have been…'' She let her voice trail off as if he should be able to fill in the blanks. Then she abandoned her search and looked directly at him. ''You're sure he got out without being caught or followed?''

Joe shrugged. ''He was invisible and split right after we spoke. No shots, no ruckus. Yeah, I'd say he made it without a hitch.''

She cleared her throat and continued searching the place. ''Humberto found out pretty quickly who I am. My prints are on file and the man had connections in the States you would not believe. He emailed my employer and demanded a ransom for me, meanwhile knocking himself out trying to convince me to stay voluntarily.'' She scoffed. ''Such a charmer, wasn't he?''

Joe didn't want to talk about Humberto charming her. Humberto had been pretty close-mouthed about it himself. Joe had just assumed the Goddess was simply Humberto's new mistress. He didn't want to think about that at all. Or the things she must have had to do to get virtual freedom within the compound. Damn, she'd even read the man's email?

She rose and dusted her hands against the legs of her pants. ''All right, we can go now. Time is short. I'll need to call as soon as we get safely away and see if Matt made it.''

"No one but me ever realized your brother was there. He must be damn good at what he does. He might have run into a little trouble on the way back, but I expect he could handle that, don't you?"

"I hope so," she said. "He's all I have."

It all sounded plausible the way she told it. Whatever the truth, the man who was supposed to be Joe's only means out of Colombia was dead. Vargas was an agent with a proven track record. But he could have turned.

Joe had come to neutralize Humberto and disrupt operations. The CIA—namely Vargas in this particular area—was more concerned with the state of the government, which faction would prevail and figuring out how to control that faction if possible. Maybe Vargas resented Joe's intrusion or simply gave him up to cement relations with Humberto. Stranger things had happened.

At any rate, the mission was over and it was time to go home.

The DEA had a presence in Bogotá, a carefully controlled presence maintaining strict cooperation with the government forces. Joe was unsanctioned as far as they were concerned. On his own. He couldn't go to them for help. If caught, he would be labeled CIA, even though he wasn't. The interference of a CIA operative would generate some truly bad press, both here and at home. The CIA *was* here, after all. Dead on the floor.

A mere DEA agent was expendable in the grand scheme of things. There was no love lost between the two agencies. That was one reason for organizing the new Sextant team, promoting cooperation. It seemed unlikely to Joe that it would work after so many years of rivalry and jockeying for jurisdiction, but ever since he'd been approached about joining he'd been fascinated by the concept.

"Ready?" Martine asked, interrupting his thoughts.

"The chopper is meeting us in half an hour and we've got about a mile and a half to run."

Decision time. Humberto's drug operation helped finance a rebel faction while he still held rank in the regular army. He had played both sides of the fence. Martine could be with either side, sent to eliminate him. She'd done that. She had probably killed Vargas, too, and had definitely shot the unidentified man who lay in the corner.

She knew about Mercier and the job and what Duquesne had been doing here, but if Duquesne had been captured, getting that information out of him would have been simple enough. Anyone under enough pressure or the influence of certain drugs would spill his guts all over the place.

That left two options to consider. She was leading him into a trap, to take him alive for purposes of embarrassing the American government, or she was exactly who she said she was and was getting him out of Colombia.

Could he afford to trust her? He closed his eyes, hoping for another quick flash of precognition, but nothing came. So much for the infamous Corda *gift*.

That aside, his ordinary instincts were usually pretty good.

Martine practiced patience while Corda made up his mind. She understood his dilemma and admitted to herself that he would be a fool to take her at her word. She had no identification on her, though even that would not convince him. ID could so easily be faked.

"Your weapon?" he said, holding out his hand.

"If we're ambushed along the way, I'll be defenseless," she reminded him. She watched him extract the mags from the AK's, including hers, and tuck the extra ammo in his belt.

He shrugged. "And if you are not who you say you are, sweetie, and that chopper we meet is full of government troops, I'm pretty much screwed six ways from Sunday.''

She sighed, turned over the Beretta she'd taken from Humberto's desk. It would be useless to reassure Corda that she was not his enemy. Better if she did what she could to facilitate his trust. ''It pulls a fraction to the right,'' she told him.

Corda looked at her oddly, as if she'd surprised him with her compliance. She felt his dark gaze slide over her as he did a slow visual check.

Pure male appreciation gleamed right through the careful scrutiny by the agent. Martine fought her response to his obvious admiration of her body without much success. Her temperature rose automatically and she knew she probably blushed.

He was a great-looking guy and in better physical shape than anyone she knew, even her brother who obsessed with working out. There were those bronzed, finely honed muscles rippling everywhere. Jet black hair set off intoxicating eyes the color of well-aged bourbon. His sensual, mobile lips quirked way too often with a hint of sexy mischief. Yes, definitely, a killer smile. But Corda's looks weren't the main attraction for Martine. It was his humor. Show her a man who could laugh in the face of danger and she was hooked big-time. This man laughed in the face of death. Tempted though she was to start something with him and see where it led, now was definitely not the time.

''You have a backup?'' he asked.

Martine held her arms out to her side, palms up. ''Where would I put it?''

The small size man's uniform Humberto had given her hugged her body like a lover, except where the trousers bloused over her boots. Maybe he wouldn't check there. The bone knife she carried was thin and the grip of it fairly slender, making no obvious bulge as even a small pistol might.

He nodded and seemed satisfied. "Okay, let's hit the road. Which way?"

"North," she said. "I'll lead."

His smile mocked her. "Wouldn't have it any other way."

She moved quickly through the undergrowth. Every few minutes, she checked the tiny, special compass built into the back of her watch, which she had turned upside down on her wrist.

Neither of them spoke, which was fine by her. The man was entirely too savvy. She was afraid he would figure out this was her first attempt at a field assignment and decide to take over. If she could just hold it together until they got on that chopper, she was home free. Then she could pretend airsickness or something that would explain giving way to the nausea roiling inside her.

She'd killed two men today. But she couldn't think about that now. She wouldn't. Read the compass again, she told herself sternly. Look professional. Look tough.

Suddenly, he grabbed her arm and jerked her to a halt. "Smoke," he whispered.

She sniffed. He was right. Oily smoke and another stench that almost overrode it. *Oh God, the helicopter.*

Carefully, he took point and led them silently through the brush until they could view the clearing ahead. The chopper sat gutted by fire, the pilot still inside.

Within the cover of the trees just beyond that, she spied two uniformed soldiers, armed and alert, scanning the surrounding woods.

The breath she'd been holding expelled suddenly. She quickly bent double and retched into the bushes. A strong hand slid under her stomach and held her. "Steady now," he whispered. "This is not the time to lose your cool, baby."

She wiped her mouth on her sleeve and sucked in a deep breath. "I'm not a baby," she snapped, her voice almost inaudible.

He didn't argue.

Martine straightened, carefully moved back through the tangled growth of forest and headed west. "Let's go."

"Where?" he asked, but he was following her.

"Bogotá," she answered. "Plan B. We'll have to fly out commercial."

"You *are* kidding, right?"

"I might lie a little, but I never kid," she said.

Six hours later, they stopped for the night, found a little overhang in the hill to protect them from the incessant rain that had been drenching them all afternoon. Both were soaked to the skin, too exhausted to do anything but slump against the rock at their backs. She was awake now, though. Joe could tell by her breathing.

It was time they got to know one another. He kept recalling that possible glimpse into the future that consisted of nothing but her face wearing a horrified expression, abject fear. The memory replayed now when he closed his eyes, a much too up-close and personal view of Martine.

If it was a premonition, he couldn't prevent seeing it for real sometime in the near future. The best he could do was try to figure out the context of it ahead of time. Unfortunately, he'd only been able to do that a time or two in his life, a life interrupted by little snatches of what was to be.

Why such weird anomalies deviled *him,* Joe had no clue, even after exhaustive study by so-called experts on psychic phenomena. After a few months, he had dropped out of the study initiated by the university and never mentioned his "glimpses" to anyone again.

Right now all Joe wanted was to gain more information

about the woman who would eventually star in the reality version of his latest episode and prepare to deal with it ahead of time if there was any way he possibly could.

"What scares you most, Martine?" he asked her, keeping his voice soft, playing to the intimacy that had been forced on them by the elements.

"What is this? Truth or Dare?" she shot back.

"Just truth. Settle down now." He slid one arm around her and drew her close. She tensed a bit, but he knew it was only a token resistance and ignored it. "I'm chilly, aren't you? Not coming on to you here or anything, just sharing a little body heat, okay?"

"Fine," she snapped. "I'm tired, wet and hungry and not in the mood to get personal, so just behave yourself."

"I will," he promised. "I've got to tell you I have nothing but the greatest respect for you, Martine."

"Thanks. Hold that thought." She shifted her body so that she fit closer, but Joe didn't mistake it for encouragement. She was cold and trying to get more comfortable, that was all.

He stifled the urge to pull her head down to his shoulder. Instead, he carefully charged ahead with his disguised interrogation. "You're one of the bravest people I've ever met, so don't get me wrong. But tell me, does anything frighten you to the point you can't function?"

Her silence stretched on for a full minute. "Mediocrity," she declared finally.

Joe laughed and squeezed her shoulder, liking the firmness of her warmth beneath the rough wet sleeve of her uniform. Her right breast pressed firmly against his side, her hip against his leg. His body responded normally, but he wasn't uncomfortable with that. Not yet anyway. He just enjoyed it, determined to press on with his original intent to find out everything he could about her.

She wasn't giving up a thing unless he went first. Maybe not even then, but he'd try anyway.

"Dying alone scares me," he admitted, sticking strictly to fact. Somebody as savvy as she was would spot a lie in a situation like this, he figured.

"We all die alone, Joe," she said.

"I know, but I mean dying the way I would have if you hadn't come along. No one would ever have known I was dead. My family would hope, pray and search for years maybe, thinking I was a prisoner somewhere or a victim of amnesia wandering around waiting to be found. The dying part I could handle, but I'd want somebody to know where I bought it and why, you know? I'd also like to be holding a hand when I go. Somebody who would care one way or the other."

"Something to think about," she granted him, her voice thoughtful.

"Now you. What's your greatest fear?"

Again she considered his question before she answered softly, reluctantly. "Subjugating myself. Not being able to make my own decisions. Being helpless and dependent. My mother was like that. My father was…never mind. I'd rather not go into it." He thought he heard her curse under her breath.

There was a wealth of information in that revelation, one he was sure she hadn't intended to make.

But she still wasn't getting what he meant, Joe thought with a shake of his head. "No, I mean an immediate scare. What would nearly stop your heart? Make you sweat bullets?"

"Oh." She was quiet for a minute. "Being tied up, I think. Confined so I couldn't move freely. That would probably do it." She laughed quietly. "I remember once when Matt and I were small. We were playing soldiers and he took me prisoner. Bound my hands with cellophane tape."

"Ah. Well, I expect he was sorry he did that when you got free," Joe guessed.

"I beaned him with a plastic baseball bat and blacked his eye," she said with another small chuckle.

"Good for you. Bet he hasn't tied up a woman since then. See? You saved him from a life of kinky sex."

She ignored that observation. "He was a horrible brat. I suppose we both were." Joe heard the affection in her voice, recognized it as exactly what he felt for his siblings.

"Why are you doing this, Martine?" he asked, trying to stay conversational and not betray the intensity of his need to know what drove her.

"I told you the truth. My brother didn't join me when he should have. I wanted to get to Vargas and find out if he had heard from him. And to get you out of there as planned, of course."

"The other reason," Joe demanded softly, wanting to know more about what she'd revealed earlier, about the subjugation thing. About her parents and how their behavior might have led her to this point.

She sighed and leaned against his shoulder. "Could you cut the chatter now and get some sleep? We have a long walk tomorrow."

"Sure," he agreed, knowing she'd given him all the confidences he could expect for now.

He still didn't know enough about her. Considering his overpowering interest in her as a woman, maybe he never would get enough. It might be better to drop it. She wasn't what he needed, not at all what he was looking for now that he'd decided to settle down and leave this kind of work behind.

As terrific as she felt in his arms, he was going to have to bypass Martine and find somebody different.

At least he had found out one thing that could put that godawful look of horror on her face. In light of that, he ought to prepare for them to be captured. It was probably going to happen in spite of whatever he tried to do to prevent it.

# Chapter 3

They had been struggling through hanging vines and palmetto fronds for hours. Joe had taken the lead, wishing like hell for a machete even if it would leave a trail a kid could follow. Though it wasn't that late in the day, the denseness of the forest blocked out most of the sunlight.

They would have to stop soon or he was going to disgrace himself and drop in a heap at her feet. Outdone by a girl. If he was a few years younger and had the energy left for any show of pride, he'd worry about that. However...

"I need a rest," he said in all candor, hoping she wouldn't kick him in the butt and tell him to keep walking.

"Thank God," she muttered, stretching her arms above her head and flexing her fingers, rolling her shoulders, generally making him sweat even more than he already was.

Joe flattened the vegetation to make a nest large enough for them to recline.

"I'll never take another steam bath as long as I live," she announced.

"Me neither." Joe stretched out and sighed with relief, thinking how nice it would be to have gills. The humidity was at least ninety-nine-point-nine percent. It was probably raining outside the canopy above them. He was as wet as if he were out there in it.

He risked a look at her to see how she was faring. Dewy was the word that came to mind. No rivulets of sweat for this chick. As Mama would say, girls didn't perspire, they *glowed*. Even in the near darkness, Martine glowed. Golden. Untouchable. Except that his leg was resting right next to hers. She raised hers just then and broke contact.

Joe grinned. "What's the matter, kid? I make you nervous?"

"Where are you really from, Corda?"

"What state?"

"No, what planet? You think every woman you meet is fair game. Catch up with the world, will you?"

Joe laughed out loud. It felt so good. Here he was in the middle of the damned jungle, half dead from exhaustion, lying next to a beautiful woman while looking about as unappealing as a guy could look and he was loving life at the moment. Just loving the hell out of it. He'd never felt quite so alive.

She turned her face to his, a look of concern clouding her features. "You're not cracking up, are you?"

He laughed again, couldn't seem to stop. Even so, he managed to shake his head. She sat up, peered down at him and slapped him. Hard!

"Damn! What'd you do that for?" he snapped, rubbing his face. She had a mean right palm.

"You needed that," she said, lying down again. "And no, you do not make me nervous. You make me tired. Now be quiet and save your energy. We have a long way to go yet."

* * *

Martine smiled to herself as she lay turned away from him, her face pillowed on her hands. He was keeping his distance, at least for the moment, but she didn't think he would for very long. His eyes gave it away. He wanted her. Badly.

She wanted him, too, but didn't plan to let him know yet. It had been a long time since she had wanted anyone, not since her senior year in college. Her engagement to Steven had been such a fiasco, it had almost turned her against men forever.

This time—if she decided to give in to this need of hers—she did not intend to relinquish one iota of control, not one. She suspected that Joe Corda would turn out to be a lot more demanding that Steven Prescott, engineer, had ever thought about being.

Her father's death had been a wake-up call for her. Seeing how her mother behaved after being left alone had changed Martine's life forever. Talk about totally lost!

The quiet unassuming daughter had realized she was becoming her mother all over again. Ripe for picking by a man who would rule her with an iron hand, dictate every aspect of her existence, choose her friends, even her clothes. Steven had been well on his way to achieving that until Martine suddenly and unequivocally rebelled. Thank God she had.

As for starting up something with Joe Corda, Martine knew very well that what was too easily gained would never be fully appreciated.

He was a lot like her brother. Even good men like these two thought of sex as a simple hunger. They'd hook up with whoever was handy and reasonably attractive, do the deed and never look back after the sun came up. It was the nature of the beast and she didn't blame them. However, though Martine was not looking for permanence, she at least wanted to be remembered past lunch the next day.

There would be plenty of time to explore what she was feeling for him, and also decide what course she should take, once they got out of this godforsaken country.

She wriggled out a comfier spot in the damp bed of fronds and barely managed not to jump when his arm slid around her, settling across her waist. His body rested along the length of hers, not snuggling precisely, just barely touching. Almost teasing.

Martine didn't panic. She also didn't mistake it for an attempt at seduction. She had felt his finger wrap snugly around her belt loop. He merely wanted to make certain she didn't crawl off and leave him there when he went to sleep. She was the one with the compass.

Oddly enough, his ability to reason while he was aroused gave her comfort. She really liked intelligent men, practical enough to control their impulses when it counted.

The next day passed much the same as the first. Joe could not believe the guts this woman had. It just boggled his mind. Once out of the forest, she led the way through the hills, directly to the outskirts of the city without getting lost once or encountering a single soul on the way.

Her instincts were damned near perfect. She never complained. She had never lost her cool again after that one upchuck when they had found the fried chopper. That little upset had lasted, what? Two seconds?

This morning as soon as they woke up, she had disappeared behind some bushes, giving him time to take care of his own business, then marched right back and took up the journey. Her stamina equaled and almost outstripped his.

The forest canopy had thinned enough to show that the rain had stopped, but the mud made the going rough. They'd been walking at a fast clip for hours and he could do with a rest.

She must have read his mind. "We're stopping up ahead. There's a stream."

Good as her word, she led him right to it.

"You've come this way before," he guessed.

"Yes, just this far in. I thought it wise to set up an alternate plan before I hired the driver to take me to Vargas."

While he was kneeling, scooping up water and washing his face, she was digging in the dirt. "What are you looking for, roots?" he asked, wiping his hands on his shirt.

He'd had it with snatching berries along the way. Roots would be good. Even grubs were sounding tasty at this point, his squeamish dislike of them during survival training notwithstanding.

"Candy," she informed him, continuing to scoop the earth out of the shallow hole. "Ah," she said with satisfaction, pulling a plastic bag out of the hole.

"You buried candy!" he said with a short laugh. "Sweet tooth?"

At last he got a smile from her. She hadn't smiled at him for almost twenty-four hours. He'd missed it.

She pulled a long slender knife from her boot and cut the bag open. Joe's mouth almost dropped open when he saw the blade. Didn't that prove he was losing his touch? Couldn't even disarm a woman. He ought to become a bean counter, it would serve him right.

But Martine was no ordinary woman, he reminded himself. No, she was extraordinary with a capital *E* in every respect. Some men might like helpless women they could coddle and protect, but for him, competence had always proved a large turn-on.

Of course, he had always known he'd have to change his preference when he got out of this racket, and that time was almost here. If he tried to settle down with somebody like her...well, they weren't the settling kind, now were they? Home and family would never be enough. Too bad, because Martine had him hot as a firecracker most of the time. He wasn't too sure he could ever go for helpless after having met her.

He promptly shoved aside the current wave of lust he was experiencing when he saw her stash. There were clothes in there. Civvies. Shoes. Grinning, she tossed him a passport.

Joe opened it. His photo stared back at him, an old one taken a couple of years ago. Made him look like a terrorist. Typical tourist picture, he thought. "You are very resourceful, lady," he said, thumping the page.

She tossed him some of the clothing. "Prepare for all contingencies whenever I can. We'll bury the uniforms. You change here, I'll go upstream. Give me about twenty minutes."

So she was typically female after all, he thought with a laugh. He could be ready in five. She handed him a pink plastic razor. He stared down at it, turning it this way and that.

"Lose the mustache," she ordered, plunking a small bar of hotel soap in his hand, "and there are some hornrims in the bottom of the bag."

"Gotcha," he replied. The girl thought of everything. "Thanks, Martine."

"The name is Guadalupé, José," she said in her perfect Spanish. "Do not forget it." Then she left to do her thing.

Joe stripped, waded into the shallow water and sat down to wash. He soaped and scraped off his mustache and the couple of days' worth of beard.

Hurriedly, he dried himself on the uniform and tugged on the clothes. She'd brought nothing flashy, only muted colors. His pants were pull-ons, the shirt a dull print with a long enough tail to cover a pistol. The shoes were leather, lightweight soles, a fair fit. Not much good for walking a long way, but he suspected they were chosen because they took up little space. He stuck the passport in his shirt pocket, dug around in the bag, located a couple of Mars bars and sat down to eat one while he waited for her.

A few minutes later, she appeared. At least he thought it was her. She was wearing worn sandals and an ankle-length skirt of dark green. A long-sleeved brown pullover hung loose to her hips. He noticed a slight padding over her abdomen that made her appear a few months pregnant. But it was the rest of her that truly astounded him.

She was also checking him out and nodded her approval. "Amazing transformation, José. The bare face makes you appear quite civilized. What do you think?" She did a slow turn for his inspection.

She was brunette now and her hair was slicked severely back into a bun at her nape, the strands still wet and straight as a die. Her eyes were dark brown. Contacts, of course. And her skin had deepened several shades. A faint tint of brown lip gloss had replaced the enticing natural rose color that he knew for a fact didn't come out of a tube. He had the stupidest urge to kiss off the fake stuff.

"Wow," he said simply. "Lupé, you are a knockout!"

"Knocked-up," she corrected with a wry smile. "And let that be your last comment in English if you know what's good for us." She pulled a purse made of dark parachute cloth higher on one shoulder. "Let's get the AK and the uniforms buried."

He nodded and quickly did as she said, packing one large weapon and their clothing into the hole she'd just emptied and covering it carefully so the earth looked undisturbed. Then they headed for the road into the city.

As they walked along, she commented idly on the scenery, pointing out several wildflowers he had absolutely no interest in. He could hardly keep his eyes off her and the amazing changes she had made in herself.

She even walked differently, affecting a much more feminine sashay with a delicate little waddle thrown in.

Pregnancy became her. Her voice sounded musical, now minus its former overtone of command. Joe wasn't sure he liked it.

Had she spoken to Humberto this way? Was that how she'd grabbed the man's interest and held it to the point of letting her do damned near anything she pleased while she was supposed to be a prisoner?

He couldn't keep thinking that way, dwelling on what she might have done. It was robbing him of any good sense he might have left. Taking a deep breath and forcing a smile, Joe joined the conversation she'd been having with herself.

"So where'd you train?" he asked.

"McLean. Quantico. Local police academy and a private dojo. You?"

"Same deal, basically, plus three years with the army. Rangers," he added.

She nodded.

"How is it your Spanish is so perfect? Bet you didn't learn that in school," he observed, still digging for more facts about her.

"My mother's Andorran. Spanish was my first language."

"And your dad?" he probed.

"American. He worked for the embassy."

Joe smiled. "Totally against what you're doing for a living, I would bet."

She shook her head. "Not really."

When she didn't follow that with an explanation, Joe's curiosity overcame him. "Well? Why not?"

"He's dead."

"I'm sorry. And your mother?"

"Gone home to her family," she said simply, emphasis on the last word, her tight expression telling him in no uncertain terms that the conversation about her family was over. Obviously, she was hurt by her mother's return to Andorra, so Joe didn't pursue it.

As they walked along, she fished in the slouchy purse and handed him a cheap leather wallet. He checked the contents, finding a driver's license to match the passport she'd given him, a few photos of little Latino kids he didn't know and a fairly generous supply of pesos.

"What, no airline tickets?" he joked.

She patted the purse and smiled. "Air fare for two!"

*Well, damn.* Joe laughed out loud. "Talk about backup plans. You really take the cake, you know that?" His admiration knew no bounds.

"*Gracias,*" she replied laconically as she bit down on the chocolate she'd unwrapped.

"Why didn't we simply head for the city and fly out to begin with? Why hire the chopper?"

She wrinkled her nose at him. "You really enjoyed that hike?"

Joe saw her point, but this plan was just way too easy to really work. This would be when they were captured, he knew it. Then he would see that look of horror on her face, the one he had conjured up accidentally out of her future.

But it seemed he worried for nothing. They entered the city where he hailed a cab that took them to the airport. On the way, Joe disassembled their weapons so he could ditch them in pieces. No point adding to Colombia's already significant arsenal of illegal firearms.

Martine headed for the nearest phone. In moments she was back, wearing a beaming smile, tear tracks all the way to her chin. "He's safe!"

"Your brother? Damn, that's great!" Joe exclaimed, giving her a hug that she promptly returned, holding him even longer than he would have expected. She had obviously been more worried about Duquesne than she had let on.

When he released her, she kept hold of his arm. "He had a fall and broke his leg. I don't know the details, but he's all right now. He's home."

Their mood was up. A happy couple. Joe kissed her cheek, loving the feel of her skin against his lips. She didn't resist, even a little, only smiled up at him as if he'd saved Duquesne himself.

Slick as a whistle, they grinned their way through customs, boarded a bad excuse for an airplane, endured a short, uneventful layover in Panama and flew on to Miami. Unbelievable.

Joe decided the minute they touched down that he was out of the business, as of now. He was going to turn in his resignation before he even started with Sextant, settle down in some podunk town on the Florida coast and become a couch potato slash beach bum. And if he could talk Wonder Woman into joining him, she could come, too. Maybe she was ready for a break.

Though he couldn't quite picture Martine just hanging out, boiling up crabs and watching the daily soaps, he could still dream of lazy walks in ankle-deep surf followed by hot nights in a beach shack. Did his heart good to think about it, even if there wasn't much hope that it would come to pass.

He resisted the urge to try for another vision. For one thing, it took more energy than he had at the moment, and for another, he was afraid he wouldn't like what he saw.

The last two hadn't been pleasant in the least and one of them still hadn't been realized. He and Martine had not been captured coming out of Colombia. That meant something else would happen. A chill ran up his spine.

In Miami, they stood in line for customs just like everyone else. A few of their fellow travelers were Americans returning from sojourns south, chattering about how different things were *down there*. If they only knew.

Joe kept his arm around Martine's waist, maintaining their charade as a devoted married couple who were expecting a child. No longer a critical disguise since they were safely back in the States, but he had gotten used to it really fast and hated to give it up.

No, acting the fond husband, lover and prospective father wasn't necessary at all now, but he still leaned into her, brushed a kiss over her cheek, gazed deeply into her eyes when she shot him a questioning look.

He caressed her face, trailing one finger across her forehead to brush away a strand of hair that had escaped, then closed his hand around the back of her neck in a gesture of comfort. Her skin was so soft, that nape of hers so vulnerable he wished he could kiss it.

After a while, he realized he might be overdoing the touching. It was hard to keep his hands off of her, no pretense about it.

She hadn't moved away from him the way he'd expected her to, so he leaned down and whispered in her ear, "Where are we going next, *querida?*"

"Atlanta."

"Is that where you're from?"

"That's home now," she answered in English absently just as they reached the customs agents who would plunder through her voluminous purse.

There would be so little time to talk about all that had happened. Joe wanted to talk to her openly, out loud and at length before they reported to the authorities about all that had gone on.

He worried a little that she would disappear on him before that. Nothing said she had to go with him and report anything at all. Joe just hoped she might agree to go with him to D.C. so he wouldn't have to leave her just yet.

They cleared customs in a few minutes and went to purchase tickets for the next leg of their trip.

He planned that they would go on to D.C. from Atlanta. He would, at any rate. He certainly had reports to turn in and a resignation to deliver. After that debriefing on the mission, he would be free to do as he pleased.

No longer would he have to think about every single move he made and every word he said. He wouldn't have to speak Spanish unless he was talking to his dad, and even then, he wouldn't *have* to. And, best of all, he wouldn't need to worry about not being able to fix all the world's troubles. It was somebody else's turn.

He was going to Florida and decided he'd definitely try to talk Martine into coming with him. Just for a little while. Beach life could be seductive, soothing. Maybe if she liked it enough, she'd be willing to quit what she was doing.

Damn, but he'd like to pursue what he had begun to feel about her. But not if she planned to go traipsing off every few months on some dangerous assignment.

"You look so tired," she commented with a worried look on her face.

"Yeah," he admitted with a pained sigh. "This gets to you after a while."

"Maybe you should take a vacation," she suggested.

He searched her eyes for interest and found it. "Maybe you should join me."

For a minute, Joe thought she might have been tempted to say yes. Then one of her fine, shapely brows kicked up and she smiled. "You wish."

"God knows, I do, and that's a fact."

Wouldn't it be great to lie around doing nothing but what he felt like doing, and doing it with Martine? Maybe it was for the best if he didn't do that, though. Someone who didn't talk shop, or didn't even *know* shop, would suit him a whole lot better in the long run. But a short run with Martine sure had a great appeal.

* * *

They barely had time to grab a quick burger before boarding the jet for Atlanta. Once aboard, Joe settled down to await takeoff, wishing for a drink, knowing he'd have to reconcile himself to something nonalcoholic.

He turned to Martine. "You know what? Soon as I get debriefed, I'm getting rip-roaring drunk," he informed her.

"Thanks for sharing that," she said, her tone sarcastic. "Big drinker, are you?" She smoothed the wrinkled skirt over her thighs.

Damn, but she had fine thighs. And great ankles. And nice breasts, not big enough to call her generously endowed, but quite large enough to make him sweat bullets.

"You don't strike me as the type," she commented.

*The type? Oh, a drinker, not a breast man.*

Joe laughed at himself, both for indulging in a galloping case of desire that was heading nowhere and for the idea of liquor settling any of his problems.

"Well, I'm no lush yet," he admitted, "but the possibility is definitely there. Yeah, I think I could adapt. Tequila. You like tequila?"

"Not much."

He watched the stewardess up front fiddling with the serving cart, stocking it with soft drinks. Bourbon would be nice, he thought with a sigh. *So* very nice.

"Until the shoot-out, you seemed to be faring well enough. You got along very well with Humberto and the others. Was this assignment really so terrible?" she asked, sounding truly interested.

"Not as bad as it could have been," he answered. That much was the truth.

She had been there almost a week herself. And surely she'd had it rougher than he had. Joe hadn't been required to share a bed with Humberto. Martine obviously had.

But then Joe reminded himself, Humberto hadn't been

ugly, despite his lack of character, and he might have been a real expert in the sack for all Joe knew.

Latin lovers got their flattering rep from somewhere, after all. He wondered if he qualified, being half-Latino himself. Probably meant he half-qualified, he thought with a laugh. She shot him a questioning look.

Joe returned it, wondering if he'd ever have a chance to find out how he qualified with present company. He'd bet she was a damn good lay. She'd done everything else with the expertise of a well-trained professional. Still it made him sick to think about her making it with Humberto.

He looked away, upbraiding himself for his silent sarcasm. No, he shouldn't judge her. He'd already decided that. She'd done what she had to do to insure a relative amount of freedom in captivity. He couldn't very well complain since that had surely saved his butt. If Humberto had locked her inside a room in the compound, she wouldn't have been where she was with that gun in her hand.

Joe felt terrible. But his conscience ragging him about being critical of her morals wasn't the only reason. Imagining what she must have done with the man was driving him crazy.

"Did I say thanks, Martine? My manners probably got lost in the shuffle down there. But I want you to know I appreciate what you did. *All* of it."

"You're welcome, Corda. Mission's accomplished and I'll get a paycheck. That's thanks enough."

God, she sounded so…well, company-oriented. "You really get off on this, don't you?" he asked.

"Your animosity is showing," she said with a smile. "And, yes, I like what I do. Otherwise, I would be doing something else. I have a pretty good head for business."

"Monkey business," he muttered under his breath while he fiddled with his seat belt.

"I beg your pardon?"

*Uh-oh.* Joe looked at her. Both brows were up now and she wasn't smiling at all. "I shouldn't have said that. Never mind, I know I shouldn't. It's just that I'm having a hard time getting my mind around you and Humberto, y'know? I mean, how could you just…let him?"

"Let him what?" she asked, all prim-lipped like his sixth grade teacher used to get when he'd said something off-color.

"Sex," Joe hissed through gritted teeth. "How could you have sex with somebody like him?"

For a long time, she said nothing, just trained her gaze out the window and ignored him. When they were finally in the air and the cabin noise resumed, she whispered, "I didn't."

Another of her lies, but he wanted to believe this one. Real bad. "No? Why not?"

"Humberto found out exactly who I was, so I didn't bother to lie about it. He didn't know why I was there. I told him I was looking for my brother who had disappeared on an assignment I knew nothing about."

"Truth works better in cases like that," Joe agreed. "So, since you were working for this company and not law enforcement, he figured he could persuade you to throw in with him?"

She shrugged. "That was his plan, I think. He treated me exceptionally well because he wanted me to be content to stay. Also, he enjoyed playing the Old World gallant. You know how pretentious he could be. I got a fairly good estimation of the man by assessing his traffic on the computer."

"How in the world did you manage that?" She never ceased to amaze him.

She shrugged, a small smile tickling her lips. "Let's just say I tend to wander a bit in the wee hours of the morning and Humberto was a very sound sleeper."

Joe shook his head, unable to hide his doubt. "And he let you have that free a run, given what he knew about you? How stupid was that?"

"I had a freer run than he knew I did, at least within the compound. Getting past the gate guards would have presented a problem, of course. At least before the distraction your leaving caused." She sighed and shook her head. "Maybe he knew why I had come and was waiting for me to identify you. I couldn't get a message to you without danger of your being caught. He'd been notified that DEA was in place undercover, but you could have been any one of the new people. He watched each of you like a hawk."

Joe grinned when he thought how successfully he had bypassed that scrutiny when he went to wire the truck. "Closer than he watched you?"

"Obviously." She continued the explanation. "When you took off, that as good as identified you. That's why the squad followed. And why Humberto did. He wanted to be in on the kill."

"And how did you manage to find that out?"

She grinned. "I'm a dedicated eavesdropper, Corda. Amazing how much you can learn when guys think you're just a wide-eyed female with feathers for brains." She examined her nails with a frown. "When business came up, he forgot I was around. Especially when you took off."

"So you followed. And shot him. That must have been hard for you after..." He let his words die off, wishing he'd kept his mouth shut. It was in the past now, over and done with. She'd want to forget it. Hell, *he* wanted to forget it. But he couldn't seem to. It bothered the hell out of him that she had slept with Humberto.

Martine expelled a frustrated breath. "After what?"

Joe shook his head and grimaced. "After how...close

you were. You don't owe me any explanations. I just wondered about it, that's all.''

She nodded. "All right.''

So that was it. Joe tried to let it go and forget it.

"I take it Duquesne's your real name? Or did you and your *brother* choose that as your alias?''

"Yes, it is real. There seemed no reason to change it since neither of us is exactly famous. You see, Ames International—''

Joe interrupted ''—liberates Americans caught in embarrassing quandaries outside the boundaries. What made you go for that kind of job?''

"I think we'd better change the subject.''

Reluctantly he agreed. "So, you coming on vacation with me?''

"Certainly not,'' she replied. A little too zealously not to have at least considered it.

"Offer stands. You could use a little R&R after shooting up Colombia, couldn't you? Just think, you could be lying on a beach down at Port St. Joe, eating oysters and watching the tide roll in this time next week. That's where I plan to be.''

"Port St. Joe?'' she asked.

"Yeah, I'm actually named for the place. Gulf Coast of Florida. My mother's a teacher at the local high school. Dad's retired. Both my sisters still live there. It's home.''

She smiled at him, a real smile that warmed his insides. "Sounds lovely,'' she said. "Thank you for asking me, but I can't join you. There'll be another assignment waiting when I get back.'' She sighed. "At least, I hope there will be.''

Joe chilled around the region of his heart. "Good grief, nobody but a newbie is that gung-ho! Tell me you're not.''

She was biting her lip, frowning, not saying squat, looking out the window instead of at him.

"You *are!* This was your first op?"

She nodded once, just a little nod.

When he got his voice back, Joe had to work hard to keep from yelling. Instead, he rasped, "You could have gotten yourself killed, Martine! Hell, you could have gotten *me* killed. What the devil was Mercier thinking about, hiring *you,* of all people?"

"Me, of all people?" she asked, definitely offended. "Why do you say that, because I'm a woman?"

"Because you're green! Damn, they don't even send green operatives down there from the Company." Joe shook his head as he ran a hand through his hair. "I gotta think Mercier didn't want me back very much if he sent somebody green."

"He sent my brother, who is very experienced!" she argued.

"Even as backup, they shouldn't send a novice." That thought alone reinforced his decision to quit the minute he got back.

"No, you shouldn't blame Mercier," Martine said vehemently. "He only contracted for my brother to go. I talked Matt into letting me go as far as Bogotá. Sort of to get my feet wet without being in on the actual operation."

Joe studied her for a minute. "So when your brother disappeared, you were the next body in line?"

"I had to make sure Matt was all right. And that you made it back, too. I'm trained to do anything Matt can do. You saw for yourself, I can shoot. No hesitation, no misses. I planned everything right down to the smallest detail and I prepared for every possible eventuality. Go ahead, tell me something I did wrong, I dare you!"

Joe couldn't. She was highly competent. No mistakes. If you didn't count sleeping with the enemy. And even that could be explained, if not condoned.

He forced himself to calm down and think rationally,

to put aside the weird swell of fury that felt a whole lot like jealousy all mixed up with a spiky wad of regret. It hurt like a sonofabitch.

"You...you did okay," he ground out. "What exactly is your job at Ames, if you don't mind my asking?"

"Technically..." She looked away, unable to meet his eyes. "Information analyst. Coordinator. That sort of thing."

He closed his eyes. His jaw clenched until his teeth ached. "A secretary?" he growled. "They sent a friggin' secretary?"

"I told you before. No one *sent* me. They sent Matt," she said with an exasperated roll of her eyes.

"Yeah, and you're the one who wound up in Humberto's bed!" Joe accused.

"He only kissed me one time! And it was just a little kiss, like a kindly old uncle's or something. We never went all the way."

Joe groaned. "*All the way?* What a quaint little old-fashioned phrase, Martine. Tell me, did you two *go steady?* Did you head him off at *second base?* God, Martine, you make my head hurt, you know that?"

"Then take a nap, Corda!" she suggested in a snippy little voice he hadn't heard her use before. "This conversation is *over*."

"You're damned right it is! I'll take this up with your brother and your boss. You'll be lucky if they don't bury you in the bowels of the files in the basement."

"That's where I *was*," she countered. The fire in her eyes was so bright, he thought he could see the blue burning through her brown contacts. "And if you get me demoted back there, Corda, I'll hunt you down and make you sorry. That's a promise!"

"Threatening a government agent, Martine? What're you gonna do, shoot me?"

"There's an idea." She crossed her arms over her

chest, gave him the back of her head and didn't say another word.

He was really glad right then that they'd had to ditch the weapons in order to fly.

# Chapter 4

Martine hated to leave things as they stood. Neither of them had said much on the flight to Atlanta, just enough to create gross misunderstandings.

She had called her office from Miami and had left Matt a message that she was on the way. Joe had phoned his old office and stated only that his mission was complete, leaving the details for his debriefing when he arrived in D.C.

The adrenaline had ebbed along with the danger, leaving them both exhausted.

They deplaned still looking like refugees. She had ditched the padding that made her appear pregnant and her clothing hung loose on her frame. She had also removed the brown contacts that had irritated her eyes and left them red-rimmed. Corda's five-o'clock shadow had grown into a near-beard. She ached for a hot shower and at least eight hours' sleep.

"Well, I'm on home turf at last," she told him when they entered the terminal, "and you soon will be."

She wondered if she would still have a job when she returned to work. Hopefully, when she admitted to her brother that she had gone to the compound after him, he and their boss, Sebastian, would see it as her taking initiative and would agree she had done as well as either of them could have under the circumstances.

They would read her the riot act, of course, and she could hardly blame them for that. But if they attempted to make her give her word she would never do anything remotely like this again, she would simply have to resign. Her days behind a desk were over.

"Is this where we part company?" Joe grinned at her, but it looked like a real effort. "I was hoping you might deliver me personally to Mercier. Plop me on his desk and demand payment for the job."

She shrugged. "Where do you go for the DEA debriefing?"

"D.C. Then on to McLean after I deliver my spiel and I'm officially released. I'll commend you to Mercier when I get there."

"Thanks." She didn't quite know what to say next. They had said so much over the course of three days. And yet so little about anything that really mattered.

The attraction they felt stood between them like a swaying rogue elephant. They both recognized it. There was no point pretending it didn't exist, but she'd been having serious second thoughts about whether they should approach and attempt to tame it. It just loomed there, promising trouble. Maybe it would be better to steal away from it in opposite directions and avoid eye contact.

Martine didn't think now that she could take a relationship with Joe as lightly as she ought to. It might mean too much to her.

He ushered her to the tram that would take them to the main terminal. Just before it reached there, he cleared his throat. She looked up at him.

"Could I buy you dinner?" he asked, then patted the folded currency they had exchanged for in Miami. "Your treat?"

She smiled. All those second thoughts she'd been having evaporated. "Sure, why not?" In the back of her mind, she knew it was a bad idea. This was leading directly to a one-night stand. They both knew it. It was there in his eyes, a promise clear as could be.

Maybe she should be offended. He thought she was promiscuous, that she had slept with Humberto as part of her cover. And that she would sleep with him for no other reason than he was there and willing. That last assumption might be a shade too close to the truth, but there was a bit more to it than that. Damn. He was looking serious and she couldn't afford to do serious.

She'd have to make certain she stayed uninvolved emotionally. And that he did, too.

"Want to hit the shops here and get you some clothes?" she asked. "I'll bill Mercier."

He laughed and plucked at his shirt. "I guess I do look a little scuzzy for a night on the town."

"Or for reporting in…tomorrow," she added, giving him the suggestion to wait until then to fly out instead of seeing him off after the dinner he promised.

His reply was nonverbal and non-tactile, but his acceptance was clear in the heated look he gave her. He would stay over.

They went to several vendors of horribly overpriced merchandise where he bought a small Swiss Army knife—he confessed it was a ritual comfort purchase he made every time he landed weaponless in an airport. He also picked up a sports bag to hold his purchases.

Next he selected a change of clothes and a few toiletries. He boldly plunked down a box of condoms with a raised eyebrow that dared her to comment.

She lifted her chin, looked him straight in the eye and said nothing. Silent consent.

No turning back now, she thought. She was committed. A frisson of excitement vibrated through her. The adrenaline was pumping again. Danger did that.

They took a cab to her apartment. On the way, he kept throwing her speculative looks that often approached the boiling point, but their conversation remained impersonal. How the weather here compared to Colombia's, the atrocious Atlanta traffic, the gold dome of the Georgia capitol, anything other than what they were both thinking about.

When they reached her place, a modest two-bedroom in LeJardin, a sprawling complex with a faintly French flavor, he hummed and nodded his approval. It wasn't terribly pricey, but it had charm and the neighborhood was nice enough. She led him up the stairs, punched in her code and opened the door.

He stood just inside for a minute, looking around. "Now, *this* is just not you. I was expecting…I don't know…not this. More sophistication, I guess. It's too homey." He looked down at her and winked. "You'll simply have to move."

"You think?" She had to laugh. Her rooms were shabby chic, so she supposed she should feel complimented.

He examined the exotic travel posters she had framed for the wall. Her globe-trotting brother had sent her souvenirs from all around the world, so her taste in accessories must seem wildly eclectic.

Nothing matched very well, but she didn't really care. One cohesive style or single identifying preference in her surroundings would be boring to live with. Her home suited her better than he knew.

"You remain an enigma," he declared, flashing that charming grin of his. "So, which way to the shower? I'll race you. Or we could share."

"How sophisticated is that? Let you watch me scrub off this disguise? I don't think so." Martine pointed to the guest bedroom. "I have two. Yours is through there. Help yourself to anything you need that you forgot to buy."

The moment he disappeared through the door, Martine hurried to her own room. The message light on her answering machine blinked like crazy. She deliberately ignored it. There would be time enough to sort things out with her brother tomorrow after Joe left for D.C.

Tonight was hers, a reward for her daring, a benefit she meant to claim. No matter what happened in the future, she would have this adventure to remember. A time when she had used all her senses, all her wiles, all her knowledge and training. A mission where she had experienced every emotion from the depth of fear right up to—she hoped—the height of passion.

When she said goodbye to Joe on Saturday morning, she would have lived to the max for once in her life.

She scrubbed away the dusky makeup easily enough. Then she shampooed out the substance she had used to temporarily darken her hair. She'd stolen that from Humberto. The man did like to cover his gray. Unfortunately, the dye left a residual shade of red in hers. She would have to bleach to get the original color back, but there wasn't time. She slathered on conditioner and hoped for the best.

At least she knew what to wear. Joe had only the black long-sleeve pullover, a pair of gray slacks and casual deck shoes, things he had purchased at the airport. Her little black dress would be perfect if she kept it simple. Gold hoops for her ears and a plain gold chain. Her black sandals with the medium heels would do.

She dried her hair, applied her makeup and dressed quickly. By the time she found her purse and went into the living room, he had already raided her fridge and found the wine. Faintly embarrassed that it was only an inexpensive bottle of Riesling, Martine blushed a little.

"Nectar of the gods," he said, handing her a glass. "Hope you don't mind. I made myself at home." His voice was a low, seductive Southern drawl. Though his dark good looks gave away his Latino heritage, his voice did not unless he spoke Spanish. She wondered which language he would use when they were intimate.

He looked very comfortable in her kitchen, very comfortable in his skin. She liked that about a man. She liked Joe. A lot.

The wine was deliciously fruity, despite the fact that it was cheap. She sipped, meeting his gaze over the rim of her glass. He looked fantastic. Very hip. Very macho. Her pulse fluttered when he smiled that way, like he knew secrets that would make her incredibly happy once he shared them.

"So, where shall we go?" he asked, rocking his wineglass a little and glancing down into it with a thoughtful expression, then back at her.

Martine frowned at the motion, wondering if he had little cork pieces floating. She stared into her own and saw nothing but clear amber liquid. "You like Chinese?" she asked.

"Not much," he admitted and took a sip of his wine.

She watched the muscles in his throat, saw the drop of wine cling to the corner of his upper lip when he lowered the glass. Her mouth almost watered, anticipating the taste.

"You know what? I'd kill for a pizza," he told her. "You have more of this." He rocked his glass again, again watching the liquid as it swirled. "We could order out."

"It's white wine. Red goes with pizza."

"Since when do you follow rules?"

She reached to pick up the phone. It rang just before

she touched it. Her brother's number appeared on the caller ID. Reluctantly she answered.

"Hi, Matt," she said, her gaze still locked with Joe's.

"Where the *hell* have you been?" he shouted. "Never mind, I *know* where you were! What happened?"

Martine had jerked the receiver away from her ear and winced at the volume. "Glad you made it back, Matt. I'll explain everything, but not now. See you Monday," she said and hung up.

"He's a bit testy," she explained to Joe. "Must be the heat."

"Right. Temperature's definitely rising." He stepped closer so that they were almost touching. He lifted his hand and touched her face with one finger, drew a featherlight line from her brow to her chin. She shivered.

His lower body pressed hers to the wall. She could feel his breath on her cheek, his heart beat against her breasts, his leg between hers. "I thought...you were hungry," she whispered.

"Yeah. Famished," he whispered as he possessed her mouth.

Martine returned the kiss, sliding her arms around him, pulling him even closer, reveling in the pleasure of his hands. They seemed to be everywhere at once, gliding, grasping, claiming.

The growl in his throat reverberated through her, a primal demand. She pressed herself to him and undulated, an intimate, urgent age-old invitation. Her heartbeat thundered in her ears, blocking out all sound.

Suddenly he stilled. He released her and backed away as far as he could with her hands fisted in the back of his shirt. "Martine?"

"Umm?" She clung to him, her body still seeking.

"Somebody's at your door," he murmured between kisses. "I don't think they're going away."

The doorbell was buzzing, an insistent staccato as

someone punched it repeatedly. How had she not heard that?

Reluctantly, she uncurled her fingers and let him go. "Must be Matt," she said with a heavy sigh of frustration. "Sorry."

When she looked through the peephole, she saw she was right. He must have been nearby, calling from his cell phone.

"Tell me you didn't go where I think you went!" he demanded the minute she opened the door. "You were supposed to hotfoot it back here if I was even a day late returning to Bogotá! Dammit, you weren't here when I finally made it back yesterday and I was getting ready to fly back down there!"

He had pushed in past her, the cast on his foot thumping against her hardwood floor.

His hand flew to his weapon the instant he spied Joe.

Martine grabbed his arm and gave him a pinch. "Matt, behave."

Matt's assessing gaze flew back and forth between them. Joe had moved behind the kitchen counter, probably to hide his arousal, and was calmly sipping his wine.

"Hey, Duquesne," he said. "How's it going?"

"Am I…interrupting something?" Matt asked, his voice tight with disapproval.

Martine pinched him again. "Yes, you are. And I'll pay you back. Count on it."

He turned on her, ignoring Joe. "Sebastian's gonna fire your little ass, you know that? He swore if I was right and you'd gone into the middle of that mess alone, you were through at Ames. Terminated."

She smiled sweetly. "Maybe not. Corda's back in one piece. I'm okay. No problem. Want some wine? We were just about to order pizza." She closed the door and headed back to the kitchen.

She had almost reminded him that he was the one who

failed to bring Joe home. He was the one who broke his leg and was late making the rendezvous in Bogotá. But she had to hold her tongue. If anyone could talk Sebastian around to keeping her on, it would be Matt.

"Wait a minute! I want to know *exactly* what happened." He seemed to remember Joe then and stopped. "What the hell's he doing here with *you?*"

"He followed me home. Can I keep him?"

"Damn you, Martine!"

She admitted Matt had reason to be upset, but she wasn't about to apologize. Still, an explanation might be in order. "Look, you were overdue coming back. I couldn't contact you. Sebastian was...out of pocket, and Nestor was, well, you know where. There was no one else left to go looking for you. And for Joe, of course. So I went."

He looked ready to explode, speechless and fuming. Sebastian would be worse, she knew. And he would not be speechless. Better if she downplayed the whole mission.

She rubbed Matt's forearm and squeezed it gently, soothing where she had given him the sisterly pinches. "Look, Matt, I'm home now. Everything turned out fine. You don't need to worry about me. I'm sorry I upset you, okay?"

He looked over at Joe and expelled the breath he was holding. "I guess I should thank you for getting her out of there, Corda."

Joe glanced at her and smiled, took another sip of his wine and set down the glass. "Getting *her* out? Are you kidding? If she hadn't been such a great shot, I'd be rotting in the woods right now. She's a real piece of work, your sister."

Martine's breath caught in her throat. Joe must think he was helping.

Matt's mouth had dropped open. He snapped it shut, then said very quietly, "She...shot somebody?"

Joe shrugged and leaned forward, resting on the counter. "Oh yeah, I lost count how many." He shook his head as he pretended to count. "Fourteen, fifteen...can't say for sure. Then when the chopper blew up and we had to run for it, she really showed her stuff." He held up the short lock of hair he'd brushed down over the graze on his forehead. "Dazed me big-time."

Matt continued to gape.

Joe went on, picking up his wine again. "Hell, man, she carried me half the way to the airport, fed me to get my strength back and hauled our butts out of there on the first plane. Never seen anything like it. Girl's a wonder. I owe her my life." He tossed her a sappy look of gratitude over the rim of his glass.

She was going to kill him.

"Matt, he's exaggerating. I promise you..." She broke off when she saw his expression of pure disbelief. "What's the matter? Don't you think I'm capable of that? Of...of what he said?"

Matt turned without a word and slammed out of the apartment. They heard him thumping down the stairs. She rounded on Joe, throwing up her hands in sheer frustration. "What the devil did you think you were doing? You probably got me fired, you know that? I wanted him to think..."

What had she wanted Matt to think? What had she expected when she set out on this venture? That Matt and Sebastian would be so delighted when she'd proved herself, they would promote her to field work permanently? She slumped against the nearest armchair and blew out a sigh.

Joe came over and grasped her shoulders. He bent just a bit so that his face was right in front of hers. "So I beefed it up a little. They won't fire you, Martine. You really did save my life. You got me out. Maybe Matt's just ticked off because I refused to get out when he tried to get me to, and then I came back with you. What you did was well-planned and executed right down to the last detail. They can't possibly argue with your results.''

She shrugged, but she couldn't agree with him there. Matt and Sebastian would argue all right. And Sebastian Ames would probably terminate her employment immediately because she had seriously overstepped and gone way beyond her job description. But that was a worry for Monday morning. Not tonight.

She dismissed it for now. "I'll handle it. Let's forget about it for now and get that pizza. You call it in. I need to… God, I need that glass of wine.''

He laughed, straightened to his full height and planted a playful kiss on top of her head. "Lighten up. Before I'm done, they'll be giving you a citation and a raise.''

"Joe, please!'' When he turned, eyebrow raised in question, she continued, "Please, don't do me any more favors.''

He walked back over, his gait lazy, his dark eyes gleaming wickedly. She stood while his hands cradled her face and his lips met hers. The kiss had a different flavor than those Matt had interrupted. This one tasted like gratitude, something she appreciated, but not right now.

She raised on tiptoe and increased the pressure, pulling him to her, hoping to regain ground lost by Matt's unfortunate interruption.

Joe pushed away and smiled down at her. "No, Martine. Not now.''

"Why not?'' Her breath shuddered out, causing the words to wobble. Like her knees.

"Because I don't want to be a player in your little rebellion, that's why.'' He looked amused, but she sensed he meant it. "I admit I was all for this before your brother showed up, but I've changed my mind. I sense you're not a one-night stander, Martine. To tell you the truth, neither am I." He gave her a grim smile. "At least not any more."

"Fine," she snapped, angry with herself for revealing how much she wanted him. He obviously had more control and wasn't nearly as affected by their mutual attraction. "Forget it."

He slid his hands down her arms and clutched the hands she had fisted. "No, I'm not about to forget. But I think I *will* postpone until I know it's *me* you really want. It looks like you're still trying to prove something here. Maybe show your father you're no different than your brother, even if you are female?" He paused and sighed. "Dangerous work and casual sex. Not what a woman usually leaps at unless there's a reason."

"Spare me your pop psychology. I told you my father's dead!"

"Yeah, but he's still dictating what you do in a way, making you feel you have to be everything your brother is. If it means anything to you, I don't think you'd ever have turned out a wimp, Martine. Not under any circumstances. But I don't think I want to be a party to establishing your thrill-a-minute lifestyle. Nobody likes being used."

"*Used?* Why, you…" She jerked her hand free and almost slugged him. He was waiting for it, but she stopped just in time. Taking a deep breath, she released it slowly, unclenched her fists and regained a little of her tattered dignity. "I think you had better leave."

He nodded and stepped through the door, but turned back to face her. "I should. And I'm going to. It's not that I don't want you, Martine. I want you too much."

"It was just a few kisses, Corda. Get over yourself." She held his gaze, willing herself not to shake.

"I wish you had wanted more than a night's worth."

He frowned thoughtfully as he paused again. "You know, I don't think I've ever said that to a woman before?"

She slammed the door in his face and then leaned against it.

*Oh God, could he be right about her?*

Joe walked to the nearest gas station and called a cab. The ride seemed long. And sad. He had met the one woman he could really go for in a big way, but he couldn't take her on the terms she offered.

He almost had, physically at least. Only seeing her as some guy's sister had made him stop and think how he would feel if it were one of his own crazy little sisters in her place and Matt Duquesne were the one doing the seducing.

He had also told Martine the absolute truth, how he felt about being used. If she wanted him for real, not just what he represented, then maybe he could handle it. Or maybe it was the excuse he had needed to let her go.

He knew Martine didn't realize she was still riding the adrenaline high. True, her heartbeat might have slowed down to almost normal. But the fever of success, the exhilaration of defeating death was clouding her judgment more than she knew. He'd been there, right where she was. As recently as a half hour ago.

Once she settled down, figured things out, she'd be relieved that he hadn't stayed tonight. His body was still humming with arousal. He would probably spend some sleepless nights between now and the time he got over her.

Forty minutes later, Joe arrived back at the airport to book his flight to D.C. He was paying the cab driver while scanning his surroundings out of habit. It was mere chance that he caught sight of the all-too-familiar profile of Carlos Humberto as he and two associates entered a taxi.

Shock at seeing a dead man walking held Joe immobile

for all of two seconds. Then he spent another few kicking himself for not climbing into that ravine and checking the body for signs of life after Martine shot the bastard. Humberto had to have been wearing a Kevlar vest.

Humberto couldn't have been right on their tail coming out of Bogotá. He would have had his hands full then arranging his own escape. But he was here now and there could only be one reason for his being here in Atlanta. He knew where to find Martine.

Joe jumped back in the cab and headed straight back to her, praying Humberto had not somehow discovered her home address.

He arrived, slung a fistful of bills at the driver as he leaped out of the cab, and tore up the steps at top speed. He had no weapons other than his hands and a stupid pocket knife. If Humberto had beat him here, he knew they had little chance of surviving.

After all he and Martine had done to the man, Humberto would have a vendetta going that no one could reason with. He would be out for blood, because there was nothing left for him to be after. Not the money, not the drugs and no possible restitution of his former life at all. Nothing but revenge.

# Chapter 5

"**M**artine! Open up!" he called, banging on the door with his fist, punching the doorbell repeatedly.

He stopped when he heard her—at least he hoped it was her—sliding the chain off the lock. The breath he was holding huffed out when she swung the door open. "Let's go!" he ordered, grabbing her by the wrist.

"What?" She dug in her heels.

"Humberto's here. I saw him at the airport. If he knows where you are, we've got to get the hell out of here. Do you have a weapon?"

She nodded, looking dumbstruck by his news. He noticed for the first time that she was only wearing a night-shirt.

"Give me your gun. I'll stand watch while you grab some clothes. Make it snappy. And bring a cell phone."

To her credit, she grasped the urgency of the situation and flew to follow orders. He did a hurried check of the Glock she shoved into his hands. The feel of it soothed him a little.

Humberto and his friends would also have to find a way to arm themselves before coming here. They could not have brought weapons on the plane. With the spot checks of baggage, it would have been too dangerous to risk arrest. No, they would either have contacts here who could furnish weapons or they would steal them.

Several minutes crawled by as Joe stood in the shadows outside her door, peering into the night, every nerve on edge. He shuddered to think what might have happened if he'd not gone back to the airport. And with the size of that airport, he could so easily have missed seeing Humberto at all. Hell, he had thought they were home free.

"Let's roll," Martine said, handing him the sports bag he had left behind earlier and the overnight bag she had packed for herself. She pulled the door closed behind her, keys in hand. She had donned a pair of dark-brown slacks and a matching silk blouse. Her leather shoes were flat-heeled, stylish but practical. She wore a brown sweater draped over her shoulders, the sleeves tied in front. Very preppy, he thought. So not her.

He followed her to a dark Jeep Cherokee parked in the well-lit lot nearby, where she popped the locks with the remote and went straight to the driver's side.

Joe almost demanded she relinquish the keys, but told himself she knew the city better than he did. He climbed in the passenger side and took the small bag she'd brought with her into his lap. "Your cell phone in this thing?"

"Big pocket on the side."

He fished it out.

"Call Matt. Speed dial 2," she ordered.

Joe was already shaking his head and punching at the numbers on the little instrument. "If ol' Hummy knew where you'd be, he knows where your brother is. We'll give Matt a heads-up, but we aren't going there."

"Then where?" she demanded.

Joe put the phone to his ear and waited. A message

machine on the other end spat out the number of the duty agent for the local office. He tapped it in and waited some more. A woman answered. "Cunningham."

"Agent Cunningham. Joe Corda from the D.C. office here." He hesitated as she asked how she could be of help. How could she? How could he explain that he'd just come off an assignment he'd thought completed and found himself and a civilian being chased by a drug lord who had serious retribution on his agenda?

"Do you recognize the name Carlos Humberto? From Colombia?" he asked her.

"No. Do you need some information concerning this individual?"

"I have more info than I need, thanks. But look him up. He's just arrived in your city with two of his men. This is a seriously disturbed individual with murder on his mind and he has local contacts. I have reason to believe he will show up shortly at the LeJardin apartments, unit 205, loaded for bear. Get all the backup you can and take him down."

She cleared her throat. "Agent...Carter, is it?"

He spelled his name. "Listen to me, please. Humberto's entire operation in Colombia has just been shut down. He's mad as hell and about to wreak some serious havoc. Are you with me on this?"

Another small hesitation. "I have no immediate way to verify what you're saying, sir. Or even who you are. If you want to leave a number, I'll contact my superior, meet him at the office and get back to you."

Joe gritted his teeth and banged his head back against the headrest. "Look, lady, I've just delivered what amounts to the collar of the century. Can you handle this or not?"

"As soon as I have contacted and coordinated with my office and yours, of course I can," she snapped. "But I can't very well commit agents to this without some sort of—''

"Thanks anyway," Joe snapped and punched the Off button. He quickly hit the speed dial for Matt Duquesne, who answered immediately.

"Duquesne? Listen up. Humberto's here. I saw him at the airport and have reason to believe he's after us. I'll keep Martine out of his reach. Call in some troops, do what you gotta do. He knew what Martine was doing in Colombia so he'll know about Ames and its employees. Watch yourself.''

"Where are you?" Duquesne demanded.

"On the move. We'll be in touch.''

"If you let him within a mile of Martine, I'll—''

"Save your breath, okay? We're not planning to make a stand and shoot it out with him. We're headed for D.C. She'll be safe with me.''

He rang off before her brother could argue that. And there were several arguments that would be valid. For now, Joe intended to do precisely what he'd promised Matt. He'd keep Martine and himself alive and reach familiar territory where he could depend on getting help from either DEA or Sextant. Or both.

He had no clue how many contacts Humberto actually had Stateside, but there was no point waiting around for some of them to show up.

"I'm not going to Washington with you," Martine declared, slowing the car to an unreasonable speed for the six-lane they were on.

He shot her a steely look. "Don't you test my determination, Martine. Put the pedal down and get us out of this city." When she scoffed, he shouted, "Do it *now!*''

She gunned the accelerator so hard, his neck almost snapped. "I can't believe you're running," she said.

"You damn well better believe it. Our little Humbuddy probably knows a hell of a lot more people in Atlanta than I do. Maybe more than *you* do. And they'll still be believing they have to depend on him for their steady supply of dope. By the time the people here get the word he's history with the cartel in Colombia, we could be dead as last week's catch.''

''Won't someone call and tell his contacts here?'' she asked.

''Not likely. They won't want to admit it—not yet anyway—and besides, they're probably still looking for him there. How much gas you got?''

She glanced down. ''Half a tank.''

''How much money?''

''A few dollars. Fifteen, maybe. You?''

''Not enough. Get off at the next exit. Find an ATM,'' he ordered. ''If we both withdraw the max, it should be enough to get us there. We'd better not leave a paper trail.''

''Don't be ridiculous. He couldn't trace us that way.... Could he? Why don't we just fly? We'd be there before he knew we were gone.''

''Maybe. Unless he has someone watching for us at the airport. We just don't know how many people he has here. That's the problem. I've been on this guy's case for nearly a year now and his reach is incredible. You said yourself he's got contacts up the wazoo. That probably won't change unless he tries to arrange a deal involving the Colombians or until word filters through the grapevine. By that time, it would be too late for us.''

Her worried gaze flashed his way briefly, then back to the road where cars were zipping past despite the fact that she was speeding big-time. ''You think he's come specifically to find you?''

''To find both of us. Absolutely.''

They managed to find a bank within a block of the exit and drew out the daily limit allowed from the automatic teller machine. Joe felt a bit better. They had a good vehicle, a fair head start and enough money to get them to D.C.

She filled the gas tank and then took the access road to the northernmost route that would take them to Chattanooga, Tennessee. Joe had never been there and didn't particularly want to go now, but he'd go to hell itself to keep Humberto from catching up with the woman who had shot him.

Martine checked her watch as they reached the outskirts of Chattanooga. While they had not been driving all that long, she needed to take a break. They also needed food since they had never gotten around to ordering that pizza. But they had drunk the wine. "I'm starving," she told him.

He sighed impatiently. "Pull off at the next exit and hit a drive-through. We can eat on the way. I'll take over if you're tired of driving already."

"I need to go inside," she said pointedly.

"Oh, okay."

He might sound amused, but unless he had a bladder the size of Texas, she knew he would welcome a pit stop, too. "There's a place." He pointed to the towering sign advertising a chain restaurant at the next exit.

Their meal took less than twenty minutes and when they returned to the Jeep, he asked for the keys. "You sleep a while. I'll wake you when I get too tired. We should take turns and drive straight through if we can."

"Why? There's no way Humberto can find us on the road like this. He won't know what kind of vehicle I have."

"Want to bet your life on that? I don't. He's going to come after us with every resource he's got, Martine. There's nothing left for him to lose. After we blew his operation sky-high, there's no way he could have gone back. We made him a marked man."

Martine shivered, rubbing her arms to restore warmth. "I guess he couldn't even risk going to his wife and family, could he?"

"No. His missus will surely side with her old man and he'll be out for Humberto's blood. So our boy's got nothing left now but a very temporary power here in the States and whatever funds he had access to before he left the country. That gives him a limited time in which to exact revenge on the people responsible for his downfall. Namely us."

"It could be he was only getting out of Colombia, seeking safety. Maybe you're just being paranoid," she suggested as she fastened her seat belt.

"If that's so, why would he come to Atlanta? And hey, paranoia's my friend," Joe said easily and pulled back onto the interstate. "Can't live long without it in this business."

"How long have you been doing it?"

"Too long. Way too long," he answered, his tone weary. The dash lights cast a weak glow that angled upward, exposing the planes of his features and emphasizing lines hardly noticeable in the light of day. His strong fingers flexed a few times, fitting themselves to the steering wheel as he settled his large body for the long drive ahead. He rolled his shoulders slightly. He looked exhausted.

"Joe, is something else wrong?"

"Why? That's not enough?" He smiled and tossed her a weary glance. "No, there's nothing else. You know all I know. Go to sleep, Martine."

"I meant with you. Is there something wrong with you, Joe?" she persisted.

"Nothing a few weeks on the beach wouldn't cure. When this is over, that's where I'm headed. Just me and a cooler full of Dos Equis." He glanced over again. "Offer still holds. You come, too. That is, if you want to and promise not to talk shop."

Martine laughed, leaned back and closed her eyes. "Nice dream, Joe," she said, letting exhaustion claim her. She hadn't lied. It was a nice dream.

As the purr of the motor and shimmy of slightly out-of-line tires morphed into waves rhythmically rolling onto a shore, the dream proved better than nice. It became real.

Joe, wearing only ragged remnants of the gray trousers, strolled down a sandy beach, beer in hand, grin revealing those straight white teeth as he approached. The glare of a tropical sun bounced enticingly off his heavily muscled shoulders, arms and chest. Strong, bare feet tracked through sugary white sand, bringing him ever closer.

She wore a sarong tied loosely allowing the warm ocean breeze to caress her skin as the soft garment billowed out from her body. A heady sense of anticipatory awareness created a tingle in places he had yet to touch. She quivered as she held out her arms in welcome.

He walked right into them, those amazing hands of his sliding beneath the silky fabric, creating havoc with her senses.

She breathed in his scent, a peculiar mix of cool fresh limes and hot ready man. The low timbre of his voice vibrated through her as they embraced, the landscape of his body melding perfectly with hers. She writhed in pleasure, the sun hot against her bare back, his hands even hotter against her bare flesh.

Something began tugging at her arm, calling to her, warning her to…

"Wake up!"

"No," Martine groaned in protest, even as she opened her eyes. Reality hit her like a slap in the face. Headlights from oncoming traffic flashed, causing her to squint. She gulped in a deep breath and quickly pushed herself upright in the seat, embarrassed by the fact that a dream of Joe had aroused her. She risked a glance at him and saw him frowning.

"It was just a dream," he assured her. "You groaned like you were in pain or something. Thought I'd better bring you out of it. You all right?"

Martine nodded, afraid to speak and maybe betray what she'd really been up to in that dream. What *he* had been up to. But he couldn't know. How could he? There was no way he could even guess she'd been dreaming of him. Of them together.

She released the breath she was holding and smoothed her hands over her face, raking her fingers through her hair and shaking her head to clear away every vestige of the dream. But the erotic images of them together remained, teasing her mercilessly, even as he watched.

"That bad, huh?" he asked, sounding concerned.

Not taunting her, Martine decided. He was worried. She smiled to herself, her secret safe. "I'm fine. You want me to drive now?" Her voice trembled, sounding almost as shaky as she felt.

"Not on a dare in your condition," he replied to her question about taking the wheel. "There's an exit up ahead. I think we'd better stop for a few hours. I noticed you didn't get much shut-eye on the planes. Apparently you have trouble sleeping while you ride."

Fully alert now, Martine almost laughed. The fool had no clue *he* was what disrupted her sleep. She cleared her throat and switched on the radio. "Don't worry about it. What kind of music do you like?" Anything to get his mind off that dream of hers. To get *her* mind off of it. "Oh, I remember, oldies. Right?"

He reached over and switched it off. "No music. We're finding a motel. You're too dopey to drive and I'm getting there fast."

"Let's not do that," she said, trying not to sound as if she were pleading. All she needed was to be shut up in a motel room with him, especially with that lingering vision of him half naked still clear in her head.

But Joe ignored her and slowed for the turnoff. He looked pretty determined. His jaw tight, his lips firmed, his eyes narrowed as he checked out the signs along the way advertising lodgings for the night. Vacancies everywhere. She lost the will to argue.

Surely after making it clear he wasn't interested in a brief sexual encounter with her, he would keep his distance a lot more carefully than he had before. Martine knew she wouldn't risk another rebuff like the one he'd given her after Matt left. It would be all right, she assured herself.

He bypassed the better-known chain hotels where they would need a credit card, and found a small place about two miles off the interstate. "This looks like a strictly cash establishment," he said, more or less to himself.

He was right. It certainly did. She doubted if any customers who stopped here ever gave their correct identity. Or did much sleeping, either.

Even Martine had no idea exactly where they were, which was reassuring. Humberto would never locate them here, wherever *here* was. Even if he somehow figured out they were headed for D.C., there must be thousands of motels between there and Atlanta.

"One room," Joe said pointedly, though there was no suggestiveness whatsoever in the declaration. "We need to save our cash for emergencies."

"Okay," she agreed. This wasn't a hotel where she'd like to be left in a room by herself. She could handle whatever happened, of course, but she certainly wouldn't be able to close her eyes for a minute. Then the rest of what he'd said registered. "What emergencies?"

He parked to one side of the office and unfastened his seat belt as he turned to look at her. "I saw a sign advertising a gun show at the civic center in Carnton. We might need another weapon."

"Get real. You can't buy a decent slingshot with what

we have between us now and we'll still need to eat. Plus, this," she said, shooting a dubious glance at the rundown hotel, "will cost us."

"We'll see what we can do," he said and went into the hotel office.

The room surprised her. Though the furnishings had probably been in place since the sixties, the linens actually looked clean. So did the bathroom. "Not so bad," she quipped. "The bed's king size anyway."

"Yeah," he said, eyeing the bed, then her, then the bed again.

"Don't worry," she told him, her voice a little bitter. "You're entirely safe with me."

He sighed and tossed his duffel onto the chair. "I came off a little high-handed at your apartment. Sorry."

Martine ignored him, went into the bathroom and closed the door. She stayed there for some time, until she ran out of things to do in a five-by-six tile-surfaced box with nothing but towels, T.P. and paper-wrapped soap for company.

There was a mirror, too, but she didn't really want to study her reflection for longer than it took to rake her hair back and check the circles under her eyes. The woman looking back would probably try to convince her she should go out there and make another pass at Joe and damn the consequences.

He knocked softly. "You asleep in there?"

She jumped up from the edge of the tub where she'd been sitting and unlocked the door. "Sorry," she said, brushing past him into the bedroom.

Damn, but he made her nervous now. She would have to watch every word she said and think about every gesture she made, so he wouldn't get the idea she was coming on to him again.

With that in mind, she curled up on the far side of the

bed fully clothed and closed her eyes. When he came out of that bathroom, she meant to be sound asleep.

Of course, the very intent kept her wide-awake. That, plus the fact that she had napped in the car. Dream-sleep must count because she was in no way sleepy now. She'd have to pretend, because she certainly didn't want to have a *can-we-sleep-in-the-same-bed-and-be-nice* conversation.

Her senses went on full alert the minute he returned to the bedroom. There was a long silence, filled only with the overly long breaths she drew in and released.

When he did move, he wasn't particularly quiet about it. He checked the gun. She heard it click. He sat down heavily on the far side of the bed and toed off his shoes. Then he stretched out full-length beside her, not touching. "Those are some slow-moving sheep you're counting," he said finally.

Martine didn't respond. She crunched the pillow impatiently and snuggled deeper into the too-soft mattress. In less than five minutes, she could tell by his breathing—almost a soft snore—that he really had fallen asleep. Moving slowly, she carefully turned over so she could see him.

He was facing her with his eyes wide-open. And he was smiling. "That's how you fake it."

Infuriated, she snapped, "This is the first time I've ever *had* to fake it."

He laughed. "I promise you you'll never have to fake it with me again."

Martine turned over so fast, she almost fell off the bed. It was going to be a very long night.

Joe awoke with his hand cupped around a very shapely butt. His chest rested comfortably against Martine's back. It was her restlessness that had wakened him, a sinuous backward snuggling he hated like hell to resist. But he had to. They should have been out of the motel and on the road hours ago.

He removed his hand, backed away a little, flicked on the lamp and gave her fanny a firm pat. "Up and at 'em, slugger." Before she could react, he had rolled off the bed, pulled on his shirt and stepped into his shoes. The pants looked as if he'd slept in them because he had. He tucked the pistol beneath his belt and fished the toothpaste and brush out of his duffel.

She bypassed him without so much as a good morning and disappeared into the bathroom with the small bag she'd brought with her. "Ah, not a morning person," he muttered. "But I knew that."

He recalled their trail to Bogotá and how silent she had been for a while after they'd awakened. Though she'd moved quickly and surely then, he had realized that it took her a while to gear up for the day.

Joe always came awake at full throttle. He could hardly help wondering then what it would be like to coax her awake slowly with touches and kisses. And now that he had the opportunity, the wondering almost became compulsion.

"No," he said to himself. "Not just yet." If he ever had Martine Duquesne—and it was looking more and more like that *if* was a *when*—he wanted all the time in the world and no distractions. He also wanted more tomorrows with her than she would promise him now. Shared danger was not enough of a connection to sustain anything more than a quick fling. Joe knew this woman was worth more than that. He'd do something about it, too, if he thought she would give up her current job.

The water turned off. "Hey, babe, get a move on, would you?" he called to her. She'd hate being called *babe,* but Joe needed the distance that little insult would throw up between them right now, or else he'd be tempted to stay right here in this dump of a motel making love to her until Humberto died of old age.

She stormed out of the bathroom looking like a sixteen-year-old who'd been stood up for her favorite concert. "If you call me that word again…!"

"Yeah, yeah, I hear you," he said and left her standing there fuming while he went in to shave. "Just what I love, sharing a bathroom with a girl. My sister spent *days* primping while I had to stand outside, waiting to pee." He quickly closed the door, grinning when something thunked against the outside of it. He felt to make sure the gun was still where he'd put it.

"You're crude, rude and…"

"Delightful to know!" he added, laughing as he heard a muffled curse through the door.

He had just lathered his face when the door flew open.

"Joe, come look! There's a dark car out there by the office. Three men just got out and went inside."

He rushed to the window and pulled the drape aside. It was impossible to see into the motel office. Though the whole front was glass, it was covered with blinds.

"Get in the Jeep," he ordered. "You drive. Pull up right behind that car and be ready to fly."

He had never seen her move so fast. She grabbed her bag, jumped into the vehicle and in seconds, she braked where he'd told her to. Joe climbed out, slashed the back tires on the black Camry and dived back in. She was peeling out of the parking lot before he had the door shut.

Shots erupted, several thunking into the back of the Jeep. Tires screeched as Martine careened onto the access road and gunned the motor.

"Turn right!" he ordered. "We'll take back roads. I hope you've got a map."

"Compass," she assured him, lifting her left wrist to remind him of the one in her watch.

"Right now any direction away from here is fine. They have us outgunned." He studied her carefully as she drove. "And you have a transmitter of some kind somewhere on you or they would never have found us."

She gasped, almost veering off the road.

"On me?"

He shrugged. "Well, I've been checking *me* daily while I was there and never found anything. Besides, you were money in his pocket, remember.

"There's no chance they put it anywhere on the car because we were gone with it before they got there," he said, thinking out loud. "We've got to find and ditch it," he told her. "And we have to do it before they get those tires fixed."

# Chapter 6

"Next place you see that could give any kind of cover, pull over," Joe ordered.

She chose a used car lot, fairly well lighted, and parked in between a truck and a van.

The second she cut the engine, she yanked off the watch and handed it over. "It's got to be this. Can you tell if it's in there?"

"Not without tools to open it."

"Smash it!" she insisted.

"No. We'll put it on something that's moving, preferably going south."

"Truck stop. Back to the interstate," she suggested and fired up the engine.

She drove top speed, surpassing the limit, but it seemed forever before they reached any place like what they were looking for. A Stuckey's loomed ahead and she took the exit.

Quickly, Joe jumped out when she stopped, looped the

buckled watch over the antenna of the nearest large vehicle and returned to the Jeep.

"Okay, hit it. Only go that way," he said, pointing away from the interstate.

For hours, they drove, taking turns, saying little, stopping only to refuel once. The back roads took them seriously off the nearest route to their destination in D.C., but the farther away they got, the more they relaxed.

It was nearing noon when Joe suggested they stop and rest. Food was high on his list of needs, but contact with someone who might help them came in a definite first.

When he mentioned that again, she nodded in agreement. "I guess DEA would be thrilled to get their hands on Humberto, especially if they can take him alive."

"Oh, they've had chances before. What do you think I was doing down there trying to get rid of him? They can't arrest him until he commits some crime on American soil that can be proved."

"Cold-blooded murder? Duh."

"Yeah, but if they wait until he succeeds, what good does that do us?"

"Point taken."

Joe nodded. "They can turn us over to the Marshal Service, get us in the Wit Program on the basis of what we did down there. But you know what that would mean."

She scoffed, just as he knew she would. It would mean giving up her family, her life, everything she knew. For his part, Joe knew he'd rather have a showdown in the middle of the street and be done with it. If only Martine were not involved. He couldn't stand the thought of her getting hurt, maybe even killed. She had already faced more risk than she should before they ever reached the States.

"I vote for the nearest police station, maybe call in the

State Patrol," she told him. "I suggested that as we were leaving Atlanta, and now I think I have to insist."

Joe shrugged. "If I thought they could deal with this, I'd have already done that. But those are fully automatic weapons our boys are using, not something a small-town force would be likely to have or be able to compete with in a showdown. Also, the locals won't believe us at first—you have to admit it sounds unbelievable—and there might not be time to check our story if the transmitter wasn't in that watch."

"Well, I don't know where else it could be," she argued.

Joe had a pretty good idea where it was. But he didn't want to tell Martine that it could possibly be a part of her body now. A transmitter inserted when she was sedated and unaware. The devices were so small now they could be implanted damn near anywhere. He'd made it a habit to check the surface of his skin every morning when he had showered, but who knew? She was simply the most probable carrier.

It had most likely been placed there so Humberto could track her down if she had decided to escape. Or maybe he'd been waiting for her to make contact with someone outside the compound, go out to meet whoever had sent her in to spy.

"How about the FBI?" she questioned. "Wouldn't they be able to do something?"

"I don't imagine they have anything more concrete on Humberto than DEA does. I told you that's why I infiltrated his organization in the first place. My job was to destroy the operation and put the head honcho out of business."

"Well, you certainly did that," Martine said, shaking her head.

"Yeah, but before I left to go down there, there were only rumors he was the one running the cartel and trucking with the rebel forces to get the drugs out. He's been incredibly careful not to break any laws here. Not a one.''

''What about all the drug deals? They must have been big ones with lots of people involved.''

''He met with major dealers all over the place, but someone else made the actual arrangements. Unfortunately, none of them are in custody to testify that they were doing them on his behalf. So, we have nothing to present to any law enforcement agency except our own belief that he and his men are here specifically to get rid of us. We can't even prove he's done anything since he's been here this time.''

''I saw him about to kill you in cold blood,'' she said with a shiver.

''Even if he had committed murder there, no one could arrest him for it.''

''He put bullet holes in the back of my Jeep and would have killed us.''

Joe nodded. ''Yes, but you didn't actually see him shooting, did you?''

She sighed. ''No. Too bad he's not a terrorist, everybody would be all over him.''

Well, there it was. Joe laughed and slapped her on the shoulder. ''Out of the mouths of babes! My girl, you are something else.''

She shot him a dark look. ''Yes, I'm something else all right, not your *girl*. And definitely not a *babe!* What is it with you?''

''C'mon, Martine! You've hit on something here. Don't go all PC on me while I'm doing cartwheels!''

''What do you mean?''

''Terrorists. That's the answer.'' He kissed her soundly on the mouth and laughed again when she drew back looking stunned. ''We'll call Mercier. What would you label three foreigners using illegal weapons to shoot up a motel parking lot, endangering American citizens? That fits a terrorist in my book. You know how to reach him?"

"I certainly do." A smile slowly crept across her features. It was like the sun coming out after a storm. Joe dearly wanted to kiss her again. But they had a phone call to make.

Here was his chance to see what the Sextant Team was all about and whether he wanted to be a part of it. *If* he lived to be a part of it.

First off, he'd request that they stash Martine somewhere safe until all this was over. Surely they could do that much even if Mercier and his new hires turned out to be desk jockeys, simple window dressing for the new HSA organization, a show to illustrate how well agents from the different agencies could work together.

Chances were pretty good that they weren't that. After all, they had hired him, a DEA cowboy who had never been particularly photogenic. Or tactful. God help *them* if they were front men for the new outfit and expected him to deal with the press in any way. He'd wind up in Leavenworth.

"Joe?" She glanced up into the rearview mirror again and then over at him. "There's a car trailing us about a quarter of a mile back, and it's made the last two turns I have. If it's them, I figure they're hanging back until we stop again."

"How're you doing on gas now?" Joe asked as he turned around to look for the tail.

"Quarter of a tank."

He reached for the 9mm for all the good it would do against an AK-47. "We'll call in the cavalry later if we get the chance, but it looks like we'll have to handle this next skirmish by ourselves."

Martine knew they were outgunned and outmanned. They needed a plan if they were to survive Humberto's catching up with them when they stopped for gas, which would need to be soon. She had believed that once they unloaded her watch with the transmitter, they'd be good to go. They had crossed the Virginia line about five minutes before and were traveling parallel to Highway 81.

"How do you suppose they found us?" she asked Joe.

Busy checking the weapon again, he merely shrugged.

"What aren't you telling me?"

"The transmitter," he said. "It's gotta be an implant. They make 'em about the size of a grain of rice now. Shoot it in with a hypodermic. Track you with a cell phone or global positioning system using a laptop or handheld."

A chill ran through her just imagining something foreign within her that she hadn't even known about. She racked her brain, trying to recall if she'd ever been so out of it that Humberto could have injected her with something without her knowing about it. She was a very light sleeper and as far as she knew, had not been drugged to make her sleep through such a thing.

He glanced over his shoulder again at the car following them. "If we can lose them for half an hour, maybe we can find it and get rid of it."

She was afraid to ask. "How?"

"Minor surgery," he muttered.

Martine cringed, imagining what that would involve. She promised herself it was only like removing a splinter. "Funston City's about four miles away. Maybe there's a mall there. They'd know we were there, but not exactly where. That would give us time to hide somewhere inside and look for it."

"And if we can't find it? Can you imagine the havoc if these goons open fire in a mall? Besides, I don't think there is a mall in Funston City."

"You know the place?"

"Been there to buy supplies for camping trips. An old

college buddy of mine is from Roanoke. We used to come out this way when we were in college. Beautiful country with pretty good fishing.''

Another idea occurred to her. "How about the police station there? They wouldn't follow us inside, would they? Surely the cops could help us if they did.''

"Might work.'' He didn't sound too hopeful, however. Humberto would still be waiting for them when they came back outside, even if they were minus the transmitter.

"Somehow we've got to get them off our tail until we can stop broadcasting our location,'' she said, stating the obvious. "Could the signal be interrupted somehow?''

"In some place where there's a lot of interference maybe. There's no way to know how sophisticated the little gadget is. It could be as simple as the one used to track pets when they're lost or stolen.''

"Or not,'' Martine said, almost under her breath.

"Yeah. Or not. But I think we have to hope for that and run on that assumption. You can bet Humberto's not planning to trail us much longer without making another move. I've got an idea.''

"What?'' she demanded.

He looked behind them again, then turned around to peer into the darkness ahead. "If we haven't passed the turnoff already, there's a place we used to go caving once in a while. I don't know if a ton of overhead rock will block the signals we're putting off, but it's worth a try. At any rate, we ought to be able to evade for a while, even if he can track us. Caves are my thing.''

"Well, they certainly aren't *mine*,'' Martine muttered, but she didn't elaborate. This probably wouldn't be a great time to admit to claustrophobia.

They rode in silence for another ten minutes. Then he pointed at a sign half overgrown with vines. "Yeah, there we go! Peebles Ridge. Cut the lights and hang a right.''

She swerved onto the paved, two-lane side road, blinking rapidly, trying to adjust her vision to the weak light of the half moon.

"Now watch for a break in the foliage. There's a dirt road on your right about a half mile ahead if I remember right."

It was less than that. Martine turned too sharply and almost ran into the ditch. "How far?" she gasped once the wheels were straight. "Are they back there?"

He looked. "If they are, they're running dark, too. Go left when I tell you. Good thing we've got four-wheel drive. They don't, so we're ahead of the game and should have a little lead time."

She turned when he told her and after a grueling five minutes of bumping over brush and deep ruts, he ordered her to stop. "We're here. Come on."

He brought his duffel and she grabbed her bag and they hurriedly exited the car. Brambles snagged her clothing and branches raked her hair and face as he half dragged her through the heavily wooded terrain.

She'd always been pretty good in the rough, but the last few days had taken their toll.

"Through here," he commanded, disappearing into a dark hole in the rock, about two feet wide and four feet high. Martine froze.

"Hurry up!" he added when she remained outside. Before she could protest, he reached back out and grasped her arm, yanking her inside with him. "Now stay put until I check it out. Don't venture farther in yet."

"Like there's a chance of that," she gulped.

Martine clung to the damp wall of the cave while he stepped back out. She heard him break off and drag several dead branches, she guessed to conceal the entrance. What sounded like a huff of relief whispered through the stygian darkness that had swallowed them whole. She shivered and a small whimper escaped in spite of her resolve.

Joe found her hand and gripped it. "We'll have some light in a few minutes, soon as we get deeper in. Stay stooped over so you don't bump your head."

Her head swam as if a rock had already smacked her. She felt disoriented by the total lack of light, but she placed one foot in front of the other as he pulled her along. Walls closed in, damp, fetid as bat guano and scary as hell.

She heard Joe's shoulders periodically brush the outcroppings of rock, a soft swish of fabric dragging against rough stone. She secured the shoulder strap of her bag and trailed her free hand along the wall to steady herself.

*It will not collapse. We will not be crushed. The opening will get larger. There is an exit. Several exits.*

She moved her lips with the made-up mantra, but allowed no sound to escape them. Joe could not know her fears. Apparently he had none, the idiot. Didn't he know they would suffocate and die in here? If the rocks didn't collapse and kill them first?

She sucked in a deep breath, more or less to prove there was enough air for that. There was nothing for it but to tough this out. If she planned to do this kind of work, she must endure whatever came along. God, even dodging bullets didn't scare her like this did.

"We'll have to crawl through here so kneel down," he told her.

*Crawl?* A small, hysterical laugh burst out before she could stop it. At the same time, a light came on. At last, the flashlight. Martine almost wept with relief. Then she spied the tunnel he expected her to enter.

"I'll go first," he offered.

"You'll go last, too," she gasped. "I can't, Joe. I can't do it."

"Sure you can. You have to." His voice sounded so logical, as if he weren't telling her she had to do the impossible. "On your knees for me, babe." The flashlight illuminated his grin from below, giving it a truly evil cast. "Not a phrase I'll ever repeat if you're a good girl to-night."

"You… You're trying to make me…angry…aren't you?" she panted, glancing fearfully between him and the small gaping maw that waited for them. She clung to his arm for support because her legs were quivering badly. "Angry…because you know I'm…"

"Yeah, it'll be okay, though. Is it working? You mad enough yet?" His hand came up to brush her hair back from her face and lingered to caress her cheek and ear. "Where's that kickass kid who dragged me halfway across Colombia? Is she gonna wimp out on me now?"

Martine took a deep breath and knelt. What else could she do when he put it that way?

He smiled, nodded and went ahead and crawled into the tunnel, taking the light away from the larger corridor where she waited. Through sheer force of will, Martine climbed in behind him.

The temperature must have been around fifty degrees, but she was covered with sweat. Her fingers slid on the slippery rock, wet with its own perspiration.

"This too shall pass. This too shall pass," Martine kept whispering to herself through what seemed an endless passageway.

Slivers of light dodged around Joe as he held the flash-light in front of him and low-crawled through the narrow opening cut by some ancient underground flow of water.

Several times, he grunted almost painfully while squeezing his wide shoulders past a particularly narrow point. Humberto might fit through here, Martine thought, but given the size of his two cohorts, he'd have to come in alone.

She and Joe seemed to be steadily descending since entering the tunnel. Blood must be pooling in her brain because she could hardly think now. Sensory overload, she suspected. Or oxygen deprivation. She prayed she wouldn't faint.

Suddenly Joe disappeared. An almost perfectly round exit to the tunnel loomed in front of her and his hands reached back inside to lift her out. She almost fell on top of him.

"Here we are. Careful where you step when I put you down." He had rested the flashlight on one of the stalagmites protruding from the floor of the cave room they'd entered.

The light only illuminated the immediate area of what appeared to be a very large chamber. Musical plop-plops of water echoed in the stillness as she looked around warily.

"Living cave," he explained, smiling. "Great place, isn't it?"

She frowned at his impaired mental acuity. His "great place" was her worst nightmare, second only to the narrow space she'd just experienced. "How…how deep are we?"

"You don't really want to know that, do you?"

"Maybe not." Her voice sounded very small, the way it had when she'd been a child. That would normally have made her furious with herself, but she was too wrapped up in terror at the moment to spare any other emotion. The vastness of the cave room seemed to shrink by the second. The tonnage of solid rock above and all around them, more threatening.

"Okay. Here's how I figure it," he was saying. "They'll take a while to find the entrance. Then they'll have to decide which hole we crawled into. We passed a number that are wider to enter, but will narrow too much to get through or will dead-end."

Martine took a deep breath and made herself pay attention. She could get through this. *She could. Be practical.*

*Think.* "We should block up this one so that it looks like it dead-ends, too, but I don't see how we could." She pointed. "Knock off some of these little tower things. We can block it with them."

Joe glanced around at the eerie formations protruding out of the ground and hanging from the ceiling. "Sorry. Against Virginia law. Can't deface anything. *Take nothing but pictures, leave nothing but footprints,* code of the caver."

"I'll pay the damn fines!" she cried in a desperate whisper.

"Not necessary," he assured her. "There are so many bends in the tunnel, the little bit of light we have won't show through to the main cave."

"You're sure?" Martine stood frozen, struggling anew to control her breathing. It wasn't so bad in here now if she didn't let herself think about having to crawl her way out again.

"Martine?"

She jumped, brushing back against a slender waist-high point that snapped under the pressure. The sound of it hitting the floor of the cave seemed to echo forever.

"It's all right, honey," Joe told her. "Just try to relax for a minute. Don't worry about that."

Yeah, getting slapped with a misdemeanor for defacing a cave was not exactly high on her worry list right now, Martine thought, catching back a sob that threatened to unleash hysteria if she let it go.

Joe was rubbing her arms, doing his best to comfort her, but it wasn't working very well. "Now comes the really fun part, I'm afraid," he said.

She was already shaking her head. "Not another crawl!"

"Nope, not yet."

"Then what?" What in the world could be worse?

''Body search,'' he replied, looking a little apprehensive of her stunned reaction. ''We've got to find that implant.''

Joe had dearly wanted to get Martine naked, but certainly not in a situation like this. She obviously wasn't that enthusiastic about it herself right now, though she was gamely unbuttoning her shirt. His gaze followed her fingers and he winced a little when he saw them tremble. ''Wait.''

She halted what she was doing and just looked at him, wide-eyed, awaiting further instructions.

''Let's check your neck and arms first. Maybe undressing won't be necessary.'' God help him, he didn't need to see her without her clothes on. Not right now. He had enough problems without arousal sapping all the blood from his brain.

When she offered one arm, he pushed up her sleeve and ran his fingertips over her skin, sliding them up to her shoulder beneath the fabric. Smooth as cream. He nodded and then began checking the other. ''Any bumps you've noticed anywhere lately?'' he asked, hoping for a reprieve. If not, he was in for a really uncomfortable hard-on he couldn't do anything about.

''Maybe a few bug bites, but I got those when we were hiking to Bogotá.'' Her voice sounded breathless.

He released her arm and slid his fingers along the sides of her neck, checked her nape, hairline, then massaged the scalp beneath that gloriously silky mane. Nothing. He sighed. ''Shirt first, I guess.''

She removed it. Joe held the flashlight close to her skin as he examined every visible inch, sliding her bra straps off her shoulders.

Impatiently she yanked the thing down around her waist, freeing her breasts. Joe watched her hands slide carefully over the surface of her body, her fingertips pressing against her softness, checking for any blemish that might indicate her skin had been perforated.

Breath stuck in his throat. He couldn't tear his gaze away. Her breasts were beautiful, the dusky nipples erect. Due to the cold inside the cave? He sweated as if it were ninety degrees. Or was she as turned on as he was? *Now was not the time.*

"My back?" She turned away and presented the smooth expanse of skin. Joe shut his eyes tight for a couple of seconds and flexed his fingers. Gingerly he placed his palms so that they spanned her rib cage and drew them inch by careful inch until he'd covered the area between her waist and underarms. The curve of her waist drove him crazy.

Fanning his fingers out, he caressed her shoulder blades, the indentation of her spine and on up to the smooth curve of her neck and shoulders. She shivered.

He groaned. "Lord, I wish we were doing this somewhere else," he muttered.

"And for some other reason," she added in a small voice, reminding him that she was suffering from both fear for her life and claustrophobia, not arousal.

"Pants next," he told her with a new determination to keep this businesslike. "Put your shirt back on so you won't freeze."

She tugged up her bra and put her arms through the straps, then pulled on her shirt. Without pausing, she pushed down her slacks, panties and all, so that they bunched around her ankles. Then she straightened.

Joe swallowed hard, praying for strength while he examined the enticing roundness of the nicest ass he'd seen in years. Maybe ever. She jumped a little when his fingers strayed into dangerous territory.

"I'll do that," she gasped. "Get the backs of my legs."

He crouched and did as he was told, beating back the wildest urge to kiss the backs of her knees. Though the light was too weak, he imagined he could see the faint veins there in that tender spot, the crease of thin skin, sensitive as hell. His lips tingled at the thought. He ached to taste her against his tongue.

He deliberately avoided even thinking about what she was doing to her front while he was busy at her back.

"All clear," she told him, moving a step away and hurriedly dragging her pants up. "Now for my feet. But I'd know it if it was imbedded in one of my feet. Don't you think?"

Think? Who could think? He couldn't even stand up. Instead he leaned back against the wet wall of the cave, still crouched, and patted one knee. "Balance against that stalagmite and put your foot up here."

She placed her hand against one of the sturdier-looking waist-high towers and did as she was told. Joe removed her shoe and cradled her bare foot in his hand, memorizing the shape of it right down to the length of her delicate toes. Reluctantly, he relinquished it and slid her shoe back on. "Other one," he muttered, both glad and sorry as hell he was almost done.

Near the back of her ankle was where he found it. A small, raised nodule the size of a mosquito bite. He cursed.

# *Chapter* 7

"What? What is it?" she demanded. "You found something?"

"Looks like it," he growled. Now he was going to have to damage that beautiful skin of hers to get the transmitter out. He would have to hurt her. The thought of it made him sick, but it had to be done.

"Well, that's a relief!" she said with a protracted sigh. "That figures. It would be in the last place we looked, wouldn't it? What can you use to remove it?"

Joe placed her foot on the ground and got up. Without answering her, he pulled a clean T-shirt out of his sports bag and then found the Swiss Army knife he'd purchased at the airport gift shop when they'd bought his clothes.

He rummaged in the corner of the pocket for the cigarette lighter. Though he'd never smoked, he did possess the primitive notion that a man should carry fire wherever he went. He couldn't count the times it had been a life-saver.

He tried never to be without a lighter and a pocket

knife, two things that were very handy to have in some situations. Every time he flew, he had to ditch a knife and buy another when he got where he was going. Thank God he had one now even though he was cursing what he needed it for.

"This will have to do." He opened the smallest blade, flicked the lighter on and ran it over the blade to kill any bacteria. "Sit down and get as comfortable as you can. This is going to hurt a little."

She sat, looking so pale and vulnerable against the bare rock he could hardly stand it. He sat facing her and gently lifted her foot to rest in his lap, her leg braced between his knees.

"Lean forward and hold the light close. Brace your arm on my knees," he ordered, bracing himself, trying to see her foot as an inanimate object. "Be as still as you can."

"Just like removing a splinter, right?" she said with blatantly fake cheer. "Go for it, doc."

Joe made a careful incision, slicing open the layers of skin with the sharp point, regretting he had nothing to anesthetize the area. If only they'd still been in the jungle, he knew certain plants he could have used for that. Even the enzyme from certain frogs, he could have used topically to deaden the tissue.

She hadn't made a sound or jerked her foot the way he'd expected. Blood trickled out, the flow increasing the deeper he went. He mopped at the incision with a corner of the T-shirt he had wadded beneath her heel.

Sweat beaded his face as he worked, separating the small wound, searching for the foreign object he was sure would be there. *Nothing!* The tissue beneath the skin looked totally undisturbed except for the incision he had made.

"Damn!" he growled, grabbing the flashlight and holding it directly over the cut. Again he stanched the blood and searched, probing with the flat of the blade until he was sure. What he was looking for simply wasn't there.

"What? What's wrong?" she asked, her voice higher pitched than usual.

Joe sighed heavily and shook his head as he looked up and met her worried gaze. "Looks like it was just a mosquito bite." But now it was a gaping little wound that was bleeding profusely and probably hurting like the devil.

"Then where could the transmitter be?" she demanded in a small voice. "Where could he have put it?"

Joe was already cutting a portion of the clean shirt to tie around her ankle as a bandage. "Looks like you might be able to pay me back for this little mistake. I guess it's my turn."

Martine watched, knowing her attention was a little too avid, as Joe sat back on his heels and hastily ripped off his shirt. Muscles rippled and gleamed in the glow of the flashlight. He wore a grim, narrow-eyed expression and she knew hers probably matched it.

"Must have slipped me a mickey one night and put it where I wouldn't notice. Dammit, I thought I'd gained his trust."

"He didn't trust anyone," Martine said with a huff.

"Start with the upper back," he ordered. "That's the most logical place to put the thing since it's the hardest to reach and the place I'd be least likely to notice a blemish." He turned as he spoke.

Martine brushed her hands over his skin, feeling the warmth and dampness against her palms.

"C'mon, you'll never find it like that. Punch around," he demanded. "Do it harder."

*Do it harder.* Yeah. When the lightest of touches only fueled the fire he'd started with his examination of her own body's surface.

She exhaled noisily and pressed her fingertips more

firmly into the muscles, covering every inch, wondering how much more stirred up she would get if he had to remove those pants of his and search more intimate areas of his body. Probably too physically excited to remember why she was doing this. At least it was taking her mind off where they were.

"Joe?" Just to the left of his right shoulder blade, she had felt something. She zeroed in on the spot, circling the small pea-sized lump. "This could be it."

"Dig it out," he demanded. "Don't be fussy about it. Think of cutting the eye out of a potato. And hurry up. Those batteries need to last long enough to get us out of here when you're finished."

Oh, God. The light! Crawling out with no light. She didn't want to think about that. She wouldn't.

Her hands shook when he handed her the knife and lighter and took the flashlight in his hand. He braced one palm against the wall of the cave and draped the hand holding the light over his shoulder so that it shone down on the area she was probing.

Martine shook her head to clear it, took a deep breath and concentrated on the job at hand. She had to forget about the problem of getting out of here and do what she had to do. If they didn't unload this transmitter, there was no way they'd make it to D.C. without Humberto catching them. They probably wouldn't even make it out of the cave if the transmission wasn't blocked by all this rock.

No. She couldn't think about all the rock bearing down on them from all sides. Not now.

"Do it, Martine!" he demanded. She jumped and almost dropped the knife.

To give herself a moment to focus, she wiped the knife on the knit shirt he had cut in pieces to make her bandage, and then clicked the lighter to sterilize the blade.

Joe remained steady as the rock that supported him while she gingerly drew the sharp tip of the blade over the bump she had found. Steel struck something foreign. His blood obscured whatever it was, so she patted it away with the shirt and cut a bit deeper. And there it was.

Hissing in sympathy, she pried the small cylinder free and caught it in her palm. "Got it."

"Give it to me," he said, his voice gruff, impatient.

She reached around him and he took it from her, moving the flashlight to look at what she had found. Martine quickly pressed a pad of fabric hard against the wound, though she could no longer see it. Her own incision pulsed like a bad bee sting. His must be hurting even worse.

After a few seconds, he moved away from her and rose to his feet. "We'll leave the thing here," he said, speaking in a near whisper as he placed the transmitter on a small ledge in the cave wall. "Now we need to go."

He gave her the light and pulled on his shirt. When she moved toward the tunnel they'd come through, he stopped her with a hand on her arm. "Not that way. We'd probably run right into them."

She heard his weary sigh. Something was wrong. "Joe? What is it?"

He squeezed her arm. "You trust me, don't you?"

"Like I have a choice? Yes, I do trust you." Her heartbeat had kicked up to double speed again when she'd heard the apprehension in his voice.

"Good, because I need you to do something you're not going to like." When she remained silent, he continued. "You'll have to go first this time because I'll have to lift you up."

She shivered. Quaked, really. Her nervous gaze scanned the shadows around the top half of the cave room. As if he read her thought, he directed the beam of light to an opening about six feet off the floor.

"There," he said. "It will be a longer corridor than the one we came in through and a little narrower in places. We'll have to leave the bags here, so anything you can't live without, get it if it will fit in your pockets. Your I.D. and money, maybe a comb.''

She was already kneeling, digging out the things he'd listed. Fighting off her dread as best she could.

"Put your sweater on. We might have to spend the night in the woods if they've disabled the Jeep. It's not that chilly outside, but sleeves will protect your skin from the brush and bug bites.''

As they moved toward the hole in the wall that he had pointed out, he kept talking steadily. Martine grasped at his every word, at his every implied reassurance that they would exit the caves and go on to other challenges she knew she could handle. But her heart was in her throat and it pounded mercilessly.

When they reached the place where he would have to lift her up, he grasped her shoulders and lowered his mouth to hers. His mouth was warm against hers, his lips parted, his tongue searching out hers. She wanted to respond, meant to. But all she could manage was mere acceptance while trying hard to lose herself in the moment. Much too soon, he pulled away, taking all the warmth with him. All the comfort.

The kiss scorched her inside and out, not dispelling her fear very much, but imbuing her with a new determination to get the hell out of this hole and see where a kiss like that could lead.

She sighed after he released her and rested against him for a couple of seconds, trying her level best to soak up some of that confidence of his.

"Up we go now," he said, shaking her firmly but gently. "You can do it, Martine. One arm over the other, push with your feet. We'll be climbing this time, so it'll take more energy. Think of surfacing, seeing that moon.''

"How…how deep are we? I need to know now.''

He hesitated as if remembering, measuring in his mind. "About ninety, maybe a hundred feet. Maybe not that far,'' he said. ''Piece of cake. You can do that.'' His voice was gentle, coaxing. ''Come on now, let's get it over with, okay?''

*A hundred feet of rock?* She caught back a moan, cleared her throat to cover it, and tried not to shiver uncontrollably when he turned her around and grasped her by her waist to lift her up. Then she remembered. ''The flashlight!'' she cried.

''Once I get up there behind you, I'll pass it to you, but we'll have to leave it off unless we run into an obstruction and need to see—''

She gasped, a horrible little sound of terror, then clamped a hand over her mouth.

He surrounded her with his arms and held her tight. His lips pressed against the side of her neck, then whispered into her ear. ''You can leave the light on. All the time, Martine. It will be okay. But you'll need to crawl in the dark far enough that I can get in there behind you. Then I'll give you the flashlight, all right? Can you do that for me?''

She nodded, a jerky movement that made her even dizzier than she had felt before. ''Let…let's go.''

The hardest thing she'd ever done was crawl into that small dark place. Fear of being confined and crushed almost overwhelmed her the second Joe's hands left her.

Suddenly she couldn't help scrambling forward just to make sure she could. *Up and out,* she huffed, hyperventilating, anything to get free, to feel open space around her, the night air, anything but all this…rock. *Faster,* the terror urged, *go faster. Get out. Get out! Now!*

Dimly, over the frantic thundering of her heart, she heard Joe call to her. But she couldn't listen, couldn't slow down. Not even for the comfort of light to lead the way. Her mind worked in fits and starts, rapidly grabbing at anything else when it touched on the thought that she wouldn't make it.

Suddenly the passageway narrowed, her hand pushed through a hole smaller than a basketball. Light bled around her body, flickering on the solid rock in front of her, on the small jagged opening. Desperately, she pushed at the obstructing wall around the aperture.

*Oh, God! No room, no way through, no way out. Trapped!* She screamed. And shut down.

Joe grasped Martine's ankles. She was totally limp. Probably fainted. If he dragged her backward to the right branch of the tunnel, the one she'd scrambled past, her face would be a bloody mess from scraping against the rock. Her hands were probably already ruined. This tunnel was way too narrow for him to crawl up beside her, but maybe he could turn her over and slide her back out of the dead end.

He pushed his arms up beside her as far as they would reach and gently flipped her over on her back. She didn't even moan. Joe paused to check the pulse in her ankle, terrified she might have suffered heart failure or something. The beat was fast, but steady.

He breathed a sharp sigh of relief and wiped the stinging sweat out of his eyes. Then slowly, carefully, he began to wiggle back the way they had come and pull her inch by inch to relative safety.

Though he had caved for decades and loved it, Martine's fears were insidious. He had never experienced anything like claustrophobia, but understood how debilitating fears like that could be. Now more than ever since he'd just seen it happen firsthand.

Martine was no coward. He admired the way she had bravely faced right up to the problem. Before she'd climbed into the tunnel, he had finally seen that look of abject terror on her face that had appeared to him in the premonition. But she had crawled right in to meet her worst fear head-on. Then what she dreaded most had come to pass when she'd reached that dead end. He began to feel a little antsy himself.

No use speculating what might happen if the other branch of the tunnel was blocked. It was considerably wider than this one after it branched off, but who knew what the years had brought? This was a living cave and living things changed constantly.

He almost hoped Martine would stay unconscious until he got her out, but accomplishing that would be tricky if he had to drag her all the way. They still had some forty feet or more to go.

When he reached the turnoff they had passed, Joe backed into it, relieved to have more wiggle room. Ten feet later it widened, almost large enough that they could have crawled the rest of the way on their hands and knees if she were conscious.

He might be able to bring her around and they could make it out pretty quickly. But he worried she might wake up screaming and they were now too close to the other entrance. If Humberto and his pals were already outside the caves, she could draw them right to the place where he planned to exit. That opening was not as well concealed as the one they had entered.

He continued pulling her along, wincing as the floor grew rougher and her head bumped. "Sorry, kid," he mumbled. "You're gonna have a hell of a headache, but it's better than the alternative."

Joe shifted to a sitting position and let himself collapse for a minute once they approached the opening. He could actually see it, a flattened hole about four feet across and three feet top to bottom. It was filled with blue-gray moonlight and striped with stalks of sparsely leafed weeds.

He squinted at them. They looked too evenly spaced. It gave him a little jolt, a second's worth of shock that somebody had actually installed bars. Surely not.

But he risked leaving Martine alone in the dark while he scrambled over to check, to be certain no one had put up a locked gate. He laughed silently, sheepishly when his fingers touched the stickers along the dead stalks of thistles. He and Martine weren't trapped. But he knew right then, that very second, that his days of spelunking were all behind him. Those few seconds of panic instigated by Martine's phobia had done the trick. He could not wait to get out of this cave and into wide-open spaces.

He scuttled back to her, cursing himself for leaving her there where she might wake up hysterical and get them both killed. Once she was settled in his lap, Joe rested his hand near her mouth in case he had to muffle her once she came to.

He had until then to decide whether they were safer here or out there bumbling around in the dark.

Humberto contained his rage outwardly, but inside him it roiled like lava under pressure, threatening to erupt at any second. "I would give my right arm for explosives," he muttered, shoving Thomas aside to take the lead as they exited the cave.

He kicked at the weedy ground covering of plants he did not recognize or care to. This was his first time in the wilds of this country. Aside from the major cities he flew into for business purposes—the posh hotels where he had stayed and the carefully manicured golf courses where his contacts often took him for the pleasure of a game—he had seen little of the United States. Certainly nothing this rural.

Now here he was, virtually ruined, unable to return home and left with nothing but a burning desire to punish the ones who had done this to him. And at the moment, even this final quest of his seemed doomed to failure.

"I will not give up," he muttered, looking up at the

stars that seemed to mock him, the moon that cast its bluish glow over the alien landscape.

"What do we do now, Carlos? Wait here for them to come out?" Thomas asked.

Humberto shook his head, more in frustration than to provide a negative answer. Poor Thomas, for all his bulk, possessed so little intelligence he was incapable of anything but following the most specific of orders. The other cousin, Manuelo, was little better, though he did have an imaginative flair when it came to inflicting pain. A useful talent.

What a pity these were the only two to be trusted now. Two loyal cousins with barely half a brain between them. But they were family, the only family he had left after that damned DEA agent and the bewitching Martine had destroyed his business and therefore his life.

Hatred filled his soul and fueled his determination. "There will surely be another exit to that damned hole in the ground," he explained, his voice tight with the necessity of spelling out everything. "Corda knew where this cave was, so he has obviously been here before. He would not trap himself inside without knowing there was another way out. Manuelo, go and disable the car."

"But Carlos, how will we leave this place if—"

"Disable *their* car, you imbecile!" Humberto exhaled sharply and rolled his gaze heavenward, praying for patience. "Take this pistol and give me that automatic."

"Oh, *si*," Manuelo replied, nodding. He quickly switched weapons and then lumbered off toward the vehicles.

"Thomas, you wait over there. Remain concealed and watch this entrance while I search for the other one."

"Good thinking, Carlos."

Humberto added, "Hold them at gunpoint if they emerge. Do not kill them."

"But if they try to escape, what am I to do?"

Humberto ground his teeth against a curse. "Shoot at their legs, Thomas. Disable, but do not kill them. That is for me to do? Can you understand this?"

"Of course, Carlos. You know I am a very good shot."

"Thank God for small favors," Humberto murmured as he stalked off through the weeds, his eyes scanning the rock formations for any possible openings.

Until he found and disposed of Corda and the woman in the most painful way he could devise, he would not leave this place. All he must do was wait until they emerged. Here in the wilds would be the ideal place to dispose of them.

Thank God he'd had Ramos plant a transmitter in Corda. He should have done so with Martine, but Humberto hadn't trusted the man to be in the room with her. He had similarly drugged and tagged all his men, at least all of those with full knowledge of his operations. One must always prepare for an unexpected betrayal. Corda had been the first to fool him. The only one to elicit trust and then prove to be the enemy.

The transmitter he had placed under Corda's skin obviously did not project its signal to outside the cave that concealed the couple. However, once out of there, even if they evaded capture right away, they would not be hard to follow. Unless...

Suppose Corda had deduced how he had been tracked thus far? He was a wily one. If he had somehow found and removed the transmitter, this might not be so easy after all. That possibility must be taken into account.

At any rate, the two were now trapped belowground without food or water. Sooner or later, they would have to come out. And when they did, they would pay for their treachery.

Humberto knew he could not destroy the entire force of agents who had been regularly and systematically denuding the crops in Colombia. However, this one man had reduced this to a personal battle.

Joseph Corda had successfully secured his trust. Then, not only had he destroyed the largest shipment of heroin ever attempted out of the midcountry operation, but he had somehow cracked the safe and spirited away the payment received for the last delivery. That had been earmarked for a huge purchase of weaponry slated to arrive from Jordan within the next few days.

Repercussions for these monumental losses would fall upon the head of the man in charge. Humberto would receive all the blame. A sentence of immediate death would be carried out if he allowed himself to be found.

There was no way to redeem himself, but Humberto vowed if it was the last thing he did in life, he would make Joseph Corda suffer.

And the woman. He had found out, of course, that she was the sister of the mercenary, Matthew Duquesne who worked for the Ames Company. Running a check on her identity had been child's play, accomplished in a matter of minutes on his computer. All he had needed was her prints. She hadn't even bothered to deny it.

He had treated her extremely well, offering her no insult, nothing but kindness. He had been confident that Duquesne would pay an enormous ransom to have her back, but that the soldier of fortune would also seek the ultimate revenge if she were harmed in any way.

It embarrassed him still that he had fervently hoped she would stay with him. He had so admired her cool demeanor, her class and her unearthly beauty. He had even courted her, given her his respect. He could have loved her. Unlike his wife of fifteen years, Martine would have been *his* choice.

But she had also betrayed and made a fool of him. And she would pay. The bitch would also answer for shooting him point blank without even blinking an eye.

Thank the gods he always wore a vest. He brushed a
hand absently over the uncomfortable bulk of the one he
wore now. Obtaining it, plus the two AKs, the SIG Sauer
pistol and ammo for the three weapons had cost him
dearly in terms of risk and dollars.

The money was running out, but he would conserve
what he had very carefully. It only had to last until he
accomplished what he had come to do. Then he would
notify the general. His father-in-law must understand that
he was no traitor, even if the general could not forgive
Humberto's misplaced trust and the losses that resulted.
It was all he could do. Then he would disappear forever.

# Chapter 8

Joe held Martine in his arms. She had awakened with a tremor and one sharp little cry that he immediately silenced. Once she noticed the moonlight shining through the cave's opening, she grew calm and regained her composure. She didn't draw away from him, so he simply held her.

"You took a beating when I dragged you out. How's your head?" he whispered.

"Hard as ever," she whispered back with a scoff. "My hands are sore."

He examined them gingerly with the tips of his fingers. "The skin's not broken much, but they'll need a good soaking."

"Joe...I'm so sorry I—"

"Don't be. We made it out, didn't we?" He cradled her against him and brushed his lips over the top of her head. "That's all that counts. Will you be okay if I go take a look outside?" he said directly into her ear.

She nodded and gave him a little push of encouragement.

Joe crept to the opening and peeked between the tall stalks of the weeds. His vision was limited, but he heard the crunch of footsteps on the ground's dry vegetation. Not close by, he thought.

Carefully, he parted the weeds enough to poke his head between them and gain a panoramic view of the sparsely wooded field surrounding the outcropping of rock.

The silhouette of a man passed a good fifty yards away, headed for a much larger rock formation. Joe could clearly see the outline of an automatic weapon braced in one hand as the man crept toward his destination.

They could remain where they were, but it would not be safe for long. Humberto had obviously decided there was another opening to the cave and was looking for it. And there were not that many places for him to search. Eventually, almost surely within the next half hour, he would find this one.

He crawled back to Martine and advised her of the situation. Then he gave her their alternatives. "We could shoot him when he discovers us, but that would bring the other two down on us. Or we could wait until he rounds that rock cliff and then get out before he comes back this way."

"What about his friends?" she asked, her voice steady as his now. "Where are they?"

"That's the problem. Unless he's a total idiot, he's got one with the vehicles. The other's almost certainly at the primary entrance to the cave. We can't hope to out-shoot them with only the pistol, so we'll either have to hide, or run again while we call in help."

"I vote run," she said, squeezing his arm with her fingers. "At least we can lose them now that the transmitter's gone. How's your back?"

He felt her hand slip around him and slide lightly over

the back of his shirt. She gave a brief little hum of satisfaction. "It's dried so it must have stopped bleeding, but we need to get that looked at, get you some antibiotics or something."

"Least of our worries," he said and deliberately set out to make her angry. "Are you steady? I don't want to take off out of this cave and have to carry you all the way."

She stiffened and inhaled sharply. "I can keep up. Just because I lost it back in there—"

"Save it for later. Right now I want you to do exactly as I do, exactly what I tell you. Don't think. Don't question. Got it?"

"Got it," she huffed.

"Let's go." He crawled toward the hole in the rock and looked out again. No sign of anyone now. He bent the tall thistles aside, ignoring the prickles of the sharp spines. Silently, he wiggled through them and low-crawled along the ground until he was a few feet from the cave. A glance over his shoulder revealed a messy shock of blond hair emerging from the cave. He pivoted around on his belly and gave her a hand.

"Stay low and move slowly," he whispered, knowing he need not add that she should stay as quiet as possible.

They crawled through the brush, Joe scanning the field in all directions, until they reached the copse of trees some fifty feet distant from the rocks. He leaned close. His lips actually brushed the tender shell of her ear as he rasped, "The car is on the other side of these woods. Stay right behind me."

They waded slowly through the undergrowth, virtually soundless as they progressed. Visibility was limited, but he was glad for the leaves that gave them cover. The trees were hardwoods for the most part and if this had been late fall or winter, they would be almost as exposed as they would be on open ground. He halted when he saw moonlight glint off the chrome and the stationary glow of a flashlight.

A grunt and a foul curse in Spanish emanated from the direction of the vehicle. Joe moved closer, keeping only one large oak trunk between him and the clearing. Both vehicles were there. And one of Humberto's cronies was half hidden under the open hood of Martine's Jeep.

He reached around and patted Martine's shoulder, then pressed down on it until she sank to the ground. Then he signaled her to wait there.

Joe pulled her pistol from the back of his belt, checked the safety, then turned it around to use as a club. He couldn't afford to rouse the other two men's attention with a gunshot. He moved silently out of the trees until he was directly behind the figure beneath the hood.

Unfortunately, there was no way he could do what he had to do without giving the man time to yell out. So he waited, listening to the rasp of metal against metal, disgruntled mumbling and then a final chuckle of satisfaction.

The bulky fellow emerged from his work, a distributor cap in one hand and a wrench in the other. Joe jumped forward and struck, landing a solid blow directly behind the man's right ear.

When the big figure crumpled at his feet, Joe motioned hurriedly for Martine to join him in the clearing. Meanwhile he searched the Colombian's pockets, looking for the keys to the sedan parked about ten feet away.

"No time for repairs," he explained, keeping to a whisper as he stood with the key and the goon's pistol in one hand, Martine's Glock in the other. He handed that to her and checked the one he'd just appropriated, wishing it was one of those automatics the other two had.

Quickly they hopped into the sedan, Joe behind the wheel. With the flashlight, he checked the fuel gauge. "It's got half a tank. Enough," he said. "Ready?" All hell was going to break loose when they cranked this baby up. They'd have to tear out of here at top speed and hope the resulting hail of bullets didn't damage the tires. Or the occupants.

"Shouldn't we take that distributor cap so they can't follow us?" Martine asked, grabbing his forearm.

"Nope. They'd probably kill someone to get another car. This way, they'll think it's less trouble and probably quicker to fix the Jeep."

"And we'll also know what they're driving!" she said. The girl was no slouch in the brain department. Joe smiled, proud of her. And a little proud of himself that they had gotten this far, he admitted. It bothered him that he felt that way. He was supposed to be looking forward to giving up all this and here he was sort of enjoying it again. Adrenaline did weird things to the mind, he decided.

"Stay down," he told Martine. He shoved into neutral gear, pushed in the clutch and accelerator and twisted the key in the ignition. The sound of the engine rent the night, announcing their departure like a noisy brass band. As he gunned the motor and spun out of the clearing onto the dirt track that led to escape, the shooting began from two directions.

Five minutes of bumping over the washed-out ruts and they were home free for the moment. When they reached the highway, he floored the sedan, hoping to attract any law enforcement personnel who might be conducting speed traps. Nothing.

Finally, some ten miles down the road, they approached a crossroads community with only one gas station/convenience store, closed. But the phone booth out front was a welcome sight. He didn't want to use her unsecure cell phone for his call to D.C. Joe whipped into the parking lot. "Get on the phone and dial 911," he told her. "I want everybody in the state on this. Tell them that the three guys who shot up that hotel parking lot are on a spree, targeting civilians. I'll give you the location coordinates to repeat. Then you give a description of your Jeep complete with tag number, just in case they get it in running shape before they're surrounded.''

She did as he said, injecting just the right amount of hysteria sure to bring out the cavalry. Hopefully it would result in a convergence of forces like the 2002 shootings here in Virginia. At any rate, Humberto and his playboys would be entirely too busy to stick to their original mission. ''Well, it's over,'' he said.

''We hope,'' Martine added. She stared at the receiver in her hand as she replaced it in its hook.

Joe placed his hand over hers and stood there looking at her for a full minute. ''You okay?''

''Peachy,'' she answered. ''Shouldn't you make some calls?''

She slid her hand from beneath his and moved away to give him better access to the phone. He dialed the D.C. office and related the pertinent information to Drewbridge, the duty agent for the night. Agent Drewbridge promised to send a chopper to Roanoke first thing in the morning to pick him up.

''What will you do now?'' Joe asked Martine as he hung up.

She shrugged, eyes closed, hands clutching her arms as she hugged herself. ''I don't know. Fly home, I guess.''

''Come with me to D.C.,'' Joe insisted. ''DEA could use your input since you were there, too.'' He smiled at her. ''You were in charge of cutting Humberto's purse strings. I expect you'll get a commendation.''

She smiled back and sighed wearily. ''Maybe. But before I do anything, I want a bath.''

He took her arm and led her back to the car, opening her door for her and settling her inside. How could he expect her to make up her mind about anything when she was totally exhausted? "Tell you what. Let's go in to Roanoke, get a room and catch a few hours' sleep. I don't know about you, but I'm beat."

"Sounds like a plan," she said. Though she was nearly dead on her feet, her words didn't slur and she exhibited no signs of the weeping fit he would have expected after her harrowing ordeal. Martine was a highly unusual woman. She had shown him nothing but sheer courage, even when dealing with the claustrophobia. He was almost glad she had an Achilles' heel. Perfection would be hard to live with.

Not that he would be the one living with it, he thought with a half laugh. What had made him even think of it? Martine seemed to thrive on danger—at least as long as she could avoid closed-in spaces—and he was definitely not in the market for a girl with her proclivities. Nope. He needed a soft, willing homebody, one whose idea of a bad day was missing her favorite soap opera on TV or choosing the wrong hairdresser.

But dammit, in light of all they'd been through together, one night together would be okay, wouldn't it? One night to last him a lifetime.

Martine woke up when the car stopped. She brushed her hands over her eyes, feeling actual grit in the creases of her eyelids. Her hands stung from the prickles of those thistles they had crawled through and her ankle throbbed from the knife cut. She was such a mess, she didn't even want to face a mirror. And she didn't much want to face Joe, either, after disgracing herself in that cave. Elevators made her a little nervous, but she hadn't realized just how serious her claustrophobia was until she had to face it like that. She really owed him a profound apology for cracking up, if he would just let her say it.

"Here we are," he said. "I thought maybe we

shouldn't go for really swanky, given our current condition. I could sure stand a Jacuzzi, though.''

He had such a great smile, Martine thought. Those straight white teeth and sensuous lips were enough to drive any woman right to the edge of caution. His deep brown eyes with their long lashes and teasing glint pushed her right over. ''You're my hero.''

''Yeah,'' he said laughing. ''And you'll be mine if you swing your little hiney in there and get us registered.''

Her breath stuck in her throat. *His, if she did that?* She clicked off her seat belt and reached for the ID she'd tucked in her pocket. If that's all it took…

He followed her inside the motel office, ignoring the stares the sleepy desk clerk offered. Martine almost laughed out loud. She certainly wouldn't take any customers who looked the way they did.

''We would like a double,'' she said in her haughtiest voice, presenting her charge card with a flourish.

The clerk nodded as he took her information and scribbled it on the form in front of him. ''How long?'' he asked as if he expected her to answer in hours.

''One night,'' she confirmed, retrieving her card and tucking it away.

''Could we possibly get room service at this hour?'' Joe asked him.

''Yes, sir,'' he said hesitantly. ''Sandwiches or something like that. Breakfast isn't for…another three hours,'' he added after glancing at the clock. Then he leaned forward over the desk, looking concerned, first at Joe, then back at her. ''Are you all okay? Were you in an accident or something?''

''Yes. Something like that,'' she agreed with a nod. ''But we're fine now. Just need a little rest.''

He handed her the key card. ''Do you have any luggage?''

''Lost,'' she told him with a shake of her head.

"We have laundry facilities," he offered, "but I'm afraid the maids are not on duty yet."

"Not to worry," Martine told him with a smile. "We'll manage."

He gave directions to the room.

"Well, that went well," Joe said laughing as they got back in the car to drive it around to the room. "Think he'll call the cops on us?"

She sighed. "If he does, they'll have a devil of a time waking me up when they get here."

"Not me. I'm starved." He parked, took the key card from her and went to open the door. Martine trailed in behind him. "You take a bath. I'll order some food," he told her.

She luxuriated in the shower for a good quarter hour, using well over half the shampoo provided and scrubbing her skin until it grew bright pink. Then, wrapped in a huge white towel, she left the bathroom without even glancing in the mirror. "All yours," she said to Joe.

"God, I wish," he muttered, appraising her with his eyelids at half mast. He gave new meaning to the description *bedroom eyes*. That look jacked up her temperature several notches and made her glance at the nearest bed with anticipation.

But he obviously had his priorities a little straighter than hers at the moment. He got up and passed her, offering only a little hum of appreciation while staring at her legs, disappeared into the steamy bathroom and closed the door.

Martine sat down on the edge of the bed, ruffling her wet hair with the small hand towel she'd brought out for that purpose. Her imagination ran wild thinking about Joe.

He was in there right now, shucking that shirt, those pants, those shoes. The tap was turned on as she listened. Streaming jets of water massaging all those well-defined muscles, easing, soothing, touching what she wished to touch. His eyes would be closed, his head leaning back. Before she knew it, Martine had her hand on the door-knob, about to invade that place of dreams.

A sharp rapping sounded. Damn. Room service. She groaned, backing away from the forbidden door to go and answer the other one. But just before she unlocked it, she paused, her fingers resting on the dead bolt that remained fastened. What if it was not their early-morning snack?

What if Humberto had managed to get that distributor cap back in place and had somehow followed them without their knowing? She didn't think it was possible, but who knew? It could be that she also had one of those damned transmitters and she and Joe simply hadn't found it.

She moved toward the nightstand where Joe had left her gun. She checked to make sure her Glock was loaded, clicked off the safety and went back to the door. Looking through the peephole might get her a bullet in the eye. Instead she crouched to one side, careful to stay away from the drapery-covered window.

"Yes? Who is it?" she called, her heart racing, her body braced for whatever came next, a couple of over-priced sandwiches or an immediate hail of gunfire.

Martine swallowed hard, then called out again, louder, "Who is it?"

"Room service, ma'am," came the reply, muffled by the door. Sounded like a southern accent, she thought. Couldn't be Humberto or one of his men. She lowered the gun, shook her head sharply and tried to relax her tensed muscles, wondering if she had gone around the bend to be jumping at shadows this way. She was sup-posed to be proving herself in this business, not stacking up reasons to go back to what she had been.

"Just a second," she answered, looking down at what she was wearing. Or wasn't wearing. In her mad scramble to grab the weapon, her towel had come untucked and was now lying across the room on the floor by the night-stand. A low chuckle caused her head to snap up.

Joe stood in the doorway to the bathroom, his towel securely draped around his body just below his waist.

He walked over, scooped up her towel and tossed it to her, picked up some of the bills she had left on the night-stand, then went to answer the door. She noticed he did risk a look through the peephole before he unlocked it.

That reassured her a little that she was just being para-noid. Paranoia wasn't a bad thing. Joe once said it was his friend and had kept him alive. She laid the gun on the floor and hurriedly covered herself.

By that time he was positioning the tray on the round table in front of the window. "I ordered decaf," he ex-plained as he turned the cups right side up to pour. He cast her a look that spent a little too long on her bare legs, then went back to what he was doing with the coffee.

Martine felt a concentrated heat wave. That was the only way to describe the sensation that began around her shaky knees and undulated right up her body, playing havoc with the torso, stopped the breath right about the region of her neck. And probably fried her brain com-pletely because she totally forgot about the sleep she needed, the food her stomach was growling for and the fact that when this was over she probably would never see this man again.

He looked too damned good in that towel. How shallow was that? she asked herself sharply. How many times had she castigated Matt for mentioning how hot some girl or other looked? Now here she was doing the same thing. Guilty as she felt about it, she didn't even want to deny the excitement Joe generated.

"Rye or white? I got one of each," he said. She didn't miss the smile in his voice that told her he was not really thinking about bread. The body-flaunting rat knew exactly what she was feeling. He had already turned her down

once. Damned if she was going to give him another
chance. If he wanted her, he was going to have to make
the first move. Nothing, however, said she couldn't egg
him on a little.

She adopted a bold, wide-legged stance as if she were
about to fire the weapon she held, then shifted her weight
to one leg, causing the slit in the towel to open and grant
a pretty good view of her left thigh, hipbone and the area
just above it. Good, she had his attention.

Then she tilted her head a bit as she examined the nine
millimeter she held out in front of her. Her two-handed
grip on the pistol squeezed her breasts together enough to
provide a decent line of cleavage. *There, ignore that, hot-
shot.*

When she raised her gaze from the gun to meet his, he
had abandoned any pretense of pouring coffee. Motion
arrested, mouth open, he stared.

She raised a brow in question.

He closed his mouth, swallowed hard, then set down
the coffeepot. "You planning to shoot me?" he asked, his
words laconic. Infuriating.

Martine stiffened. "Just maybe," she answered, then
stalked over to the nightstand and plunked down the pistol. "Damn you, Joe! You make me so mad!"

"Yeah," he said, exhaling audibly. "And you scare the
hell out of me."

Well, that was unexpected. "Scare you?" she repeated
with a bitter laugh.

"Absolutely," he admitted. "And if you don't get
away from that bed and get over here and eat, I'm about
to face up to my fear. In a very large way."

"Bragging, are we?" As warnings went, Martine
thought this might be the best one she'd ever had. But
obviously Joe was fighting his need for her at least as
hard as she was trying to stoke it. There had to be a reason
for that, one even more meaningful than the one he'd

given her back in Atlanta. Until she discovered what it was, she decided not to try anymore to seduce him. A girl could only take so much rejection, reluctant or not.

She huffed once, flounced over and plopped down in the straight chair next to the table. She knew her movements were not provocative. They weren't even the least bit graceful.

*Bite me, Joe Corda!* She thought as she grabbed up the sandwich closest to her and sank her teeth into it. She chewed furiously, hardly tasting the food.

"I guess you think we need to talk about this some more," he said, fiddling with his own food, not wolfing his down the way she was doing. "This…whatever it is between us."

Martine shook her head and took another bite.

"No? Well, you're the first woman I ever met who didn't talk a thing to death."

As if talking could change a thing. As desperately as she wanted to know the real reason he wouldn't take her up on what she offered, Martine was determined not to play the role he expected her to play here. She gulped down the bite of sandwich and slurped a swig of her coffee.

"Shut up, Joe," she ordered, and busied herself picking off the limp lettuce and flinging it down on the side of her plate. "Just shut up and eat."

"You think I don't want you, right?" he asked, sitting back in his chair, drumming the fingers of his right hand on the table where he rested his arm.

Martine shrugged and took another bite. Damn, she hated this sandwich. The bread was stale, the tomato grainy and the ham barely there. And the mayo was old. Probably tainted. She slapped the remainder of the sandwich down on top of the lettuce, choked down what she had in her mouth and leveled him with a glare. "Get stuffed, Corda. And I mean that in the very worst sense of the word!''

With that, she pushed out of the chair and slammed into the bathroom to wash her clothes as best she could. She crumpled them into the sink and turned on the hot water.

Tonight was obviously a total bust, so she would concentrate on tomorrow. If nothing else, she had come through this mission alive and well. Crawling home looking like a dirty ragamuffin would only lower her in Matt and Sebastian's estimation and God only knew she felt low enough in Joe's already.

He had seen her at her very worst. But he had seen her at her very best, too, she reminded herself as she scrubbed at the dirt, watching it muddy the water to a murky gray-brown. Besides, what did looks matter?

She drained the sink and ran more water using the remainder of the shampoo as detergent, then rinsed it away. Imagining herself wringing the neck of that mule-stubborn man in the next room, Martine twisted the water out of the fabric, rolled the garments in a dry towel, then hung them over the bar that supported the shower curtain.

That done and still so angry she could spit, she wasn't about to go back in there and make a bigger fool of herself. Instead, she washed the clothes he had left piled in the corner of the bathroom.

''God, what am I doing?'' she muttered as she flung them on the rod beside hers. ''He'll think I'm Suzy Homemaker!''

''Actually I think you're Rambo,'' he said from the doorway.

Martine whirled around, grabbing at the towel as it shifted. When had he opened that door?

He shook his head, pushed away from the door frame and approached her. ''Okay, you win. I give up.''

# Chapter 9

Words just failed her. Martine knew if she could just draw a breath, she would scream invectives that would curl his hair. Instead she just stood there letting his hot gaze incinerate her good sense.

Then his arms surrounded her and enveloped the rest of her in his heat. Dimly, she was aware of moving backward, felt the coolness of the wall tiles press against her back. But, oh, the glorious warmth that encompassed her front! A wall of muscle created the most delicious friction.

His mouth devoured hers. Her palms smoothed over his wide shoulders, glided up the sides of his neck. Her fingers threaded through his hair, reveling in the crisp texture of it. His deep, visceral growl of possession reverberated through her body like a powerful current.

Strong hands gripped her hips and lifted her. Still lost in the kiss, she felt she was flying, swept away from the wall, whirled around and spirited out of the steamy bathroom to the softness of the bed. Her mouth sought his again, desperately, when he broke the kiss.

"Minute," he gasped, as she felt his hand between them, a brief break in body contact as he took care of protection. Then he renewed the welcome onslaught, covering her completely, his movements sinuous and inciting. He pressed that ridge of pulsing promise against her belly.

"Now!" she demanded, her word half lost as she struggled for breath, for surcease. Blood pounded in her ears and stars burst behind her eyes.

"Not...yet," he groaned, his weight pinning her as he stopped moving. "Too fast."

"No!" What the hell was he waiting for?

A harsh breath rushed out past her ear. His hand tightened on her hip as he slid lower and entered her in one smooth glide. Pleasure flooded her with such intensity, she felt tears push from beneath her eyelids. Joe was so right, so good, so necessary.

She moved with him, against him, her total focus on increasing the sensations he caused within her. He set the pace and held to it no matter how she pleaded with her body for him to increase it.

Suddenly, she shuddered, came apart in all directions at once until there was nothing left but pure white ecstasy of motion. All senses coalesced into an explosion that rocked the universe. Her cry, his. An indrawn breath that captured his unique scent. The slick sweet feel of his skin on hers. She forced her eyes open and looked directly into the deep brown depths of his.

What she saw there both frightened and reassured her. No wonder he had said she scared him to death. He had known before she had. Martine blinked and looked away, then closed her eyes again, unwilling to put voice or even more thought to what she had realized.

This had been a mistake. A gloriously wonderful terrifying mistake. One that she doubted could be undone. One night was all she had wanted with him. One experience, one adventure. Not a soul deep connection. So she'd thought.

"Oh, no," she whispered. This felt like love.

"Yeah," he agreed with a heavy sigh. "Yeah." Then he lowered his head, resting it on the pillow beside hers, their bodies still joined, their awareness perfectly attuned. Neither of them was ready for what they had discovered in the other.

After a few moments, he slowly disengaged and moved off of her, leaving the bed. Martine kept her eyes shut and curled away from him. She snuggled into the quilted bedspread when he draped it over her, then retreated into herself, trying not to think, trying to obliterate the need to have him hold her and tell her that somehow they would resolve this.

Totally exhausted and her body sated, she needed to sleep. But that proved impossible with Joe lying so close. This might never happen again. She couldn't hold on, but neither could she let go.

Joe knew he couldn't love her. Didn't dare. Talk about a patently counterproductive thing to do.

"Falling for you would make me crazy," he said, his words barely audible. "I'd worry myself to death."

"I can take care of myself," she answered, her defiance evident even in the softness of her voice.

Being without her would make him crazier. He'd been this close to plenty of women without even thinking about a future with them.

He couldn't even remember the last time he had thought about that. For the last few years, he had doubted he even had a future to think about. Well, that had changed.

When Humberto was out of the picture and Joe began the new job—if he decided to take it—maybe he wouldn't be risking his neck on an hourly basis. Oh, there would almost certainly be danger involved in some of the assignments, but his days of constantly living under the scythe of the grim reaper were over. Maybe he could actually have a life.

How could he possibly hook up permanently with a woman who planned to keep doing that? He had never asked a woman to put up with that kind of worry about him, so why should he have to endure it himself?

But how could he not? Even if they shook hands right now and faked a cheery little goodbye, how could he not worry about where she was and whether she was safe?

This just wasn't like him, this asking for trouble. He might appear to be a devil-may-care risk taker, but he was secretly a planner. That's how he'd survived this long on missions that outwardly seemed suicidal. He sure hadn't intended to get this involved.

He had been in the field way too long. His brain must have been affected. This should be a simple decision, quickly made and implemented. But he kept on vacillating. One minute, figuring he'd better kiss her off for good and the next, struggling like mad to think of a way to make it work out.

"Joe?" she said softly, turning to him, her graceful hand sliding lightly over his chest, one finger threading through the hair, her nail gently scoring his skin. "Are you all right?"

He grasped her hand in his and squeezed lightly. "Poleaxed. Too confused to think straight. You?"

She sighed, a luscious sound that sent his temperature climbing, and stretched that gorgeous body like a satisfied cat. "I'm hungry again."

"That makes two of us," he muttered, giving up without a fight. He kissed her again, answering the demand she hadn't even made yet. As surrenders went, it beat any kind of victory to hell and back.

* * *

Martine awoke to his shaking her shoulder gently.

"Come on, sleepyhead. You need to get up and get dressed. I called in our location. They'll be here soon to pick us up."

She wanted to resist and kept her eyes closed.

He persisted, caressing her arm, but it felt impersonal somehow. Distant. "They'll impound the rental car and arrange a flight for you." He sounded very businesslike, she thought.

How should she respond to that? As determined as she was to present a woman-of-the-world face to him this morning, Martine didn't think she was capable of it. She certainly couldn't do flip, not after they had turned the world upside-down. About the best she could hope to do was to answer in kind.

She sat up. "All right. I'll be ready in ten." With all the dignity she could muster, she got up and walked naked into the bathroom and shut the door.

He had removed her clothes from the shower rod and folded them neatly on the counter by the sink. She wanted to cry. Instead, she turned on the shower, waited patiently for the water to run hot, then stepped under the spray.

Her body ached but not nearly so much as her heart. It was not simply sex. The connection had gone much deeper than that, just as he had known it would. It had provided the culmination of all the feelings, risks and hidden hopes they had experienced and shared since they met.

Joe had not wanted to make love to her and now she understood why. Their goals in life were so opposed.

She was only just coming into her own, realizing her potential, waking up from a slumberous life lived under a heavy cloak of male protection. First her father had kept her wrapped in batting. Expected her to stay safe, weak, dependent, like her mother. Even before he had died, Steven had stepped in, determined to guide her into teaching. Her attempt to assert herself had ended that, but had fallen flat when Sebastian hired her, then refused to let her do anything meaningful. Even Matt still tried to shelter her.

At last, with this initiative in Colombia, she finally felt alive. Capable of doing anything.

But Joe craved peace. He had lived on the edge for so long that he had earned the right to a comfortable life free of danger and worry.

His concern was very real. Flattering, but it would be stifling, too, if she let it.

What a great beach bum he would make, she thought with a wry smile. The spray of water on her face obliterated the tears and sluiced over her body to wash away the traces of their lovemaking. She only wished it could take away the memory they had made together, but nothing could ever do that. There would never be another man who could measure up to Joe Corda. She'd just have to get over him somehow.

Dressed in her wrinkled pants and shirt, her damp hair slicked back behind her ears, she took a deep breath and went out to face the music.

"Coffee?" he asked, sipping his own and pointing at the cup he had poured for her.

"Yes, please." Room service again. She could use a decent meal, but food was running a distant second to what she really needed.

"I don't recommend the pastries for taste, but they'll help to fill you up."

Martine sighed. Nothing would help do that. "Thanks, just the coffee," she said, taking the chair across from him, glad of the distraction the meager breakfast provided.

"Martine…" Oh God, he sounded apologetic. She didn't want an apology, one that she'd have to echo. What had happened was definitely her fault.

"Let it go, Joe," she advised, not meeting his eyes.

"These things happen. Hazard of the occupation, I guess."

He remained silent for a few long seconds. "We could give up the occupation and see if we still—"

"No." Not an option, she thought, shaking her head for emphasis. She could not become what she once had been. Not that clueless, plain vanilla, too-eager-to-please copy of her mother. God, she might as well move back to the old country.

"I've seen too much, Martine," he said, his voice only slightly above a whisper. He pleated a paper napkin between the fingers of one hand, worrying it, shredding it, then crushing it in his fist. "No matter how hard I try, I can't stop the evil. If I thought I could, I'd keep going, you know? But it grows like kudzu, covers everything. Kills it."

She drew in a deep breath and let it out slowly. "Yes, but if we all stop trying, where would we be?"

"I know what you're saying. I'll give the Sextant team my best shot. At least for a while. But I know I can't watch you put your life on the line every day and then die for nothing in some godforsaken jungle."

He reached over and took her hand, held it, caressed it hard with his thumb in that way he had when he grew intense. "I'll stay with it. Forever, if you'll just get out of it now. If you don't, you'll be where I am one of these days."

She reached up and brushed her fingertips over his forehead, then traced the healing scar where the ricochet had nicked him. "I'm sorry."

He nodded and leaned away, releasing her hand and breaking all contact. It wasn't an angry move, she could see that. He just seemed resigned.

For a long time, they didn't speak, didn't look at one another. Martine felt a keen sense of loss already. How much worse would it be when he was out of her life forever? "Joe? I know this sounds like the world's worst cliché, but we could stay friends."

To her relief he smiled. "Yeah, that's what they all say."

The next silence proved more than she could stand and as she struggled to find something to say to show she was holding up better than he was, she heard someone knocking on the door. She got up.

He beat her to the door to check out their visitor. "Who is it?" he called out.

"Jack Mercier," the man answered.

Joe's eyebrows rose as he cast her a glance of surprise. Then he opened the door, one of the pistols in his hand. "Identification?"

Mercier flashed a badge and picture ID. "Your office notified me after you called in."

Martine thought he looked much like he had sounded over the phone. She had taken his call to Matt about the mission to Colombia and they had talked at some length about it. Mercier was definitely on the spring side of forty, well built, deeply tanned. Early silver streaked his dark hair and his eyes were the color of polished steel.

Mercier was handsome and distinguished, but with an edge she imagined could turn menacing if he were crossed. That gray hand-tailored suit he wore fit to perfection both his body and the current image he was projecting. He wore it extremely well, but it seemed a disguise all the same.

Now he was assessing her. "Ms. Duquesne? I believe we spoke on the phone when we hired your brother."

"Martine," she affirmed and shook his hand. "Nice to meet you in person."

He smiled, transforming his face into a charming expression of determined diplomacy. "Surviving to do that must give you even greater satisfaction. It has been a near thing, so I hear."

She shrugged, risking a glance at Joe to see what he thought of Mercier. He was frowning now. She slid her hand through the crook of Joe's arm. "It was, but Mr. Corda knew precisely what to do in every instance. You'll be very lucky to have him on your team, sir."

Mercier looked from one to the other, his smile fading. "No doubt."

"What are you doing here?" Joe asked him.

"You'll be debriefed by your supervisor at our office in McLean since you're one of us now. I thought the trip back would give us a chance to get acquainted."

"I'm not one of you yet. What about Humberto? Have they got him yet?" Joe demanded.

"No. They found the Jeep abandoned five miles from the turnoff that led to the caves. He could be out of the country by now."

Joe cursed. Martine felt like it. She knew as well as Joe did that Humberto would never give up and go away forever. Unless he was found, they could expect him to turn up sooner or later to complete his vendetta. Now no one knew where he might be or what he was driving.

Mercier studied Joe for a moment. "There's a chopper waiting for us."

He continued, speaking directly to her as they left the motel room. "Martine, we have arranged for you to be interviewed separately, of course. Standard procedure. We'll part company at the airport, and you'll be flown directly to the D.C. office with an escort from the DEA. After that, they will see that you get back to Atlanta and have protection until Humberto is apprehended."

Martine looked at Joe. When he said nothing, she nodded at Mercier. "Thank you."

"We're good to go then," Mercier said. "I'll need the keys to the car you drove here. We'll see that it's returned."

Joe handed over the keys, then opened the front passenger door of the Ford that Mercier indicated was his. He waited for her to get in. Martine hesitated. "No good-byes, okay?"

He glanced at Mercier who seemed to be ignoring them. "A clean break is better."

"Clean break it is, then," she muttered as she climbed in the car. "So much for the friendship."

Joe didn't answer. He simply got into the back seat where he remained silent for the entire fifteen minutes it took them to reach the airport.

Once they met her contact, a clean-cut young agent by the name of Willowby, and were about to go their separate ways, Joe grabbed her hand and turned to her. "Look. I'll call you once in a while. Just to make sure you're all right."

"Will you?" she asked, noting that Mercier was stu-diously looking the other way and pretending hard not to listen. "You were right, Joe. Let's keep it simple. Clean break."

He released her hand, his dark eyes holding hers for two full seconds. Then he gave a decisive nod and turned away abruptly, striding for the gate to the runway where the helicopter waited for them.

Had that been anger in his eyes? Or regret? Martine supposed she would never know, but the question troubled her.

Even after a week to get over what had happened, Joe felt a large gaping hole in his chest where his heart ought to be. That part of him had gone on back to Atlanta, he guessed. The old heart, wherever it was, certainly wasn't in his work.

He liked Jack Mercier. He liked the other members of Sextant, too. But he just couldn't get worked up about throwing himself right back into the fray, even if it was a slightly different fray. Instead of insinuating himself into some drug lord's confidences or portraying a potential big-shot buyer in order to make a bust, he would be playing other roles, ferreting out terrorists. And he wouldn't be working alone anymore.

He sat in front of one of the computers in a security-cocooned inner office in the heart of McLean, pretty much up to speed now on an aspect of the world situation he had so far touched on only marginally.

For fifteen years, the drug culture had permeated his professional life. At times he'd become so immersed in the horror of it, it seemed that's all there was. Now he knew there were even worse threats.

Mercier entered, took one long assessing look at him and drew up a chair. "You're not ready yet, are you?" he said, his voice father firm.

"No," Joe admitted. "I'm not." He swiveled away from the desk and leaned forward, hands clasped between his knees, and faced his new supervisor. "I might never be."

"There's no great rush. This is a big decision for you."

"Jack, I'll be honest. I'd hoped the change of pace, the difference in focus, would make a difference." He sighed wearily. "What you've got to deal with here needs someone clicking on all cylinders. The missions are critical, more so that what I've been doing."

Mercier nodded and sat back, drumming his fingers on the arm of the chair. "You're exhausted. I still think you're the man. You just need a break, Joe. Take a couple of weeks. Go lie on a beach."

Joe laughed. "Is there anything you don't know about me?"

"I know what's good for you right now. Just go. We're pretty much in the organizational stages here and the alert level's low right now. You still have to go through a little training before taking on an assignment. The job will be here when you get back."

"You're not going to *let* me quit, are you?"

"If I thought you really wanted to do that, I wouldn't have you here right now."

Joe nodded. "I'll go down to the Gulf. See the family. I promise to give you an answer within a couple of weeks. How's that?"

Jack grinned, another stab at the camaraderie he worked hard to establish among his crew. "Think you might swing by Atlanta on the way?"

"That's not an option."

"Giving up personal relationships is not a requirement of the job, Joe."

"It's definitely a requirement as far as Martine's concerned."

"What's the matter, you don't trust her?" Mercier asked, frowning.

Joe shrugged. "Worse than that. I think I love her." He managed a wry smile. "But I'll get over it."

Mercier nodded thoughtfully. "Well, you'd know best about that, I guess. But if you do decide to see her, give her my regards."

Like hell he would, Joe thought. The relief he felt at actually being encouraged to abandon his duties for a while made him almost forget that avid perusal Martine and Mercier had given one another when the two first met. Joe had experienced an unreasonable spurt of jealousy and he knew it was unfounded, had known it even at the time. He certainly didn't need a woman who clouded his judgment that way.

But maybe he'd just layover in Atlanta for a few hours and check in with Matt Duquesne at Ames International. He didn't even have to see Martine while he was there and stir up anything.

Wasn't he sort of obligated to make sure she had adequate protection? Even if Humberto had seemed to drop off the face of the earth, Joe knew he was still out there, biding his time, waiting for defenses to drop.

"I'll finish out the day and leave tonight," he told Jack. "Thanks."

"No problem. That next weapons training session at Quantico doesn't begin until the first of the month. You'll need to be back for that." He gave Joe a friendly slap on the shoulder and left.

A few minutes later, Will Griffin appeared. "Black, right?" He set down a cup of coffee just to the right of Joe's mouse pad and didn't stick around for thanks.

Now what had precipitated that? Joe wondered. Griffin stuck his head back around the door. "Good luck. Let us know how it goes, okay?"

"How what goes?" But Griffin was gone again. Joe sipped the coffee. Last night he had joined Will for a drink at Christa's, a quiet little pub within walking distance of the office. It had become a sort of hangout when the work day was over and they had nothing else to do. But Joe couldn't recall discussing anything important there with Will. What the hell was the guy talking about?

Holly Amberson, the one female member of the team, strode in with a sheaf of papers in her hand. She flattened them against her truly admirable chest and crossed her arms over them. "I don't know you well enough yet to be giving you any advice, Joe, but don't you be stupid."

Joe sat up straight and stared at her. "Excuse me?"

Her black eyebrows climbed up to her perfect hairline and dark chocolate eyes pinned him with a warning stare. "You go see that girl, you hear?"

Joe stood, his chair rolling back and banging against a file cabinet. "Now wait just a minute—"

"No, you wait a minute," she ordered, shaking her finger with its long crimson nail very close to his nose. "You don't drag a woman through two countries, give

her a quick squeeze, then cut her loose and leave her to
the sharks. You go see about her. And play nice.''.

Joe uttered a short cough of disbelief. Who did this
woman think she was, his mother? She was younger than
he was by at least four or five years. And what the hell
did she know about Martine? He opened his mouth to tell
her to buzz off. Instead he heard himself saying, ''I'm
going. I'm going.''

She smiled and slapped the papers on the desk. ''Good
boy. You'll want to check this out before you go. It's the
final report on what happened after you left Colombia.
Great work, Joey. Good to have you aboard.''

*Joey?* Nobody had called him Joey since third grade
when he'd beat the hell out of Mike McCann for telling
him Joey meant a baby kangaroo.

Did they all know everything about him, up to and
including his sex life? Well, what did he expect working
with a bunch of spies?

The whole bunch probably thrived on personal gossip
since they couldn't share any secrets with anyone else in
the world. Joe wasn't used to this, at least not at work.
An agent's private life was just that. Private.

He picked up the report Holly had brought him, but
didn't need to read it. That mission was history. So was
his brief relationship with Martine. New life. New leaf.

Joe glanced around the six hundred square feet allotted
to what they called The Vault. The room housed all the
company's electronics and was protected from the world
by lead-encased walls, scrambling devices and the latest
access mechanisms.

It contained no windows and was completely secure.
Even the outer offices, Joe's included, were invulnerable
to intrusion of any kind except maybe a bunker buster. In
the case of that, they would all be smithereens anyway.

He did like his office, never having had one all his own.

Sextant was six months old now, experimental, working better than anyone had reason to expect, so Mercier said.

Joe now knew that Jack had been with the NSA. His talent for organization and brilliant analytical ability had put him in charge. If anybody on the planet could construct a cohesive unit from alumnus of the FBI, CIA, DIA, ATF and DEA, it was Jack Mercier, the voice of reason, proponent of the big picture.

The Sextant team had become tight as a guy-wire. The five in place were already friends. Four men and one woman. One black, one Native American, and three WASPS. And now Joe, last hired, was the resident Hispanic. Holly had dubbed them the Crayola Kids and treated them all like children. *Her* children, though she wasn't even a mother for real.

Sextant was a great concept, a dream team. On one level, Joe wanted to belong. On another, he clung to his status as a loner, a real master of surface relationships. Could he fit in here?

He closed his eyes, massaging them with his thumb and forefinger.

That's when the picture appeared, clear as a well-focused photograph. One lone frame of the future behind his eyelids. Martine's face. Covered with blood.

Joe tore out of the computer vault, the vision still filling his mind. Down the corridor, passing the offices, his only thought to get to the airport as fast as possible.

Eric Vinland caught him in a headlock, effectively halting him in the hallway. ''Hey, what's up?''

Joe struggled, desperate to fly to Martine, to save her. But Vinland held on, a forearm almost cutting off his air supply. It took a moment for reason to take hold. Martine was in danger, yes, but at this rate, he would kill himself getting to her.

He stopped fighting and Eric released him, even

straightened his tie. "Okay, spill it, Joe. What set you off?"

"I've gotta go. I saw...never mind." He shook his head and started to push past Vinland.

He felt a tight clamp on his arm. "A premonition?"

Joe was so stunned, he simply stood there, his mouth open.

"Yeah. We know." Eric smiled, a benign-looking expression beaming behind innocuous round-rimmed glasses. A young Brad Pitt, the picture of boyish innocence in specs and Brooks Brothers. "I have a similar...talent," Vinland admitted with a shrug.

Still Joe couldn't speak. What the hell was going on here? Was this another damned government study he was getting sucked into?

"Do all of you...?"

"No, not really. We'll talk about that later. Right now, I think you're too worried. It's the woman, right?" Eric guessed, his voice soft, cultured. Concern seemed out of place in this muscle-bound *boy* with the weird, steely eyes.

"Yes," Joe answered in spite of himself.

"We'll help," Vinland said simply.

Humberto had now relinquished all hope of regaining anything resembling the life he once led. He replaced the receiver and put the telephone back on the nightstand, handling it very gently, afraid if he gave physical manifestation to his fury, he could never regain control. Things were worse than he thought. Much, much worse.

His sweat mocked the pitiful effort of the air-conditioner cranked as high as it would go. Miami might be considerably cooler than equatorial Colombia, but a much more dangerous heat, one more difficult to escape, had been combined with that of the climate.

Other than the relatively meager amount he had managed to shift to a recently established account in the Cayman Islands, his wealth was gone. He had expected Rosa to transfer funds from their bank in Bogotá to the one he had selected in Miami. He'd thought perhaps she would even join him there once he could safely bring her out of Colombia. She was, after all, the mother of his children, the daughter of the general who had recruited him and treated him like a favored son. But no. She would not come to him. And neither would she send money. The general knew everything. Including Humberto's former fascination with the Duquesne woman.

He had lost Rosa, their life savings and all that he had invested. All of it gone. Transferred to her father's accounts for her to spend at leisure. She had laughed so bitterly.

She had been told how he had kept the woman at the compound. He wished now that Rosa had good reason to accuse him of infidelity, since he was paying the price anyway.

He should have taken the Yankee bitch instead of treating her like an honored guest. But he had enjoyed the willing company of a beautiful, cultured woman. He had been the envy of everyone in the compound. She had enthralled him, tricked him and then betrayed him.

He did not have to worry that Rosa would divorce him. She would not have to do so, he had just been informed, because he was as good as dead.

Nowhere could he find protection. The whole organization had blown sky-high. The fields were now useless, sprayed with glyphosate, a result no doubt of Corda's revealing their precise locations. Corda and the woman had ruined him more completely than he knew.

His father-in-law had put a price on his head as if Humberto were a criminal to be hunted down and shot. Miami was no longer a safe place to be now that he had phoned Rosa.

The hatred he felt for Joseph Corda and Martine Duquesne increased tenfold. Using the families of his enemies to exact revenge seemed less than honorable to Humberto, but the time had arrived when honor was no longer a luxury he could afford.

# Chapter 10

Martine jumped as lightning cracked nearby, followed immediately by a jarring rumble of thunder. The weather suited her mood. Gloomy. It described her future. Unpredictable. And it made her only more eager to leave Atlanta, a place that seemed worse than inhospitable in every respect at the moment.

She couldn't believe she'd really been fired. Sebastian had been livid, much angrier than she could ever have imagined about her using her initiative. She had to admit that her reaction to his hadn't been conducive to continued employment with Ames. Tempers had flared and now she was out of a job.

Matt's loyalties were torn and he was threatening to quit, even though he agreed with Sebastian's assessment that Martine was too impulsive and foolhardy to be trusted with field work.

On top of that, she still had to worry about Humberto surfacing unexpectedly. And worst of all, she had heard nothing from Joe.

True, she had told him a clean break was best, but she had secretly hoped he would be as awed by what had happened between them as she was and his resolve would crumble. But if that had been the case, he would have called her by now.

Joe had that undefinable something that simply set her on fire. He was the kind of guy she had always admired, a real honest-to-God hero who never bragged, just did what needed doing and never took a bow. She knew that mission in Colombia was only one of many thankless assignments.

Joe's abilities and confidence in them had wowed her more than his good looks, but those sure hadn't detracted from his appeal.

He could be exasperating, but that was to be expected with a personality as forceful as his. Maybe that was part of his problem with her. He didn't want to compete for control constantly as they always seemed to do. Martine shrugged. For her, competition was a huge turn-on.

Joe might have felt the same thing she did when they'd made love. She had thought so at the time. It seemed as if they both had realized afterwards that sometimes love was just not enough.

He obviously thought she ought to give up the kind of work she was doing to prove how she felt about him. But she knew that if he couldn't love her unconditionally, then it would never work as a long-term thing. She stared out the window at the rain. Well, she wasn't changing herself for anybody, not even Joe.

It was probably just as well they had parted when they did. The longer she was with him, the stronger her feelings grew. The real problem was, now that they were apart, what she felt for him hadn't begun to subside. Not even a little.

Her life was a mess at the moment. But she had plans. It was impossible to control everything in her life, but she didn't have to settle for simply reacting to events. She had to be the one to make things happen.

Her résumé was out there making the rounds again, and even if her experience was fairly light, her credentials were nothing to sneeze at. Her grades at university had been excellent. She had maxed all the extra courses Ames had funded. She was fluent in three languages, an expert with small arms, qualified in two disciplines of martial arts and her security clearance was up-to-date for government work. Somebody was going to want to hire her.

In the meantime, she was packing to move. None of the jobs she had applied for were located here in Atlanta. It was time for a change and she meant to be ready for it when it came.

The phone rang. Probably Matt. He had been checking on her several times a day since her altercation with Sebastian. But she checked the caller ID and didn't recognize the number. *Joe?*

She snatched up the receiver. "Hello?"

"You got canned. It was my fault, wasn't it?"

Martine clamped her mouth shut on a cry of glee. Patting her chest to calm her racing heart, she inhaled and released it slowly before speaking. "Hi, Joe. What's up?"

"I just talked to Matt. I'm going to go speak with Sebastian Ames."

"No!" she cried, then lowered her voice to a reasonable level. "That's not necessary. Please don't bother."

"He needs to know just how good you are, Martine. I won't overdo it like I did with Matt. I'll just tell him how flawlessly you planned everything. How much I owe you. He'll come around."

"No, Joe. The truth is, it's high time I made a career move. Matt will never see me as anything but a kid sister and Sebastian's been like an uncle to me ever since we moved to Atlanta when I was twelve. I know they just want to keep me safe, but I have to get away and be on my own, you know?'' When he didn't answer, she changed the subject. ''So, how's the new job?''

She heard him expel a deep breath. ''Iffy. Look, I had this...sudden feeling you might be in some kind of danger or something so I called Ames to see if you were okay. You are, aren't you?''

''Sure, I'm fine. Are you calling from D.C.?''

''No, I'm in Atlanta. I just stopped by on my way to Florida.''

''Great! I'd love to,'' she said, unable to hide her excitement.

Long pause. ''Uh, Martine...''

''Sorry, Joe,'' she said with a laugh, tossing her hair back over her shoulder and wriggling out a comfy spot on the sofa, ''but you already invited me, remember? Twice, I think.''

Long silence. ''Well, that was before.''

''So this is after,'' she argued. ''I'm not after promises or commitments, Joe. Just a week on the beach.''

Another pause. Her heart fell, collapsed like a pricked balloon. She squeezed her eyes shut and tried not to cry.

''All right, bad idea,'' she said, making her voice bright, sunny as the day was dark. ''You take care now, Joe. Enjoy your vacation and—''

''Be ready in half an hour.'' *Click.*

She threw the receiver down and growled with frustration. He made her crazy. But a smile grew when she started thinking about retribution. She could make him crazy, too. She had done it once and now she knew exactly how. The red bikini would be a good start.

Joe settled into the narrow seat next to the aisle, wishing he had splurged on first class. Martine was gazing out the window, waiting for takeoff. The flight into Tallahassee would be short, fortunately, giving them little time to discuss much of anything. Joe wasn't ready for any deep discussions.

He hadn't even been ready to see her again. All he had meant to do was check with Duquesne, make sure adequate protection was still in place. What the hell was he thinking bringing her to Florida?

His mother and sisters would be planning the wedding before he set his suitcase down. Other than his girlfriends in high school, this was the first time he had ever brought a woman home with him. Well, maybe it was best this way. At least he could make sure she stayed out of trouble for a week.

He rested his elbow on the outer armrest and massaged his brow. Scrunching his eyes shut, he willed away the beginning of a headache.

Suddenly a swirl of white flashed behind his eyes, a face materialized. *Oh, God.*

"What is it?" Martine was shaking his arm. "Joe? Are you sick?"

He must have gasped or something. Joe opened his eyes and she was almost nose to nose with him. Her worried expression a direct contrast to the serene face she had worn in the vision. She'd had her eyes closed then as if waiting for a kiss.

Now her long graceful fingers grasped his forearm. Her subtle perfume threatened intoxication. He turned away.

No. That hadn't been a vision, not really. Not Martine in a wedding veil. What he had seen had been brought on by that thought just before it. The one about his mother and sisters misunderstanding his motive for having Martine with him when he arrived. That was all it was. No way in hell was he destined to marry Martine Duquesne.

Maybe it only indicated she would be a bride soon. *Someone else's bride?*

"I need a drink," Joe muttered, pressing his head back hard against the headrest of the seat, careful not to close his eyes too tightly. That's when he always got the mind pictures, when he forgot and did that. "Soon as they get this crate off the ground." He felt her fingers squeeze his and looked down. When had he taken her hand?

They hadn't even kissed or touched when he went to pick her up at her apartment. She had been on the phone with her brother when Joe arrived, telling Duquesne where she was off to and with whom.

Matt Duquesne must have been deliriously happy to have that information. Joe could just imagine his own delight if one of his sisters had called to tell him she was flying off to the beach with some guy he barely knew.

All that considered, he held on to Martine's hand through the takeoff and after, his fingers laced through hers, their ambivalent relationship remaining as up in the air as the plane in which they flew.

What would happen after they landed was anyone's guess. Maybe he should just live in the moment, enjoy the feel of her shoulder next to his, the warmth of her palm, the sound of her breathing. He turned his head to look at her, see what she was thinking.

"Excuse me, sir?" one of the hostesses said, leaning near, her voice little more than a whisper. "You're Agent Joseph Corda, right?"

Joe snapped to attention, his first thought leaped to a possible hijacking. "Yeah, what's the problem?" He was not carrying, but had registered his weapon with security and it was in his bag in the hold.

"We've had an emergency call for you, sir, from a Mr. Duquesne. He asks that you call him back immediately at the number he gave. The matter's urgent."

Apparently so. It was highly unusual for anyone to get clearance to contact a plane's cockpit directly to reach a passenger. Had to be life or death, he would imagine. He reached for the phone on the back of the seat. "The number?"

The hostess frowned at Martine, then glanced briefly to either side at the other passengers. "If you'll come with me, you might want to use the phone up front," she said, then added, "for privacy."

"Joe?" Martine started to get up when he did.

"Stay here. I'll be right back," he told her. He couldn't imagine what Matt Duquesne had to tell him, but he felt fairly sure the man wasn't calling just to warn him off Martine. It would take a damn sight more than brotherly outrage to get that kind of clearance.

"Could I get anything for you?" the attendant asked.

"Jack and Coke," Joe replied as he dialed.

The hostess remained nearby, pretending not to listen. Her face was a study in concern, so she must have been told what the problem was.

"Duquesne here," Matt answered in the middle of the first ring. "Corda?"

"Yeah, what's up?"

"It's Humberto again. I hate like hell to tell you this, man, but he's got your sister and your niece. I'm sorry, he didn't give me any names, so if you have more than one, I don't know which sister it is."

Joe almost dropped the receiver. "What? How did he...no, where? Where is he holding them?"

"He called from Panama City and asked for me here at the office. He said I'd better find a way to reach you. He's wanting to make a trade. He's demanding you and Martine for your sister and the child."

Joe felt his stomach plummet to his feet. He had no frame of reference for this. No idea what to do. His instincts were not kicking in, not where the safety of his family was concerned. His immediate urge was to find Humberto and blow him away. Not a productive idea for a rescue plan.

Matt paused for a second, then continued. "He assured me he doesn't plan to kill Martine. Not that I believed

him. I told him she was with you and that it would take
a while to locate you in D.C. because I wasn't sure where
you worked. Since he has no idea you're almost to Florida
already, that might give you some time. I'm leaving here
now, getting a friend to fly me down. Where you want to
hook up?''

"Stay there," Joe ordered. "Please. You're his point
of contact. With that cast on your leg, you couldn't do
much anyway. Martine will be safe. I'll send her back to
Atlanta the minute I can get her on another plane."

Reluctantly, Matt agreed. "Anything else I can do?
How about calling Mercier? Wasn't he with the FBI?''

"No," Joe answered absently, his mind shooting off in
all directions, trying to form some kind of plan. "Look,
I need to get off the phone and think. Call me on my cell
with any further developments." He rattled off the number.

"You bet, and tell Martine—"

"You can tell her yourself. I told you I'll put her on a
plane home.''

"Good luck doing that," he thought he heard Matt say
as he snapped the receiver back into place on the wall
unit.

The hostess put a hand on his arm. "The captain said
this has to do with a kidnapping in your family. Is there
anything else I can do to help?''

She handed him a plastic cup filled with ice and Coke.
She also offered him a miniature of Jack Daniels, which
he had ordered earlier.

He downed the soft drink in a few gulps, but refused
the liquor. "Ms. Duquesne and I will need to exit first
when we land.''

"Of course. Could I make any calls for you while we're
in the air? Have the authorities meet you?''

He pulled out his credit card and handed it over. "No,
but if you could please, call ahead and have a rental hel-

icopter standing by. I'll need my bag off-loaded right away. Also Ms. Duquesne's.''

''Certainly. Describe your bags and I'll have them rushed to you. We'll be preparing to land in about twenty minutes.''

Joe told her what the bags looked like, then turned around to head back to his seat. Martine was standing directly behind him. ''Who's been kidnapped?'' she demanded.

''My sister and niece,'' he told her. ''Let's go and sit down. We'll be landing soon.'' They quickly settled in their seats and he turned to her with the rest of the story.

''Humberto didn't give names, but I think it's most likely Delores and her oldest, Nita, who is six. My other niece is just an infant and Humberto did mention a child, not a baby.'' He hurriedly explained how Matt got involved and what Humberto was demanding.

She remained quiet for a minute, thinking, then gave one succinct nod. ''Then we'll have to agree to the exchange,'' Martine said. ''Humberto will let them go once he has us. He'll want his pound of flesh before he gets rid of you and me, so that will afford us a little time to act after we turn ourselves over. We can take him.''

''Or he could kill all four of us immediately,'' Joe argued. ''We can't risk it. We'll have to locate him beforehand and get Delores and Nita safely away. Then I'll move in.''

She raised one perfect eyebrow. ''*You'll* move in, huh? All by yourself.''

''That's the plan,'' Joe said, holding her gaze with one even more determined than hers. ''I promised Matt I'd send you home.''

''I'm not going.''

''Then I'll put you somewhere safe.''

''How about a cave? Got any caves around Panama City? That's about the only place you could *put* me where

I'd be incapacitated enough to let you do this alone. You're never going to let me live down that one weakness, are you?''

"That's not fair, Martine. Did you hear me recount anything to anybody about your claustrophobia? Did you?''

"No, but you're thinking about it right now," she declared, clasping her hands in her lap and looking out the window. "You don't trust me to pull my weight."

Joe heaved out a heavy breath and shook his head. "I would trust you with my life, Martine, but I can't stand the thought of Humberto getting his hands on you. And I'll do damned near anything to prevent it."

"I can handle Humberto," she said with a huff of indignation.

Her overconfidence really worried him. "Well, we have to find him before anybody can do anything. Right now we need to decide what Matt should tell him when Humberto calls back to set up the exchange."

She shivered, chafing her arms with her palms. "We don't dare keep him waiting too long before giving him some kind of answer. He's not well known for his patience." Her gaze bored into his then. "Your eyes look a little too wild, Joe. You know you have to keep your cool."

Joe blinked, forcing himself to take a deep breath and exhale slowly, to channel his almost overpowering rage into an energy that wouldn't get everyone involved killed.

Martine slid her hand into his again. "You've got to let me help you with this. Nothing you do will work if Humberto thinks I'm out of the picture."

Damn it all, she was right. Joe just couldn't reconcile himself to putting her out there with a target on. He recalled that quick click of a vision he'd had in McLean. Martine with blood all over her face, her eyes closed.

But his visions always came in sequence. The other one he'd had more recently, right here on the plane, where she was swathed all in white was the only thing that gave him a little measure of hope. It came after the one with the blood, so didn't that mean she would survive to become a bride?

He looked at her again, that earnest expression, those beautiful features. His heart caught in his chest. Had the white been a bridal veil? Or the white satin lining of a casket?

Less than half an hour after they landed in Tallahassee, Joe boosted Martine into the chartered helicopter and they were off to Port St. Joe. He needed to make some calls, but knew there would be too much noise in the chopper.

His parents would be insane with worry if they already knew what had happened. He could only hope that they weren't aware of it yet. If they were, his dad would have immediately called the authorities and the local cops and FBI would be all over this by now.

Martine had said little and remained silent as the chopper lifted off. She appeared to be lost in thought, no doubt planning how to effect the exchange with the least risk of his family being hurt. It touched him that she would not only volunteer to surrender herself to Humberto in order to save two people she didn't even know, but that she also seemed convinced that right would prevail in the end. She just hadn't been in the business long enough to know that the good guys didn't always win.

He watched for coastline to appear on their left when they'd had time to near the Gulf. Something settled inside him when it finally came into view.

This was home, waves lapping foamy tongues at the shelly sands, shacks and quaint private cottages dotted among time-share condos and pastel hotels. Souvenir shops sporting garish signs, atmosphere provided by decrepit, peeling boats half buried in the dirt outside. There would be the ever-present gulls darting for fish and scraps from tourists. Not the most beautiful beach in the world, but it was his beach.

If not for the nightmarish circumstances that marred this homecoming, Joe knew he would be feeling an incredible rush of peace now. It's what brought him back here every chance he got. He couldn't, for the life of him, remember why he'd ever left in the first place.

This return was different, a result of his failure in Colombia, his reticence at becoming a straight-out assassin and killing Humberto with a couple of rounds to the head or a swift twist of the neck. He'd had numerous chances to do both but he hadn't.

Didn't that decision prove he should get out of the business?

## Chapter 11

"It's beautiful!" Martine mouthed. Joe couldn't hear her words over the sound of the chopper. He smiled as she leaned over him to look down at the coast. He knew that up close the place wouldn't be all that impressive unless you already knew and loved it.

The sand wasn't Daytona white and the waves weren't surfer high. In the stretch fondly called the Redneck Riviera, you'd find only a few upscale amenities. But it had been a great place to grow up, a family place. He wouldn't trade it for the ritziest coast in Hawaii.

Joe directed the chopper to land on a flat section of beach near the causeway just off Highway 98. They ducked their heads against the downdraft, hefted out their two bags and Joe waved the pilot off.

They would have to hoof it for about a mile. He could call his folks to come get them, of course, but then he'd have to explain over the phone what was going on. Better to do that face-to-face.

Instead of heading for the highway where they might

have caught a ride, he took Martine's weekender from her and nodded toward the east. "That way. Kick off your shoes, but watch out for broken shells."

The whap-whap of the chopper blades had faded in the distance and left only minor traffic noise, the squawking of a couple of gulls and the swishing rhythm of the waves.

Joe drew in lungsful of the salty air as he began his trek home, welcoming the scent and humidity like old friends.

"Your family lives right on the beach?" she asked.

"Mom and Dad do. The others are farther inland. Linda lives about ten miles north. Delores has a house here near the school. I figure that must be where she and my niece were snatched. She walks over to pick up Nita at noon."

Shoes in hand, she trudged beside him, staring out at the Gulf. "We'll get them back, Joe."

"I know. Just a matter of time." He had to believe that. But he didn't have the faintest idea how to go about it. They had no clue where Humberto was. There was nothing for it but to wait until he made further contact.

Martine's cell phone chirped. She quickly snatched it out of her purse and answered. Her eyes widened as she offered it to Joe. "It's Mercier!"

Joe dropped the bags in the sand and took the phone, remembering that he had turned his off on the chopper. This must be important for Mercier to have gone to the trouble to get Martine's number. "Corda here."

"Matthew Duquesne called and told me what's going on. We're in."

"No way," Jack argued vehemently. "Humberto warned against calling in the troops. He says he'll kill my sister and her little girl."

"Hear me out. You'll be running the show. All I'm saying is that you have all our resources at your disposal, Joe. Every agency represented by Sextant. Anything you need—info, manpower, weaponry, supplies, funds—you name it.''

Joe felt overwhelmed by the offer. It was a godsend and he wasn't about to turn it down. ''Breaking rules, aren't you? This is not within Sextant's scope. National security's not threatened here.''

''Hey, you said yourself that Humberto's a foreign national, a known criminal working against his own government, who has entered our country to do deliberate harm to U.S. citizens. Four citizens targeted so far, two of them women and one, a child. Not to mention a government agent. As far as I'm concerned, that's terrorism at its most personal.''

He paused for effect, then added, ''So tell me what you need and let's take care of this.''

''We need everything. Right now we're at square one,'' Joe told him.

Martine piped in with specifics. ''Trace on the phones at Ames for the call back. Check on local rentals in the past few days. And abandoned properties. Get photos of Humberto if they can find any.''

Joe repeated what she said verbatim.

''We're on it. Turn on your phone and keep it on so we'll have two numbers to reach you. When either of you think of anything else you can use, give us a buzz. I'll get back with you soon. Oh, and give my regards to Martine,'' Mercier said.

He had used her first name. Joe wasn't sure he liked the note of familiarity.

''Yeah, sure.'' Joe thanked Mercier, signed off and returned Martine's phone. ''That's quite a deal. Sort of stunned me for a second.''

''He's wonderful, isn't he?'' she said with an encouraging grin. Then she picked up her suitcase before Joe could grab it and walked on down the beach.

He felt another stab of jealousy. Jack Mercier would

definitely appeal to a woman like Martine. To any woman, Joe suspected. Jack probably had some smooth moves. Definitely had a position of power and impressive resources. Those were resources Joe desperately needed himself at the moment, so he knew he had to squelch any personal animosity toward Mercier, deserved or not. It wasn't that Joe didn't like the guy. He did. He just didn't want Martine to keep noticing how great Jack was.

That worry was quickly supplanted by another more immediate concern. A wave of dread rippled through him as they passed the Williams' rustic little beach house and approached his parents' home.

He felt like the snake in the garden of Eden. He had brought this ugliness to paradise. If not for his damned job, this would not be happening. He should have quit sooner. Just one mission earlier and everything here would still be fine.

He stopped at the bottom of the steps leading up to the deck of the sand-colored stucco dwelling and shifted the bag in his hand.

"Well, this is it. My dad's gonna go ballistic and want to call in every law enforcement agency on the planet. Mom will probably have a heart attack."

God, he hoped not. There was no way to break this gently. How were their hearts? Had he even asked about their health lately?

She placed a palm on his back, just a comforting touch, support that he really needed right now. He looked down at her and she smiled encouragement. "I'm right behind you. If I see I'm in the way and they want privacy, I'll retreat and wait for you outside. If it goes the other way, I am trained in CPR."

Prepared for all contingencies, that was Martine. Joe wished he had time to hug her and tell her how much he appreciated her no-nonsense attitude. But that would have to wait.

* * *

Martine knew Joe was too preoccupied at the moment to focus on the investigation. She would have to pitch in until his equilibrium was restored. Thank God she had called Matt in private earlier and instructed him to get Mercier's number and tell him everything.

Any boss who would go the distance that he had to get Joe safely out of Colombia, even to paying a merc like Matt to bring him home early, would surely go all out to show Joe what the Sextant team was all about.

This kidnapping would provide a perfect opportunity to accomplish that if the rescue proved successful. It would also obligate Joe to stay with the team after everything was resolved. Mercier was no dummy. Martine had counted on that.

Once Joe got through this ordeal of telling his parents, she would question them, get the particulars on where the sister and her daughter might have been picked up and how long they had been missing. Hopefully, that information, combined with what Mercier would glean, might provide a starting point.

Joe knocked. In a couple of seconds a dark-haired little girl skipped across the glassed-in porch and unlatched the door. "Hi, Uncle Joe! Grandma, Papi, it's Uncle Joe!" She flung herself at him and clung like a little spider monkey. "What'd you bring me?"

"Nita?" His voice was a broken whisper as he clutched her with one arm. Then he cleared his throat, dropped his bag on the steps and peeled her off of him. Holding her by her slender shoulders, he crouched and looked her straight in the eye. "Where's your mama, Nita?"

The child beamed. She was a beauty except for the gap where her front teeth used to be. "She's making cookies. C'mon." She grabbed his hand with both of hers, tugged and danced backwards as she led them inside, through a living/dining area and to the doorway of a large eat-in kitchen. "Mama! Look who's here!"

Joe seemed to be having trouble assimilating the fact that his niece and sister were accounted for and safe. His other sister, the Cordas' youngest, had an infant. Martine feared she knew what was coming next, but she kept silent.

The living area, its wall of windows facing the view of the Gulf, had three other doors in addition to the kitchen, that opened off of it. There was a staircase leading up to what were probably more bedrooms. Joe's parents' home was very large, airy and comfortable. The rooms she could see were decorated with family photographs, handmade crafts and wicker furniture. She wished to heaven she'd been invited to the place under happier circumstances.

Joe embraced his sister fiercely, ignoring her laughing protest that she was sticky with cookie dough.

"Where is Linda?" he demanded, obviously having come to the same conclusion Martine had reached. If Humberto didn't have this sister, then he must have the other.

"At work, I guess. I haven't talked to her today."

"Aha, Joseph, you've come home!" A man, obviously Joe's father, rushed in, slapping him on the back and planting a kiss on either side of Joe's face. Then he noticed Martine. "And you bring pretty company. What a wonderful surprise!"

"Martine Duquesne," she said, holding out her hand. Instead of shaking it, he raised it to his lips.

"Welcome to our home. Son, you should have—"

"Where's Mama?" Joe interrupted, his impatience evident. He squeezed his sister's arm and gave her a little push. "Go and get her, Delores, while I make a phone call. I'm afraid I might have some bad news."

The happy expressions worn by Mr. Corda, Delores and the child, Nita, sobered instantly. Joe's father looked to her, his dark brows drawn together in question, probably figuring the bad news must have to do with her.

Delores returned less than a minute later with the mother. The older woman obviously had been asleep. Her short blond hair was a bit tousled and the shirt and shorts she wore looked wrinkled. She hardly looked old enough to have a son Joe's age.

"Joe, honey? What's wrong?" his mother asked, her Southern accent even more prominent than Joe's when he wasn't speaking Spanish. Her arms went around his waist as he hugged her with one arm.

He carefully replaced the receiver of the phone on the handset as his gaze met Martine's. He shook his head. No answer at his sister's house.

"Let's sit down," Joe told his mother gently, leading her over to the brightly patterned sofa that sat facing the bank of windows.

Martine looked out. You could see a panorama of surf from here and faintly hear its breathing. Even inside the house with doors closed and the air-conditioning on, the fresh scent of the ocean added its fillip to the tantalizing smell of homebaked cookies.

How the senses could lie, Martine thought sadly. All was not right with the world. And here, in this peaceful place, it should be. It really should be. She knew she felt only a trace of the awful betrayal Joe must feel at that. This was his haven. *Invaded*.

She and the rest took the chairs as Joe began. "Mama, have you spoken with Linda today?"

She shook her head. "Not since yesterday afternoon. I phoned early this morning, but... What's happened, Joe?" Her voice rose with every word.

He sighed, worrying his bottom lip for a moment before he went on. "We think Linda might have been kidnapped. Her and little Consuelo."

"Oh, my God, no!" Mrs. Corda cried. She reached out,

grasped at his shirtfront. Delores clutched Nita to her and held her protectively. They stared at Joe, speechless and wide-eyed with shock.

His father was already on his feet, fishing his keys out of his pocket. "It is that no-good man of hers! This time I will destroy that—"

"No, Papa. This has nothing to do with Paul. He's not involved in any way." He urged his father to sit back down. "Be still now and let me tell you what we know."

"Who has them and where are they?" his father demanded, still standing, his hands fisted at his sides. Martine could see where Joe got his fierce determination.

"I know the kidnapper. He's not from around here and his name is Carlos Humberto."

Joe Senior's eyes narrowed. "You know this man? From your work? This has to do with drugs?"

Martine watched Joe nod, guilt written all over his features. "We don't know where he's taken them yet. But you have to keep your head and not go off half-cocked. Agreed? We can't call in the authorities. He might panic if we do. I can handle this."

Mr. Corda exhaled harshly, finally dropped down in the chair again and pressed a hand to his face. He nodded, his conflict evident. A loving father and grandfather forced to relinquish taking an active role. His jaw clenched and his hands fisted, he narrowed his eyes at Joe. "You find them, Joseph. Today."

"I'll move heaven and earth, Papa. You know that," he promised.

Martine could see that Joe was clearly over his shock and back in control now, thinking logically, able to handle whatever came.

"But we must call the police," Mr. Corda announced.

"Joe's co-workers have offered to help, sir," Martine said. "Believe me, that's a much better alternative in this case."

All they needed was a bunch of uniforms muddying up the waters, maybe initiating tragic results if Humberto saw them as a threat. "We're advised to keep things quiet and wait for further word from the kidnapper. Then we'll know how to plan."

Joe gave her the ghost of a smile and a nod of approval as he stood up. "Martine will explain further while I go over and check at Linda's. There might be evidence there that can help me find her."

"Then go, go," his mother urged, pushing at him.

He spoke to Martine. "I'll be back as soon as I have a look around."

"I'll be here," she said, amazed when he cradled her face and brushed a quick kiss on her forehead.

"Take care, Joe," she told him as he was leaving.

When the door closed behind him, Mr. Corda pinned Martine with a worried glare. "Why did you say that to him? To have a care? Is our Joseph in danger, too?"

"A figure of speech, sir. You know Joe can look after himself. And as for your daughter and her baby, I don't believe the man who has them would harm them. I was hostage to him myself not long ago and he treated me very well, like a guest. Once he gets what he's after, he'll let them go."

"What does he want?" Delores asked. "Do you know yet?"

Martine hedged. "We're waiting on instructions."

"You were a hostage? Joe saved you?" his mother whispered, hope flaring in her wide blue eyes.

"Of course," Martine said with a wide smile to reassure the woman. "And if your son went to that much trouble for me, someone he hadn't even met before, you *know* he'll find his own sister and niece. He's the very best person to handle this."

Little Nita came over and climbed on the arm of Martine's chair, bumping one foot against the side, studying the stranger her uncle had brought home with him. "Are you going to marry my Uncle Joe? He kissed your head."

Martine noticed the others were staring at her as intently as Nita was, waiting to see what she would say. Would they be glad or upset if Joe really had brought her here with serious intentions?

A small laugh escaped. "No, no, sweetie. We're not that kind of friends. I'm only here to…well, help if I can."

"Tell us about this man, this kidnapper," Mr. Corda ordered. "What sort of person is he and what do you *think* he is after? Money?"

"Humberto's after me." She figured she could admit that much. They didn't know her so that shouldn't upset them. But Martine didn't want to be the one to tell them he was after Joe as well. "I believe he wants an exchange, and if Joe can't find and rescue Linda and little Consuelo right away, then we'll make it."

"We know something of what Joseph's job entails. This man is a drug runner," Joe's father said. "Does he also use drugs?"

Martine shook her head emphatically. "No, sir. Humberto is not your run-of-the-mill drug lord. He views himself as a very savvy Colombian businessman, not as the criminal he is. Self-delusion on his part, I know, but he behaves accordingly."

"He behaves as a gentleman?" The father of any abducted daughter would desperately hope that was true.

"Yes, sir. He always did with me," Martine said, hoping to alleviate a little of their worry.

She watched relief deflate Corda's chest. His wife and daughter looked a lot more skeptical. Did they suspect what a rosy colored picture she was painting about all of this? Of course, they must.

Martine took the little girl's hand. "Now if you would come show me where things are, Nita, we could finish baking those cookies your mother started and make some coffee or something. I don't really know anything else to tell anyone, and I'm sure your mother and grandparents will want to discuss this without little ears tuned in.''

''Or stranger ears,'' Nita retorted, squinting at Martine's. ''We can talk to each other while they say secrets.''

''You bet.''

Nita gave her a look that acknowledged Martine's frankness, almost a thank-you for not inventing some phony excuse to get her out of the room. Children were so much more savvy than people gave them credit for. Martine could never understand why some people talked down to them.

Mr. Corda was already comforting his wife. Delores had set about reassuring them both about her sister's strength and how little trouble the baby was. Everything would be all right, Martine heard her say. Joe would take care of it. Linda and little Connie would be home before breakfast tomorrow. Martine prayed to God she was right about that.

All in all, they had taken the news much better than she had expected. The Cordas were a strong family who apparently bred strong children.

She smiled down at the six-year-old who exhibited a bold confidence that was pure Joe. A sudden and unfamiliar longing stirred in Martine's heart.

Her children would probably look just like this if Joe were their father. Beautiful, fearless kids with wisdom and warm humor shining out of deep brown eyes.

He would be so gentle and loving with them, but firm, she imagined. He wouldn't just demand, but would earn their respect as they grew up. He seemed to have a good example to follow. Yes, Joe would make a fine father. She would be the one lacking in the parental department, but she still had this incredible urge to give it a try.

What a rotten time for dormant maternal instincts to kick in, she thought with a sigh. This was *so* not good.


Joe hated it when his worst fears were realized. Linda's purse was on the floor in the small foyer, its contents scattered. Quickly he searched the five small rooms of the little tract house. None of the sparse furnishings were disturbed. She must have decided not to put up a fight. He was relieved about that.

In the baby's room he found the diaper bag, empty except for a crumpled paper, the daily report form from the nursery listing feedings and changes. The coverlet in the crib was wadded to one side. Joe touched it, willing his rage down to a manageable level, then hurried back to the kitchen.

There were two prepared bottles in the fridge, one lying on its side.

He propped his hands against the edge of the counter to keep from trashing the kitchen himself.

The sugar bowl was tipped over. In the spill of sugar a finger had hastily carved out the number three. Linda had left the message, probably when she'd been allowed to grab a bottle for the baby. *Three,* signifying there were three men involved, he guessed. It was all she would have known at that point.

Joe looked around more carefully. Near the sugar was an electrical outlet. And an unplugged cord which led to a cheap plastic alarm clock. Another message. The hands had stopped at six o'clock. This morning or yesterday evening?

She usually picked up Connie at the Playhouse Nursery and got home from work about five-thirty. If Humberto and his men had been waiting to take her then, the diaper bag would not have been in the nursery waiting to be packed with diapers and bottles for the next day. He would have found it with or near her purse.

Hoping against hope someone would have seen something, he went house to house and questioned her neighbors. No one had seen her leave. But the couple across the street had been outside working in their yards until long after six the day before. Her car had still been in the driveway at nine. Now it was gone. So they must have taken her this morning, at six o'clock.

He drove his dad's car back to the beach house. He had been gone for a couple of hours. It was nearly seven. They could be anywhere by now, but he felt they wouldn't be too far away. Humberto would need to have the hostages handy when it was time to make the trade.

Joe pulled out his cell phone to touch base with Mercier, knowing it was too soon for him to have found out anything significant. He was right, but at least things had been set into motion.

He pulled into the driveway and sat there for a minute wondering what in the world he could say to reassure his parents that Linda would be all right. She was their baby girl, only twenty-five. And little Consuelo was only four months old.

His father came out of the house and hurried to the car just as Joe got out and slammed the door.

"You were gone for so long! What did you find?" he asked, his dark eyes searching Joe's face.

"Linda and Connie were taken, just like I figured. Any calls?"

"None. Any sign that they were hurt?"

"No, and no indication that she resisted, which was smart." Joe quickly filled him in on his findings based on the clues Linda had provided.

"She is smart and brave, our Linda. But I worry she will anger them. Her temper is too quick."

"You know she won't endanger the baby."

His father nodded, hands on his hips as he looked off down the main drag. Traffic was fairly light, even for this late in the season, but Joe knew his dad wasn't gauging that right now. He was lost in his thoughts of what might be happening to two people he loved. "What are we to do, Joseph? How can we find them?"

"We'll find them. Let's go inside."

"This woman you brought with you, she is also working for the DEA?" He led the way back to the house, his gait weary, his head bowed.

"I'm no longer with the DEA, Papa, remember?" He didn't want to bring up anything about battling terrorists right now, but Joe wondered if the agency he *did* work now for might trigger situations every bit as bad as this one if he stayed with the job. His dad sure didn't need to hear that. "Martine is with a company out of Atlanta. A hostage rescue outfit. I met her in Colombia when I was on my last case. I thought she would have told you all that."

"She only said that you saved her from this man. That you are very good at what you do." There was more than pride in his father's voice. Joe detected profound hope that what Martine had told them was true.

"Yeah, she would say that." He tried to change the subject. "What do you think of her, Papa?"

"She knows the right things to say at times like this. And she seems willing to do what must be done. She has said that if she goes with this man, Humberto, he might release Linda and the baby. Is this true?"

"Only if he gets me, too. Did she tell you that? He plans to kill us. If I thought he would honor his word on the trade, I might try it."

"Even if it meant the death of Martine Duquesne?"

Joe looked his father straight in the eye and meant to answer, "Even then." But he couldn't form the words.

He kept seeing Martine's pale face in that vision he'd had back in McLean, her beautiful features covered with blood, her eyes closed.

# Chapter 12

His father's strong hand gripped Joe's arm. "Go inside your mind and see what will happen, my son, for I can see nothing. The future hides from me."

"And it only teases me with random glimpses, Papa. None of them good. It's a curse."

"It's a gift and you must use it when it comes."

Joe shook his head and pushed open the front door, needing to see Martine alive and well and free of the gore in the vision. "It's a half-ass gift, then, one that can't be trusted."

"It is more than the gift you do not trust, Joseph," his father argued. "You would never be still long enough to search your heart." He flung out his hands. "Always moving, moving, try this, try that! The one thing I could not teach you is to have patience with yourself!"

In the open doorway, Joe turned on him. "The one thing you *did* teach me is to stand for what I believe is right, old man. I would die for any one of my family and

you know it, but I do *not* think it's right to expect Martine—''

''I believe that's my call.'' Martine stood there, blue
eyes spitting fire.

His father's gaze flicked back and forth between them,
obviously waiting for an explosion. But Joe knew now
was not the time for a battle of wills. Martine was no
martyr and, even given her lack of experience in dealing
with men like Humberto before Colombia, she had good
instincts. Joe waited to see what else she had to say.

''I think we should try acting before we resort to reacting,'' she said. ''Time for a planning session. Tell me
exactly what you found, Joe.''

Relieved to avoid a confrontation with her when he had
so much else to worry about, Joe repeated what he'd told
his father and elaborated a little more on the details. His
objectivity kicked in while going over it. Maybe that's
what she'd had in mind.

He knew one thing: in spite of his urge to protect her,
he was damned glad she was here.

Martine took the chair Joe pulled out for her at the
kitchen table while the others took their places.

Delores had put on a Disney video for Nita in one of
the bedrooms to keep her occupied. Then she made sandwiches and opened chips and soft drinks for everyone,
urging them to eat. Martine hoped Joe's youngest sister,
Linda, was as practical as Delores. Linda would need all
her wits to hold her own with Humberto.

By all rights, Joe should be in charge of the planning,
but Martine could see he wanted to shield his mother from
thinking about the worst. He would probably send her in
the other room to lie down, not understanding that the
woman really needed something positive to do instead of
being coddled.

''All right, question,'' Martine said, jumping right in

before he had a chance to assume the lead. "Is Linda breast-feeding the baby?"

Mrs. Corda nodded, her brow wrinkled with confusion. "Yes. She expresses her milk for the daytime feedings while she is at work, but she is still nursing."

"Okay, so the baby will get fed and they won't need to shop for milk," Martine said with a nod. "But they left the diaper bag, which was stupid. After one stinky one, they'll realize they *need* diapers. So, Mr. and Mrs. Corda, you'll need to begin at one end of the strip and go to the other, questioning every cashier that might have checked out a man buying a generous supply today."

"Good thinking," Joe said. "They probably went for one of the convenience stores. Fewer customers and less time looking for what they wanted. What we're after is the make and model of the vehicle they're in. We can be pretty sure they will have ditched Linda's by this time."

Martine nodded. "Call Mercier back, Joe, and see what he has for us so far."

"I called him on the way back from Linda's. It will be morning before he can get everything to us. He's waiting for a source to get him the photo of Humberto and will then forward it. I gave him the e-mail address here."

"What can I do?" Delores asked, shoving the plate of sandwiches at her father and giving him a pointed but silent order to eat.

Martine knew Delores wasn't going to like the next suggestion. "You'll take Nita and get out of town. Humberto might just decide to up the stakes."

Delores shook her head. "I'll take Nita to her other grandparents right now, but I'm coming back here. I can help and so can my husband."

Joe answered. "Good. You two will man the phone and computer here, collect whatever Mercier sends, and call us in when you get something new. Martine and I will meet with the realtors and start checking out rental properties and get some leads on vacant buildings.''

Martine's phone rang. She looked at the display, then quickly answered, ''Matt? Did he call again?''

Martine watched Joe's face change from agent-in-charge to brother-in-pain. Delores was already standing, gripping the back of her chair with white-knuckled fingers. Mrs. Corda had paled even further, her breathing shallow, her color not good at all. Mr. Corda held his sandwich at half mast, the bite he'd just taken still unchewed. Everyone around the table was totally focused on her, waiting.

''Humberto called,'' Matt affirmed. ''He seemed nervous this time. I told him I had just located you. He said you and Joe have until tomorrow afternoon to get to Port St. Joe and be ready to make the switch. If you don't do what he says, he told me the hostages will be *sleeping with the fishes* by midnight tomorrow. Can you believe he actually said that? Guy's been watching too much American TV. We traced the number and it was a ship-to-shore phone. He's on a boat.''

''Name?''

''The *Paper Moon*. You can thank Mercier for getting with the Coastal authorities to obtain the ID. It's a forty-two-foot Flybridge, usually slipped at the Portaway Marina at Mako Beach. Captain is Harley Banks. He's a live-aboard and only hires crew when he takes her out. See if you can get a location on the boat but do it on the Q.T. The Coast Guard would go roaring in with foghorns and automatics. I wouldn't advise that. Humberto even warned me to stay where I am. Fat chance of that.''

''You'll stay, Matt. Come down here and I'll break your other leg. Any background noises on the phone?'' Martine asked, hoping for some kind of clue as to whether the boat was very far off shore. ''The motor running? Gulls or anything?''

"Too quiet except for a baby crying. Not screaming, just fussing. It was close up, so he intended me to hear it. Could have been a recording, though."

"Let's hope not."

"Yeah, let's. I gave Humberto your cell number so he'll be phoning you and Joe with directions for the swap." He paused for a second. "But don't you go for it, Marti. He'll kill you. He said again that he wouldn't, that he just wants Corda, but that was just to get me to cooperate and get you down there. I'm coming anyway as soon as I can get a flight."

"No, Matt. I mean it. I have a feeling he'll be checking periodically just to make sure you stay in Atlanta. There's no doubt he knows exactly what it is you do for a living and he'll see you as his biggest threat. Please, be sensible and stay where you are."

"Only if you promise me you won't consider the exchange. Find another way."

Martine agreed they would, but she wasn't so sure there *was* another way. She said a quick goodbye, rang off and put the phone down. It had been so deathly quiet in the room and her reception so good on the cell phone, she knew everyone had heard the entire conversation.

"We need to move tonight before Humberto realizes we're already here," Joe said. "Mercier's going to have to get us a location."

"Satellite?" Martine asked. "You think he has the authority for that?"

Joe sighed. "We're about to find out. If not, he can buy the information. Anyone with enough money can. Papa, forget the convenience stores. You and Mama drive down to the marina. See what you can find out about the *Paper Moon* and how long ago she pulled out, how much her tanks hold and when she refueled. Call back here on the land line soon as you get the info. Delores, get Nita over to Terry's folks and get back here. Martine, scare up a map of the area. There should be an atlas on the bookshelf. Meanwhile, I'll call Mercier about the satellite.''

Delores went to collect Nita and her toys. Joe had barely finished giving Mercier the pertinent information about the boat and requesting his help when his sister returned to the dining room.

''Joe, a little beach bunny just appeared on the back porch insisting she's a friend of yours. I told her you were too busy but—''

''Don't mind the disguise, Joey,'' said a sultry voice from the doorway. ''I didn't know whether anybody might be watching the place or what I'd find going on, so I played the local and walked up the beach from the hotel. Y'all ready for some help around here?''

''Holly?'' Joe was too stunned to stand up. The woman was barefoot and wearing a string bikini. She had a beach towel slung over one shoulder, probably concealing her weapon. ''What the hell are you doing here?''

She rolled her eyes and grinned at Delores. ''Tell me, girl, has he always been this slow?'' Then she held out her hand. ''Name's Holly Amberson.''

Delores hesitated, then shook her hand. ''Delores Trimble, his sister.'' She shot Joe the same look she always had when he'd gotten himself in hot water with his girlfriends. An expression that read, ''How are you going to manage two at a time, bro?'' Then she glanced toward the other side of the living room where Martine stood with the atlas in her hands.

It was obvious Delores thought Holly and Martine shared an interest in him that had nothing to do with the kidnapping. It was also clear that she was not at all happy about the probable distraction a triangle would cause right now.

''How'd you get here so fast?'' Joe asked.

Holly grinned and did a little flourish with her well-manicured hand. "Magic. We caught a hop down to Tyndal Air Force Base."

"*We?*"

"Will and Eric came, too. Matt Duquesne called Jack about the trace and I just talked with him. He's pretty sure your boy's on a boat, but the guys are casing other possibilities. It can't hurt to be thorough. As for me, I'm all yours!"

Not the best declaration to make with Delores eyeing them that way. "Holly works with me. Come on in and sit down, Holly," Joe said. "Delores, scram and do what you gotta do. Martine?" he called. "Bring the map."

It took less than five minutes for him to realize that Martine might have the same idea about Holly that Delores had, despite his explanation of the job situation.

Though she was polite to Holly, Joe sensed an undercurrent of wariness that could possibly be jealousy. He wondered if it was personal or professional. It would be nice if he had time to explore that a little, but he didn't.

Holly had never shown any indication of interest in him as anything other than a member of the team. He certainly had none in her, though he had not missed the fact that she was beautiful. Who wouldn't notice?

Her conduct right now was all business, but she sure was radiating sexuality in that bikini. Her skin—and she was displaying a *lot* of it—was pale caramel, only a shade darker than his. The catlike eyes were made for concealing secrets and taunting people with them. Her short cap of hair glistened like black watered silk.

Unfortunately, it was impossible not to notice her remarkable breasts straining against the triangles of electric-blue spandex, but Joe staunchly ignored them after one or two furtive glances. Martine was not quite so dismissive of Holly's most prominent features. She glared.

Joe attempted to drown the tension with a spate of information, hoping to direct their attention back to the main reason they were here. Once Holly was up to speed on everything, he turned to Martine. "Did I tell you? Holly used to be with the FBI."

Martine looked unimpressed. "I'm sure her credentials are...impeccable."

Holly just smiled, the picture of innocence. Joe knew she had a wicked sense of humor because he'd seen her ply it with the guys back in McLean. She knew exactly what she was doing. He felt like shaking her right now for putting him on the spot with Martine.

"Okay, here's the deal, you two," Holly said suddenly, shutting off the sensual glow around her like a light switch. "Jack will be getting with the National Reconnaissance Office tonight. Hopefully, he'll be able to see the pictures from one of the satellites over the Gulf and try to pinpoint any forty-two-footers hanging around out there and get us some coordinates to work with."

"There are bound to be quite a few, but I think we can be pretty sure he'll stay close. That should narrow it down a little," Joe said, thinking out loud.

"Timing might be a problem," Martine declared. "If the pictures are even an hour or so old, the boat might not have remained stationary."

Holly agreed. "Yes, right. He'll compare from two sources passing over at different times if possible. The sightings that are the correct size and fairly stationary will be the suspect vehicles. The satellite views will probably be more or less straight down and boat names won't be visible."

Joe had an idea. "We could do a flyby early in the morning with one of the sightseeing helicopters that sell rides. They will have been flying at intervals today, so that shouldn't send up any alert that we're using them for a search."

"We can also question other boat owners who have

been out, see if they've noticed the *Paper Moon*," Martine suggested.

"Yeah, but even if we identify the boat right away, the earliest I can get aboard is tomorrow night," Joe said. "That could be too late."

Holly raised an eyebrow. "You're to talk to Humberto by phone before then. Stall him. Then after dark, *we* do the insertion, Joe. I didn't fly all the way down here just to darken my tan."

"I'm going, too," Martine said emphatically.

"We'll see," Holly said calmly. "Right now, if you would please get on the horn and hire us a little whirlybird for the morning. Promise to double their rate if they'll have us up there first thing."

To her credit, Martine didn't argue. Joe imagined she would make up for lost time when she found out she definitely wasn't going on the boat raid, but he would deal with that when they came to it.

"I'll call around and get us some SEAL gear and an inflatable Zodiac. Joe, you'll scare us up some weapons. Get with ATF or DEA for some confiscated automatics and magazines. Throw your new weight around if you need to. Big Boss has authorized us cooperation from the top on down on every case we run. Let's see how well it works."

"Done," he assured her, already compiling a mental list of what they would need.

As it happened, his mention of Sextant worked really well. Bill Cole, an old associate working with the local DEA, promised to fix them up with a virtual arsenal.

Civilian companies obviously weren't required to co-operate quite as fully, Joe discovered. Martine hit a stumbling block.

"FlyRight wants a cash deposit up-front and an explanation of what's going on," she said. "One of us needs to go to Panama City and make the arrangements tonight if we want the helicopter tomorrow.''

As soon as Delores returned from taking Nita to the in-laws an hour later, she and Martine headed out to take care of it, which meant a forty-mile drive. Martine didn't look all that happy about leaving him there alone with Holly.

Joe decided he didn't mind Martine's little pique all that much. Payback for her deviling him about Jack Mercier and what a great guy he was. Still, he was too worried about Linda and the baby to give it much more than a passing thought.

Even so, he followed her out to Delores's car. When Martine turned, her hand on the car door, to see what he wanted, he showed her exactly what that was with a kiss.

It was over too quickly and her surprise too great for her to give much of a response. Joe had to be satisfied with her ghost of a smile and that smug little glance toward the door of the house where Holly stood observing them.

He sighed when Delores backed out of the driveway and took off. He used to be a lot more adept at managing women. But he suspected most women were a lot more manageable than Martine would ever be.

Time crawled by as the night wore on. ''I can't understand why they're not back yet,'' Joe said, checking his watch again, then glancing at the kitchen clock to make certain the two jibed. How many times had he done that already? ''It's been four hours. The cell phone is off and that worries me,'' he added. Surely she wouldn't have turned it off. He had swapped his for hers since Matt had given Humberto her number. Maybe his was just out of juice. He couldn't remember when he'd last charged it.

Holly poured them another cup of coffee and nodded at one of the chairs in a silent effort to get him to sit down. He couldn't seem to be still no matter how hard he tried.

"Your parents got some good info at the marina," Holly said. "We know at least two of them are out there on the boat. We should be able to find it easily enough with the chopper once Jack gets us the coordinates from the satellite pictures. How much do you figure Humberto knows about boats?"

"Not a lot, I guess, but we can't count on that," Joe warned. "He's smart. What he doesn't know, he'll find out or at least make sure he has someone around who's an expert. When I knew him, he left very little to chance. In which case, the captain might still be alive." Joe surely hoped that was so.

His parents, exhausted by worry and their trip to the marina, had gone to bed an hour before. It was after midnight already. Joe was so wired, he didn't figure he'd sleep at all tonight. Not that he'd even consider it until Martine and Delores returned and he knew everything was set for the search in the morning.

Holly looked as bright-eyed as ever. She wore one of his mother's robes over her bikini, so she wasn't quite as distracting now. He felt a little jolt of satisfaction every time he thought about Martine's reaction to Holly. He sipped his coffee and put it down again to resume pacing.

"Will you please sit?" Holly snapped, clicking one long red nail on the Formica tabletop. "You make me nervous." She shook her head and chuckled. "That girl's got you so wound up, I swear."

Joe dragged out a chair and sat. "Yeah, she does." He blew out a sigh. "You ever been nuts about somebody, Amberson?"

She nodded thoughtfully, playing with her cup, turning it around and around. "Time or two."

"How about now?" he asked, grinning at her. "I

thought I saw you looking a little cow-eyed at Will Griffin back at the office.''

She shrugged, refusing to meet his eyes. ''The boy's eye candy, what can I say?'' Then she laughed at herself, shaking her head. ''He's got a twin. Did you know that? Looks exactly like him. He's still with Alcohol, Tobacco and Firearms. Double trouble, those two.''

''So you got two shots at the gold ring?''

Again she laughed, this time more softly. ''No. No rings for me. Best I'd get out of the deal with Will would be a roll in the hay and that's not an option. Not with a co-worker. Or his brother,'' she added for good measure. ''Besides, Will's not—''

Joe jumped up as a car turned in the drive, shell gravel crunching beneath the tires. ''It's about damn time.''

He jerked open the side door and stepped out. Delores was already out of the car and running toward him, stumbling in her haste. ''He's got her, Joe!''

He caught her arms to steady her. ''Humberto?''

She nodded, catching back a sob. ''He must have been watching the house. I thought we were being followed and started to turn around. He blocked me and held a gun on us. I thought…he was going to shoot.''

''Take it easy,'' Joe told her. She was nearly hysterical. He needed a clear picture of what had happened. ''Come inside and sit down.'' He led her in, plopped her in the nearest chair and signaled Holly to get her something to drink. ''Now, step by step, sis. What happened?''

She sucked in a deep breath and plowed her hands through her hair, leaving them there as she rested her elbows on the table. ''Okay. Okay. These lights were right behind us, tailgating. I pulled over to let him pass. Before I knew what happened, he was just…there! We were blocked. He had this huge gun pointed right at Martine and ordered us out of the car. Then he hit her with it, Joe.'' She shrank into herself just thinking about it. De-

lores had never been subjected to violence of any kind
before this, he knew.

"How hard? Did he knock her out?"

She nodded frantically and sobbed again. "Then he tied
my hands with a cord of some kind and pushed me into
the back seat of the car. It took me…forever to…get
loose!" She rubbed her wrists which were red and raw in
places.

Joe forced himself to be calm. Going berserk wouldn't
help Martine. "But you did, hon. You got free. Now tell
me, what did he say to you? Did he say anything?"

Again she nodded and swallowed hard. "He…he said
he knew you would be looking for him and if you didn't
quit, he would kill Martine." She began crying, shaking
uncontrollably.

Joe had no choice but to wait until she got over it a
little, then offered her the juice Holly had brought over.
He wiped her eyes with a napkin.

"Here, drink this. You'll feel better," he said. Nothing,
absolutely nothing could make *him* feel better at this point
other than getting his hands around Humberto's throat.
"Did he say anything else?"

She blinked hard and drew in a shuddery breath.
"Bombs," she whispered, horror in her voice. "He said
he'd planted bombs. And…and he said to be sure your
phone stays turned on. He'll call." Her eyes, swimming
with tears, met his. "One of those…bombs is where Linda
and the baby are. Oh God, Joe, what are we gonna do?"

She collapsed again, weeping hard. Joe slammed his
fist on the table and cursed. Holly quickly put her hand
over his, warning him to be quiet.

She was right. If he woke up his parents, he'd have
three people hysterical. Four, if he let go, too. He had to
remain in control if he was to get Martine, his sister and
her baby out of this.

God only knew what Humberto was up to with bombs.

Could he possibly have planned all this so far ahead? Then Joe reminded himself that Humberto had to have been doing something during the time Joe was in McLean with Sextant and Martine was back in Atlanta.

He had somehow found out about Joe's family, closely guarded information when you did undercover work. Also he had known exactly which buttons to push to get Joe to Florida, even if they hadn't already been headed there.

He wished to hell he hadn't brought Martine with him. That had not been planned, but Humberto would have found a way to get to her sooner or later. Joe just couldn't stand to think of Martine at that devil's mercy, hurt and tied up.

God, he hoped she wasn't in some confined space on top of all that. Fear tightened his chest muscles to the point of pain. He had to do something.

"Sit back down, Joe," Holly ordered. "We've got the phone number of the boat. Call the jerk and let him know we'll blow his ass out of the water if he detonates any bombs ashore."

"He'll kill them!" Delores cried, wringing her hands. "He'll kill them all!"

Holly shook her head and patted Delores's back. "No, he won't. They're his ace in the hole. Without them, how's he gonna get to Joe?"

"Linda and Connie aren't with him," Delores rasped. "He said one of the bombs was planted with Linda and the baby, and he'd make it go off if he saw anybody searching for the boat."

"All right, all right, settle down. We'll find a way," he said, speaking as much to himself as to Delores.

Holly picked up the kitchen phone. "You call the ATF, Joe. I'm calling the AIC at the Panama City FBI. Let's get everybody running checks on who's been buying boom stuff in the area. If Humberto got the materials locally, maybe we can determine how much fire power he's working with. I'm also calling in EOD teams with sniffers to check out high-traffic areas. They can bring in help and arrange a quiet sweep of the entire town.''

His call accomplished, Joe located the number for the *Paper Moon*. Holly motioned for him to wait about phoning the boat until she finished the one she was making. Joe listened.

She was talking with Mercier. ''Jack, we're officially involved now. This has escalated and there's no question that this guy's a terrorist in every sense of the word.'' She replaced the receiver on the hook and nodded once. ''It's a mission.''

Joe welcomed the help with the bomb situation. If everyone got on it, they would probably find Linda and the baby in time because there weren't that many places around Port St. Joe to hide them. But he knew in his heart that he would be going to that boat alone. It was the only way, and even at that, he had a very slim chance of saving Martine.

If Humberto had even taken her to the boat. Hell, they could be anywhere, land or sea.

Joe lifted his cell phone and dialed the number for the *Paper Moon*. The ringing went on forever, but no one answered.

# Chapter 13

Martine opened her eyes, immediately aware on waking that she was on a boat. The cabin undulated, causing her stomach to lurch and her head to pound. A spot above her right temple throbbed painfully. He had hit her with the gun. A coating of dried blood pulled the skin of her face taut.

The head trauma hadn't induced any merciful bout of amnesia for her, Martine thought, catching back a groan. She remembered every detail until the split second when she lost consciousness.

Desperately, she scanned the enclosure, which consisted of wall-to-wall bed. This was the pocket cabin, she guessed, a small tuckaway space for overflow guests.

She was alone. For a few seconds, she struggled with the binding on her wrists, telling herself it was only a matter of minutes before she could work free. Don't panic, she warned herself. Stay calm.

Had Humberto killed Linda and her baby? And where was Delores? Were they onboard in another cabin?

*Oh God, poor Joe.* Both of his sisters and his niece were missing. And her, too. She knew he would include her in his worrying because he obviously cared. He was a caring man. Why hadn't she told him how she felt about him before it was too late?

She could hear the rhythmic slap of waves against the sides of the craft. The odor of mildew and sweat permeated the small space that seemed to close in and grow more confining by the second.

She took shallow breaths, battling the encroaching terror of having her hands bound behind her, of not being able to work free, of the sloped walls shrinking inward.

A screaming plea for release rose in her throat, but she choked it back, knowing the futility of crying out. It would only alert Humberto that she was awake. Seeing him, watching him gloat or perhaps do worse, was the last thing she needed right now.

Escape seemed impossible, but she couldn't simply give up. What had she trained for these last four years? Deliberately, she forced anger to replace the fear.

In desperation she recalled her shame at wimping out in the cave, depending solely on Joe to haul her out of that tunnel in a faint. Damned if she'd let herself get that worked up again. *Think! Plan!*

The first order of business was to get rid of the rope.

Her hands were swollen, but not to the point where she had lost feeling. *Don't struggle. Relax.* She twisted her fingers, carefully probing for the knot in the narrow nylon cord.

A soft curse escaped, but at least she was breathing more normally. Her second-worst enemy, panic, was more or less under control, at least for the moment.

Damned if she would let it end this way. Humberto had brought her here to lure Joe to the boat where he would kill them both. Knowing Humberto, they would not suffer an easy death. Then he would dump their bodies in the

Gulf and be docking in Mexico, the Islands or somewhere before they were found. If they ever were.

She remembered Joe's admission, his greatest fear. Dying alone and no one knowing. Well, at least he wouldn't be alone. She gritted her teeth and let fury flow through her.

She had no clue how long she had been unconscious. Maybe she had remained asleep for some time even after recovering from the blow to her head. The two tiny windows were covered but it wasn't completely dark. If that was daylight and not artificial light seeping through, she had to have been here at least five or six hours.

Joe might already be on his way and she had to be in a position to help him when he got here. She had absolutely no doubt that Humberto would have called to give him the location of the boat. And she knew for certain Joe would come.


"You're too hyper, Joe," Holly warned. "At this rate, you'll collapse before we get a plan in place."

She put her arm around his mother's shoulders and asked her if she had anything else in her medicine cabinet that would calm Joe down. Mama had already given Delores something and put her to bed. His father and Terry, Delores's husband, had run down to the marina again to see what else they could find out.

His mother was no sooner out of the room than the phone rang. Holly had made use of her contacts with the Bureau and theirs with the phone company. All calls dialed to the cell phone were to be rerouted to a regular land line so they could be taped for analysis and traced if necessary. All the equipment was in place.

Joe was amazed at how much she had accomplished by seven o'clock in the morning and was damned glad to have her help. He sucked in a deep breath and prayed for calm as he waited for the third ring.

"It's on speaker," Holly said. "Go ahead, Joe."

He punched the button. "Corda here," he snapped.

"Ah, you sound less than cool, amigo. Where is that charm you oozed when you secured my trust? Where is your confidence?"

"Cut the bull and get down to business," Joe ordered.

"Very well, we will dispense with amenities. My plans have changed. I have decided to let your sister, niece and Martine live if you will do precisely as I tell you."

"And the captain," Joe bargained. "Include him."

Humberto paused. "Ah, too late for the old fellow. You, of course, will have to die, too. I think you will not mind it so much. You seemed willing enough when propped against that tree and I had you in my sights. Or was that an act as well?"

"Spit it out, Humberto. Tell me what you want?"

"Two million will suffice. You owe me considerably more than that, but it is all I can reasonably expect you to gather by seven o'clock this evening."

*Ransom?* The demand surprised Joe, but he supposed it shouldn't. Greed was a huge part of Humberto's makeup.

Joe didn't think for a second Humberto would release Martine for any amount, but he probably would let Linda and the baby go. "Where the hell would I get two million? I can get you half that, maybe, if you give me another day."

"No room for negotiation, Corda. Get the money by seven tonight or their deaths will be on your head." His voice grew hard with the last demand. "You know I will keep my promise. Unlike some men I could mention, my word is my honor."

*Honor?* Joe wanted to shout. What man's honor allowed him to kidnap defenseless women and a baby? But he kept his temper in check. Years of experience had taught him much about dealing with scum like Humberto.

"How do you want it handled? Cash or transferral to an account?" Joe amazed himself with his businesslike tone. The almost overpowering urge to threaten Humberto nearly broke free, but Joe held it back. Loosing his cool wouldn't help. "Where and how do we make the exchange?"

"Cash, and you will bring it to me. I will call again at seven o'clock with instructions." His chuckle crawled through the receiver. "I know your mind must be working alive with plans to find me before that time. I warn you, do not try. And do not involve anyone else in this, Corda. I will be able to see anyone approaching and I have prepared for that."

Joe glanced at Holly as he spoke to Humberto. "I got the message. This stays between us."

Humberto made a small sound of what sounded like approval. "I hope you are not lying again, Corda. If you are and I see any sign of interference, I shall have to light up your precious Port Saint Joseph sky. There are explosive devices that will detonate at my command."

"I told you I'll be alone," Joe insisted.

Humberto continued as if Joe hadn't spoken. "One of these is planted with your sister and her child. If the deal goes well and no one follows me after our business is complete, the authorities will be notified of the locations I have wired. If not…" He paused. "Well, in either case, you have my word."

The connection broke. Joe glared at the phone and slammed his palm with his fist. "God, I need to kill that man!"

Holly placed a hand on his shoulder. "Can you raise that much money?"

Joe shrugged away, rubbing his eyes with the heels of his hands. "Hell no. But I'll think of something." He'd rob a bank if that's what it took. "I might need to show the cash to get Humberto to let me on the boat."

"I'll arrange it," she said. "We've used confiscated counterfeit sometimes in instances like this. It's not like he's going to get anywhere to spend it."

"You'd better put a tracker in with it, just in case he gets away. First, see how the bomb squad's doing finding those explosives," Joe told her. "And get the SEAL gear delivered now instead of tonight. I want their smallest Zodiac."

Holly nodded. "Will's picking up the weapons. Mac-10's with a couple of mags extra. A 9mm and a .22 apiece for backup. Enough?"

"Where is he now?"

"Should arrive in a couple of hours with the goodies."

Joe nodded approval. "I'll need a blade, too. I want to gut that sonofabitch. And I want a submersible, tanks and a wet suit in case I get a chance to go in before the deadline."

"You're not going in alone, Joe. Take Eric. He's had SEAL training and is the best at hand-to-hand you'll find anywhere."

His hackles rose. "I was a Ranger for three years and did my share of waterwork. I can handle it."

Holly threw up her hands. "Joe! What are we all about here, huh? Chuck the rivalry, will you?"

"It's not that," Joe insisted. Well, it wasn't *much* about that. But she was right. He had to think of the mission first. Logically. "Fine then. If it turns out I have to wait and go on schedule, Vinland can come. Okay? But I'm going in underwater if I can get a fix on him before rendezvous hour, and I'm going by myself. Let's get everything together so I can check out the gear."

"I'm on it," she assured him. "Meanwhile, play with that tape and see if you get any background noises. I thought I heard a car horn. He might not be on the boat right now."

Joe rewound the tape. "While you're at it, see if Jack's

got the pictures and coordinates on the forty-two-footers anchored off shore yet. If we can find the boat, I'll take the sub and go at sundown when there's glare on the surface.''

He pictured himself cutting an underwater wake, zooming toward that boat like a relentless shark with teeth bared, psyched up to tear that bastard apart.

His entire body hummed. Despite the current burst of energy, Joe knew he needed sleep, hadn't had any for over twenty-four hours. But he couldn't. Didn't dare. He had too much to do and too little time to do it.

An hour later, waiting impatiently by the computer for the satellite pictures, Joe looked up and saw Eric Vinland propped in the doorway of the downstairs bedroom his father had converted to a home office.

This was the first he'd seen of him since leaving McLean. The man moved like a ghost. Joe hadn't heard a sound when he arrived. ''What's up?''

Vinland smiled. ''We found your sister,'' he announced.

Joe jumped up so fast he almost upset the desk. ''Is she all right? And the baby?''

''Yeah, both fine. They were alone, locked in the basement of an abandoned farmhouse about fifteen miles north of here. Will's taken them to a motel down the coast for safety's sake in case Humberto's ashore somewhere. Holly's getting your folks to your sister's new location so they can go and be with her and the kid.''

''Thank God.'' As relieved as Joe was about the rescue, he couldn't help cursing the fact that Martine was still out there, still at Humberto's mercy. Not that the bastard had any mercy. ''Was there a bomb?'' Joe asked.

''Yeah, we found one, just like he said. He'd turned on the gas, too. All he'd have had to do to set that off was make a phone call. Spark from the ringer. Then the gas explosion would have set off the bomb. Too far inland for him to use a remote trigger. Guy knows his stuff.''

Joe sank back into the chair, his hand to his head, thanking God for the intervention. His sister and the baby were safe. "Thanks," he whispered.

"Don't mention it," Vinland said. "All in a day's work."

"How'd you find out where he was holding them?" Joe asked.

Eric shrugged. "Oh, I zoned in. Got a feeling."

Joe hesitated. "How? Exactly?"

"Will got me one of your sister's shirts. Sometimes if I touch things belonging to a person, I'll get…notions about what they're feeling, sometimes what they're seeing. You know, just their perceptions of immediate surroundings. Worked pretty good this time, so I described the place to a local real estate agent. She identified it right away. We lucked out. I guess there aren't too many houses this close to the coast that have full basements.''

"Water table's too high," Joe said, nodding. "Thanks, man. Really.'' He knew any gratitude he offered would never be enough. Obviously, Vinland had a much better handle on his so-called gift than Joe had ever had on his.

"Could…do you think you could do it again with something of Martine's? Just to make sure she's on a boat?" *And alive.* But he didn't add that. He wouldn't even let himself consider the alternative.

"I can try."

Joe hurried to the weekender Martine had brought with her and snapped it open. He handed Eric the item on top, a red bikini bottom, then snatched it back. The last thing he wanted was to see another guy fondling that. Instead he held up a white sleeveless pullover.

Vinland examined it as if looking for spots. Then Joe noticed he had indeed *zoned out,* as he'd described. Only his hands moved, gripping the supple fabric, moving the pads of his fingers over it, raising it to his face to breathe in Martine's essence.

Joe watched, both fascinated and apprehensive. In a few seconds, Vinland dropped the blouse back into the suit-case as if it burned his hands. "She's there." His voice sounded shaky.

"Is she all right?" Joe demanded.

He nodded. "She seemed kind of…I don't know, scat-tered? Her thoughts, I mean. Scared. Nothing much to see. She's in the dark or her eyes are covered. Maybe she just had them closed. But there were ocean smells, waves sloshing. Definitely on a boat." He hesitated, not meeting Joe's gaze.

"What? What's wrong?" Joe demanded.

"Does she ever, you know, panic about stuff?" Eric asked. He was rubbing his strong, pale wrists, almost clawing at them. "I sensed she was a little worse than…scared."

"Damn him to hell!" Joe cursed roundly, slamming his palm against the wall. "He's tied her up. That freaks her out. She's…claustrophobic." He winced, feeling he had betrayed Martine by admitting what she saw as her worst fault.

"Oh," Vinland said simply, nodding. "Yeah, that'd do it. Well, at least she's alive." He dropped his hands to his sides and gave a sort of shudder.

"You okay?" Joe asked.

"Yeah. It's just that the sensations are…insidious, I guess you'd call it. I'll be fine."

Then he changed the topic altogether, as if he wanted to get his own mind off Martine as quickly as he could. "Your sister was sending out signals nobody could miss. She was mad as hell." He forced a laugh.

"Yeah. Linda can be what you might call volatile." But Joe couldn't think about Linda right now. She was safe. Martine wasn't.

Vinland continued talking, hopping to yet another topic. "You know, that bomb of Humberto's was a pretty sophisticated piece of homemade ordnance. Very small in size but would have been damned effective combined with the gas. Judging by the materials we know he acquired, there's at least one more out there we haven't found yet."

"Only one?"

"Yes, and he did buy a remote garage door opener, so this second one's gonna be different. Jack tells me our perp did a stint in demolition when he was in the army down there." Vinland sighed. "Jack's got everybody on this, but a casual observer would never know it. It's an invisible op so far and it's going well."

Not nearly well enough, Joe thought. It wouldn't be *well* until Humberto and his men were dead and Martine was safe.

He leaned back against the wall and closed his eyes, pressing his thumb and forefinger against his lids for the hundredth time since all this began. But nothing came to him. Not a blessed thing.

"Relax, man, you're probably trying too hard."

Joe looked at Vinland, searching his face for truth as he asked what he had been wondering since he'd left the McLean office. "Is this why I was hired for Sextant? This...premonition thing?"

"No, but it sure didn't hurt your chances when it came to making the selection. Jack appreciates the fact that hunches play a big part in investigations and in survival. He had the records of that early study you participated in, and the results."

"Lack of results," Joe clarified. "About all we did was try to match cards and colors. I was wrong most of the time and only guessing when I got them right."

"Yeah, well, it's not as if he expects you to have any full-blown episodes on command."

"Good thing," Joe muttered, shoving away from the

wall and beginning to pace in the small confines of the bedroom/study. "'Cause I am *not* psychic."

However, he couldn't help but remember the way Martine had looked in the glow of that flashlight in the cave, terror stricken, exactly the way he had seen her in his mind not long before the reality took place.

The vision where she had blood on her face could very well have predicted what she looked like now after that blow Humberto had delivered with the gun when he abducted her last night. And that one of her surrounded by white had not yet happened.

Bride or corpse? A shiver rattled him right down to his soul. He felt dizzy and disoriented just thinking about it.

"I'm definitely *not* psychic," he repeated, arguing as much with himself as with Vinland.

Eric smiled knowingly. "Maybe. Maybe not. But you have survived missions that most agents wouldn't. Those mental snapshots you pick up occasionally are not much more than your mind's little parlor trick. More distraction than help, I expect. It's the gut instinct you run with, the one that saves you when your number should be up."

Joe frowned. "That's what Mercier was after in me?"

"Yeah. In all of us, I think. I figure you haven't realized yet how valuable a tool that can be, but you need to be aware of it. Maybe learn to trust it, and yourself, a bit more than you do."

"Strange you should say that. My father said almost the same thing." Joe studied Vinland. "You've obviously delved into all this pretty deeply."

He grinned and shrugged. "As good a hobby as any, I guess. Look, we can't do anything else for a while. You want to give it your best shot? I'll be your control. It can't hurt."

Useless effort, but why the hell not? It would at least show Vinland he ought to give up on the precognition bull where Joe was concerned. He shrugged. "Sure."

"C'mon, loosen up. Lie down over there." Eric pointed to the daybed against the wall across from the computer desk.

Joe complied, nerves skittering beneath his skin. *Loosen up? Yeah, right.* Martine was out there suffering God knew what and he was supposed to laze around playing mind games with Boy Agent?

Eric pulled a chair next to the daybed and sat down. "Fine, now close your eyes and do the muscle thing. You know, tighten and relax 'em one at a time until you're a puddle. They teach you that?"

Joe nodded. He began the exercise he had learned all those years ago. As he concentrated on that, Eric ran his mouth, yammering on and on about walking on the beach, seeing the sun go down, watching the waves roll in. The timbre of his voice melded with the actual sounds from outside the beach house. Joe focused on forcing his muscles to behave, only half listening, not even bothering to respond.

Eventually he felt the rocking motion of waves, annoyingly rhythmic, swishing over the sand, advancing, retreating, never-ending, relentless.

"Relax. Let it come at you sideways," the quiet voice droned. It was the last thing he knew until Vinland shook him awake later and Joe realized it had been a ploy to lull him into much-needed sleep. If not for his renewed energy and sharpened thought processes, Joe would have been mad as hell.

By that time six o'clock had rolled around and things were coming together. So were the principals involved in the rescue. Joe had been surprised when he woke up to see Mercier there. The entire Sextant team was, with the exception of Clay Senate who was holding down the fort in McLean.

One of the bomb squads had swept the Corda cottage last night and declared it clean. That was now headquar-

ters. Joe's family were residing at a safe house in Panama
City until the situation was resolved.

Mercier, Holly, Vinland and Joe flanked the oak table
where Joe had once done his homework. He was damned
glad to have partners for this project.

A map of the coast lay spread on the table now. Mercier
had brought it with him with the positions of all the boats
located by two satellites clearly marked. He was pointing
at one in particular, one mile and ten degrees southeast
off the elbow of Cape San Blas.

"This is it," Mercier announced. "One guy on deck
just behind the windlass, automatic weapon within reach.
One other, also armed, lounging on the aft deck." He
smiled. "The EXTER-14 satellite could have read his
magazine if he'd been holding it at the right angle."

An exaggeration, Joe knew, but not by much. If the
angle was right, it could actually identify the numbers on
a license plate.

"Big question is whether they have moved since they
were spotted," Holly declared. She shot Joe a warning
glance. "You know you can't go in without being sure.
Suppose they aren't anchored where they were and you're
out there snorkeling around looking for them when Humberto's call comes in?"

Mercier agreed. "You'll have to wait for his instructions. You'll take the Zodiac and go in above board. Eric
will take the submersible, swing around and come at the
boat from the opposite direction. While you create a distraction going aboard, he can slip in on the other side."

"I thought I was running this show," Joe argued.

Mercier inclined his head and gestured with one hand
as if offering the lead back to him. "If you have a better
plan, we're listening."

Joe felt sheepish and let it show. "No. It's sound. No
alternative."

They all looked pleased. *Joe Corda played well with others.* He figured that meant he could keep his job if he wanted to. But did he? All he cared about right now was getting Martine off that boat alive.

# Chapter 14

The sound of a motor sent Martine's efforts into over-drive. She almost had the knot undone. A cry of frustration slipped out as she twisted her joined wrists to unwind the bonds.

Even though they were free, her hands now felt like useless dead things at the ends of her arms. Her fingers were numb and swollen. Frantically, she rubbed and stretched them, coaxing circulation. No more time. She had to act now. If nothing else, she could divert Humberto's attention, give Joe a chance to get the upper hand.

Quietly she twisted the doorknob, opened the narrow door to her cabin and peeked out. It opened into the forward end of a main salon. To her left was the wheel, unattended now since they were at anchor.

Curtained windows lined the salon, most of them closed. Along one side was a built-in banquette and narrow trestle bolted to the floor. On the other, an efficient little kitchen. At the opposite end was the door to the aft cabin. The doorway to the deck was on her right just past the banquette seat and a storage cabinet.

She heard voices. But oddly enough, not the shouting she expected would accompany Joe's arrival. Martine dropped to her knees and crawled down the corridor of the salon. As she crept nearer the steps up to the deck the voices grew clearer.

She drew closer to the window nearest the entrance to the salon and risked moving the curtain a fraction of an inch to peek out. Humberto was climbing aboard via the swim ladder. His two men were hovering, almost obscuring her view of him. He must have been ashore in a smaller boat and just now returned. One of the guys took something from him as he boarded.

She recognized the men as two who had served Humberto as bodyguards in Colombia. They were strictly muscle and not too bright, but had seemed devoted to their leader.

When they found her free, they would tie her up again and throw her right back into that cabin. Martine thought that before she was discovered, she should simply run for it and dive over the rail. But she had no idea which way she should start swimming. They'd probably shoot her before or after she hit the water anyway. But wasn't anything better than being tied up again? An involuntary shudder shook her.

No. No way was she ready to die. And Joe would blame himself forever if she let that happen. She thought again about Joe's greatest fear.

As poor as her chances seemed right now, Martine resolved she would survive this. And if Joe came to find her, she would save him, too. Somehow.

She watched Humberto peer out over the water. He and his men were dressed like tourists or fishermen in Bermuda shorts, Hawaiian print shirts and deck shoes. His bodyguards looked ridiculous, too beefy to be anything but what they were, especially with automatic weapons worn as accessories.

Humberto looked dashing as ever, wiry and fit, his bearing only a little less soldierly in those casual clothes. She had at first thought maybe he possessed a code of honor, warped as it was. But though he had treated her well, she had soon discovered the layer of cruelty beneath that veneer in watching him deal with his men.

The man—Thomas, she thought his name was—who stood closest to Humberto wore an AK-47 on a strap slung over his left shoulder. He was holding a small box very carefully with both hands and staring at it as if it contained poisonous snakes. The other guy was hurriedly climbing down the ladder into what had to be the boat in which Humberto had arrived.

Humberto, his back to her now, was now talking on a cell phone. She could hear his voice, but couldn't make out his words. Suddenly he finished his conversation, tucked the phone into the pocket of his shorts and turned to speak to the man holding the box.

"Thomas, place that on the console just in front of the wheel. Make certain this side faces the front window." He pointed. "Understand?"

Thomas said something Martine didn't catch.

"Don't worry. It will not explode unless I give the cue." Humberto raised one hand and gingerly touched something, the top of which was just visible, in the pocket of his shirt. It appeared to be a remote control. He added, laughing, "But do be careful not to trip."

Then she heard him ask, "How is our guest?"

An engine started, obliterating anything else they might have said. She saw a small motorboat cutting through the water as it departed. Humberto and his friend with the box turned toward the salon entrance.

Martine scrambled quickly back to the door of the pocket cabin. There was no place inside the boat where she could hide for long and she'd surely be caught before she made the railing if she ran. Worse than that, she could startle Thomas and make him drop that bomb.

She closed the door quietly and climbed back into position on the bed. The cord lay taunting her. She picked it up, put both hands behind her and wound it around her wrists, knowing it wouldn't stand close inspection, but if he only looked in on her, she hoped it would fool him.

She needed time to think, time to form some kind of plan before Joe got here.

Meanwhile preparations for the rescue were under way at the Updike Marina off Port San Blas. Humberto had called promptly at seven o'clock with instructions. Joe was to leave precisely at nine from this particular place and travel due south at twenty-five knots per hour for ten minutes, then stop and await further directions. It would be pitch-dark by then. The sky was overcast and there would be no moon visible tonight.

"Humberto's obviously changed location. Eric's gonna play hell finding that boat without coordinates," Holly grumbled. "That rigged-up underwater running light on the Zodiac's not sufficient to follow with the submersible."

"It will be if he stays close behind me. We can't risk anything else. If it fails and he loses me, he can surface for a visual check. As dark as it is, he shouldn't be detected, but he'll be able to see me since I'll have lights." Joe was stating what he felt was obvious while he doggedly inspected his gear. He was trying like hell to stay as busy as possible, and not dwell on what Martine must be going through at the moment.

Humberto had ordered him to wear fitted swim trunks and nothing else so there would be no place to conceal a weapon. That also meant he wouldn't be able to wear a Kevlar vest. No protection at all.

Though the April night was warm enough, Joe felt a distinct chill.

He had been told to arrive in an open craft that would seat three, do at least 35 knots per hour and to bring extra gas. There was to be nothing else in the boat except a container bearing the money and Martine's cell phone. Humberto had the number to that and had warned Joe there might be further instructions.

Whether the extra gas was to insure that Joe had enough to reach the *Paper Moon* which might have moved any distance offshore, or to augment the motor yacht's fuel supply once the deal was done, Joe didn't know. But he would comply right down to the letter. His main objective was to get aboard the *Paper Moon* alive.

"Where's the money?" he asked.

"Will's on his way. His ETA's about ten minutes," Holly said. "Sorry to cut it so close. He had a little trouble getting a big enough case with a built-in transmitter, something that couldn't be detected and removed."

Joe checked his watch again. Twenty minutes and counting. He adjusted the flesh-colored dart pen taped to the inside of his wrist. It would need to be fired at close range and carried only one dose of paralyzing agent.

All he needed was the chance to come within three or four feet of Humberto. He had practiced with dummy darts half the afternoon and felt he was as proficient as he could get with the gadget. It was his only weapon.

The minutes crawled by. Will arrived with the money contained in a waterproof aluminum case. "Transmitter's built inside the plastic handle," Will told him as he handed it over.

Joe hefted it, then climbed into the inflatable black Zodiac. It rocked with his weight, then settled when he sat down. There were three fuel bladders secured in back, clearly visible behind the case with the money.

"Good to go," he said with a shake of his head. "God,

I wish I knew how this was going to play out." He looked up at Mercier, then at the others. "Whatever happens, thanks. All of you. I owe you."

"Buy us a drink at Christa's when we get back to Virginia," Mercier said. His stony expression slowly morphed into a confident smile. "I have a feeling things will work out tonight."

A feeling, huh? Like he was supposed to trust that. "Right. Well, here goes nothing."

Good thing somebody had a positive *feeling* about this, Joe thought as he switched on the running lights and cranked the motor.

The Zodiac zoomed away from the dock on an almost silent, southerly course while Joe played out every possible outcome in his mind. There was no way of knowing what kind of reception he'd get when he reached the *Paper Moon,* but short of a bullet to the head or heart the minute he got there, he meant to get rid of the threat to Martine if he had to die doing it.

"Get up. Company is on the way and we must entertain," Humberto said, grasping Martine's ankles and dragging her half off the bunk.

He had looked in on her shortly after he'd returned to the boat, then again later. That time he had placed his fingers to her neck and felt for her pulse. It had been racing ninety to nothing and he'd immediately realized she was awake.

Martine opened her eyes to the glare of pure hatred in his and a very lethal-looking pistol in his left hand. She had thought he might kill her right there on the bed.

Instead of showing the fear he was obviously looking for, she boldly asked to go to the bathroom. He paused to consider it, then stood back and allowed her to wriggle off the bed. Roughly he grasped her upper arm to lift her to a standing position.

She had wrapped the cord loosely enough around her wrists that she could shake it free in a second and had hoped he would put down the gun and start to untie her. That would have given her a chance to disable him with a surprise move. Instead, he backed well away from her and opened the door to the small head in the forward cabin, his nine-millimeter aimed directly at her heart.

"Some *goddess* you are now. I should humble you further, but you disgust me. You should see yourself."

She did, in the mirror over the small sink. What a mess she was and glad of it. At least he didn't seem to find her in any way tempting. Humberto was too fastidious. Blood caked one whole side of her face and neck. Her hair was matted with it and incredibly tangled. One eye was purplish and swollen.

In the cabin when she first woke up, she had noted the shorts and camp shirt she wore were a mass of dirty wrinkles and her arms and legs were streaked with dark sand and scraped raw in places. She had lost her shoes. At some point after he had taken her, he must have dragged her along the ground.

When she had finished in the bathroom—no easy task since she left the rope around her wrists—she bumped against the door. He jerked it open and waited for her to exit, then shoved her back into the pocket cabin where she fell on her side across the bunk.

"Reflect on your sins. They are about to catch up with you," he had told her then.

Well, he had come for her now and she guessed this must be the time for it. *Company coming* meant Joe, of course.

One of Humberto's men was still away. She had listened for the return of the smaller boat, but had never heard one approach. That meant only Humberto and one other guy were onboard. If Joe got in a position to take one of them out, she would rush the other.

Humberto pushed her ahead of him into the salon. She risked a glance at the wheel and saw the box with the bomb sitting just forward of it facing the window. It didn't take a genius to figure out what he planned to do with it.

He and his man would take the boat Joe came in and leave her and Joe alive on the motor yacht if he could. When he was far enough away, he planned to detonate that bomb with the remote and watch them die.

He had planned this very carefully. Nothing as simple as gunning them down would suit Humberto. Unless they forced his hand.

Martine stumbled before she reached the steps from the salon up to the deck, hoping he would run into her and she could catch him off guard. But he stopped too soon, motioning with the gun for her to continue.

There were low-level lights in the salon, the drapes drawn except for the ones in front of the wheel. She climbed the steps and exited into the breeze and total darkness. There was no moon, no stars. In the distance, she could hear the drone of a motor.

She sensed movement to her right and as her eyes became more accustomed to the dark, she could just make out the large silhouette of Humberto's man. And the automatic he held. He was standing at the rail.

Humberto switched on a deck light, blinding her in the process. The whine of the motor drew nearer. Martine willed herself to be patient and hold her hands behind her rather than drop her bonds and attack. She could take out one of the men, but the other would shoot her if she did. Then he would more than likely kill Joe before he could even board.

"Go to the swim ladder, Thomas," Humberto ordered. "When he pulls alongside, take your flashlight and check out the contents of the boat. Make certain all is as I ordered. If it is not, kill him."

Martine held her breath. Joe would be a fool to come

alone. And a damned fool to come unarmed. The running lights of the smaller craft grew closer and closer until they disappeared beneath the high railing of the motor yacht.

"Ahoy," called Joe, his voice cocky. "Permission to board?"

Thomas sat astride the break in the rail where the swim ladder attached. He held on to the raised edge beside him, leaned over and pointed the flashlight downward for a long minute.

"He has the fuel," he called back. "And he is not armed." He leaned over a little farther as if to inspect closer. When he straightened, he held a silver case aloft. "The money!"

"Drop it on the deck," Humberto ordered and Thomas did. It bounced and fell over on its side. Martine looked up just in time to see Thomas disappear over the railing headfirst. His scream of surprise ended with a loud splash. Joe climbed aboard, hands out to the side to show he held no weapon. He smiled and said, "Oops."

Thomas cried out from below, sputtering, that he couldn't swim. Then silence, another gurgling yell and then nothing. Martine thought maybe he had managed to climb in the other boat. Or maybe not.

"Thomas?" Humberto shouted when all went silent. No answer.

He cursed. But instead of running to the rail to see about his man, he grabbed Martine in a choke hold, the pistol pressed against her temple. "Stay where you are, Corda. One more wrong move and she dies," he warned. "If you do exactly as I tell you, I might spare her life."

Joe shrugged and pointed to the case lying next to his bare feet. "There's your ill-gotten gain, Carlos. Don't you want to count it?"

"Open it," Humberto demanded. Martine felt the tension in the forearm locked beneath her chin, in the strong body that pressed against her back. The cold steel of the barrel dug into her skin. She could grab him where it hurt—her hands were positioned right—but he would blow her head off and might still have time to shoot Joe.

Joe knelt on the deck and unlatched the container, raised the lid and turned it toward Humberto. "All there. Come and get it."

Though he wore nothing but swim briefs, Martine wondered if Joe might have a weapon. Or maybe he was merely trying to get Humberto's focus off her. She saw Joe quickly scan the part of the deck within view and the flybridge, as if he were looking for the other man.

There was no way to signal Joe that he wasn't aboard. It was all she could do to breathe with Humberto's arm threatening to cut off her air supply.

Suddenly Humberto released her and shoved her at Joe. "Untie her!" he ordered.

Joe reached for her hands and made a low sound of surprise when he found the ropes loose. He made a show of struggling with the knots as he asked, "Are you hurt bad?"

"I'm fine." She lowered her head. "There's only him," she growled in a low voice she hoped Humberto couldn't hear.

"Gotcha," he whispered. "Do as he says. Help's coming."

Humberto shouted for her to move away from Joe. She moved, hands out to her sides.

"I don't trust your fancy briefcase, Corda. I know you are not so stupid as to leave my escape to chance. You will have made provision for me to be followed. Go to the aft cabin, woman!" he commanded Martine. "Empty the bag on the bed and bring it to me. Do exactly as I say or I will shoot him where he stands."

Martine scurried inside. She rushed to the right, found the dark canvas bag shaped like an army duffel bag, but only about half the size of one. She quickly pulled out everything inside it, tossing Humberto's clothes every which way.

He wanted to transfer the money to get rid of any hidden tracking device that might be hidden in the case? Well, she'd give him a device, all right, but no one would be able to follow him unless they went to hell.

When she returned to the deck with the bag, Humberto proved even more predictable than she could have hoped. "Took you long enough. Empty the money into that," he demanded.

Martine looked up at Joe as she knelt, hoping to signal him somehow, but his eyes were trained on Humberto. She began to stuff the money into the bag. Very carefully.

"I am curious, Humberto. How in the world did you find my family?" Joe asked.

Humberto scoffed. "I had your name from Vargas. He told me you were DEA. I knew how closely held your employment records would be, given your *occupation*." He sneered at the word. "But I also knew a man with your physique naturally would have played college sports. It was child's play to discover your school, hack into the computerized records and discover your hometown. There was only one José Corda in a small town such as yours. You see, I, too, have excellent skills in the field of espionage."

"And you found Martine, too," Joe commented, acting a little impressed. Martine knew he was playing for time.

"Even simpler," Humberto bragged. "She has a passport. Her prints were on file. Her place of employment, a matter of record with your Social Security. Your country tends to underestimate the enemy. And I *am* the enemy, make no mistake. You and your people have destroyed my livelihood. My very life."

Joe heaved an audible sigh. "That's my job, Carlos."

"Destruction of drugs, I could understand. But you even tore apart my family. I am branded a traitor."

"You *are* a traitor," Joe argued, but Humberto seemed not to hear.

"My wife, my children. I have lost them because of you." He glanced at the rail where his man had disappeared. "Even poor Thomas, drowned. He is no great loss, but he was my cousin. A fair trade for that loud-mouthed sister of yours and her mewling brat, I suppose."

"Oh, I should have told you. We found them," Joe said, a smile in his voice. "Turned off the gas and dismantled your bomb."

Humberto cursed.

"We know there were two, and I expect they've found the other one by this time," Joe told him.

"I assure you, they have not." Humberto chuckled, a truly evil sound.

Martine smiled herself. He was quite right. They had not found it, but they'd know where it was soon enough.

When she had transferred the money to the bag, she stood, hands on her hips, waiting for what she knew would come next.

"Get inside, both of you," Humberto ordered and made a threatening movement with the gun. He stayed well away from Joe and kept the pistol pointed at her. "Into the aft cabin. Corda, you first, and go to the far corner, away from the door."

Joe's gaze raked the deck again, fury and desperation in his eyes. Martine noticed his near naked body tense, the muscles standing out in relief as his fists clenched, opened and clenched again. His stance screamed attack. She knew he was ready to rush Humberto if he found a chance to do it without getting her shot. "Don't do it, Joe. You know he'll shoot. Go inside."

Finally, he looked at her. She winked and tried to put a smile in her eyes to tell him everything would be all right. It would be if only Humberto didn't check the box just in front of the wheel.

"Go!" shouted Humberto. He fired one shot above their heads and retrained the gun on her.

The cabin door closed behind them and she heard the snick of the key in the lock. Joe immediately rushed to it and tried to break it down, but it was too sturdy and there was no room for him to back up and gather any force. Hardly more than a minute later they heard the muted roar of an engine catch and Martine pictured Humberto zipping away from the motor yacht, far enough away to stop and watch the fireworks. Good, he hadn't had time to go forward and check on the bomb.

Joe was already pounding on one of the two windows with his fist. He was too big to fit through it even if he managed to break out the thick tempered glass. But she wasn't. Martine smiled. He was doing everything he could to save her. There was no use trying to stop him. He was like a man gone berserk.

Suddenly he ripped a shelf off the wall above the bunk and shattered the window. "Here, crawl through. Hurry!" he said, shoving her at the window. "Dive over the rail and swim like hell. I think he's left a bomb aboard."

"No he hasn't," she argued, about to explain what she had done.

As the words left her lips, an explosion rocked the world. Joe shoved her flat on the bunk and fell on top of her, shielding her with his body.

# Chapter 15

Joe lifted his head, sniffed for smoke, listened for the crackle of flames. He was amazed that the cabin was still intact, the glass unbroken except for the one he had smashed. "Ha. We're alive! I need to get out there and assess the damage. It couldn't have been a very big bomb."

"Yes it could." Martine could barely see his face. The cabin was almost dark, illuminated only by a meager amount of light coming from that on the deck. "But he took it with him."

Joe stared at her for a minute, then laughed, pushing up and bracing on his arms above her. "Don't tell me. You put it in the bag with the money?"

Martine nodded. "He must have been clicking that remote all over the place when it refused to blow us to kingdom come."

Joe dropped a quick, gentle kiss on her lips. Her poor face was a wreck and must hurt like the devil. His rage when he had first seen it nearly had him doing a suicidal dive for Humberto. The vision of her with blood on her face had come to pass and she had survived. He felt much better about the one of her in white.

He kissed her again, drawing out the pleasure a little longer, tasting the sweetness of life. His body was super revved, still pumping adrenaline. "Have I told you how wonderful you are, Ms. Duquesne?"

"You can start showing me any time now."

He laughed again when she moved suggestively beneath him. "Not that I wouldn't love to, but we *should* try to get out of here and let everyone know we're all right." He brushed her tangled hair away from her forehead, noting how she winced. "You are all right, aren't you, *querida?*"

"Well, I could do with some bedrest. A quarter hour maybe?"

She was revved, too, apparently. "Martine…"

Her kiss shut him up nicely and he was just getting into it big-time, his heady state of arousal blocking out all the *shoulds* and *should-nots,* when he heard a sound from the broken window. The beam of a flashlight flicked over his face. Before he could react, he heard a chuckle he recognized.

"I guess you don't really need any help?" Vinland said. The light danced playfully around the bed.

"I guess not. Where the hell were you when I did?" Joe growled.

Vinland sighed, his head and shoulders backlit by the faint light from the deck. "You had another tail besides me after we left the marina. When you changed course, I surfaced, did a three-sixty and saw him. Thought I'd better take him out before you got caught in a sandwich. Had to ram him and damaged the sub. Took me a while to get it going and then I couldn't find you. That explosion scared the bejeesus out of me. Then I spotted the deck lights and came to see if there was anyone left aboard."

"Thanks," Martine said. "Now please go drive the boat, whoever you are."

"Sorry," Joe said. "Martine Duquesne, Eric Vinland, one of Sextant's finest."

"Pleased to have met you," she said, her impatience showing.

Eric took the hint and disappeared.

"Continue," she demanded when their audience left.

But Vinland's interruption had brought Joe to his senses. "When I take you again, I want hours and hours. Days, maybe." He caressed her through her wrinkled shirt and shorts, long languid strokes that did nothing to augment his decision. "I want you in something slinky and silk. I want you in…"

"I want you," she interrupted breathlessly. "Now. No promises, no conditions. Just now, like this…" she murmured against his mouth, then melded hers to it with a white-hot kiss that swept rational thought right out of his head. He devoured her, his hands acting on their own to tear away the clothes that denied him her soft skin, the feel of her pulse around him.

There was nothing on earth but Martine. His woman. His heart. He entered her in one swift stroke, desperate to reaffirm his claim, to bind her to him in any way he could. Forever if possible. For this hour, if not.

She met him thrust for thrust, gasping words he couldn't understand for the blood thundering in his veins. All the feeling he possessed had concentrated where their bodies met, where skin slid against skin, where lips scorched paths, where they became one.

On and on into a white-hot frenzy he drove her, lurching them against the slanted wall, rolling side to side, pressing her deep and deeper into the soft foam of the bunk. He felt her legs wrapped around his, the soles of her bare feet against his calves, her nails scoring the sweat-slick muscles of his back. His own palms cupped her curves, held her to a wild, savage dance with no rhythm.

The beat grew so fierce, he abandoned any semblance of control. Her cry and the tightening of her body drew him down, plummeting into euphoria, releasing all that he was.

For a long time, he lay motionless, one hand fisted in her hair, the other clutched behind her right knee, his fingers trapped and content. "Can't...move," he gasped, a half-ass apology for crushing her, he knew, but true.

She quivered around him, a final ripple of pleasure so keen he groaned. *Now,* he thought lazily, would be the time to die. *Right now.* He was already in heaven. Nothing would ever get any better than this.

The boat was moving, he realized. How long? How many minutes did he have left to own her? When must he give her up to reality and emerge from this delicious prison?

Wearily, very reluctantly, he rolled to one side, holding her close, knowing time was nearly up. Reason was creeping slowly back into his brain, adrenaline on the wane, passion spent for the moment. Martine would want to clean up and dress before they reached the marina and someone opened that door. And he really shouldn't present himself to his boss and co-workers naked except for a satisfied grin and the scent of sex.

She was first to pull away, disengage and speak normally. "Please don't say anything, Joe. We agreed, no ties."

"We do need to talk," he argued, feeling around for her clothes. He picked up a shirt and realized it was too big to be hers. It certainly wasn't his because he hadn't been wearing one. Humberto's. They were lying in a mass of garments, probably where she had emptied the bag she'd taken outside earlier for the money.

She sat up and pawed through the clothing, tossing

some of it on the floor. "Here," she said. He heard plastic rip. "New T-shirts," she explained, shaking one out and draping it over his shoulder. She pulled one over her head and began searching again, he supposed for her shorts.

Joe found his swim trunks still clinging to one ankle and put them back on. By the time he did, she was decently dressed.

"I wish I could wash my face," she muttered. "I'm a fright."

"You look beautiful," Joe argued. "Besides, everyone will be so glad to see you, they won't care. But maybe Eric will let us out now so you can find a sink and freshen up." He banged on the door with his fist.

A few seconds later, it opened. The salon was well lighted now and Vinland stood there grinning. "Humberto left the key in the lock probably so you couldn't pick it. Our ETA's about seven minutes. I was just about to give you a warning."

Martine swept by him and disappeared into the head. Joe stood staring at the closed door, unwilling to spar with Vinland just yet. His mind still felt a little too numb to come up with anything clever. Or even remotely sensible.

"What happened, Joe?" Vinland asked.

The first thought Joe had was that he was asking about what had gone on in the cabin with Martine. Then he realized Eric meant what had gone down before that with Humberto.

He shook his head to clear it. "I had to take out the bodyguard with the dart as I came aboard. Thought it would improve the odds, but it didn't. Humberto had the drop on us. He wanted the money in a different bag and sent Martine in to get one. She put the bomb inside it and the money on top."

Eric threw back his head and laughed out loud as he walked back through the salon to the wheel. "Hot damn, what a woman! I'd like to have one like that myself!"

"Yeah," Joe muttered as he plopped down on the banquette seat. So would he. The lights of the marina grew brighter as they neared San Blas.

He knew Martine, maybe even better than she knew herself. She was definitely cut out for this kind of thing. Her mind worked sharpest when she ripped into action, when the threats were greatest, when everything was at stake. She excelled in a crisis and knew it. And loved it.

No matter how much she might care about him—and he did know that she cared—he would never be able to change her. If he tried, he would lose her anyway. But he couldn't stand by and watch her risk her neck on a regular basis. He'd already decided that would drive him crazy.

Hell, he was crazy right now, ground down to raw nerves by the last two days. He needed sleep, needed rest, needed peace. But he needed her, too. She filled something inside him that had been missing all his life.

She appeared, face clean, hair wet, rivulets of water splotching the white T-shirt she had appropriated from Humberto's discarded wardrobe.

Joe stood and his arms opened without any conscious thought on his part and she walked into them, laying her damp head on his shoulder. He cradled it with one hand and held her close with the other.

"I'll never let anything like this happen to you again," he swore.

She pulled back and looked up at him, searching his eyes. But she didn't say a word. Instead, she put her head on his chest again, snuggled close and held him.

He wished to God he felt desperation in her grip, but it seemed more like comfort or maybe consolation. The desperation was all his and as useless as his wish for peace. Some things just weren't meant to be.

How could he ask her to be other than she was? Would he even love her as much as he did if she changed to suit him?

Then the boat was docking and it was too late for talk. What could they say anyway?

Not only were Holly, Will and Mercier there waiting for them, but also representatives from the FBI, the Coast Guard and Joe's old friend from the local ATF office. And the police, of course. While the anchored *Paper Moon* had not been visible from the shoreline, the explosion of the Zodiac had been and had attracted attention.

Joe sighed, thinking of the numerous debriefings that would be necessary. Separate debriefings. When they disembarked, he made a beeline for Jack Mercier who was obviously the man in charge. "Do you think Martine and I could have a few minutes alone before the circus starts?"

Jack frowned, turned away from the crowd and spoke to Joe in a low voice. "Sorry, not likely. We called them all down here. Now we have to lay it all out for them. The Navy will be jumping up and down about the loss of their equipment. The FBI's already bent out of shape because they weren't in on the plan to start with. And we don't even want to talk about the cops. That sheriff is fit to be tied, especially about the bombs, because EOD was running all over his county while he was kept totally in the dark."

Joe winced. "Not the model of agency cooperation you envisioned, is it?"

The answering chuckle was grim. "See if you can get your local buddies off our backs while I pacify the Navy rep. Holly will handle the FBI while Will takes the official statements from Martine and Eric. He can get yours later. Let's get this wrapped up, *then* you can settle things with Martine. It's not like there's a big rush on that." He paused, then frowned at Joe again. "Is there?"

Joe looked at Martine who was already engrossed in an animated conversation with Holly. "I guess not."

After relating to Sheriff Nigel all that had happened and

why local law enforcement had not been called in from the beginning, Joe excused himself to go to his family. They had arrived in force shortly after the boat had docked and he had not yet had the chance to speak with them. Surrounded by his parents, sisters and brother-in-law, Joe watched Martine disappear around the office of the marina with Mercier.

He didn't see her again. When he finally managed to break away from the family and ask where she had gone, Holly informed him that Jack had gotten a call and had to leave for McLean. Since he'd been going anyway, Martine had requested a ride to the airport with him.

Since he had half expected something like that, Joe's sudden and almost overwhelming anger surprised him. It also kept him from calling her later, after she'd had time to arrive in Atlanta. Apparently, she'd had what she wanted from him and it had been enough.

Despite Joe's exhaustion, sleep eluded him. He spent the entire first night going over everything that had happened between him and Martine. She had gone without so much as a word of goodbye. Not even a wave.

When Holly, Will and Eric stopped by the following morning, he told them he was staying in Port St. Joe and that he might not be returning to McLean at all. The three shared a look that said they were confident he would.

Joe was anything but sure of that, but he had promised himself time to think everything through. Mercier had insisted that he needed some down time and ordered him to take it. Joe knew they all expected him to return to work with Sextant. He did feel obligated because of all they had done, but he couldn't let that sway his decision.

"Put it all out of your mind for a while, Joey," his mother advised him when the others had gone. She fed him paella, fried chicken, his favorite pie, and babied him just as she always had. It felt good to be loved and indulged. But somehow it was not enough.

"Enjoy your rest," she insisted. "You'll know what to do when the time comes." She wore that knowing smile, the one that had always encouraged him to follow his heart.

Though she had been known to meddle shamelessly and ask the most personal questions a mother would dare, she carefully avoided any mention of Martine. So did his father and sisters. Joe began to think there might be a conspiracy involving reverse psychology here. Surely he was being paranoid.

For once, Joe decided he would follow orders to the letter. He wouldn't think about Martine or the job for a while. Especially Martine. If only thoughts of her were that easily dismissed. She and Joe had been so close, he missed her like he would miss an amputated limb, as if she had been a part of him he could barely function without. But he didn't talk about her.

Mercier had called the next day. "Joe? How are you?"

"I'm not coming back," Joe announced, feeling backed against a wall, forced into a hasty decision by that one simple question.

Mercier laughed. "Of course not. I don't want you to yet. I merely called to tell you the special weapons training at Quantico has been pushed back another week because they're hiring a new instructor. So you'll have three weeks down there. I'm off on assignment today and not certain when I can touch base again. Just wanted to tell you to enjoy your vacation and congratulate you on a job well done. I hear that the government forces swept over the compound not long after you left and Humberto's old outfit is pretty much as dead in the water as he is."

"Good," Joe said, uncertain what else Mercier expected him to say. That was why Joe had gone to Colombia, after all.

He remembered to give Mercier the morning's news. "They found the captain of the *Paper Moon,* by the way. Humberto's men had tossed him overboard as soon as they were out of sight of land. But the old codger was a former Navy swim instructor, swam the distance and wound up down the coast in a hospital. They say he'll be okay."

Mercier laughed. "Good for him! Bet he's mad as the devil about his boat. Eric was Navy, too. He'll get a kick out of this when I tell him."

Joe chuckled, too, his mood lightened a little. He almost wished he could be the one to tell Vinland. And the others. Would they be in the office now or getting ready to deploy on this new thing, too? He wouldn't ask. It was nothing to him anyway. "Good luck on the mission, Jack."

"Thanks. And *you* take it easy," Mercier said. "Remember, you still owe me a drink at Christa's when we get back."

The connection broke without even a goodbye. Joe suspected it was because Mercier didn't want to give him time for any further refusals.

Curiosity niggled at him. Where was Jack off to that put that undercurrent of excitement in his voice? What was this new assignment? Was it anything remotely like what Joe had been doing and what would the real day-to-day work of Sextant involve?

He tried not to think about it.

But after eight days, one thought did keep reoccurring. This vacation business was proving to be incredibly boring. Each morning Joe would wake up with a start, sit straight up in bed and throw the covers off, feeling there was something undone, something to prepare for. He soon realized he had spent so many years geared up and in a state of physical and mental readiness that he couldn't turn it off.

No amount of time spent strolling up and down the beach, watching greedy gulls, feeling the familiar pull of the waves could quite settle him down enough to enjoy this longed-for leisure.

Joe kept busy. He bought his mama roses, fixed everything that was broken around the house that his father had ignored, went fishing with his dad, baby-sat for Linda and Delores a time or two and got to know his nieces better. But at every lull in conversation, and especially every night when he was alone, Joe's mind flew North. His thoughts kept pinging back and forth between Atlanta and McLean.

After that week, his parents decided to go to Ft. Lauderdale to visit Joe's brother and his family and give Joe some time alone. The solitude only heightened his need for Martine. And, in spite of his resolve not to, he did think about the job.

To his dismay, Joe began to realize that he missed work. How could he relax knowing there was evil out there while he was simply lying around, letting it flourish, not doing one single thing to stamp out what he could 'of it?

And he missed Martine more than anything. What would he give to have her here beside him, dressed in that little red bikini he'd yet to see her wear? But even if she were here, she wouldn't be content simply to laze in the sun. Not with all that incredible energy of hers.

The memory of the way she felt against him would suddenly rush through him, a wave of lust drowning him in need. But he fought it as hard as he would fight to survive an actual drowning. He could not give in. He couldn't possibly live with her, so he would have to learn to live without her. God, how he missed her.

Eighteen long days into his vacation, Joe sat on the edge of a deck, the boards beneath him hot from the sun while a warm breeze warned of summer fast approaching. As much as he loved it, the urge to leave almost over-powered him with its intensity. It grew worse by the minute. And he had three whole days to go yet.

This was a place to come home to and recharge. And as long as his batteries were working even a little bit, it was no place to stay.

All this fantasizing about life on the beach with no worries had been just that. Pure fantasy, probably born of the isolation he felt when immersed undercover. Who had he been kidding? He had to *do* something or go absolutely nuts. And it ought to be something productive, something he did well. Running occasional fishing expeditions like his dad did just wouldn't cut it.

Angry at the realization, Joe stood up, dusted the sand off his shorts and went inside to call Martine. If he was destined to go full tilt at the world, he might as well admit he would never be satisfied with a woman who would do any less. He loved her. There, he'd admitted it. And he loved her in spite of what she was, most likely because of it.

His sigh of resignation made him laugh at himself. Something inside him loosened as if set free. The thought of seeing her again, holding her in his arms, laughing with her and admitting what an idiot he had been sent energy zinging through his muscles like a shot of adrenaline.

He dialed her cell phone, only to find that the number was now invalid. Her land line number was no longer in service. Matt didn't answer his.

As Joe hurriedly punched in the number for Ames International, he allowed the memory of that last vision of her to drift back to mind. *Martine in white. Surely a bride.*

He felt suddenly very anxious. He needed to talk to her, plead with her if he had to, arrange a place for them to meet halfway and see where it would take them.

The receptionist at Ames informed him that Matt was

away from the office. And, no, Ames could not give him a number where either Martine or Matt could be reached.

Joe nearly panicked. He knew the feeling wouldn't go away until he found out where she was and what she was up to. God only knew how much trouble she was in right this very minute.

# Chapter 16

Martine had more to do than she had time for. The new apartment was stacked shoulder-high with boxes. Her furniture was in place but she could hardly get to her bed to sleep. The job had her in such a state she couldn't sleep much anyway.

Matt tossed her a bottle of water across the kitchen table and shoved the remainder of the pizza he had ordered to her side. "Eat, sis. You need some energy!"

She pulled out her chair and sat down, eyeing the piles of kitchen stuff that littered the counter. "Will I ever get this place straightened out?"

He laughed and sipped his beer. "It's small, but I think you'll manage to fit everything in eventually. I gotta tell you, though, living expenses up here are gonna eat you up."

She laughed. "Yes, but I'll make it. It certainly took the Bureau long enough to process my application and make a decision. What's it been, nearly a year since I applied?"

He sobered a little, tilting his bottle, staring at it. "Well, I can't say I'm sorry you got it since it's what you want. But will it be enough, Martine? The job, I mean. I know you…had feelings for Joe Corda." He looked up, his eyes narrowed, "Want me to beat him up for you?"

Martine laughed. "Like you could. It's not Joe's fault we couldn't work things out. He made it pretty clear what he wanted for the long term and I was about as far from that as I could get and still be female."

"If you had just promised to do something a little less risky than what we were doing at Ames, he would have come around," Matt argued. "He probably would, even now, if you'd just find him and talk to him about this new job. Speaking of which, will you miss the other? Instructing's not exactly a thrill a minute."

Martine shook her head as she picked a pepperoni off the pizza and nibbled at it. "No, I had about as much danger as I could stand on the Colombia thing and then Florida really capped it. I can do without that much whiplash action, thank you very much."

"You handled it, Mart. Wrapped it up like a pro." He saluted her with his beer and winked.

She sighed. "I didn't say I couldn't hack it. I could. I did. But all I wanted in the first place was a job that made a difference, you know? What I'm doing now will still do that."

Besides, she had done a lot of thinking these past few weeks. Joe had guessed right about her reasons for overcompensating.

Matt grinned back when she smiled at him. "And if you should just happen to hook up with Joe again, he'll appreciate the change in you."

She shrugged. "I don't know, Matt. I haven't really changed that much. He was pretty adamant about what kind of woman he was looking for. He wants a homebody.

I won't be any man's shadow, not like Mama was. You know what she's been like since Dad died.''

"Lost," he affirmed, nodding sadly and taking another sip of his beer. "You could never be like her, though. Even when Sebastian had you safely tucked away in the file room at Ames, you had that independent streak. Sure you're not gonna miss the challenge now that you've had a taste of the action?''

"No. I'll be fine." She avoided Matt's questioning gaze. They had always been close and he saw too much of what she was feeling.

Would she miss Joe? Hardly a minute went by that she didn't think of him, wonder what he was doing, whether he thought of her at all.

Chances were, she'd never see him again. If their paths did cross, she wasn't altogether sure she could pretend nonchalance. *Well, hello, Joe? What have you been doing with yourself all these years? Married? Any kids yet?*

No. She just hoped if they ever wound up in the same location, she would see him first so she could run like hell and not have to hear all those answers. A clean break was best. He'd said so himself once, the first time they had parted. He'd been right.

There would be a good fifty or sixty miles between where he worked and where she was now. His job would entail a lot of travel. No real reason they should have to see one another ever again. Unless he made a dedicated effort to find her, she wouldn't be easy to locate. That was the plan. She certainly didn't want him phoning her casually, asking how she was, keeping himself in the forefront of her mind.

"If you're gonna daydream instead of finishing that and unpacking, I'm out of here. Sebastian's short-handed and needs me back in Atlanta. I'm getting this cast off next week.''

"That's too soon! What about therapy for that leg?''

Martine demanded to know. "You need to be at full strength before you tackle another assignment."

"Yes, bossy-britches. It's strong enough now to kick your little butt if you get embroiled in anything else as hair-raising as your last escapade." He stood up and tossed his bottle into the trash. "So behave yourself."

"Go unearth the box with my shoes if you can find it and quit giving me orders."

He rounded the table, cast thumping, roughly mussed her hair and went into the other room to begin unpacking. Martine felt a tear leak out the corner of one eye. She would miss him when he went home. Her aloneness would be more complete then than ever before.

But missing her brother would be nothing at all compared to how she would miss Joe. How she missed him even now. She ached for him, longed for the touch of those long, strong fingers, that buff body, that deep sexy voice breathing Spanish love words in her ear.

Maybe she had become too much like her mother after all in spite of her determination not to. No way could she ever allow a man to become her whole world, her reason for being. Especially not a man who was fully capable of enforcing his will on her. Joe would never use force, but he could be way too persuasive. She had been right on the edge of suggesting compromise when she realized if she gave an inch, he'd surely grab the proverbial mile. She had to do what she had to do and that was that.

From now on she would spend her free hours arranging this place to suit her, making it a comfortable home where she could be happy with her own company.

The rest of the time, she would dedicate to the work. The job was tailor-made for someone like her. What she would be doing was vitally important to the training of women and men who would put their lives on the line every day.

That satisfaction would have to be enough.

* * *

Three weeks of beach life had been more than Joe could stand. With two days left before he had to make a final decision, he bought himself a used Explorer, a few new suits and a couple of pairs of dress shoes and drove as straight to McLean as the highways allowed. He had to work. There was no denying it, no getting around it.

Now he was enrolled in one of the advanced weapons training classes at Quantico. It was only a three-day thing. Holly had advised him he also needed to bone up on his conversational French while he was here and had signed him up for private tutoring sessions with a contract linguist.

The French lesson had to do with the next assignment, she had said, being pretty cryptic about it. Mercier was already in place over there. Joe figured he must be slated to go over with the backup team. He certainly was eager enough to get out of the country and immerse himself in something—anything—that might take his mind off himself.

So here he was at the Academy again, same place he had completed his DEA training years ago, this time for quick brush-up.

Joe had donned the blue golf shirt and khaki pants, uniform for the weapons range. He wasn't unhappy about being relegated to student status at the ripe old age of thirty-two. Nope, he had too much misery about other things than to let this training exercise bother him even a little. He lifted his blue baseball cap, ran his fingers through his closely clipped hair and then replaced the headgear, tugging the bill down to shade his eyes.

Qualifying with anything bearing a sight and a trigger wasn't going to be a problem. What he dreaded was the crash course in French later this afternoon. His mother was the one with the facility for grasping languages. Even though English was his mother tongue, Joe knew his

Spanish was damned near perfect thanks to his dad insisting they speak it at home on alternate days for as far back as Joe could remember. But he sure wished he hadn't goofed off during his two years of high school French. And that he hadn't elected to study Russian at the University. Hell, nobody spoke Russian these days, even the Russians.

With a sigh, he got off the bus that had transported him and the rest of the eager beavers to the range. They were mostly FBI vets with a few trainees from other agencies, like himself, thrown in. None were fresh recruits. The weapons they were to play with today were not the usual issue. This was the spooky stuff, some of it not yet available either in the field or on the street.

Work was the byword in his life right now. Anything to make him forget his personal life. Or lack of one. He still hadn't been able to locate Martine.

He lined up with the others to await instruction. It felt strange to be part of a group of friendlies after going it alone for so long among the enemy. He hadn't even had time to get used to working with the other five on the Sextant team and now, here he was among twenty-odd agents he didn't know, plus the two instructors.

His gaze drifted to those two individuals wearing the darker shirts. His heart jumped when he saw the long blond ponytail threaded through the baseball cap one of the instructors was wearing. Hair like Martine's. God, he was seeing her everywhere he looked. Even now he couldn't help but imagine this woman turning around to face him, Martine's smile beaming at him, ecstatic about seeing him after nearly a month. *Ha.*

Still, wishful thinking had him moving closer to her, hungrily eyeing the curve of that fine little butt in those khaki slacks, the proud set of those shoulders, the long line of that graceful neck. *Damn. So like hers.*

She turned. No smile.

Joe's knees nearly buckled.

"If you would, form a line, please," she snapped, sounding very official as her gaze slid right over him to someone else. "We'll proceed with roll call."

Joe must have managed to comply because she didn't address him again except to say his name right after some guy's called Alex Cash. And she used the same perfunctory tone of voice.

He wanted to grab her and shake her, make her look at him, speak to him. Just to him. Explain why she'd ditched without even saying goodbye. Tell him how the hell she could have left him with a hole in his chest the size of a Florida grapefruit and a brain that wouldn't work.

By the time she had finished marking that stupid clipboard of hers, Joe had worked up the worst mad he'd had on since Roy McDonald had planted pot in his locker in the eleventh grade and almost got him arrested. Must have something to do with a person trying to wreck his entire life for no good reason.

He didn't understand a word during the entire demonstration of the new sniper rifle.

When his turn came to fire it, he missed the target completely. He was too busy shooting daggers at Martine and hitting that particular target dead-on. She ignored him. Totally.

Only when the male instructor who was running things dismissed the class and Martine started walking toward the vehicle parked near the bus did Joe have a chance to speak to her. He had to hustle to catch up. "Martine? Wait!"

She halted, did a sharp, military about-face and threw up her chin. "Yes?" The clipboard hugged her chest like Kevlar. He noticed her knuckles were white.

He gritted his teeth, took a deep breath and tilted his head to look at her. "Where the hell have you been and what are you doing *here?*"

She forced a tight little smile. "Assisting the weapons instructor, obviously. Filling in. How are you, Joe? Long time, no see. How's the family?"

"Dammit, Martine! Why did you just take off that way?"

"Excuse me. I have to leave."

"Don't you think you owe me some answers?"

"I don't believe I owe you anything at all," she said, calm as you please.

They were drawing an audience, but Joe didn't care. He started to grab her arm, but yanked his hand back and stuck it in his pocket, unsure what would happen if he touched her. He wanted to kiss her so bad he feared he might break her teeth if he did.

"How'd you get this job? You're not trained for it," he said through gritted teeth. "Are you?"

"As it happens, yes. I went through police training after college. Top graduate was sent here to the Academy. That was before Ames."

"You were a *cop?* What *else* haven't you told me?" he demanded.

"I never served as an officer. I just trained." Her lips tightened and she glanced up at the sky. Probably praying lightning would strike him. Her voice dropped to a near whisper. "What do you want from me, Joe? You know damned well I'm not going to change."

"Who the hell asked you to change?" he all but shouted.

"*You* did! We can't talk about this here. We shouldn't have to talk about it at all. I know what you want and I can't be that. It's over. End of story."

"Beginning," Joe argued, getting right in her face. "It's just beginning, Martine."

She glanced around them, her fair skin reddening. "Not here, Joe," she muttered.

"Then where?" he demanded, shaking his head. "I'm

not going away. And if you do, I won't quit until I find you this time. Count on it.''

The supervising instructor walked over, hands on his hips. He was a hulk of a guy, outweighed Joe by a good forty pounds and looked fairly lethal. Joe felt he could take the man apart in three seconds in his present mood.

The hulk glanced back and forth between them. ''Problem, Duquesne?''

''No, sir. Nothing I can't resolve, thanks.'' Her gaze flicked back to Joe. ''Don't you get me fired again!'' With that, she put the hulk between herself and Joe and stalked off to the car. Joe reluctantly entered the bus in which he had arrived. This wasn't over. Not by a long shot.

Two hours later, still grumbling to himself about the encounter, Joe paced his temporary quarters waiting for the tutor to arrive. A sudden summer storm gathered outside. Though it had grown murky in his room, he purposely left off the lights. Maybe he would pretend to be out and simply skip the little French class.

Like he wanted to sit here and listen to somebody tell him *fromage* meant cheese. He wanted to slam out of here and go find Martine, rattle some sense into her. Make her see they could work things out if she'd stop being so bullheaded and just *try*. But he had to cool off first so he wouldn't blow his chance. If he hadn't already.

Someone knocked and he strode over to the door and yanked it open. And there she was.

Martine wore a wry grimace as she shoved a book at him. ''I had nothing to do with this arrangement. I didn't know you were here until I got my schedule this morning.''

Her voice sounded raspy as if she were coming down with a cold. But it hadn't been that way earlier. Had she been crying? Over seeing him again? He tossed the book on the table.

She wore no makeup at all and had that beautiful shades-of-gold hair of hers pulled straight back, the ponytail now twisted into a bun. Downplaying her looks, he decided. Probably wise, because they would be a serious distraction for anybody trying to learn anything.

She had lost weight. A little twinge of sympathy struck when he realized Martine really had suffered, too. Joe knew she cared about him. That wasn't something she would have faked. It was just that he hadn't thought he could stand her living the way she seemed determined to live. She must have had second thoughts about it herself.

He hid his smile. Being an instructor at Quantico was probably the safest job in the world. She'd be surrounded by FBI all day long. Perfect.

But he'd changed his mind, too. She'd left him thinking he'd be spending the rest of his life bumming around Port St. Joe. Only now did it occur that she might not be nearly as pleased with *his* latest plan as he was with hers.

The laid-back lifestyle he had always thought he wanted more than anything, had bored him to death in a matter of days. Now he was itching to get right back into the thick of things. Some of his future missions might make his DEA assignments pale by comparison. What would she think of that?

"Did you mean it?" she asked carefully, her gaze straying around his room, taking in the neatly made single bed, the spotless floor, the lack of personal items.

"That I'd look for you if you disappeared again? You know it."

"Not that," she admitted. "About not asking me to change. I thought about it for the last couple of hours and realized you never did actually demand that I quit. Not quite."

"Just hinted at it about as subtly as a sledgehammer, right? Sort of begged a little, maybe? Tried to do a deal?"

Joe asked, releasing the smile he was fighting. *She was going to be a teacher. Just a teacher. Safe.*

He reached for her hand, but she stepped back. Joe sighed. He should have known it wouldn't be that easy. "I love you," he told her honestly. "Just the way you are."

Her gaze rolled upward as she sighed. "Easy for you to say now that you know what I'm doing."

"Or *not* doing," Joe agreed. He kept his distance, knowing that what he said now would make all the difference.

He began slowly, carefully. "On any mission, under any circumstance, I'd choose you above anyone else to watch my back, Martine. I admire your capabilities so much. But I love you, too. Knowing you're in danger of any kind makes me a little nuts. But if you hadn't taken this job, I could have learned to cope."

She expelled a wry little laugh as she stared out his window. Rivulets of rain were streaking the glass and the stormy sky threw her into sharp relief. Thunder rumbled in the distance as Joe waited for her to speak.

"You know you're asking me to do that, Joe. I'm well aware of what Sextant does."

"How do you feel about that? Want me to quit? I almost did. I still could."

She turned to him, searching his face. "Oh, Joe. You would never be happy on the beach or behind a desk. It's good that you realized that. But I will admit I'm glad you won't be out there working alone the way you were." She did that little one-shoulder shrug thing. "I sort of know where you were coming from. About the worry thing."

Joe approached her and held out his hand again. She took it and he felt hers tremble slightly. "I was wrong about what I thought I wanted. Except for wanting you."

She smiled up at him, her features barely visible in the semidarkness. "I guess I was, too."

Joe lifted her hands and placed them on his shoulders, felt them slide up to his neck. He closed his eyes and embraced her, holding her as if his very life depended on it. Which it did. He could never let her go again no matter what.

His lips found hers, hungry for the sweet taste of her. He tugged off her cap and pulled at the band confining her hair until the silky strands came free even as he backed her toward the single bed in the corner.

When his mouth left hers, she gasped, "This…must be breaking every rule…in the book."

"So they ship us out," he growled, nipping at the sweet curve of her neck, inhaling the scent of her subtle perfume. "I can learn French anywhere. How do I say *Take off these damned clothes?*"

*"Enlevez ces vêtements,"* she muttered breathlessly, tugging his belt loose, pushing his pants down over his hips. *"Maintenant!"*

"Yeah, *now*. I know that word." He already had her shirt half over her head.

They were laughing helplessly as they fell across the bunk, messing up the military precision of it. He kissed her again, this time with his entire body, glorying in the soft, sweet feel of her beneath him. How had he lived for weeks without this? He hadn't lived, he'd only existed.

"Oh, Joe," she sighed, opening to him in every way as he sank into her with a groan of deep relief.

Instead of rushing to completion this time, he desperately needed to prolong this, to show her how he valued her, how much he treasured this beautiful connection they shared.

He withdrew slowly, his mouth trailing down the arch of her neck to kiss those remarkable breasts, concentrating on the fascinating surface of the pebbled peaks against his tongue.

Her cry of pleasure seemed to go straight to his groin,

urging him to reenter her and assuage his greed, but he held back. Determined, he slid downward, raking his teeth gently over the curve of her waist.

She moaned something in what he thought might be French, causing him to smile against her abdomen and go lower still. His hands encompassed her breasts, alternately brushing lightly and giving her what she wanted. She tasted exotic, wildly erotic, a blend of sweetness and woman.

He hummed with the pleasure of it and felt her first tremor of completion. No way could he resist. With speed to rival the lightning in the sky outside, he moved up and over her to share it.

Thunder ripped through him, shook the building and the bed. The sky opened and torrents lashed against the window while his heart pounded just as hard. Joe thought he might never experience a storm again without climaxing no matter where he was.

They lay, replete and entwined, silently savoring the aftermath. Joe just wanted to hold on to the moment, though he knew they still had a lot to resolve. Martine might be willing to give him more than this, but he wasn't yet sure about that. Maybe all she wanted was occasional sex. She had never actually said that she loved him.

He had to know. He raised up on one elbow and looked down at her. The storm had moved on and the afternoon sun was peeking through the clouds, its weak, slanted rays gently illuminating the room with errant streaks of light. One fell across Martine.

Her eyes were closed, her long lashes like small perfect fans. Her lips looked full, a result of thorough kissing and recent arousal. The sunlight highlighted her features and the folds of white on the pillowcase, the rumpled sheet that he had drawn up to her shoulders.

"Oh, God," he murmured, his former vision of her all in white replaying itself in his mind.

Her eyes flew open. "What is it?"

Joe swallowed hard, tremendous relief all tangled up with disappointment. "At least you aren't dead."

She looked confused and also a little amused. "No. You stunned me but I'm still breathing. You were great, but let's not overestimate your effect."

"But you aren't a bride, either," he muttered.

She shrugged. "No. No, I'm not. What's all this about, Joe?"

"I had a vision of you all in white, surrounded by it. And I think this is…what I saw," he said, pointing at her swathed in the white sheet, the pillow bunched beneath her head, unwilling at the moment to go into an explanation of his so-called gift. "I didn't know what it meant at the time."

"Will you marry me, Joe?"

Elation shot through him. "You want to? Really?"

She shrugged, a slight smile playing about her mouth. "I guess we'd better."

Then he realized what she might mean. They *had* had unprotected sex on the boat. And again just now. Damn, that would screw up all her plans. At least for now. "You're pregnant?"

She laughed, wiping the frown off his face with a sweep of her finger. "No, it's not that."

"Then why?"

With one hand behind his neck, she pulled him down for a kiss. When she released him, she answered, "Because if you're going to retain a vision of me in your head, I want it to be one where my hair's combed. Why do you *think,* Joe? I love you."

"You never said," he accused.

"I'm saying now," she replied, teasing his bottom lip with her finger. "But before you make an honest woman of me, I'd like at least one more adventure as a single girl if you don't mind."

"Anything you want," he promised, grasping her to him and hugging her hard. *Adventure?* "What?"

He knew that tentative question had probably betrayed his fear that she would insist on going with him on the next mission or something equally risky. It would be just like her to demand that.

"I'd like to break some Academy rules again," she said, wriggling against him to make her intentions clear.

*"Maintenant?"* he asked, just to show her he'd been paying attention to her very brief but effective lesson. He was already rising to her expectations.

"Oh yeah, Corda. *Right* now."

"That would be *tout suite!* Hmm? Oh yeah, *all* my French is coming back to me now."

Her laughter was like the bright sunshine now permeating his quarters and his heart like a blessing.

# *Epilogue*

"Dammit, I *knew* this would happen," Joe grumbled as they danced around the polished oak floors of Christa's. The old pub's oak and brass fittings were buffed to a high shine and gleamed with old world charm. Joe had rented the whole place for the evening and a judge friend of Clay's had performed the ceremony.

"Ah, don't tell me. You had a flash of me dressed in French couture?" The laughter in her voice was hard to resist.

He kissed her, still moving to the strains of the Righteous Brothers' "Unchained Melody," compliments of Christa's old-fashioned jukebox.

Earlier, as Martine and he had said their vows, Joe realized this, their wedding day, was only the second time he had ever seen Martine in a dress. That simple little black number back in Atlanta had been racy, but this...

She was gorgeous when barefaced, sporting jungle fatigues or that asexual getup she wore on the job. Dressed in this ultra-feminine, slinky, ivory satin number that looked like star-stuff out of a thirties movie, her hair and makeup perfect, she just blew him away. That was probably the whole idea, stunning him into compliance. Unfortunately, it might be working. He dipped her, just to get her off balance for a minute.

It wasn't that he didn't want to be with her. He sure didn't want to postpone their honeymoon. But Martine coming to France with the team on this mission seemed to be tempting fate. They had waited until just after the ceremony to tell him. "Language advisor, huh? This is a misuse of power or nepotism or something equally illegal, I bet, contracting a family member. Mercier will flip when he finds out Holly requested you for this."

"No, we weren't married when the Bureau approved it. And from what she tells me, Jack's in no position to object at the moment." She dropped her voice to a whisper. "He's in jail."

"Shh." He goosed her waist for emphasis, sliding his fingers over that special curve. "Remember where we are. And why we're here."

It was a small, private affair, owing to the speedy arrangements. Their immediate families had flown up for the ceremony and all the members of Sextant were there except for Jack, who was already in France, setting up the mission.

"So what's your role?" he asked with a resigned sigh, accepting the inevitable.

"I'm to be the cover." She pretended to preen, tossing her sunny mane and looking smug. "Wealthy author incognito and her entourage."

Joe released her long enough to twirl her around. "I'll be your bodyguard." Whether she wanted him to or not. From what he'd been told about this gig, they could be dodging worse than bullets. Joe wasn't sure that even he could protect her from what they might be facing.

"Nope," she informed him with a saucy grin. "Will's the bodyguard."

"I'm your driver?" He executed a turn expertly as his mother had taught him all those years ago when preparing him for the prom, then drew her close and slow danced like the randiest teenager.

"Sorry, Eric's the chauffeur," she said, one ice-pink nail tickling his neck just above his collar. "And Holly's my secretary. She has it all worked out."

"Then what am I, your cook?"

She giggled, a lovely throaty sound that stirred his insides. "You're my Latin lover, my boy toy! Can you handle it, Corda?"

He kissed her ear. "Typecasting if I ever heard it. Let's go buy Holly a drink."

She laughed out loud, her head back, her eyes shining up at him. The effect nearly caused him to step on her feet.

"Quit trying to lead, Mrs. Corda," Joe warned.

"Only for this dance, Joe," she promised, her laughter subsiding. "This one last dance." They both knew she was referring to the decision she had made without him.

"And after France?" he asked, praying there would *be* an after.

"The world will be a little safer for our children," she said as the music faded. She touched his brow. "Close your eyes, Joe, and tell me what you see."

He didn't need a vision. "Us. Together forever. Whatever comes."

\* \* \* \* \*

# Undercover Virgin
## BECKY BARKER

*Intimate*

First Published 2004
First Australian Paperback Edition 2004
ISBN 0 733 55277 3

Published by
Harlequin Mills & Boon
3 Gibbes Street
CHATSWOOD NSW 2067
AUSTRALIA

HARLEQUIN MILLS & BOON INTIMATE and the Rose Device are
trademarks used under license and registered in Australia, New Zealand,
Philippines, United States Patent & Trademark Office and in other countries.

Printed and bound in Australia by
McPherson's Printing Group

### BECKY BARKER

is a multipublished author whose novels have been translated into more than a dozen foreign languages, converted to electronic format and have been reissued in trade paperback as well as large-print library editions.

Her personal hero is a former marine who helped her create three terrific children. Rachel and her husband, Jerramy; Amanda and her husband, Jay; and Thad and his wife, Dara, all live within a few miles of Mum and Dad in rural Ohio.

Besides spending time with her family, Becky enjoys music, gardening and reading. She loves to hear from readers and can be reached at P.O. Box 113, Mt. Sterling, OH, 43143 or through her Web site at BeckyBarker.com.

I'd like to dedicate this book to my siblings
and their spouses, because the older I get, the more I
value them and our big, extended family. With love to
Judy and Randy, Cathy and Larry, Tim and Luana, Thom
and Sue, Peggy and in memory of Michael. Also,
with love to Dee Dee, Sue and Dave.

And as always, special thanks to Buzz,
the wind beneath my wings!

# Chapter 1

It had been too easy. Too damn easy, thought Kyle
Tremont as he surveyed the elegant ballroom of Gregory Haroldson's estate. The plan to get him into the
employ of the wealthy banker had come together without a hitch. It had all gone like a perfectly choreo-
graphed dance.

The ease of it only made him edgy and more vigi-
lant.

Some unseen sharpshooter had taken a wild shot at
Haroldson, and Kyle had been on hand to shield the
other man with his body. Instant gratitude and a generous job offer. Kyle had wondered, several times, why
he hadn't shoved Haroldson into the path of the bullet.
Dead was a more sure-fire way to punish a man than
the prospect of a jail term.

Only five days into the operation, and he wanted out.
He'd cursed himself a thousand times over for letting
Donald Sullivan coerce him into helping. The daily

doses of Haroldson's arrogance were more than he could stomach. The urge to strangle the man with his bare hands grew stronger every time he laid eyes on him.

Undercover work had definitely lost its appeal. The innate hunger for a challenge that had motivated him in his younger days was nonexistent now. He had retired four years ago when the taste for intrigue died along with his partner.

Despite being on Haroldson's payroll, he'd yet to be contacted by the elusive agent with the code name Phantom. His assignment was to help the undercover FBI agent escape Haroldson's heavily guarded compound. Deputy Director Sullivan had lured him out of retirement with a promise that Phantom had gathered enough concrete evidence to make Haroldson pay for his crimes.

Kyle was tired of waiting and at risk of losing his patience altogether.

"She's a first-class babe, ain't she."

Kyle glanced at his fellow employee. Damon was young, cocky and a little dim-witted, but basically an okay guy. The two of them were usually paired as driver and bodyguard for high-ranking members of Haroldson's little empire.

Tonight, they were enjoying the annual staff appreciation dinner. Haroldson knew how to keep his people happy and loyal by pretending they were important to him. The ballroom's many chandeliers had been dimmed to a soft, intimate glow. Food was abundant, booze flowed freely and a small orchestra played music for dancing.

Damon's admiring gaze was fastened on their hostess for the evening.

"You mean Haroldson's fiancée?"

"She's a real knockout, and damn nice, too. Always doin' something for the staff and their families."

*Nice* wasn't exactly the word Kyle would use to describe Haroldson's very young, very blond girlfriend. Definitely a May-December relationship. Gossip had it that she'd moved in with him as soon as they'd announced their engagement. Apparently, he adored her and refused her nothing.

"I guess she can afford to be generous."

"Yeah, but I seen plenty of those rich bitches who turn their noses up at guys like us. 'Fraid they'll get dirty if we touch 'em or somethin'. Samantha, she's not that way."

Kyle had never been introduced to the lady in question. Nor did he want to be. He couldn't summon much interest in a woman who'd sleep with a bastard like Haroldson.

"I don't figure I'll be getting up close and personal with the boss's woman."

The younger man laughed. "That's what you think. She's makin' her way toward us now. She and the boss, they have this little routine. When he hires a new employee, she's the one what gets up close and personal. The boss gets a kick out of watchin' the hired help drool. She'll have you pantin' after her in a few minutes."

Oh, hell, thought Kyle. Damon usually knew what he was talking about when it came to his boss's habits. He ground his teeth in frustration. The last thing he needed was attention drawn to him, especially for Haroldson's amusement.

Their hostess slowly made her way through the throng of partygoers, stopping to speak to several people as she crossed the room. Everyone wanted a word with the lady of the manor. He watched her graceful, unhurried progress and steeled himself to suffer her attention. It wouldn't do to make his distaste evident. Better to play the dumb but awed hired hand.

"Damn, but she looks hot in that red dress," muttered Damon. "Too bad she never strays for real. I'd be first in line to jump her delicate bones."

Haroldson's fiancée wasn't what he'd call petite— probably five foot seven or eight, with a slender but generously curved figure. As she drew closer, Kyle's gaze drifted down her elegant neck, across the bare, unblemished skin of her shoulders and chest to an enticing view of softly rounded breasts displayed by the strapless dress.

The full-length evening gown managed to look both tasteful and wickedly provocative. A man would have to be dead not to react. Her heavy mane of platinum-blond hair parted in the middle and framed an oval-shaped face in feathery layers. Although not classically beautiful, her features were striking, attractive and enhanced to perfection.

The best money could buy. She had to be an unprincipled gold digger who'd sold her soul to the highest bidder. That alone should leave him cold, but his body wasn't listening to common sense. It was just reacting.

Wide-set, exotically highlighted blue eyes captured his attention and held his gaze as she came to a stop in front of him. He felt the impact of her gaze clear to his toes. Her expensive perfume teased his senses, and set his nerves alive with reaction. The sizzle of attraction hummed through his veins at the sultry challenge in those beautiful eyes.

"T. R. O. U. B. L. E." The lyrics to a country-western song popped into his mind. Haroldson's ladylove packed a sensual wallop that could mean nothing but trouble.

"Mr. Jackson." She greeted him by his alias and offered her hand. "I don't believe we've been introduced." Her voice was low and sexy, barely audible above the noise of the party. "I wanted to personally thank you for saving Gregory's life."

Kyle briefly grasped her hand, but kept his grip limp. She responded with a warm, firm grasp. Her touch made his skin sizzle with awareness.

She smiled, transforming her features to unexpected loveliness. It gave him another jolt. Not just because of the physical difference, but because of the genuine warmth and charm she emanated. No wonder she had the staff ready to jump her bones or jump through hoops for her. Warning himself to beware of wolves in sheeps' clothing, he briefly returned the smile.

"It's a pleasure to meet you, ma'am."

"There's no need to call me ma'am. We're all one big family here. My name is Samantha," she said, and then asked, "And your first name is Anthony?"

"Tony's fine."

For this assignment, he was keeping his hair dyed inky black. Thanks to tinted contacts, his blue eyes were temporarily brown. He'd even added a mustache. His naturally dark complexion had always made it easy for him to take on a Mediterranean look.

"Well, Tony, I certainly hope you're enjoying yourself. Did you get enough to eat?"

"Yes, ma'am— I mean Samantha."

She smiled again—a smile meant to reach right into a man and make him relax. Maybe even threaten his control. Kyle felt another unexpected zing of physical awareness, but hardened himself to the response.

"Do you dance, Tony?" she asked.

He glanced toward Damon, who was giving him a cheesy grin and a sly thumbs-up behind her back. Then he looked toward the dance floor. Several couples were shuffling around to a slow tune, but he wasn't eager to join them.

"I'm not much for dancing," he insisted.

Samantha curled her fingers around his forearm, smiled and batted her lashes with the finesse of a siren.

"Please, don't be shy. I promise I won't step on your feet," she teased. "I'd feel honored if you'd share at least one dance with me."

He glanced toward Haroldson. "Sure the boss won't mind?"

Her husky laughter shivered along his nerves. "I promise the boss won't mind. He thinks it's important for a hostess to mingle with her guests."

She gently but firmly led him to a shadowed corner of the dance floor, and then fitted herself snugly against his body. Heat radiated through him at every point of contact. Her hands slid up his chest to settle lightly on his shoulders, and she tilted her head back to study his face.

Kyle returned her steady gaze while his senses feasted on her warmth, the sweetness of her scent and the full, firm breasts pressed against his chest. He slid his hands to her waist and enjoyed the feel of the taut feminine body wrapped in soft, silky fabric. His fingers tightened convulsively.

It felt good to hold her. Really good, yet disturbing. Wrong place, wrong time, wrong woman, his brain insisted while his body vibrated with pleasure. It had been too long since he'd felt such a rush of sexual response to a woman. His deprived hormones were going haywire, but there was no sense fighting the reaction. Might as well enjoy the moment, he thought with a mental shrug.

"Tell me about yourself, Tony," she coaxed, sounding as though she really cared.

He wondered if the attentive attitude was all part of a well-orchestrated game she played with Haroldson. Her lover never made a move without a carefully thought-out plan. Did she support him in his sick games? Would she tempt him with her smile and body, then chuckle about his response in bed tonight?

At the thought, a shaft of anger pierced Kyle, but he swiftly controlled it. Samantha's eyes widened a little, making him wonder if she sensed his tension. Maybe she'd attribute it to sexual frustration.

"There's not much to tell," he finally answered.

"Everybody has something to tell," she urged, subtly shifting closer to him.

He grew even more tense as she swayed against him, held his gaze with her beautiful, beguiling eyes and pleaded for a response.

"Everybody has likes and dislikes," she said. "Favorite books or TV shows or movies."

When he failed to respond, she continued, undaunted. "I enjoy movies myself, but I'm especially fond of the theater. Have you ever seen the classic *Phantom of the Opera?*"

Kyle froze. His muscles locked and his mind went blank for an instant. *"Phantom of the Opera."* The code for recognizing Sullivan's undercover operative. He'd been waiting for someone in the organization to use that phrase. A phrase no other member of Harold-son's family or staff was likely to use.

He stared at the perfect, pouting lips, wondering if he'd misinterpreted the message. The undercover agent's nickname, Phantom, registered in his brain, but he couldn't reconcile the fact that the beautiful, possibly treacherous woman in his arms was one of the FBI's top operatives.

Haroldson's lover? Sullivan had said Phantom was deep in the organization, but this staggered the mind. He couldn't imagine any agent being dedicated enough or reckless enough to sleep with the enemy. Nor could he imagine the deputy director condoning it, however badly he wanted Haroldson brought to justice.

He had to be missing something.

She gently nudged him into motion, and Kyle automatically took the lead again. He stared into her eyes. Were they glittering with satisfaction, or warning? Was her expression taunting him for his unprofessional reaction?

Her husky voice interrupted his thoughts. "Am I boring you, Tony? You seem to have gone into a trance."

He didn't have to be a genius to realize he'd blown his cover like a raw recruit. At least where she was concerned. Allowing himself to be caught so totally off guard could get him killed. Might still get him killed if he didn't pull it together.

He continued to stare at her, studying the creamy skin of her cheeks, highlighted with a hint of natural blush, the lips that glistened with lipstick as red as her gown.

He silently cursed Sullivan for setting him up to extricate a female agent. His last partner had infiltrated

Haroldson's organization, too, but she hadn't made it out alive. Margie—his partner, best friend and lover. The thought of her made his breath hitch. She'd given her life for the job, and he'd never forgiven himself for not being there to protect her.

Samantha slid her hands to his chest and flexed her fingers against his shirt, her nails scoring him through the lightweight cotton and jarring him back to the present.

"Cat got your tongue?" she whispered.

Her touch lit a fire beneath his skin, making his blood run hotter. Kyle fought the wave of heat and racked his brain for the code Sullivan had given him to verify his own identity. He recalled the answer and recovered some control.

"I don't know nothin' about no phantoms," he declared exactly as he'd been coached. "I don't go for that high-brow stuff."

Her smile widened. She batted her lashes flirtatiously even though her eyes sparkled with keen intelligence. A paradox, to be sure, but could he trust her? Kyle continued to scrutinize every feature of her face, his mind still coming to terms with all he'd heard about Phantom, all he'd learned about Haroldson's fiancée, and what a helluva tangle the whole assignment had just become.

According to his instructions, she was the agent in charge of the rest of the assignment. Once they'd made contact, he'd been ordered to let Phantom orchestrate the escape strategy. He waited, barely breathing, for her to make the next move.

"I like you, Tony. I think I'll have Gregory reassign you as my personal driver."

Her throaty announcement was accompanied by a

seductive thrust of her hips, just as the music came to an end. But the ploy to tease him backfired. Heat simmered between them; the intimate connection sparked and crackled. Blood sizzled beneath his skin, and he knew she felt it, too.

Her brow creased at the undeniable attraction. Annoyance shimmered briefly in her eyes before being quickly replaced by iron determination, then her more proper hostess facade.

In any other circumstances, Kyle would have laughed out loud at the telltale crack in her armor. He wasn't the only one who'd been caught off guard by a spark of desire. Maybe in the future she'd be more careful about teasing a man.

"What do you think, Tony?" she prodded, her tone edged with impatience. "Want to be my personal driver?"

"That sounds just fine, ma'am."

"Samantha," she insisted. Then she slipped out of his arms and strolled off the dance floor.

He watched her closely, appreciating the gentle sway of her hips as she moved across the room, and wondering if he'd just signed his own death warrant.

One thing was for sure: this assignment would be coming to an end soon. Adrenaline pumped through his veins at the knowledge. He'd finally been offered a real challenge, to get Phantom out of harm's way and to the FBI's safe house. Sullivan had sworn the evidence she'd collected would be enough to nail Haroldson.

Both prospects spurred his excitement, fueling a long-suppressed need. He could have done without the sexual jolt, but he was an expert at tamping down those flames.

"What'd I tell ya, Tony?" Damon met him as he left the dance floor. Handing him a cold beer, he elaborated. "She's something, ain't she? I'll bet that's the first time you ever held such a classy piece of sugar in your arms. You looked a little starstruck."

Kyle glanced sharply at the other man. So Damon had noticed his momentary confusion. Damn. How many others had witnessed his involuntary reaction? He'd been so distracted that he'd lost objectivity. A good agent had to be observant at all times. Lives depended on it.

Swallowing a long drag of beer, he comforted himself with the fact that he wasn't a field operative anymore. He was a woodcrafter from a sleepy Texas town who'd been dragged back into service. Just a civvie doing a deferred duty. His pride still stung, but he figured he could live with another dent in his ego.

"Haroldson must be crazy to turn her loose on his employees," he finally said, wondering if the slight insult to their boss would be tolerated.

Damon just chuckled.

"He's crazy, all right. If she was my woman, I'd keep her chained to the bed. Preferably in the buff."

Kyle felt a spurt of annoyance at the lewd suggestion, but he quickly stifled it. An explicit, erotic image followed, teasing him with a slender, shapely body all soft and naked and needy in bed. Regardless of her name or game, he wouldn't mind getting more intimate with the body.

For that reason, he avowed sexy Samantha/Phantom off-limits. He prided himself in learning from his mistakes, and the biggest of his life had been getting involved with a female agent. His relationship with Margie had sent up all sorts of red flags, yet he'd arrogantly ignored the warnings. Her death had been an emotional blow he never wanted to repeat.

Foul play or fair, the lovely Phantom had prostituted herself to the scum of the earth. He believed in honor and duty, but not if it meant selling your soul to further your career. Nothing she could do or say would ever erase the facts, and that dropped her desirability to zilch.

Samantha made her way back to Haroldson's side on legs that weren't as steady as she'd have liked. Her heart pounded, her breasts felt full and tight, and her skin was flushed with heat. The intensity of her arousal was unsettling. She didn't appreciate the way her body had come alive in a stranger's arms.

For most of her adult life, she'd existed in sexual limbo, devoid of any burning desire beyond professional duty. She'd met and dated a few men she found attractive, but none who'd made her wild with desire. She'd never been easily aroused, and had resigned herself to the fact that she must somehow be lacking.

The emotional and physical reserve was an advantage to her career, if not her personal life. Now, all of a sudden and at the worst possible time, she'd experienced the hots for a total stranger. It had to be the mental strain and incredible tension of the situation, she decided, shaking her head.

She reached Gregory's side, and he pulled her hand through the crook of his arm. His touch was cold compared to the masculine heat she'd just experienced. She repressed a shiver of revulsion.

A head taller than her, Haroldson was trim and fit, his spine ramrod straight. He had handsome, aristocratic features with dark brown eyes. His personal hairstylist made sure the color of his hair stayed the same dark brown, so that he looked younger than his sixty years.

His expression was affectionate and approving. She gave him a practiced smile that hid her true feelings. It wouldn't do for him to know how much she despised him, from his polished good looks to his ugly black soul. When they'd first met, it was all she could do to keep from recoiling at his touch, but she'd hardened herself to that emotional weakness.

The past few months had been an ongoing nightmare. The only thing that kept her sane was the knowledge that it would be over soon. Haroldson had destroyed her family, and now she had the evidence to prove it.

She forced herself to slip back into the role of fiancée and hostess. She'd made it her life's work to bring him to justice, but the only way to do that had been to get close, really close. It meant drawing on incredible reserves of strength, and it got more difficult each day, but she'd worked too long and hard to fail now.

"What did you think of the new guy?" he asked.

"He seems nice enough. A little lacking in personality, perhaps, but pleasant. Is he a good driver?"

"Nearly as good as Damon."

"In that case, you should have Damon driving for you again. You're on the road more than I am. If the new man is good, I'm sure I'll be safe with him."

Gregory patted her hand. "Your wish is my command," he insisted. "You'll be perfectly safe with Tony. He knows that I'm fanatic about my future wife's welfare."

She smiled, forcing her expression into one of

warmth and gratitude. It was imperative that she keep up appearances. He thought her a well-bred, sophisticated socialite, so that's what she'd become for the past few months.

He'd proposed to her in an effort to garner more respect. For Gregory, image was everything. Respect was a living, breathing entity. He'd spent a lifetime accumulating wealth and power in hopes that it would buy him the respect he so badly craved.

That's why he'd decided to pursue a partnership with one of North Carolina's oldest and most reputable import-export companies. He wasn't satisfied with ruling his own small empire. He wanted to prove his respectability to the whole community.

As a prominent banker, he was welcomed into many social circles but he wanted a foot in the door of the most elite. He'd been advised to marry someone who'd be an asset to his home and social life. That's where she'd stepped into the scene.

He boasted that he was a hardworking man who'd realized the American dream. The story he gave the media was one of rags to riches: a life so dedicated to work that he'd had no time for personal relationships. In reality, his wealth stemmed from a lifetime of carefully coordinated crimes. He owned several offshore banks where he laundered drug money and practiced tax evasion.

But that wasn't why she wanted to bring him down. He had far greater sins to answer for. One was the murder of an undercover FBI agent. Another was the slaughter of a small, law-abiding family. Hers. She had put her life on the line to bring him to justice. And when she did, maybe, just maybe, she could shed a heavy burden of guilt that never seemed to ease.

Another glance at Gregory sent a shiver down her spine. She wondered, yet again, whether he was somehow aware of her double life.

## Chapter 2

Three days after the party, Kyle got orders to drive Samantha to a beauty salon in Elizabeth City. He deliberately thought of her by her alias to distance himself from the woman behind the facade. Every time his fantasies drifted toward the feel of her in his arms, he quickly slammed the door on his memory.

She preferred to travel in a Mercedes, and he had no complaints. It handled like a dream, and had plenty of power plus bulletproof windows. He hoped her escape plan didn't include a shoot-out, but he wanted to be prepared for any eventuality.

Rudy, one of Haroldson's most trusted bodyguards, accompanied them. Big and muscular, he looked like a brainless bull moose, but looks were deceiving. He moved faster than a jackrabbit and was nobody's fool. His responsibilities included escorting Samantha into the salon and waiting there while she had her hair styled. Haroldson was notoriously protective of all his possessions, especially his fiancée.

Kyle waited in the car, surveying the area for any sign of other guards on Haroldson's payroll. Security had tightened in the past few days, making him wonder if their assignment had been compromised. He sensed that Samantha would make her move soon. He expected her to enact her plan in the dark of night, not the middle of a bright summer day, but he wouldn't be caught off guard again.

An hour after entering the salon, she exited, looking every inch the pampered socialite. Her jeans were designer tight, accenting rounded hips and long legs. She wore red again, this time a full-sleeved blouse, unbuttoned down the front to display a white knit top that hugged soft, full breasts.

Despite the casual wear, there were diamonds at her throat, on her wrists and fingers. The brilliant sunshine caused them to shoot sparks in every direction. The only difference he noticed in her personal appearance was a fuller hairstyle. As well as a purse that was big enough to pass for a suitcase, she also carried a shopping bag with the salon's name on it.

A ripple of masculine interest spread through Kyle as he watched her slow, graceful movements. He felt a punch in the gut when she smiled at her escort, but he swiftly stifled the reaction.

Rudy followed a few steps behind her. He opened the back door of the car and held it, while she took a seat, filling the car's interior with her unique, expensive scent. Then he closed the door, opened the front passenger door and settled in the seat beside Kyle.

"Where to? Back to the house?" he asked, glancing at Samantha in the rearview mirror.

"I need to go to Anderson's Jewelers and have the safety catch on my bracelet checked. Do you know where it's located?"

Kyle had spent his spare time learning his way around the city. He knew every alley, intersection and parking lot, but not every business.

"What's the address?"

"It's out near the strip mall," offered Rudy.

"The south side of town," she added.

Bingo. So this was it. Her side trip would take them to the edge of the city, close to the freeway interchange. The safe house was to their northwest, but it would be smarter to head south, and then change directions once they were sure they weren't being followed.

Showing no reaction, Kyle nodded and put the car in gear. His muscles tightened, tension slowly coiling in him as he tried to anticipate how she'd neutralize Rudy. The big man wouldn't be easy to handle.

He waited, alert, as she started rustling through the shopping bag.

"Paulo gave me some samples from his exclusive new perfume line," she told them chattily. "I can't decide which one I like best, so I need a masculine opinion."

The high seat backs and headrests prevented the men from having a clear view of her, but they heard the *hiss* of an atomizer. Then her hand reached between the headrests. She put a tissue near Rudy's face and let him inhale the perfume.

"This one's called Ambrosia," she said, shifting the tissue toward Kyle so he could get a whiff before she withdrew it.

He heard her spraying another sample, then another

tissue was held toward Rudy's nose. "Now this one is called Sweet Nectar. It has more of a fruity scent, don't you agree? I'm not sure I want to smell like fruit. What do you think?"

Rudy mumbled a vague reply.

Damn. She was good. Kyle hid a grin as he obediently sniffed at the second sample she held near his face. Haroldson's henchman wouldn't know what hit him when she finally made her move.

They heard the spray of another atomizer, and she was reaching around the seat again. Then she slapped an ether-soaked cloth over Rudy's face, holding it tightly with both hands. He grabbed at her wrists, but she'd locked his head in a vice between her hands and the headrest. The bodyguard struggled briefly before realizing he couldn't break her hold, then he reached for the beeper at his belt.

Kyle grabbed his wrist and held tight until the big man sagged into unconsciousness. Then he hit the window button to let some fresh air into the car so the ether wouldn't affect them.

"So which do you like best?" She continued the charade in case the car was bugged. Then she slithered over the seat and slid between him and Rudy. The action had her body bumping against his, her thigh brushing his shoulder and chest. Kyle steeled himself against the feel of her wiggling form.

He offered a noncommittal grunt in response to her question.

"You guys aren't much help with the perfume preferences," she said on a heavy sigh as she shoved Rudy's limp body closer to the door, maintaining a conversational tone. "I guess I'll leave the choice to Gregory. How about some music?"

Kyle switched on the radio and cranked the volume to cover their conversation.

"What next?" he muttered.

"Anyone tailing us?" Her husky tone had been replaced with a crisp, no-nonsense whisper.

"Damon in a dark green SUV. I can't see who's with him."

"Lose 'em. I want to dump Rudy out of here before the ether wears off."

Considering the bodyguard's size, it wouldn't take more than a few minutes for him to recover. Kyle altered their route and headed for a less congested area of town. Once they'd cleared the heaviest traffic, he had a better view of the car following them. He made a couple of unexpected turns, and Damon started closing the distance between them.

"He's suspicious," she grumbled, dividing her attention between Rudy and the car behind them.

The traffic began to thin out as they reached an industrial park. The area was nearly deserted on Saturday, so Kyle made a sharp turn between two huge warehouses. They were nearing the end of the connecting alley when the SUV came into view again.

For the next few minutes, they wove in and out of alleys, slowly increasing their lead. Then Rudy started to stir.

"Stop in the middle of the next one," said Samantha.

He did as she said, slowing the car enough for her to open the door and nudge Rudy onto the pavement. The big man fell with a *thud* and a grunt. She slammed the door, and Kyle floored the accelerator, peeling rubber, as she settled into the bucket seat.

The plan went like clockwork. They were just pulling out of the alley as Damon was forced to stop for a groggy and stumbling Rudy. The few minutes it took their pursuers to get the extra man into the SUV gave them the time needed to disappear.

Kyle shot out of the complex and turned onto the nearest residential street, and then another, tires squealing. Meeting minimal traffic, he sped up for another few streets, then made a third turn onto a deserted, tree-lined street.

Pulling into the drive of a small ranch-style house, he quickly punched the code of a remote garage door opener. It slid upward, he drove inside, and the door closed to conceal them from the street.

As soon as he'd switched off the ignition, he motioned toward the dusty, nondescript black pickup truck parked next to them in the two-car garage. Samantha grabbed her bags, and they jumped from the car.

"Good plan, Jackson. I was afraid we'd have to elude Gregory's men in his Mercedes."

"No. Too easy for him to track." He'd rented this place to store a getaway vehicle and a few of his personal things. Haroldson would probably track down his car if he had it bugged, but not until they were long gone.

They climbed into the truck. He stripped off his dark shirt, leaving him in a white T-shirt. Then he reached for a baseball cap on the dash, tugged it over his head and hit the ignition.

"Shouldn't we wait a while?"

"Too risky. They've already called for backup, but they won't be looking for a truck with one occupant." He gave her a meaningful glance.

"Got it," she said, sliding to the floor and crouching

out of sight just as Kyle activated the overhead door. He backed the dusty truck from the garage.

Heart racing and adrenaline pumping, he found it hard to control the urge to speed, but he wove back through several residential streets at a sedate pace. As he approached the intersection that led back to the main highway, he spotted the SUV, but it didn't follow as he made the turn.

Within another two miles, they'd reached the freeway ramp leading south. As he paused at the yield sign, he spared a glance for his passenger, and then did a double take. She'd lost the long blond hair, apparently a wig, and now had short, spiky red hair. She'd also shed her blouse for a white knit top and ditched the jewels along with the pampered princess look.

The new look suited her new role.

Their gazes met, and something dangerously sexy arced between them. His muscles clenched as the unwelcome heat curled through his bloodstream. Undercover girl became more fascinating with each layer she revealed.

Her instant frown and the tightening of her jaw convinced him that she didn't appreciate the unexpected attraction.

"Got another ball cap?" she asked, breaking the strained silence. "I'm getting a little cramped down here."

He glanced in the rearview mirror again, then handed her a hat. After donning it, she slowly eased into the passenger seat and fastened her seat belt. Her tone was terse when she spoke.

"Where are we headed?"

"South for a while," he explained, easing into traffic. "Then we'll be turning north toward the safe house in Virginia."

Samantha nodded.

He thought she relaxed a little, but she kept a close watch on the traffic around and behind them for an unexpected tail. After a few minutes of silence, he offered a compliment.

"You handled Rudy like a pro."

Her tone chilled. "I am a pro."

Kyle hid a grin. Touchy. He didn't doubt that the mysterious Phantom was one of the best, but she also had to be insane or inconceivably ambitious to live with a slimeball like Haroldson. What could possibly motivate a beautiful young woman to that extent?

Despite doubts about her mental stability, he was finding her more intriguing by the minute. Which meant, the sooner they parted ways, the better. He didn't want or need involvement with a sexy, lunatic secret agent. He couldn't deny his yearning for uncomplicated feminine companionship, but there was nothing uncomplicated about his current companion.

He'd be glad to have his end of the job finished. A heady sense of freedom rushed through him. In a couple of hours, he could head home to Texas and know he'd done his part in bringing Haroldson to justice. The thought brought a sweet surge of satisfaction.

Samantha withdrew a cell phone from her bag. She punched in a series of numbers. He heard ringing and a pickup. She punched another series of numbers, and then snapped the phone closed.

"Notifying someone?"

"Sullivan. He'll know we're on our way when he gets a coded message from this number."

It pleased him that she had mentioned Sullivan's

name and that the two of them had the operation so
ingeniously coordinated. That meant less chance of
confusion or errors. Fewer risks meant higher achieve-
ment rates.

"So you're the infamous Kyle Tremont?"

He gave her a sharp glance. How had she learned
his name? "You've been in regular contact with Sullivan? Wasn't that risky considering how close Haroldson has you guarded?"

"I haven't talked to him, but I knew he planned to
contact you. He promised me someone who couldn't
be compromised. I've seen your photo in old agency
files and read about a few of your accomplishments. I
don't remember your hair being so dark. Dyed?"

Kyle nodded, a wave of nostalgia tightening his gut.
She was one of them, one of the FBI's elite force of
undercover agents. He'd known a few female officers,
and they had his utmost respect. Margie had worked
twice as hard as a male agent and rarely got the rec-
ognition she deserved. The law-enforcement world was
still a male-dominated profession.

"You shed your blond locks pretty quick. Are you
a natural redhead?"

"No."

She didn't elaborate, which stirred his imagination.
When he realized how curious he was to know more
about her, he abruptly halted the direction of his
thoughts.

She continued. "You earned quite a reputation with
the agency."

"Not all good," he qualified. "I hated the political
games."

"Is that why you quit the agency at the ripe old age
of thirty? You just got fed up with the politics?"

''Partly,'' he said.

''So what made you decide to come out of retirement for this job? Did Sullivan call in markers or do you have a personal vendetta against Gregory?''

Kyle ground his teeth to keep from growling that it was none of her business. Her questions ticked him off, but he supposed she had a right to ask.

''I don't owe Sullivan any favors.''

His passenger wisely didn't pursue the subject. She could believe whatever she wanted, because he didn't plan to offer any details. She didn't need to know about Margie or the guilt that had haunted him for four years.

Margie would have admired Samantha, he thought, his chest going tight. She'd always wanted to do undercover work. When she'd finally gotten her big chance, she'd walked into a trap that had cost her life. The memory made him angry and restless, so he changed the subject.

''Do you have a name besides Phantom or Samantha?'' he asked, studying her profile while she stared out the windshield. ''Is that your real name or is it a top-level security secret?''

She hesitated, glancing his way and then turning her attention forward. It was the first time she'd acted tentative about anything. Kyle found himself wanting her to trust him, yet annoyed that it mattered.

He'd almost given up on an answer when she finally responded. ''You can call me Rianna, if you'd like.''

Rianna. He liked it. It sounded soft and feminine. A little inconsistent with what he knew about her, yet appealing.

''That's a pretty name, but unusual.''

She hesitated another instant, then added, ''My given

name is Marianna, but I've always shortened it in one form or another.''

Not a giant leap of faith, but a baby step. He didn't expect much more. He knew how hard it was for an undercover agent to trust anyone after months of being constantly on guard, when a slip of the tongue could blow your cover and end your life. He didn't know how long Rianna had been hiding behind a phony name and background, but he knew it would take her a while to unwind.

Neither of them was inclined to make small talk, so conversation came to a halt. As the miles passed by, they watched the passing scenery, kept an eye on the traffic behind them and gradually relaxed.

Kyle grew increasingly aware of her scent, the warmth radiating from her body and even the soft, steady sound of her breathing. His senses absorbed everything about her in an intense, disturbing fashion, even while he argued the idiocy of the reaction. He comforted himself with the thought that their forced alliance wouldn't last much longer.

It took them a little over two hours to reach the state border and cross from North Carolina into Virginia. Their destination, a single-story house on the outskirts of Emporia, was easily found. Surrounded by several large bushes and evergreen trees, it sat apart from any neighboring houses.

Kyle turned into the drive, pulled to a stop near the front porch and shut off the engine.

Tension hiked upward a few degrees as they faced a new and unknown territory. He and Rianna both studied their surroundings for a long time before considering it safe to get out of the truck. He reached for her bags, but she halted him.

"Leave them for now."

His gaze held hers for the first time since they'd left Elizabeth City. More tension flashed between them, complicated by a touch of suspicion. Her wary expression didn't surprise him. She wasn't prepared to trust anyone or anything right now. He nodded, understanding the reaction, and climbed from the truck.

Rianna let him lead the way to the front porch. He found the key where he'd been told to look and preceded her inside the house, then stopped.

"Stay put a minute," he said, reaching for the gun he'd tucked in the waistband of his jeans.

She ignored the command and accompanied him as he searched the house, checking each room thoroughly and making sure they were alone.

"Everything looks okay," he said a few minutes later as he slowly replaced his gun. "Sullivan should have gotten your message by now. He'll have a couple of agents here to guard the place in an hour or so. They'll be coming from D.C., so it shouldn't take them long."

"You're not staying?"

Their gazes met, hers slightly accusing. He ignored a brief pang of guilt.

"My part of the plan was to get you out of Haroldson's estate and to this safe house. That's all I agreed to do."

"So you're ready to disappear?"

The antagonism in her tone had him clenching his jaw. "A week of playing lackey to Haroldson is more than any man should have to take," he argued grimly. "As soon as your bodyguards show up, I'm outta here."

Rianna snorted indelicately. "Meantime, I'm

starved,'' she said. ''I think I'll see what kind of food
we have stocked.''

His annoyance vanished at the thought of food. It
had been a long time since breakfast, and a meal now
. would help him avoid making extra stops on his way
home. He decided not to argue.

''Sounds good.''

Kyle followed her to the kitchen and watched while
she rummaged through the refrigerator. He admired the
way her jeans molded the feminine curves of her hips,
thighs and long legs. A man would have to be emas-
culate not to notice how well she was put together, but
that's as far as his interest went.

He quickly redirected his attention. Moving to the
window, he surveyed the backyard for as far as he
could see. The house was secluded; there was no sign
of neighbors and everything was quiet.

''Are you eating?'' asked Rianna.

''Sure.''

He turned back and helped her get the food on the
table. They put together some sandwiches, opened a
bag of potato chips and ate in silence. Kyle studied her
as he chewed, familiarizing himself with her new punk
look. It suited her oval face and delicate features as
well as the seductive blonde image. He wasn't sure
which he preferred.

It seemed Phantom was a chameleon, as well.

''Do you mind if I ask what you do now that you're
not with the agency any longer? Do you still live and
work in D.C.?''

He'd never been comfortable discussing his personal
life, but he didn't see the harm in small talk. ''I moved
out west a few years ago.''

''You still work in law enforcement?''

"No, I'm just a private citizen who minds his own business."

Her brow creased in a frown, and he realized how censorious his comment sounded. She abruptly stopped asking questions and grew quiet, which should have pleased him, but perversely didn't. They finished their meal in silence, and then worked together to clean the kitchen.

After they had taken turns in the bathroom, he switched on the TV in the living room while Rianna paced around the house, checking the contents of cupboards and closets.

She had just stopped her restless prowling and joined him, when a knock at the front door startled them.

"Stay out of sight," he told her, heading toward the front of the house while she headed toward the back.

A glance through the peephole showed two familiar faces, Dan Hoskins and Ted Blaine, both experienced agents he recognized from his days at the bureau. Tucking his gun back in his jeans, he opened the door. They shook hands and exchanged greetings, then he lead the way back to the kitchen.

They found it empty. Kyle glanced at the door, then toward the window, annoyed and confused until noises from the bathroom helped him pinpoint Rianna's location. He heard the toilet flush, some clinking of the toilet tank, and then she called to him for assistance.

"Kyle, could you help me again? This toilet still isn't flushing right."

He had no idea what she was talking about, but he decided to find out. "You guys help yourselves to some lunch. I'll be right back," he said, walking down the short hallway to the bathroom.

To his surprise, his reluctant charge was slipping

backward out the narrow window. She spared him a fierce glance, jerked her head toward the front of the house and disappeared.

He flushed the toilet again, stalling for time and making more noise to cover her actions. Then he followed her out the window, feetfirst. It was a tight squeeze, and he muffled a grunt as he hit the ground. By the time he'd rounded the corner of the house, she was flattening the tires of the agency's sedan with a pocketknife.

"Let's go," she said in a terse whisper, climbing into the truck and quietly closing the door.

"What the hell?" Kyle demanded, but he didn't hesitate to follow her lead. All he could do was trust her instincts until he knew what had spooked her.

"The guy who called you a renegade retiree."

"Blaine?"

"I don't know his name, but I recognized his voice. I've heard it on Gregory's private phone."

"Sonofabitch!" Kyle's hoarse oath echoed in the cab as he hit the ignition. His first instinct was to confront Blaine; to beat some answers out of the rotten, low-down traitor. Personal need warred with common sense. As much as he wanted to grill the other man for answers, he had to consider Rianna's safety first.

There was nothing lower than a cop on the take. How long had Blaine been on Haroldson's payroll? How long had the man been dirty? Long enough to have orchestrated Margie's disappearance and death? Kyle ground his teeth in frustration, clenching the steering wheel and slamming the truck into gear while mentally vowing to get some long-overdue answers.

They heard shouts behind them as they sped down the street, but lost sight of the house when they turned at the next intersection. They were both too busy checking for other threats to worry about the stranded agents.

Sure enough, the green SUV pulled from the curb as soon as they hit the connecting street. Kyle pushed the accelerator to the floor.

"Damon and Rudy."

"I saw them," she said grimly, pulling a semiautomatic out of her bag. It looked big and heavy in her small palm, but she handled it skillfully, checking the load and flipping the safety.

When they turned onto a nearly deserted, straight stretch of road, she opened the passenger window. "Swerve to the right."

"And give them a clear shot at you? Hell, no."

"Give me a clear shot at them."

"You're a better marksman?"

"I'm good. Now, swerve."

Kyle did as she asked, veering the truck to the right so she could have a straight shot at the SUV gaining on them. He heard her squeeze off four successive shots, then she swung back into the cab and stayed low.

There was no return fire.

He steadied the truck again, changed lanes, then glanced in the rearview mirror. One of her shots had shattered the windshield of the SUV, but Damon hadn't slowed his pursuit. Kyle knew how skilled he was at the wheel.

"Haroldson wants you alive."

"For a while, at least," she agreed. "He always has a master plan and his own agenda."

They hit the green light at the next intersection and turned into heavy, two-lane traffic. Another look in the mirror showed Damon running a red light, but steam was starting to roll from beneath the hood of the SUV.

"Did you puncture their radiator?"

"That's where I aimed," she said, lifting her head long enough to check behind them. "I figured it would be the fastest way to disable the car."

"You're right."

Within a few minutes, the tailing vehicle was engulfed in a cloud of steam.

"They'll have to slow down now."

Kyle took advantage of the pursuing vehicle's problems and wove in and out of rush-hour traffic until he'd put a good distance between them and other pursuers. After traveling several more miles, he thought they'd probably lost the SUV. He turned his attention to his passenger again.

"What now?"

"I have a contingency plan."

"Glad to hear it." His tone and expression were harsh. "Care to fill me in?"

Rianna didn't respond right away, but she eased herself upright and faced forward, pulling her seat belt around her. "If we get on the interstate and head south, I know a small town where we can stop over and switch vehicles again."

"Another safe house?"

Her lips tightened. "At this point, I'm not trusting my life to the agency. I'll find my own safe place and then make new arrangements with Sullivan."

"And what do you figure my role will be in your alternative plan?" he grumbled, his hopes of a speedy return to Texas fading fast.

Tension sizzled in the silence that followed. They both knew he didn't want any further involvement, but he'd promised Sullivan to keep her safe until she had adequate protection. He didn't make idle promises, and this one had just taken on a whole new perspective.

"That's up to you," she said. "You can drop me off in Hendersonville or you can accompany me to my destination."

"Which is?"

"Ultimately, Kentucky."

"What's in Kentucky?"

"It's not what's there, but who and what *aren't* there."

"Haroldson and the strong arms of his organization?"

"Right."

Kyle had little alternative but to follow her plan of action. It grated that he'd been so close to making his solitary getaway, but he couldn't just dump her alongside the road. He'd have to stick with her until alternative plans could be coordinated with Sullivan.

Reining his frustration, he focused his thoughts on Blaine, mentally reexamining every aspect of the agent's participation in Margie's last assignment. Not for the first time, he wished he knew more about what went wrong that day. The lack of details was a constant thorn in his side.

They drove through the late afternoon with minimal conversation, each lost in thought. Much to his annoyance, Kyle grew increasingly aware of his sexy, enigmatic companion. He became attuned to every subtle move she made; his nerves jangling when any part of her shifted closer to him.

They passed a car with a kid mushing his face against the window, and Rianna chuckled softly. The sound punched him in the gut, making him feel things that weren't safe to feel.

Despite his fundamental longing for a woman, he knew better than to get physically or emotionally tangled with this one. She was trouble with a capital *T*. She represented everything he knew he should avoid— federal bureaucracy, undercover activities and Gregory Haroldson's criminal dealings.

And she was another man's lover. The circumstances were strange, to be sure, but that still made her off-limits. He tried not to focus on her quiet, undemanding presence or wonder what she was thinking and feeling.

To keep his thoughts off his hormones and his companion, Kyle replayed the events of the day over and over in his mind.

He wondered if Hoskins was as dirty as Blaine. They'd seemed surprised to see him at the safe house, so Sullivan must have kept his involvement a secret.

How much of the agency's security had been compromised? Blaine had been an agent for years. How much money did it take to buy a man's soul? How much to make him betray his comrades or sign death warrants for co-workers?

How widespread was the corruption? He wanted a few words with Sullivan, but didn't want to make contact through the agency. He'd wait and call his home number later. It was long past the time for some answers.

Frustrated with his own thoughts, Kyle's attention turned to Rianna. She lifted a hand to rub the back of her neck, the first small indication of weariness. She had to be exhausted, yet she hadn't uttered a word of complaint.

In profile, she looked deceptively young and innocent. Her lashes had a pretty, feminine sweep of curl. The soft curve of her cheek made her look almost delicate when you couldn't see the stubborn set of her chin or the iron determination in her eyes.

She was a paradox, to be sure, one that challenged him more than any woman had done for several years now. Off-limits, he reminded himself sternly, turning his gaze back to the road.

# Chapter 3

They reached Hendersonville just as the sun was setting. Rianna gave him directions to a small, private storage unit. Once there, she produced a key to unlock one of the garage stalls. He lifted the overhead door and triggered an automatic light switch. They did a quick check of the space, and then she climbed into a small car and started the engine. Kyle stepped aside while she backed out of the narrow space.

Now it was decision time. He could either send her on her way alone or break his self-made promise not to get more deeply involved. Even as he cursed his own streak of chivalry, he knew there really wasn't any choice. Call him a chauvinist and a fool, but he couldn't desert her while she was being hunted by the likes of Haroldson. Despite his disapproval of her methods, she was trying to bring the other man to justice.

As soon as she'd cleared the building, he hopped

into the truck and drove it into the storage unit. After grabbing their bags, he pulled the door back down and secured it. He'd planned to drive the rental back to Texas, but he'd have to take care of it later. Now it could be recognized.

When Rianna approached to relock the storage unit, their gazes tangled and awareness crackled between them. Her expression softened with gratitude. The slight chink in her tough-guy armor stabbed him with unreasonable pleasure, but he stiffened himself against the emotion.

"I promised Sullivan I'd stick with you until you were safe," he said, making light of his decision.

She nodded, accepting without comment. When she moved close enough to grab her bag from him, every hair on his body reacted to her warmth and scent. He clenched his fists to keep from touching her, and searched for something to break the tension.

Turning, he took a good look at their new transportation. Then he swore. "Pink? You expect us to hide in a pink car?"

"It's mauve," she insisted. "And it's perfect. Who'd ever believe we were on the run in a mauve economy car?"

He grumbled, but couldn't argue the logic. Neither Haroldson nor the FBI would be searching for a compact sedan.

"I'll drive," she said as she headed for the driver's side and stowed her bag in the back seat. "You have to be getting tired, and I'm used to driving in the mountains."

He didn't argue, just moved to the passenger side and threw his bag in beside hers. The space was cramped, the bucket seat small, but he slid it back as far as it would go and strapped himself in. She did the same, and they were on their way again.

Hendersonville was little more than a crossroads with a couple of streetlights. Traffic was minimal. They found a convenience store, made use of the bathrooms and filled a thermos with coffee.

Rianna bought a variety of supplies, making him wonder where she planned to take them. Another safe house? A rental? The home of a friend or family member? He hoped it was someplace he could safely leave her and head back to Texas with a clear conscience.

She stood by while he used a pay phone to call Sullivan's private number. There was no answer, so he left a short, terse message on the answering machine: ''Blaine's your mole. We're on the run, but we lost our tail and Phantom is okay.''

Though rarely comfortable with another driver, Kyle climbed into the passenger seat, and Rianna drove back onto the highway. He remained tense for the first few miles, but soon realized that she could handle the car with the same ease she did everything else. Was there no end to her talents? He relaxed a little, deciding to pry some information out of his cohort.

''Sullivan told me you were in deep, but he didn't hint at how deep. My reaction to your identity could have gotten us both killed.''

''Rookie mistake,'' she taunted.

The barb stung, but Kyle knew he deserved it. ''Retiree mistake,'' he corrected sharply.

''Whatever.''

Her voice held a teasing note, making him wonder if superwoman might have a sense of humor.

''How'd you manage a marriage proposal?''

She hesitated briefly, but then explained. ''Gregory

wants legitimacy and the image of a normal, healthy lifestyle. I played the part of an impoverished but highly eligible socialite with a pedigreed background.''

''The perfect bait?''

Her features tightened mutinously, making him realize how disparaging his tone had sounded.

''It worked.''

The succinct reply held a touch of hurt and made him feel like a heel. He cursed himself for not being more diplomatic. She'd been under a tremendous amount of strain, yet it bugged him to think of any woman offering herself as bait to a man with so few scruples. Her deception would be all the more personal and galling to an egomaniac like Haroldson.

Was she a total rebel? Some power-hungry female who enjoyed living on the edge? A lunatic who thrived on danger? Hadn't she realized she'd be flirting with certain death if he ever got his hands on her again?

A mental image of Haroldson touching her made Kyle grind his teeth. He didn't want his protective instincts roused, yet she kept getting under his skin.

He had to ask. ''Why did you move in with the guy?''

''I had to have unlimited access to the estate without him watching my every move. I tried for weeks while we were dating, but finally decided there was no other way.''

Kyle made an effort to sound curious rather than accusing. ''So why you? Why would any woman put herself in such a dangerous, compromising situation? Just to prove yourself with the agency?''

The silence stretched until he thought he'd pushed too far. Finally, she responded in a tight voice.

''We all have our crosses to bear, Tremont. I have

my reasons, but they have nothing to do with proving myself or advancing my career. I can't be bought, and I'm not motivated by greed or glory, so that's all you need to know.''

He cursed the fact that her passionate response only served to make him more curious.

''How about a change of subject,'' he suggested.

''Okay by me,'' said Rianna. ''Why don't you tell me about yourself. Where's home for you now? That's not classified information, is it?''

''Far from it.'' He remembered how well-informed Sullivan had seemed about his current lifestyle. ''I live in Texas, not too far from El Paso.''

The small bit of casually supplied personal information caused a slight relaxing of her rigid posture. Her shoulders sagged a little, and he wondered how she was handling the unrelenting stress.

''I've always been curious about Texas but I've never been there,''. she said, then asked tentatively, ''Is that where you grew up?''

''I grew up everywhere. I was a military brat.''

The urge to see her at ease had him offering details about his private life. ''Both my folks were Air Force officers. We moved around a lot, but I spent my early years and most of my summer vacations with Granddad Tremont in Texas. He was a craftsman. I inherited his knack for working with wood, and his home. I moved back there when I retired from Uncle Sam's employ.''

His granddad had also been a decorated Second World War veteran. From the time Kyle was old enough to listen, he'd heard tales of the war, the cost of freedom, and a man's duty to serve his country. They'd watched old movies and cheered when justice triumphed over evil. He'd hung on every word of his granddad's lectures, vowing to live by the same high principles. He'd taken it all to heart—but it had nearly cost him his soul.

"Did your parents retire to Texas, too?" she asked.

Her tone sounded wistful, and he studied her profile. What did her family think of her career? Maybe she didn't have anyone. That might explain why she'd been willing to risk her life for a job.

"Dad died about four years ago, and Mom remarried. She and her new husband are stationed in Germany right now."

"Sounds like she's really dedicated to the service."

"Yep, that's how I was raised. Everything's right or wrong, black or white, with no in-betweens. That's why I got fed up with the FBI."

"Too many shades of gray?" she asked in a tone that suggested she really understood.

"Yeah, way too much gray."

They were quiet for a few miles, each lost in thought, and then she spoke again. "Donald said you left because you lost a partner and blamed the agency. Is that true?"

Kyle stared out the window, watching the scenery flash past as his memories fixed on Margie. She'd been more than a partner. So much more. Impotent rage still churned in him when he dwelled on the unfairness of her death.

"Margie went undercover while I was on leave for Dad's funeral. She went in alone, but with standard backup from the agency. She understood the risks."

Logically, Kyle knew he might not have been able to save Margie, but emotionally, he still felt responsible for not being there for his lover and friend. After years of trying, he'd finally realized he couldn't be content until the man responsible for her death was brought to justice.

Rianna broached her next question softly and cautiously. "The records suggest that she might have turned bad."

"That's a filthy lie!" Kyle snarled, making her jump and go tense again.

He tempered his next words, but they still quivered with underlying fury. "That's what pisses me off the most. An agent gives her life for her country, and what does she get in return? A damn blight on her record? Rumors that she was on the take? That's why I hate the freakin' politics. The FBI lost an agent, so they try to save face by suggesting she's the one at fault!"

A thick silence fell in the car, but the unbridled strength of his emotion pulsed between them, intimately binding them in its intensity. Kyle took a deep breath, uncurled the fingers he'd fisted, and forced himself to relax again. It was futile to give in to the long-simmering frustration.

His loss of control unnerved him and made him realize he was bone-tired. Otherwise, he wouldn't be wasting time and energy on useless venting.

Rianna spared him a glance. "That's the gray part you hated so much?" she asked quietly.

"Enough to make me call it quits."

She nodded, and something about the small, supportive action clutched at his gut. It had been a long time since anyone had really cared or understood his feelings. He needed to shut her out before she had a chance to undermine all his good intentions.

"I think I'll take a nap."

Rianna kept her attention on the winding, mountainous road, but stayed alert to every move and sound her passenger made. Tremont reclined his seat, stretched out his legs and crossed his arms over his chest. Finally, he settled his long, lean body in the tight confines.

The tension in the car eased along with him, like the cleansed calm after a storm.

"Sure you're all right to drive?" he asked, tipping the bill of his hat over his face.

"Positive," she said, still too wired to relax. "I rested earlier."

"It's been thirty-six hours for me. I could use some shut-eye."

"I imagine you could. Will it bother you if I listen to cassettes?" Music was one of her greatest passions, probably because it was a continual, no-risk pleasure that warded off loneliness. "Our radio reception won't be very reliable for a while."

"Music doesn't bother me unless it's that rap stuff."

"No rap or heavy metal, I promise."

"Glad to hear it."

There was just a hint of teasing in his tone. It surprised and warmed her, so she responded in kind. "Then, go to sleep. If I get drowsy, I'll wake you."

"Do that."

His comment sounded more like a command. Rianna shook her head, but didn't respond. Men, she thought, they always want to be the ones in charge. She recognized and could tolerate the attitude as long as it suited her purposes.

A half-hour outside of Hendersonville, she heard his breathing turn slow and steady. The sound of his soft snoring was strangely comforting, which worried her.

It made her wonder at her own reactions to the FBI legend.

She'd been shocked by her physical response during the brief moments she'd spent in his arms on the dance floor. She'd held her own emotions under rigid control for so long that she'd begun to feel like a zombie. The sting of attraction had been so alien that she almost hadn't recognized it. Now that she had, it had become an unwelcome complication.

Being cooped up in their current tight quarters stirred her senses again. Heat radiated from Tremont, enveloping her. His sheer size and stature tugged at something elementally feminine in her, something she couldn't quite analyze.

Maybe a compact car wasn't such a good idea, but she hadn't given a thought to prospective passengers when she'd bought it. She'd always been something of a recluse, and her lifestyle didn't allow much time for men or long-term relationships. Her greatest strength was the ability to function in any given situation while maintaining emotional distance—protected in her own insular little world.

So why was she having such a strong reaction to this man?

His service record had fascinated her from the beginning—dedication to duty coupled with a renegade personality. He'd been both praised and damned by his peers, but his devotion to job and country had never been in doubt. The fact that Donald Sullivan trusted him implicitly was testimony enough to his integrity.

That didn't mean she fully trusted him. She'd been alone for too many years, fiercely independent, working toward one goal with steadfast, obsessive determination.

Did she find Tremont attractive because he represented an end to her self-imposed isolation? The light at the end of the long, dark tunnel? Or because he represented all that she'd given up to accomplish her goal?

She was twenty-eight and had bypassed the usual coming-of-age flirtations—the dating games and variety of partners most people took for granted. She'd never trusted any man with her heart or her body, and didn't plan to start now.

As a teenager, she'd had a serious crush on an upperclassman. Her family had been in the witness protection program because her dad testified against his former boss, Gregory Haroldson. They had feared their location had been compromised and wanted to move, but she'd begged to stay for the high school prom. It had cost her mom, dad and brother their lives. Since then, she hadn't let anyone get too close, nor had she let anyone interfere with her quest for justice.

To Gregory, she'd been a possession, a means to an end, just another collector's item. She'd told him she wouldn't have sex until they were married. It had been a condition of their engagement, and he'd agreed. He had other women, but they were more than welcome to his amorous advances.

Men like Tremont—handsome, smart and reeking of sex appeal—usually had a bevy of women vying for attention. He could even have a wife or lover or significant other. She glanced at his left hand. He didn't wear a wedding ring, but that could be for any number of reasons. Why hadn't she thought to ask when he'd been talking about his family?

It annoyed her that she'd missed the opportunity to pry some more. He'd been unexpectedly forthcoming

about his parents, his dead partner, and his grievance
with the agency. His exhaustion had probably contrib-
uted to his candor, but it wouldn't hurt to give it another try when he woke.

Rianna gazed into the unending darkness of the
mountains, broken only by her headlights and an infre-
quent passing car. For the most part, the skies were
cloudy with random glimpses of a star-studded sky.
The slivered moon did little to illuminate the winding,
ascending road.

She didn't mind the darkness. Her thoughts were
equally dark. Over the next couple hours, she reviewed
the past six months in her mind—the conversations
she'd overheard, the records she'd unearthed and the
security she'd breached. With her testimony, they could
put Gregory Haroldson behind bars for the rest of his
life.

It had taken every ounce of courage she possessed
and a strength born of necessity to carry out the assignment. Pretending to accept his proposal and moving into his home had taken nerves of steel, but she'd
sworn to make him pay for destroying her family. That
pledge had seen her through the worst of it.

In her mind's eye, she projected the image of her
mother, dad and brother. It was a vision that comforted
her in times of extreme stress. They'd been the axis of
her world until Gregory Haroldson had ordered their
deaths. If she'd been a little stronger, a little wiser, or
a better person, she could have prevented what happened. The knowledge ate at her like a disease. The
only way she knew to counteract the guilt was to make
Haroldson pay for his crimes.

No jury in the country would fault her for the engagement deception. Not once they heard the whole

truth. She and Donald were banking on that fact. There was no way their undercover operation could be labeled entrapment. Haroldson's corruption dated back too many years to afford him that defense.

*We have him. We have him. We have him.* The litany ran through her mind like the constant spinning of the car's wheels. *We have him. We have him.*

When Rianna realized she was becoming mesmerized by the sound of her thoughts, she reached out and touched Tremont's arm. Heat and muscle. The warmth of another human being. The comfort it offered unnerved her a little because it was so unexpected. It was a pleasure she rarely enjoyed with anyone but her adoptive parents. The contact soothed her, subduing the painful turbulence of her memories.

Her passenger stirred, tilted his hat back and glanced up at her. She watched him in her peripheral vision, feeling her own body come awake with tingling alertness as he uncoiled his arms and straightened in his seat.

They'd reached the peak of the mountains, shrouded in late-night fog. She dimmed her lights to cut through the haze, and then spoke to Tremont.

"There's a roadside rest area a few miles ahead. I thought we might get out, take a break and stretch our legs. I'm starting to get numb."

"Sounds good," he mumbled.

His voice was so low and husky and incredibly sexy that it snapped her senses to alertness. A tremor of reaction tingled along her spine. It was a quick fix to her lethargy.

"Any of that coffee left?"

"About a cupful, but it's only lukewarm." She

handed him the thermos, then wrapped her fingers around the steering wheel.

"I want to try and reach Donald again if the pay phone's working at the rest area." She'd already decided to call, but threw out the comment for conversation's sake.

"I don't mind waking him in the middle of the night. I hope he's sound asleep. I owe him one." After all, Sullivan had called him at four a.m. to request his help.

"Even if someone traces the call, there's no way to pinpoint our exact location," she expanded. "Once we clear the mountains, we could go in any direction."

"Do you have a specific destination in Kentucky or is it just an unlikely spot for someone to find?"

Rianna deliberated, but then decided to trust him even further. "I'm familiar with the Cumberland Lake area, so that's where I'm headed."

"A resort lake?"

"Miles and miles of man-made lake. It's all buried in a deep valley between jagged, boulder-lined hills topped with a thick wall of evergreen trees."

"A nice place to get lost?"

"That's what I'm hoping." She wanted nothing more than to disappear, to fade into the background after months of constantly being in the spotlight and on display.

The rest area was nearly deserted as they pulled to a stop in the parking lot. Rianna climbed from the car, grabbed her bag and headed for the rest room with Tremont close beside her. They parted ways inside the utilitarian concrete structure.

She used the toilet in the women's room, splashed water on her face at the sink, brushed her teeth and restored some order to her hair. It took a while, but she managed to tame some of the spiky tufts of the punk hairstyle. The result wasn't very flattering, but it was a whole lot less noticeable. The last thing she wanted to do at this point was draw attention to herself.

Feeling more human, she rejoined Tremont near the pay phone. He'd freshened up, too. His hair was damp and a shade lighter, evidence of his attempt to wash out the dye. He'd shaved off the mustache, which drastically changed his looks. Rianna's admiring gaze traced the smooth curve of his lips. A firm, sexy mouth, she thought, before quickly redirecting her thoughts.

He'd already dialed the number and was greeting Sullivan when she stepped closer. Their gazes met, and she was taken aback by the crystal-clear blue of his eyes. He'd shed the dark contacts, altering his looks even more. The clarity of his steady gaze caused her to shiver. It felt as though he could see right into her soul, and she knew it wasn't a very pure place.

Tremont turned the receiver so that they could both hear.

"I got your earlier message," said Sullivan. "But Blaine's dead. Killed by Hoskins. According to him, Blaine pulled a weapon and tried to shoot at you when you left the safe house. They scuffled over the gun and Blaine was fatally shot."

Kyle and Rianna exchanged frowning glances, neither sure what the latest twist could mean.

"You'll be watching Hoskins?"

"For sure, and we'll do some serious checking on Blaine's record. I'll personally interrogate everyone he's worked with."

"When are you having Haroldson arrested?" asked Tremont.

"First thing Monday morning, but there's a glitch.

His lawyers will demand he be released on bail, and there's a good chance we won't be able to keep him long.''

"What about his flight risk?" insisted Rianna, her heart sinking at the word *glitch*. Gregory wouldn't want to leave his little empire or the U.S., but once he realized how damning the evidence was against him, he had the money and connections to disappear. "I thought once we had him jailed, we could keep him there indefinitely.''

"I did, too, but as soon as you disappeared today, he made a public announcement that you'd been kidnapped. He's conducting a media circus, featuring himself as the devastated fiancé who's bravely coping with a great tragedy.''

The information had Kyle and her staring at each other in disbelief.

"So that's his master plan," she whispered. "He wants the world to believe I've been kidnapped. That way he gains a lot of sympathy without having to deal with me himself.''

"He also gains the means to get us permanently out of his hair," Tremont added grimly. "That's why it was so easy. He's been playing us all along. If we turn up dead, he'll have an alibi, someone to blame for your murder. Then, if I'm conveniently killed by one of his men, the murder will seem justified.''

"You're probably right, but that won't help him against the indictment," said Sullivan.

"He's not aware of that yet," she reminded. "We're still the only ones with access to that information, aren't we?''

"Yes, and that has to stay a secret until I get the arrest and search warrants. If not, there's a risk of him fleeing. Meanwhile, he's playing the media for all it's worth. I'll have to publicly acknowledge your identity or risk having a judge release him on bail,'' explained Sullivan.

''How bad's the risk for Phantom if you expose her identity?'' Tremont asked. ''Haroldson must know she's a federal agent by now.''

''Even if he does, it won't keep him from putting a contract out on both of you. Her disappearance threatens her standing with the bureau, since we don't have her in protective custody. If I can't verify her whereabouts, that leaves us without a witness who can support the indictment.''

''You're suggesting we come to D.C.?''

''Are you staying with her?''

''I said I would.''

Tremont's tone was getting harsher by the minute. Rianna studied his fierce expression and wondered what concerned him most—the risk to her safety, the risk of weakening their case or the thought of prolonging his own involvement. It worried her that she was beginning to care about his motives.

Sullivan took his time answering. ''No. I'll swear I know where she's being held. You two disappear for a few days until we see how this is going to play out. Keep in touch with me through this number. If I'm forced to produce a witness, we'll worry about additional security then.''

They ended the call and Tremont replaced the receiver. Only then did Rianna realize how close the two of them were standing. Her right shoulder and arm were pressed against his chest, the heat of him permeating the thin layers of her clothes. It seemed so natural, yet disturbing. She had an unprecedented urge to press closer, and that wouldn't do at all.

Once they stepped apart, she felt a chill and shivered.

"You're cold. We need to get back in the car," he insisted, and surprised her by wrapping an arm around her as they moved toward the parking lot.

Her first instinct was to shift from the warmth of his touch. She didn't want to seem weak or needy, but she was cold and tired and trying to ward off an emotional collapse. She'd been warned by bureau psychologists about a dramatic letdown after an undercover assignment.

Maybe she'd be wise to accept a little impersonal support. Just as long as it remained impersonal. So far, she and the renegade retiree were making a pretty good team.

Kyle offered to drive, but Rianna insisted that she'd rather continue until they were through the mountains. She drove while he caught a few more hours of rest. Then they exchanged places, but she still wasn't able to sleep.

They shared a comfortable silence, passing the time listening to music and studying the darkness beyond the windows of the car. Rianna had picked up a map at the rest area, so she navigated them through southern Kentucky. By daybreak, they were nearing their destination.

"Where are we heading now?"

"I think Somerset is one of the largest towns in the lake area," she said. "It's not too big, but it offers the basics. If I remember correctly, there are several docks, and check-in times at the marinas are about the same as most hotels."

"Marina?"

"I'm planning to rent a houseboat if there's one available," she explained, glancing at him and wondering if he was going to bail out on her now. "The lake is huge, so you can disappear for days at a time without anyone checking up on you."

"You can actually stay out on the water?"

"It's been years since I was there, but I remember cruising around until we needed to refuel. At night, we'd set the anchor near the shoreline and stay put. Either way, you avoid contact with civilization."

"You've vacationed there in the past?"

"Once, a long time ago." The thought made her melancholy, but she tried to shrug it off. "How about you? Are you interested in staying or do you want to head on home? I don't see any possible way I can be traced now, so you don't need to feel obligated."

"I said I'll stick with you until Sullivan makes other arrangements."

"What about your family? Do you need to get home to a wife or kids or a partner of some sort?"

Tremont threw her a rakish grin. "'Partner of some sort'?"

"Partner, as in significant other or anyone who expects you home soon."

"Fishing for more details about my private life?"

The man really could be maddening. Rianna gritted her teeth. "I think it's important that I know the basics," she insisted.

"What you see is what you get," he finally said. "I don't have to account to anyone for my whereabouts. Not even Sullivan, since I already honored my promise to help you escape Haroldson's estate."

"No regular job? Are you one of those independently wealthy men who risks his life for kicks?"

Tremont's gruff chuckle rippled over Rianna like a sweet, sexy melody. Her heart thudded uncharacteristically. She scolded herself for the foolish reaction, realizing how desperately she needed sleep.

"I'm not rich, that's for sure. Unless you count the fact that I own my own little place. I'm self-employed. Nothing out of the ordinary."

No way would Rianna ever consider this man ordinary. He might prefer to think of himself that way, but she couldn't.

"Do you know anything about boating or fishing?"

"Not much."

Neither did she, but they were intelligent, resourceful adults. They could learn.

Conversation lagged as they covered the last hundred miles of their journey. The sun was rising behind them as they reached the outskirts of Somerset.

Their first stop was another convenience store and refueling station. They filled the gas tank and bought souvenir T-shirts. Then they freshened up with a change of shirts to cut the risk of being recognized. They'd drastically changed their looks since leaving the coast, but it didn't hurt to cover every angle.

Next they found a small roadside restaurant and took their time over breakfast and coffee. When the place started to get crowded, they drove into town. Rianna asked Tremont to stop at the local post office.

He stayed in the car while she rented a post office box and bought two padded envelopes. In one, she mailed herself extra cash and a fake driver's license at her personal P.O. box, knowing the post office was the safest place to hide it in case of another emergency.

She used the second envelope to mail all her jewelry to her adoptive aunt Margaret's address in Maine. It was a risk to mail anything so valuable, but the neck-lace, bracelet and rings were all gifts from Gregory. They held no sentimental value. If she ever got a chance to sell them, she'd make good use of the money, but she wouldn't be destitute if the jewelry got damaged or lost.

They spent the next couple of hours driving around the town and familiarizing themselves with the area. When the stores finally opened, they purchased additional clothing, more groceries and a few other necessities.

Rianna found a brochure with information on boat rentals, so she called several marinas until she found one with a recent cancellation. After learning that a houseboat was available immediately, they headed for the lake.

"What's the name of the place?" asked Tremont.

"It's called Beaver Creek Resort, and it's near Monticello. There are several marinas with docks and fuel stations, but the only one with an availability is Beaver Creek. This is the height of their tourist season, so we got lucky. I think they said they have one good-size houseboat for rent."

"What's good-size?"

She showed him the picture in the brochure. "There are several types, each in a different price range with different amenities and the capacity to sleep a different number of people. I guess ours is over sixty feet long.

"According to the brochure, it features a galley with a gas stove, refrigerator, running water, generator, central heat, AC, microwave, electric lights, deck furniture, gas grill, swimming ladder, power steering, and a sliding board off the top deck."

Tremont whistled softly. "Sounds like a small yacht, and looks like it must be top of the line."

"Nope, top of the line is a lot bigger, sleeps more people and costs more."

He shot a glance at her. "Which brings up the question of how we're going to pay for this rental. I don't carry around that sort of cash, we can't charge it to Uncle Sam, and we sure can't use plastic."

"I have several thousand dollars' worth of cash with me," she told him, earning herself another, longer, sharper look. "When I moved in with Gregory, he insisted on giving me an allowance and buying me designer clothes. I've been hoarding the money and even selling a few designer gowns."

His laugh wasn't pleasant. "So your lover is paying for our little hideout."

Rianna managed to keep her temper reined, but just barely. "He and all the people he's swindled out of money, including Uncle Sam," she returned succinctly.

The reminder of Haroldson cranked the tension between them again, so they grew silent, speaking only about directions. The road that led to the marina was sharply winding, and they drove downhill at a forty-five-degree angle for more than fifteen minutes before Tremont complained.

"You're sure this dock isn't in China?" he asked, as they kept going downward, mile after mile, in the seemingly endless spiral of a roller coaster.

"I told you the lake was carved out of solid rock. It takes a while to get down to the water."

She hoped the high rock walls would be an added barrier between them and Gregory's far-reaching network of criminals.

## Chapter 4

The marina came into view just as she finished explaining, and she caught her breath at the sight. There were boats in all sizes and shapes. Some were moored while others were coming or going on the water. The whole place was bigger, more modern and a lot more commercial than she remembered, but the overall beauty still held her in awe.

Her heart thudded heavily in her chest as emotion ballooned inside her. She could visualize her parents holding hands, laughing and teasing while her brother chased after them, always skipping and chattering. There hadn't been many happy, carefree times for her family, but they'd shared one wonderful week here.

The precious memories brought a lump to her throat and a rush of rare tears to her eyes. She swiftly blinked them away as Tremont parked the car.

He turned more fully toward her, and Rianna knew

he sensed a change in her. His demeanor underwent a subtle change, too.

She clenched her teeth and turned her head to avoid his probing gaze. She hated feeling so emotionally fragile. The memories were private and cherished, so she kept them carefully guarded in her heart.

"You okay?"

She wanted to allay his concern by responding in a crisp, no-nonsense fashion, but her voice failed her. To cover her awkwardness and give herself more time, she grabbed her bag and searched for a wallet. Once she'd found it, she opened the door and climbed from the car without a word.

Tremont got out of the car and followed her toward the marina. "Better tell me how we're registering," he insisted.

That had her pausing to regroup. She swallowed the last of her silly tears and turned to him. "Think we can get by with separate names and IDs?"

"Sure, it's common practice these days. We don't have to pretend we're married. We can just be lovers," he explained, his eyes challenging her to refute.

The suggestion sent a shiver of awareness over her, but she humphed, pretending the idea was too annoying to consider.

Since she was handling the money, the houseboat was rented under the alias Donna Elise Simons. The normal check-in time wasn't until three p.m., but due to the last-minute cancellation, their boat was ready to be boarded.

They left the car in a hillside parking area and hauled everything onto the boat. A dock attendant gave them a quick tour and basic watercraft instructions. Shortly after noon, they were casting off and making their way toward less congested waters.

Rianna quickly accustomed herself to the hum of the engine and its steady vibration as they glided over water as smooth as glass. The sun shone brightly, making everything sparkle with a freshness that soothed her nerves within minutes.

Tremont settled behind the steering wheel, just inside the combined living room and kitchen area. He wore a short-sleeved blue T-shirt that made his pale eyes look darker and deeper. She alternately admired the beauty all around them and his physique. His shoulders and chest were broad, the strength in his arms apparent as he easily maneuvered the big boat.

His thighs, encased in tight, worn jeans, also contracted with solid muscle. The rest of him was lean and just as appealing. She silently admonished herself for mental drooling and tried to concentrate on the water.

"It really is gorgeous here, isn't it."

"Yeah, and probably one of the last places Haroldson would expect his high-society lover to hide."

"I'm not really, you know," she insisted. At his searching glance, she bit back the words she'd almost blurted in self-defense. Knowing it was safer to let him believe she had the morals of an alley cat, she rephrased her response. "I'm not really a high-society type."

"If you say so," he muttered.

All of a sudden, Rianna felt the strength drain from her limbs. Exhaustion overtook her with unexpected speed and force. She stared blankly at the water, then Tremont.

"Something wrong?" he asked, concern creasing his brows.

"I'm tired."

His laugh sounded more like an abrupt bark. "I'll bet you are. You've been running on nothing but caffeine and nerves for days. Ready to crash?"

"Yes" was all she said. Then she moved toward the sleeping compartments, her feet and limbs feeling like lead. She fell across the first bed she found and dropped off to sleep within seconds.

Kyle spent the rest of the afternoon learning his way around the lake. A map hung above the steering compartment that displayed the overall size and shape of the waterways, but he needed to get his bearings.

Over one hundred miles long, the lake had winding waterways that covered sixty-three thousand surface acres with twelve hundred miles of wooded shoreline.

The entire shoreline was dotted with sandy-beach coves surrounded by twelve-foot-high, boulder-strewn banks. They'd been told that boaters could drop anchor in the coves to picnic, swim or fish during the day and to sleep at night. He liked the idea of being able to find their own private niche.

When hunger and thirst eventually had him stirring from his perch at the helm, he let the boat idle and went to check on Rianna. He found her sprawled, face-down, on one of the double beds. She was down for the count.

The total abandon of her position made his stomach muscles clench. Her slim, pale arms were flung, spread-eagle, across the mattress. A wedge of creamy skin was exposed at the small of her back. Her jeans-clad rump was slightly elevated, and he had an insane urge to crawl into bed and wake her with caresses.

"Whoa, boy."

He issued the soft, urgent warning to his body as blood began to pool in his groin. An unexpected arousal burgeoned against the zipper of his jeans, pulsing to life and sucking the air from his lungs.

Heat crept up his neck as he fought the temptation to slide his body over hers and wake her with greedy hands and mouth. He wanted to explore every dip and curve of her feminine form, and lose himself in her softness. The urge was so primitive and shocking in its force that he shuddered. What the hell had prompted the sudden, intense hunger?

It was the ultimate in stupidity—a risk neither of them could afford. Kyle shook his head to rid it of lecherous thoughts. As tempting as he found his sexy partner, he couldn't afford to get any more involved with her.

Instead, he slowly slipped her shoes off her feet and eased her more fully onto the bed. She didn't so much as flinch, testimony to how soundly she slept.

He soothed himself with a cold beer, and then another, as he tried to shove Rianna from his thoughts. She'd probably sleep through the night, so he was left to his own devices. Normally, he preferred his own company, but her proximity kept him restless.

After slapping together a couple of sandwiches, he washed the meal down with a third beer, his personal limit, then went back to the helm. He found a cove to anchor in for the evening, where he could do some fishing. By the time dark had fallen, he was ready to call it a night himself.

He secured the front and back doors, and then carried his bag to the small compartment opposite the one Rianna had chosen. The bathroom was smaller than a phone booth, but Kyle showered, brushed his teeth and donned a pair of clean sweatpants.

After steeling himself to check on his companion again, he grabbed a blanket and covered her lightly, then quickly retreated to his own full-size bunk. He didn't expect to drop off easily, but the soothing sounds of the country night and gentle rocking of the boat soon lulled him to sleep.

The rising sun coaxed him out of bed the next morning, and Kyle quickly checked on Rianna. She was still fast asleep, but she'd apparently been up during the night. She'd shed her jeans and crawled under the covers, leaving only one long, bare leg exposed. The sight of the slim calf and thigh caused his blood pressure to rise, so he swiftly shifted his attention to her upper body.

His eyes widened a little as he studied her head. The red hair, obviously another a wig, was gone, tossed aside like lifeless vermin. In its place was a cap of light brown hair that parted down the middle and curved across her cheek. It looked as soft and shiny as corn silk.

Something inside him went soft, too, as he glimpsed yet another layer of the woman. Both the elegant blonde and the brassy redhead had been fascinating, but easily abandoned. Now Rianna looked sweet and natural and so desirable that he had to fight another fierce shaft of desire.

The real woman was slowly being revealed, like a flower opening its petals, and each new revelation intrigued him more. He wondered if her personality would undergo a similar transformation. She'd be experiencing an emotional letdown, so it would be a while before she even recognized her own personality. Not much use in speculating.

With that thought, he moved into the kitchen area and brewed a pot of coffee. While it was perking, he watched the early sunshine glisten on the water. A light morning haze hung on the air, but there were no other watercraft to disturb the view—just soothing, unblemished isolation.

It looked as though they'd have another warm, calm day on the lake. Maybe he'd swim in lieu of his usual run. Or maybe he'd check out paths along the upper bank. It was always good to have an escape route, however safe and isolated the location.

When the coffee was ready, he filled a cup and turned toward the narrow hallway. Rianna materialized in the doorway and they collided with a soft *thud.* She fell against him like a limp rag, her face buried against his shoulder. Kyle clutched her close with his left arm while he set down his cup. Then he tentatively rested his right hand at the small of her back.

Instead of moving out of his grasp, she burrowed closer, like a sleepy child. Her arms encircled his waist, a ring of fire that seared him. The feminine warmth and scent of her made his pulse leap wildly, and his body come to full sexual alert.

''Coffee. I smell coffee,'' she mumbled innocently against his shirt.

The feel of her mouth moving against him, even through the cloth, made his muscles clench with excitement. Her breasts pressed into his chest, branding him with erotic fire.

He closed his eyes, savoring the sensual pull, then took a deep breath. He wanted to lock her tightly in his arms, ravage her mouth with his own until he'd forced her to wake up and accept the consequences of her actions.

Desire raged through him as Rianna drifted back to sleep in his arms. She obviously wasn't a morning person. Kyle clenched his jaws in frustration. He considered carrying her back to bed and having his way with her. As much as the idea appealed, he wasn't the sort of man who took advantage of women, especially vulnerable ones.

That didn't mean he couldn't enjoy having her close, he thought.

He tightened his grip, pulling her body snug against his own. A moan escaped him at the exquisite feel. Rianna moaned, too, then suddenly went rigid in his arms. Kyle grinned as her head jerked backward, and she stared at him in sleepy confusion.

He slowly loosened his hold on her. She eased her grip on his midsection, allowing her enough room to splay her hands on his chest. More heat.

"What?" she muttered huskily.

"You came in search of coffee and ran into me."

"You're—" she began, then cleared the huskiness from her throat and licked her lips.

Kyle wanted to suck each glistening lip between his own and then devour her whole mouth. The need was so strong that he had to fight for control. How the hell had he gotten so needy?

"You're very hard," she finally managed to say.

And getting harder with each breath he took. "It's a morning thing," he supplied.

Her brows puckered, lashes sweeping upward as the drowsiness cleared from her eyes. As she came more fully awake, she began to withdraw.

"A guy thing," she clarified for them both, then stepped out of his reach.

"Yeah."

"I'm sorry if I made it harder."

Kyle watched a rosy blush steal up her neck and over her cheeks as she realized what she'd just suggested. The flustered color made her all the more alluring.

"I'll survive," he teased, then decided to give them both a break from the escalating tension. "I just need some coffee."

"Coffee," Rianna parroted.

He reached for his cup, sipped it to see if it was still warm, and then downed the whole thing. Maybe the caffeine would knock some strength back into his knees.

After she filled her own cup, she refilled his.

"Thanks," he said. "I was just heading outside to welcome the morning. Care to join me?"

"Sure," she said, then preceded him through the narrow hallway between their sleeping compartments.

Kyle reached around her to unlock the door, held it open while she passed through, and closed it behind them.

"I want to go up on the deck," she said, turning toward the ladder.

The roof of the houseboat doubled as a sundeck with chairs, tables and an attached sliding board for swimmers. Kyle took another sweeping glance around the area, noting that all was still quiet. He followed Rianna up the ladder, feeling his body respond to the sight of her shapely bottom, clad only in gym shorts that left a whole lot of leg exposed. Smooth, sleek legs that could feed a man's fantasies.

He forced himself to concentrate on security. "You

can't get too comfortable up here. We're as close to being sitting ducks as we can get.''

"I suppose," she said, easing herself onto a lounge chair and stretching out her legs. "But it's just about the most perfect spot anyone could want to be."

Kyle had to agree. He settled into the chair opposite her and allowed himself to relax a little. The sun was beginning to sparkle on the water, burning off the morning haze. The waves were gently lapping at the boat in a peaceful rocking motion. Birds were singing as gulls squalled and dove for breakfast. The morning was clear and bright with a slight nip in the air.

"Are you warm enough?"

"I'm chilly, but it's invigorating, not uncomfortable."

He nodded, feeling the same. The sun would warm them before too long. It had already cleared the horizon and was moving upward like a brilliant ball of fire.

They sat in silence for a while, enjoying their coffee and absorbing the peaceful beauty around them. Neither of them had known much peace these past few weeks, so it seemed a rare and welcome pleasure.

"I guess I really conked out on you last night. You didn't have any problems, did you?"

"Not a thing. I explored a little, had something to eat and did some fishing."

"Did you see anything out of the ordinary?"

"Just a few other boats and some late-night fishermen. Nothing suspicious or threatening."

Rianna sighed, resting her head against the back of the chair and closing her eyes. "Sounds wonderfully dull."

"It was," agreed Kyle, gazing out over the water.

Margie would have loved it here.

The image of his former partner slipped into his thoughts, unbidden. She'd had dark, wild curls that were always out of control. Her eyes had been dark brown, too.

Normally, the memories were too painful, so Kyle kept them buried where they couldn't rub him raw with bitterness and frustration. But Margie had been on his mind a lot during this assignment, a result of working with another female operative.

She'd tackled life head-on, as if it were a great, unending adventure. Born and raised in the city, she'd loved doing anything outdoors, exploring new places and tackling new challenges, but it was that same daring personality that had cost her life.

Even the good memories made his jaw clench and his chest tight. For a long time, he'd been mad as hell at her for risking her life and abandoning him. Now he just felt sad at the loss of her life. Sad, and determined that Haroldson should pay.

Shaking his head to dismiss the images, he turned his attention back to Rianna. She could easily distract a man from troubling thoughts. He studied the smooth curve of her cheeks and noticed how perfectly her hair framed her face.

"I'm guessing that's your natural hair."

She reached up to tuck the ends behind her ears. "This is the real thing, and what a relief to be rid of those awful wigs."

"I'll bet. I'm sure glad to be rid of the mustache. It itched like hell."

"And contacts," they chorused, sharing a grin.

Kyle stared into her lovely, smiling eyes for a moment. Their natural color was a mixture of green and gray. It surprised him to realize how much pleasure he derived from just her smile. It warmed him.

The temperature cooled when she averted her gaze.

He watched as a frown marred her features, and suddenly wished for the power to keep her safe and smiling. He wanted to destroy anything that threatened her, to eliminate anything that might motivate her to put her life at risk. The depth of the emotion made him edgy and restless.

''How long do you think we'll be able to stay here?'' she asked, obviously sensing a need to distract him.

''A few days. Maybe through next weekend. I'm betting Sullivan will want you in D.C. the following week, at the latest.''

She nodded and closed her eyes again. Kyle couldn't seem to drag his gaze away from her. He knew it was dangerous to let his attraction escalate, yet he couldn't stem the increasing desire to know what made her tick.

Neither could he ignore the surge of impotent fury he felt every time he thought of her engagement to Haroldson—living in his home, accepting his touch, being intimate with a man twice her age.

How could she do it? How could she sell herself in such an obscene manner? What would make an intelligent, capable woman take on such a compromising assignment? She'd hinted at a deeper reason than ambition, so what could it be? A family vendetta?

He'd only known her a few days and the questions were eating him alive. He wanted answers, yet knew better than to ask. Even if she'd be willing supply answers, he wasn't sure he could handle the whole truth. Better to guard against caring too much. All that had ever gotten him was more pain and disillusionment.

''I'm starving,'' Rianna announced, breaking into

his grim thoughts. "Since you made the coffee, I'll cook breakfast. Any preference?"

"I'm not particular, but I'm hungry."

"Bacon, eggs and toast?"

"Sounds great."

He watched her rise from the chair and walk across the deck. Her smooth, supple movements had his body stirring in interest again, hungry for more than food. He clamped down hard on the desire and spent the next few minutes trying to convince himself that self-denial would make him a better man.

They pulled up anchor after breakfast, and Rianna took the helm for a couple of hours. There really wasn't much driving involved, she mused, just a gentle steering as the big boat chugged across the water.

Tremont had taken a seat on the small front deck, so her attention shifted back and forth between the lake and him. The temperature had climbed to eighty already. He'd replaced his T-shirt and sweats with a pair of gym shorts. The rest of him was gloriously, tantalizingly naked.

A fine sheen of sweat made his bronze skin shimmer in the sunlight. Every time he moved a muscle, the ropelike flexing sent a frisson of sensation through Rianna. She didn't suppose a woman would ever get tired of looking at his tight, flat stomach or his equally tight rear end.

What she didn't dare do was get too excited about his great body. As much as she'd like to explore every inch of it, she knew it would be a monumental mistake. Her assignment for the agency was far from finished. Even if she survived to testify against Gregory—which the odds were against—the trial and appeals could go

on for years. She had no business getting involved with
anyone.

That didn't mean she couldn't do a little daydream-
ing about the hunk she'd hooked up with, she thought
with a grin. Would he be an impatient lover? Or the
slow, thorough sort? Did he like partners who were
wild and uninhibited, or shy and innocent? She didn't
have any personal experience, but that didn't mean she
was totally ignorant about sex. A person could learn a
lot through the media these days. Movies, television
shows and books were pretty explicit.

Tremont stirred her feminine curiosity more than any
man she'd ever met, yet she knew any interest he
showed in her would be strictly physical. He wore his
emotional detachment like a Mylar vest, shielding his
heart.

He chose that minute to reenter the cabin, and
Rianna felt a blush rising up her neck. She hoped he
didn't have a clue what had prompted her flush.

He offered a convenient excuse. "It's getting a little
warm in here, isn't it."

She jumped on it. "Yes, I was just thinking we
might want to turn on the AC during the heat of the
day."

He moved to the controls and turned on the central
air. "I'll set it low enough that it doesn't get cold—
just not too hot."

She mumbled her agreement and then turned her attention to the lake again. Tremont stepped behind her,
and she was enveloped in the musky male scent of him.
He radiated as much heat as the sun, raising her temperature even more. It was all she could do not to fan
herself.

As they traversed the main waterway, the traffic was

heavier, with ski boats and Jet Skis zipping around on all sides of them. The boat rocked in the rough wake, and he braced himself with hands on her chair. Even the casual brush of his fingers seared her, and she mentally admonished herself to get a grip.

"How about finding us another place to drop anchor. A place with some natural steps or handholds up the embankment would be nice. I'd like to scout around the area this side of the lake. Maybe have a run if I can find a smooth enough path up there."

Rianna steered around the next jutting of land, then another before turning into an uninhabited cove with a boulder-lined bank. She cut the engine and let their boat drift as close to shore as possible.

"The brochure mentions cottages and other rental properties, so I'd think you could find a decent path somewhere near the shoreline," she said.

"I'll try. Are you a jogger?"

"No, but after you're done exploring, I'd like to swim for a while. I'm used to a good daily workout, and I'm getting stiff just sitting so much," she said.

Once she'd shut off the engine, Tremont stepped away, and she drew a calmer breath. He lowered the anchor, and then grabbed a pair of running shoes.

"Keep your gun handy while I'm gone. I won't be more than an hour. If you even suspect trouble, get off the boat."

"I'll be careful. If I need to escape, I'll follow you onto shore and then stay as close as possible until you get back."

"Okay."

They both moved to the front deck, and he dove into the water. Once he surfaced, she handed him his shoes. She noticed socks were tucked in one and a small handgun in the other. He held the shoes over his head as he waded the last few feet to shore. She watched until he'd climbed the steep bank and disappeared into the trees.

Her emotions were mixed about her sexy bodyguard. There was no denying the physical attraction. Though neither of them spoke about it or acted on it, it kept intensifying. It wouldn't be smart to let her increasing desire fog her judgment. There was so much more at stake than personal satisfaction.

She wanted to trust him, yet she'd been trained to consider every angle, the potential risk in every situation. What if Donald Sullivan was wrong about Tremont's reliability? What did she really know about him? Even though his service record was impressive, he'd retired under less than favorable conditions.

What if both sides had enlisted him to keep her under surveillance? Where did his loyalties lie? What if he'd just headed for the nearest pay phone to contact the men who wanted her dead?

Hating the paranoia that had been a part of her life for so long, Rianna shook her head in disgust. She'd have to wait and watch Tremont until she could decide whether or not to trust him. Right now, being with him held more appeal than being alone. She was so tired of being alone.

Thoughts of the loneliness brought memories of her family and their vacation on a similar houseboat. Her brother, Jimmy, had been so full of energy and enthusiasm. He'd wanted to investigate every nook and cranny, to learn how everything worked. He'd wanted to fish and swim and steer the boat. He'd asked a million questions that her parents had patiently answered.

Jimmy had called her Rianna instead of her given

name, Marianna. It had been too much of a mouthful for him, so he'd created the nickname. Tremont was the first person she'd mentioned it to in nearly a decade.

She couldn't say why she'd shared it with him, except that she'd grown sick and tired of aliases. Once this case was over, she vowed to find a new line of work: one where she never had to assume another name and identity. With Gregory out of the way, it might finally be possible.

Deciding it was a good time to take stock of the clothing she'd bought, she dragged out shopping bags and sorted through the hastily purchased collection. In addition to a few pairs of shorts and tops, she'd chosen four bikinis, two matching navy-blue ones and two neon-green ones. She set them aside and stashed most of the other clothes into the drawers under her bed.

Her biggest purchase had been panties. She took fourteen pairs of them, plus the bikinis, and moved back into the kitchen. After getting herself a can of soda, she settled down to sew, pausing every few minutes to check for unexpected guests.

Nearly an hour later, she heard Tremont shouting at her from the beach. She went onto the deck and waited until he'd swum close enough to toss his shoes onto the boat. Then she gave him a hand to board.

"Have a nice run?" she asked.

"Yeah. The path's a little rough, but it felt good. Any problems?"

"Nary a one," she said. "I saw a few boats pass by on the main waterway, but nothing came close."

"Good. Ready to swim?"

"Almost. I have some sewing to finish. Then I'll be ready."

"Sewing?" he asked, following her back inside the cabin. He glanced toward the table. "Have an underwear explosion while I was gone?"

Rianna gave him a grin. "No, I'm just practicing an old trick my mother taught me."

"And what's that?"

"Well," she explained as she went back to work, "you buy two matching pairs of underwear, then you cut part of the front panel out of one and sew it to the front panel of its mate. That makes a neat little pocket that can be sealed with thin strips of Velcro."

"For hiding something?"

"For hiding a small plastic pouch with cash, an ID, and, in my case, the key to a post office box."

"Nice, neat little package?"

"I never go anywhere without one."

"Even to swim?"

"Even to swim. That's why I bought matching bikinis. The plastic protects everything, so the shower's about the only place I go without my backup supplies."

"Clever. Your mother taught you this?"

"Yes, and it's a trick that's saved me on several occasions."

"I imagine it has," he said.

Conscious of his scrutiny, she lifted her gaze from her handiwork. Tremont had a strange expression on his face. It almost looked like compassion.

"Why are you staring?"

"I'm curious. I know parents teach their kids survival tactics, but why in the hell would your mother teach you something like that? What ever happened to the basics, like putting overzealous boyfriends in their place or protecting yourself against would-be muggers?"

Rianna dropped her gaze again. "My dad taught me that kind of stuff. Mom just expanded on the teachings."

"Why?"

"What do you mean?" she asked, but knew exactly what he meant. How many mothers taught their children strange survival tricks? Hers had done so out of necessity.

"Why did she think you'd need that sort of security?"

"We moved a lot when I was younger."

"So did we, but not without a chance to collect our stuff first. Why would you move with no more security than money tucked in underwear? Were you running from someone or something?"

Rianna debated telling him the whole truth. Instinct told her to trust him, yet it didn't come easily. She held his gaze for a few minutes, and then returned her attention to her work.

"Don't!" He ground the word out harshly, surprising her into looking directly at him again.

"Don't what?" she asked lightly.

"Don't shut me out. Just give me the basics. I can deal with whatever you have to say, and I know how to keep a secret."

Something about the intensity of his demand made her heart stutter. Did he really care? Why? His tone suggested more than idle curiosity, but what? Rianna found herself telling him a little about her childhood.

"When I was twelve, my family got moved into a witness protection program, but we never felt safe. As soon as we'd get comfortable, the location would be compromised and we'd have to move. My parents taught us to be prepared."

"Witness protection? I know about it from the agency's end, but I never gave much thought to living that way. How could your location be jeopardized that often?"

"I don't know." Having finished her project, she gathered up the panties, tossing the ruined ones into the trash. "I was just a kid, so I didn't know all the specifics—just what my parents told me."

"Which agency was in charge of your relocation? Sounds like someone screwed up royally and kept putting your family in danger. Who do you blame for a breakdown in the system?"

She considered his questions as she put her panties away with the rest of her things. He didn't need to know that the FBI had failed her family. Or that she and Donald still didn't know who the informant had been. Blaine had been with the agency for years, so maybe he was the key to learning more.

"I don't know all the answers. I wish I did, but I don't," she said. Having already donned the navy-blue bikini, she headed to the rear of the boat.

Tremont followed, but she ignored him and opened the door to the back deck. "I'm going to swim now," she said, then dove cleanly over the side.

End of conversation.

## Chapter 5

Rianna swam for a while, and then did a little sun-bathing. She tanned easily but hadn't been exposed to much sun lately, so she wanted to be careful not to overdo it. After coating herself with a liberal amount of sunscreen, she stretched out in a lounge chair on the upper deck of the boat.

Tremont stood near the railing with a collection of fishing gear scattered around him. She decided to lie on her stomach, but turned her head so that she could admire his casting techniques. Every hard line of his body was aesthetically pleasing.

She couldn't help remembering how solid he'd felt when she'd latched on to him this morning. Even the memory of his reaction heated her blood hotter than the sun baked her skin.

It had been so long since anyone had held her, tightly and securely. Just held her. Without pretense, without making demands she couldn't accept.

He'd wanted her this morning. At least, his body had
hungered for hers. The thought thrilled a very private,
feminine part of her. She found him wildly attractive
and was pleased that he reciprocated the feeling, even
if neither of them planned to act on it. It still gave her
ego a much-needed boost, a warm, fuzzy feeling to hug
to herself.

Gregory hadn't wanted her in a physical sense. He'd
had plenty of women willing to satisfy his carnal de-
sires. He'd been openly affectionate in public, but very
impersonal in private. The setup had suited her needs,
yet it had kept her isolated. She'd had no one she could
trust or be comfortable with for months.

Tremont had to be applauded for not trying to take
advantage of their forced intimacy. She hadn't known
whether his legendary honor extended to personal relationships. She supposed it did, yet she had an insane
urge to entice him beyond his control.

What would it take to make him lose control? What
kind of woman would it take to make a man like him
forget everything but raw, primitive need? Did such a
woman exist? Was she stupid to even speculate? Probably. She'd never been the type to stir men to unbridled
passion.

Deciding her backside had been exposed long
enough, Rianna turned to offer her front to the sun.
Tremont had fussed about her staying on deck too long,
but it felt as close to heaven as she'd ever known.

Gregory, Sullivan, the agency and its moles were far,
far away while she basked on her tiny island of freedom. She tilted a visor over her eyes, but managed to
keep Tremont in full view. She loved watching the play
of muscles in his arms and shoulders as he swung the

fishing pole to cast out his line. His subdued but obvious strength fascinated her.

The midday sun soon had every inch of her skin tingling from prolonged exposure. Flesh that had been cooled by the water was now sizzling. Heat penetrated her bikini top to tighten her nipples, spreading the nerve-titillating sensation throughout her body. Watching her hunky companion increased her arousal, so she shut her eyes and tried to get a rein on her wayward libido.

Dozing and unaware of the passing time, she continued to rest until a shadow fell over her body. At the same time, she felt the gentle splash of something cool on her neck. It sizzled on her overheated flesh. Peeking from beneath the visor, she glared at Tremont. He stood beside her chaise, dribbling bottled water on her sun-drenched skin.

It felt like a liquid caress against her bare flesh, so cool and sensual that her breasts grew full and tight. For that reason only, she gasped and glared at him. He returned her gaze with an unrepentant and totally wicked grin.

"Time's up."

"Uh-uh, I'm not on a schedule."

"Oh, yeah, you are. You've had enough sun and enough exposure for one day. It's not safe to stay out here too long."

"Go away. You're just mad because you can't catch any fish."

"What makes you think that?"

She couldn't confess to having watched his every move, so she improvised. "I haven't heard any of those triumphant male whoops," she drawled. "I think they're a must for you macho types."

"Macho, huh? What if I'm just a kind, sensitive guy who throws the fish back in the water?"

Rianna rolled her eyes in disbelief, and then she returned his grin. In that instant of teasing, something hot and electric flashed between them. So hot that her muscles tensed and her breath got caught in her throat.

Tremont's eyes grew hooded, his features a taut mask as he stared down at her. She licked her lips, feeling wary, yet wildly excited by the fierce hunger throbbing between them. She needed to diffuse the situation before it erupted into passion, yet the look in his eyes held her mesmerized.

"If you're going to waste your water, dribble some into my mouth," she said, never imagining that the simple action could take on the impetus of sexual foreplay.

He did as she asked, watching her with an unblinking concentration as she swallowed, then lapped the excess off her lips. The unbridled flash of excitement in his eyes caused her breathing to grow shallow. Her heart banged against her chest as every nerve ending in her body quivered with excitement.

Closing her eyes against the ferocity of desire in his, she struggled to regain control of her rampaging pulse. Counting to ten and practicing her deep-breathing technique seemed the most practical course of action. At least, until he began to paint her body with the remaining water.

She felt the cooling stream of liquid start at her fingertips, run up her arms, across her chest and then down the other arm. Her skin sizzled, the cool water on her hot flesh causing a potent reaction in every cell of her body.

Next, he bathed her left foot, letting the water tickle

over her toes and then zigzag its way up her calf to her thigh. She felt its pooling coolness on her stomach, where he painted a slow, leisurely pattern of water that caused her breathing to falter and her muscles to contract.

Her right leg got equal treatment, from toes to thigh, then the water settled in her naval. Rianna was coming apart at the seams. The erotic bath made her breasts swell against the confines of the bikini top, her nipples aching for attention.

She didn't think she could get any more aroused, until Tremont aimed the water directly onto those rigid peaks. He slowly and painstakingly saturated each nipple through the cloth until her nerves sung with tension and she felt like launching herself off the chaise.

Her sharply indrawn breath signaled the devastating impact his caresses were having on her self-control.

''Kyle!'' The exclamation was a tangle of shock, reprimand and excitement. His first name slipped out, inadvertently destroying another small barrier between them.

''I'm cooling you off.''

The words were simple, but his husky tone conveyed a more primitive message. His voice was thick with wanting. He wanted her. Maybe as much as she wanted him. Rianna dragged in a breath and opened her eyes, leveling her gaze at his body. He stood so close that his arousal was directly in her line of view. It bulged beneath the thin fabric of his shorts, signaling his own undeniable hunger.

She knew she should close her eyes and block out the sight, but her body wasn't obeying the frantic mental commands. This man had the power to make her forget all her carefully formed plans. Feeling suddenly overwhelmed and out of her league, her panicked brain searched for a way to shatter the escalating tension.

"I think I'll take a swim. That should cool me." She intended to make a firm announcement, but the words came out all low and shaky. Clearing her throat, she tried again. "Maybe we both better take a dip."

Kyle took a step backward and offered her his hand, his gaze never wavering from hers. The blue in his eyes had gone dark and hazy with need, but he allowed her some space. She slipped her hand in his and let him draw her to her feet. The touch of skin on skin lit more fires along her nerves. Another minute of contact and she'd disintegrate into a pile of ashes.

"Race you?" Her challenge lacked spirit, coming out all confused and breathy.

"Not until I get a drink of that water," he said on a low growl, pulling her tight against him and taking her mouth with savage hunger.

He tossed the empty water bottle aside and clutched her head with both hands as he ground his mouth onto hers. The force of his kiss left Rianna helpless to respond or withdraw, until he gradually eased the pressure. Then she opened her mouth and welcomed his tongue with abandon, stroking and sucking until she drew a moan from deep in his throat.

Her hands clutched at his waist, the feel of the taut, warm skin making her eager for closer contact. He continued to cradle her head, devouring her mouth, while she strained to fit their bodies more snugly together. The rigid pressure of his arousal against her lower body made her insides quiver. Her legs began to tremble, and soon his strength was all that kept her upright.

Kyle finally lifted his mouth, allowing them to gulp in air, and then he nibbled at her lips while she fought to regain some control. Her desire for him was too strong, frighteningly so. She'd never wanted a man as much as she wanted him, and that scared the hell out of her.

Desire warred with common sense, but then he captured her mouth for another long, deep kiss. He coaxed her tongue into his mouth and sucked deeply. She felt the pull of it deep in the pit of her stomach. Moaning and rocking against him, she felt herself falling off a dangerous precipice and fought to pull herself back from the edge.

"Kyle, please!" she whispered against his hard mouth, unclear of what she begged for most.

"Tell me you're protected," he insisted gruffly, grasping her hips, lifting her and pulling her legs around his waist.

The action brought his arousal to the juncture of her thighs, and she gasped at the exquisite feel. So close. The satisfaction she craved was so close, his body straining and throbbing against her. She rocked herself against him and then swallowed his groan in another ravishing kiss.

"Protection," he repeated, while his fingers dug into her flesh and pulled her still closer.

She took birth control pills. A female agent in a potentially dangerous situation had to protect herself against the possibility of sexual assault. But she couldn't get the words past the lump in her throat. She wanted him, ached for him, yet something kept her from making the final commitment.

"No!" She almost screamed the word.

Kyle jerked his head back as though she'd slapped him. She felt every one of his long fingers pressing into her skin as his features underwent a frightening transformation. Rianna watched in horror as contempt replaced the passion in his eyes.

"Forget yourself for a while?" he snarled in a soft, dangerous tone that sent a shiver over her. "Or are you as skilled at teasing as you are at everything else? Another day, another conquest? Is that how you operate?"

For just an instant, she felt a shiver of fear. Kyle's demeanor had changed in the space of a heartbeat. The drastic change shook her, and then it made her sick with shame.

She shouldn't have screamed, but her instinct had been to protect them both. He believed her capable of selling herself, body and soul. It only proved how little they really knew each other. Succumbing to passion would satisfy a temporary urge, but ultimately make their situation worse.

She tried to pull out of his grasp, but he wouldn't let her go. Instead, he swung her into his arms. Stifling the desire to scream, she clung as he moved across the deck.

"Hold your breath," he commanded harshly.

The next thing she knew, they were catapulting down the sliding board. They hit the water hard and sank so deep that she nearly panicked. Quickly disentangling herself from his arms, she fought her way to the surface and dragged in a much-needed breath of air.

He swiftly put some distance between them, swimming toward the shore with strong, sure strokes. Rianna watched him, her heart heavy. What must he think of her? And why did it matter so much? He'd been equally guilty in the explosion of passion, but *she* felt like a fool and a phony.

After dragging in a few long breaths, she floated in

the water until she'd recovered her composure. When he started swimming back toward the boat, she climbed from the water and headed straight for the shower.

Once she'd finished, Kyle took a turn, and she made them a light lunch. They ate in silence, each having withdrawn into a protective shell. Then he spent the next couple of hours boating around the lake while she watched a movie on the VCR. Despite their separate pastimes, each was acutely aware of the other's proximity.

Toward late afternoon, Kyle realized the fuel tank was getting low. He turned to Rianna, allowing himself to study her for the first time since he'd had her in his arms. His muscles tightened at the memory, but he determinedly ignored the reaction.

Once his hormones were under control, he had gotten over the anger at her rejection. She'd prevented them from committing a major act of stupidity. Pregnancy might not be a concern, but he didn't have any condoms with him. It shook him to think he would have engaged in unprotected sex with a woman who'd shared her body with scum like Haroldson.

The thought both disgusted and infuriated him. The disgust was normal, the anger wasn't, and that worried him. He had no business getting more deeply involved.

Aside from Margie, there hadn't been many serious relationships in his life. In his early years, he'd been too focused on his career to think about long-term commitments. Since Margie, he'd been too wary. Anytime he got involved, it was with the clear understanding that he wasn't looking for permanency.

He should be thanking Rianna for calling a halt to an explosive situation, but he couldn't find the words.

She'd put on a pair of pink shorts with a white, cropped top that partially bared her midriff. Her hair looked clean, soft and shiny. Her arms and legs already looked a shade darker and just a little sunburned.

He'd been aware of her activity ever since the movie ended, but now he realized she'd been baking. The scent of cookies filled the galley, making his mouth water. He couldn't remember the last time he'd had freshly baked cookies.

"We need to refuel," he said, capturing her attention.

She looked directly at him, but her expression remained guarded.

"According to this map, there's a huge dock called Burnside at the other end of the lake. I'm heading there now."

Rianna nodded. "It might be better to steer clear of the dock where we left the car. That way none of the staff will get too familiar with the sight of us."

"We need to call Sullivan," he added, "but we can't use a local pay phone. Do you have a cellular?"

"Yes, but it's probably of no use out here. It should work once we get to a little higher elevation."

"Okay, then, we'll dock, refuel and take a hike until we can get a signal."

Rianna merely nodded, looking more subdued than he'd ever seen her. It made him feel guilty, yet irritated by the guilt. He searched for a way to ease the disturbing tension between them.

"You sharing any of those cookies? They sure smell good," he said, his tone light as he offered an olive branch.

The innocent pleasure that lit her features made a knot in his gut. She offered him a tentative smile along with the cookies, and the knot tightened, a sure sign that he was beginning to care too much. He knew better than to get emotionally involved, yet she made it hard to maintain an impersonal distance.

"They're just the packaged kind you slice and bake," she warned, easing more of the strained atmosphere.

"Beggars can't be choosers," he said, taking a handful. He thanked her and turned back to the wheel.

The refueling didn't take much time. After they'd finished, Kyle steered them into an empty birth where he secured the boat. Rianna grabbed her oversize bag and they started climbing the winding path toward the highway.

People and cars came and went, but no one paid them much attention. They were just another couple of strangers in an area swarming with vacationers. They walked steadily uphill for half an hour, and then settled onto a wooden bench while Rianna called Sullivan.

"The call's being forwarded," she said. "He's probably not home from the office yet."

Kyle leaned his head closer so that he could hear any conversation, but the move brought his face disturbingly close to hers. Close enough that he could smell the flowery scent of her shampoo. His pulse reacted, and then he heard the *click* of a connection.

"Sullivan."

"It's Phantom," said Rianna.

"You and Tremont okay?"

"We're fine," said Kyle. "How's everything on your end? Is Gregory behind bars?"

Sullivan's tone was grim. "Not yet."

"Why not?" they demanded in unison.

"The district attorney got the indictment, but we're

waiting on a search warrant for his estate. As soon as
we have it, we'll arrest him. I don't want to give him
an opportunity to have evidence destroyed. We want
to take him and his cohorts by surprise, or they'll go
into hiding behind a bunch of high-priced lawyers.''

"Sounds like a solid plan," said Tremont.

"Is there anything I should look for besides his business records?"

"My suite of rooms is on the northeast corner of the
house," explained Rianna. "The closet has a circular
clothes rack with a center section portioned off for
shoes. That's where you'll find the videotapes I
couldn't smuggle out with me. There should be five.
It's important that you keep the one labeled 'Party.'
The rest can be turned in to the agency."

"Why should I keep any of them? You know it
won't be valid evidence unless it's legally confiscated
during the search."

"It's not part of the evidence," she insisted. "It's
personal and so important, Donald. You have to get all
the tapes and keep that one for me. Don't trust another
soul with it."

"Whatever you say. I'll take care of it myself."

"Promise?"

"On my life," he assured her, then added, "We're
going to get him."

Kyle felt Rianna relax, only then realizing how tense
she'd been during the conversation. His curiosity about
her just went up a couple more notches. What kind of
tape had she hidden? Was it personally incriminating?
Maybe an x-rated video of the two of them? The
thought made his gut clench.

He supposed it could be some kind of weird or de-
viant game Haroldson played. Maybe he'd taped her

without her knowledge, or in a compromising situation. She wouldn't want it to fall into the wrong hands. The idea made him furious.

His voice held a low throb of anger as he spoke to Sullivan. "We've got to go. What next?"

"Stay low and call again tomorrow about the same time. I should have good news by then."

"Is Haroldson still proclaiming that his fiancée's been kidnapped?"

"Yeah, but I didn't have to disclose Rianna's identity. Someone tipped the press off to another possibility."

"What possibility?"

"That Haroldson's fiancée wasn't kidnapped, but ran off with her lover. A much younger man."

Kyle tilted his head enough to lock gazes with Rianna. He watched her eyes darken at the suggestion, and then she lowered her lashes to hide her reaction.

The ploy amused him, easing some of the tightness in his chest. "You wouldn't have been responsible for that bit of gossip, would you?"

Sullivan's response was all innocence. "I'm just doing my part to keep my FBI buddies in North Carolina informed. And you know how the media always jumps on every new angle."

Kyle smiled and glanced at Rianna again. She looked equally pleased by Sullivan's tactics.

"Sounds like you've got everything under control. We'll get back to you tomorrow."

Rianna said goodbye and closed the phone. Then she looked up at him. "Is there someone you'd like to call?"

He shook his head, wondering if anyone aside from Sullivan worried about her. During his years at the

agency, he had found it impossible to sustain close relationships, but then, he'd always been a loner.

Except for Margie. Friends who had tolerated long
absences were rare, but Margie had understood and
been a true friend. He'd never forgive himself for not
being there when his partner needed him most. On that
last fatal assignment.

All the more reason to see that Haroldson rotted in
hell.

"We'd better get back to the boat," he said.

Kyle studied their surroundings as they retraced their
path to the dock. When the path narrowed, Rianna took
the lead. She stepped around a rock, and he accidentally bumped into her, but they quickly severed the
contact.

One touch was enough to stir his imagination. He'd
fought to suppress the mental image of her on that
chaise—her lush body glistening in the sunshine and
clothed in nothing but a few narrow strips of cloth.

Her breasts had been plump, their peaks beading into
fat buttons when he'd teased them with water. Her
mouth, so eager and responsive. God, what a luscious
mouth. He could have feasted on it for hours.

And her legs.

Kyle stared at her backside when she stepped ahead
of him again. Her hips were slim but nicely rounded.
She had long, well-toned legs. Great legs. He could still
feel the strength of her thighs wrapped around him, and
the heat of her body arching against his. He'd almost
lost it completely.

He had never wanted a woman more, had never
wanted to bury himself in someone and claim full possession. He wasn't the possessive type. Never had
been. He'd never experienced such a fierce desire to

conquer and possess. Not until this morning, and Rianna.

Need still clawed through him, but there's no way he'd act on it now. The timing was all wrong. She might have been as hot as he'd been, but she hadn't minced words when she'd wanted to shoot him down. Her panicked ''no'' had been as subtle as a knee to the groin.

They boarded the houseboat with no more than a passing nod to a couple of strangers. Everybody had their own agenda and nobody had the time or inclination to chat, which worked in their favor. Blending into the crowd had never been more satisfying.

''You want to take it out this time?'' he asked, after making a quick security check through the houseboat.

''Sure.''

Rianna preceded him into the cabin and took a seat behind the wheel. She started the engine while he untied the mooring ropes. Then she slowly steered them through the maze of docks and boat traffic until they were in the main waterway again.

''My turn to cook.'' He joined her in the cabin area and helped himself to another cookie. They were delicious. ''What'll it be?''

''What can you cook?''

Kyle rummaged through the refrigerator. ''How about some grilled pork chops and baked potatoes? I can handle that.''

''Perfect.''

They ate their meal a half-hour later after dropping anchor in another small cove. She complimented his cooking skills and ate everything on her plate. Both were careful not to make too much eye contact or broach sensitive subjects. Studied politeness became the rule of thumb.

The sky grew cloudy at dusk and a small shower kept them inside the cabin. Kyle watched a baseball game while Rianna curled up on the sofa with a book. He divided his attention between the TV and her, until the hunger in him reared its ugly head again.

By the time the rain stopped around ten o'clock, he was more than ready to escape the confines of the cabin. The sky had cleared, so he wanted a last look around the area.

"I'm going up on deck for a while."

Rianna glanced up from her book. Then she closed it and laid it aside. "I'm getting tired, but I'd like to sit outside for a few minutes before I call it a night."

"Grab a towel for your chair. It'll be wet."

He followed her up the ladder, trying hard to ignore the gentle sway of her behind and the legs that were driving him crazy. As soon as they reached the deck, he distanced himself and flopped down in one of the lounge chairs. Rianna sat in the one she'd used earlier in the day.

A silent groan rumbled in his chest at the sight of her. She appealed to him even more than she had earlier. Her cautious reserve made her all the more alluring.

"Do you have a headache?" he asked.

Rianna glanced at him with a quizzical expression. "No, why do you ask?"

"You're rubbing the back of your neck again. I've seen you do it several times in the past few days. I thought maybe you suffer from tension headaches."

"No, I just have a sore spot on my neck."

She hesitated, making him wonder if she intended to explain or leave him in the dark. Then she continued.

"I had a weird little accident while I was at Gregory's estate. I'm still not sure how it happened. I guess Gregory and I bumped into each other at the bottom of the stairs. I cracked the back of my head on the corner of the newel. It bled so much that it needed stitches."

"He took you to the hospital?"

Rianna laughed softly. "When you have the kind of money and clout Gregory has, they bring the hospital to you. Some doctor friend of his rushed to the house. He administered a local anesthetic, put a couple of stitches in the back of my neck, and went on his way again. I hardly felt a thing."

"You were never unconscious? You're sure Haroldson wasn't somehow responsible?"

"At first I wondered if I'd blown my cover, and he was planning to drug me or something, but he seemed genuinely concerned. He and the doctor were very solicitous."

"Don't you need to have the stitches removed?"

"He said they'd dissolve naturally."

"And the cut is still hurting?"

"It doesn't hurt, it just throbs once in a while."

"Maybe it's infected. Lake water is full of bacteria."

"It's not that sensitive. I meant to have Paulo check it when he did my hair. I forgot, but he'd have noticed if it looked red or irritated."

"I can take a look at it in the morning if you want," Kyle offered, knowing she wasn't likely to ask.

"Thanks, I'll let you know if it starts to bother me again."

He doubted that, but let the subject drop. Looking

at her and thinking about her was distracting enough. So much so that he forced himself to focus on their surroundings.

The inky sky was brilliant with its canopy of stars. Water lapped lazily against the shore, the waves rocking them in their wake. Breathing deeply, he let the warm, rain-washed freshness of the air seep into his senses.

It soothed, while arousing, creating a sensual delight and bringing his body to full, aching awareness. The kind of awareness that no amount of moonlight would soothe. He wondered if she felt it as strongly as he did.

The night was meant for loving, for oh-so-slow caresses, hot, tangled bodies, and deep, drugging kisses. But making love wasn't on their agenda. The woman he lusted after didn't want involvement, and had ruthlessly reminded him of that.

It might be a very long night.

# Chapter 6

The next morning dawned clear and bright. Rianna heard Kyle moving around the galley as soon as the sun had peaked over the horizon. She'd slept fitfully and knew he'd been restless, too. It didn't help to be sleeping within a few feet, wanting each other so desperately, yet knowing they dared not succumb to the attraction.

The smell of coffee drew her from her bed, just as it had the previous morning. This time, she carefully entered the galley area, making sure she didn't collide with his hard, male body. Still, he pinned her with a probing gaze that made her heart stutter. She offered a tentative smile, and he offered a caffeine fix. By mutual agreement, they carried it to the upper deck.

After a few minutes to appreciate another new day, Kyle decided he wanted grilled fish for breakfast.

"I hate to sound negative," she reminded, hiding her

grin, "but so far, the fish seem to have eluded capture."

He flashed her a very male frown before his eyes lit with challenge. "Maybe you think you can do better?"

Rianna chuckled, shaking her head. "I know my limitations, and I know absolutely nothing about catching fish."

"Any reasonable, intelligent person can learn," he taunted.

Never one to resist a challenge, she took him up on it. Then he hauled out the fishing gear and began coaching her in the basics of freshwater fishing.

The lesson involved a lot of detailed instruction, concentrated effort and good-natured banter. The attraction between them heightened with each touch of a hand, brush of a shoulder or shared laugh, yet they didn't allow it to sabotage their pleasure.

"The fish aren't cooperating very well, and I'm starved," she said after an hour without success. "How about I fix some breakfast, and we put fish on the lunch menu?"

He sighed and shook his head in disgust, then offered her a rare grin. It stole her breath. His eyes were as blue as the morning sky, his expression softer than she'd ever seen it, and her stomach did a crazy little flip-flop.

Hunger. It had to be hunger, she argued to herself. A man's eyes and smile couldn't really make a woman's stomach do somersaults. That only happened in the fictional world, never in real life. She'd just gone too long without food.

Her voice sounded rusty when she spoke. "How about milk, cookies and a banana or two to hold us until we catch some unsuspecting little fishes?"

"Okay by me."

She quickly made her exit and collected some food from the galley, all the while breathing deeply and lecturing herself on the idiocy of their attraction. When she returned on deck, she was calmer and managed to ignore the tension while they shared a snack.

Shortly after they'd eaten, the fish started biting. Rianna caught two nice-size bass, and couldn't believe how much she enjoyed the small success. She caught a third one, then turned the pole over to Kyle, who caught a couple more.

Once they had enough for a meal, they decided to call it quits. The traffic on the lake had increased, and they'd been on deck long enough. She went to the galley to get a pan of water while Kyle cleaned the fish.

When she returned, he surprised her by scooping her into his arms. "Hold your breath," he commanded.

Not again, she thought. Sensing his tension, she didn't bother to argue, just wrapped her arms around his neck and clung. Then they were whizzing down the slide. This time she gulped some air and prepared herself for the chilly depths. Instead of trying to fight her way free of Kyle's grasp, she clung to him and they surfaced together.

The first thing she did after catching her breath was pound on his chest. "What the hell was that for?"

"Helicopter," he warned as he urged her toward the shadows at the back of the boat.

They each grabbed a rung of the swim ladder and ducked out of sight. Arms and legs tangled, then they went as still as possible, making no visible waves. They watched, barely breathing, as a helicopter slowly made its way along the main body of the lake, from east to west.

"It has some sort of logo on it," she whispered.

"It could be a television news crew. Or some kind of law enforcement 'copter."

The helicopter flew over the center of the lake without veering from its straightforward path or coming too near their cove. It didn't hover long in any one spot.

Kyle had her sandwiched between the boat and his big body. Rianna couldn't move, so she finally slid her free arm around his waist and let him tread water for both of them. A shiver raced over her as her palm slid over his hard, flat stomach, but it had nothing to do with fear. She pressed herself closer, peering over his shoulder and putting her mouth near his ear.

"You don't think we could be seen or attacked from the air, do you?" She found it hard to believe that anyone could have tracked their escape. They'd been so careful.

"Tracked maybe, but not attacked. Haroldson's men wouldn't be that stupid, but they could be searching by air."

"That logo looks more like a resort emblem. The owners probably police the area, don't they? Or maybe they're doing some promotional tours."

"It wouldn't take much for Haroldson to finagle a free ride for his goons. He's a wealthy man and could pretend to have an interest in the resort operation."

"They probably take prospective clients out for joy rides," she said, absently wondering how his body could be so warm in the chill of the water. Everywhere they touched, she felt the heat of him. "I'll bet this place is impressive from the air."

He nodded, and they watched the helicopter depart, knowing they shouldn't move out of hiding until it could no longer be seen or heard.

As the drone of the engine faded, she became even more aware of how their bodies were entwined. The hair on his thighs tickled hers, sending little shivers of reaction over her skin. Her breasts, stomach and thighs were tightly pressed against his broad back and tight rear, stimulating every tiny nerve.

Excitement sung through her veins. This sexy renegade stirred her senses as no other man had ever done. It wouldn't do to let him know how easily he could throw her hormones into a tizzy. She tried to ease some space between them so that he wouldn't feel how tightly her nipples had hardened.

"I think it's safe now," he said, pulling free of her grasp and shoving himself clear of the boat.

Missing the feel of him the instant he moved, Rianna took a slow, deep breath. After regaining some control, she hauled herself up the ladder on legs that quivered. Kyle threatened her hard-won independence. She was beginning to care too much. So much so that his smile and his touch made her ache with longing. And he'd slipped past her emotional guard—that worried her even more.

She showered while he finished cleaning the fish, then he took his turn in the shower. Subdued, and lost in their own thoughts, they grilled their fish and shared a quiet lunch.

Shortly afterward, they pulled up anchor and headed back toward the cove where he'd found the jogging trail the previous day. Rianna contented herself with watching the speedboats, tubers and Jet Skiers who zipped by them, but she didn't venture on deck.

By mid-afternoon, they'd dropped anchor again, and Kyle announced that he wanted to take another run. He warned her to keep her gun within reach and to listen for a return of the helicopter. They repeated the transfer of his shoes, socks and gun. She watched until he'd swum to shore, strapped the gun to his ankle and donned his socks and shoes. Then he climbed the boulders that lined the bank.

Once he'd disappeared from view, she changed into her lime-green bikini and pulled a white T-shirt over it. She'd swim and work on her tan when Kyle returned, but in the meantime, planned to finish her book while she waited.

As interesting as she found the story, she quickly grew too restless to concentrate. An instinctive edginess propelled her toward the back of the boat. It was hard to stay cooped up inside when the sunshine and water beckoned, but she knew that wasn't the real problem. The scare this morning had her senses on high alert. She decided to watch the water traffic from the back of the boat until her partner returned.

Moving to the windowed back door, she watched one speedboat cruise by pulling two skiers. It looked like so much fun that she promised herself to try it someday. Another boat passed pulling an inflated rubber tube with two teenagers clinging to the sides and bouncing wildly. That looked like a rough ride. Laughing softly, she decided she'd have to think twice about trying that.

Two jet skiers, driving dangerously fast, went zipping by next, then a pontoon and a slow-moving houseboat. The decks were crowded with people of all ages whose laughter drifted across the water. Rianna felt a pang of envy as she remembered her own family's carefree vacation.

What would it be like to live a normal, happy life without the constant fear of discovery? Without the need to run and hide like a criminal, always fearful? She'd given up much hope of ever knowing that particular contentment.

Love and marriage had never been part of her long-term goals. Those goals hadn't stretched beyond bringing a murderer to justice. She wanted Gregory to pay for the death of her parents and brother. Although she loved children, she'd always feared her biological clock would run out long before she could consider a normal relationship.

As the next speedboat passed, her lungs constricted on a harsh gasp, then her pulse lurched into overdrive. The boat held four big men and not one of them had the look of a vacationer. The silhouette of one in particular looked too much like Rudy to be a coincidence.

Rianna's survival instincts kicked in, her only thought, *escape.* There was no time to gather belongings other than her gun. She checked the safety and tucked it into her bikini bottoms as she raced through the boat. The last thing she heard before diving off the front deck was the sound of the speedboat throttling to turn and head back her way.

She dove deep and swam underwater, kicking and pulling with all her might. Knowing she wouldn't have time to reach the shore and climb the bank where Kyle had gone, she headed for the outcropping of land that separated one cove from the next. If she could get around it before she was spotted, she'd have a chance.

A few minutes later, she surfaced to catch her breath and get her bearings. With the houseboat between her and the intruders, she couldn't tell how close they'd gotten, so she dove again and swam until her lungs burned and threatened to explode. The third time she

surfaced, she found herself at the edge of the neighboring cove.

With one final sprint, she rounded the bend of land
and put the outcropping of solid rock between her and
the speedboat. Confident they couldn't see her now, she
surfaced and began to swim across the wide stretch of
water.

The sound of men shouting gave her the extra
strength to drag herself ashore. Her chest heaved and
her limbs trembled from exertion. Her pulse roared in
her ears. Catching some much-needed air, she squeezed
excess water from her hair and shirt, frantically searching the bank for a place to climb.

She cursed herself for not remembering shoes, then
stumbled across the beach and started up the slippery
ascent. Years of strenuous workouts paid off as every
muscle in her body strained to the max. Clawing and
dragging herself up the rocky bank, she reached the top
in a burst of adrenaline, and then lunged between two
giant boulders.

For the next few minutes, she lay sprawled, face-
down where she'd fallen. The semiautomatic poked her
in the stomach, still secure, yet unreliable now that it
had been immersed in water. Her breathing was harsh,
but she smothered the sound in the tall, thick grass
while struggling to regain some strength.

Kyle.

She was going to kill him. Maybe with her bare
hands. Her fists clenched at the thought. Various methods of punishment and torture drifted through her mind,
gradually replacing the terror she'd just experienced.

How could he have betrayed her?

There was no other explanation for the timely arrival
of Gregory's men; no possible way they could have

tracked her down. Grinding her teeth in frustration, she wondered if she'd been a fool to trust him.

Her heart felt cold and heavy, clutched in a viselike pain, he'd been the rare exception to her longtime rule of not letting anyone get too close. She'd started to care for him.

Had it all been an elaborate scheme? His disgust for Gregory, his concern for her safety, and all the cautions he'd suggested? She didn't want to think she could be so wrong about someone, but she intended to find out for sure.

Lifting her head, she searched the immediate area for the jogging path he'd described. At least that part of his story was true. She saw a path and let her gaze travel to where it disappeared into a line of trees. Her pulse had begun to quiet, but it went berserk again when she caught sight of him about a hundred yards distant.

He ran at a slow, steady pace, his arms and legs moving with an economy of motion. His body glistened with sweat, and his chest heaved gently. Rianna's pulse skipped another few beats. He looked so normal, so sexy and so damn unconcerned.

She frowned. Could he be that good an actor? If he'd brought them here, why hadn't he just disappeared? He looked so natural, as though he'd been enjoying a carefree run. Why hadn't he just kept running toward the marina? Did he plan to help them trap her, or continue his vacation after she'd been hauled away?

Or could he be as much a victim as she?

Rising slowly to her feet, she reached under her T-shirt and locked her hand around the gun. It might not work, but neither of them could be sure of that. At least for now, she had the upper hand.

Kyle had covered most of the distance between them before she stepped clear of the boulder and into his line of view. He stopped immediately, his features tightening in concern. His gaze dropped to the gun and then back to her strained expression.

"What the hell?"

"You tell me," said Rianna as she leveled the Glock at his midsection and flipped the safety off. She braced her right hand with her left, and her attention never wavered from his face. She desperately wanted to believe his confusion was genuine, but her life depended on caution. She couldn't let her heart rule reason.

"Why'd you leave the boat?" he asked, panting as he tried to catch his breath. "What's going on?"

"We've got company."

Kyle's gaze swiftly flew toward the embankment, searching for the intruders. After aiming a blank glance at her, he headed to the bank above the cove where they'd left the boat. He turned his back to her without hesitation, as though she didn't present any real threat. Or, like her, he realized she couldn't afford to fire and alert anyone to her whereabouts.

Rianna gritted her teeth, clutched the gun and called herself a fool, but went with her instincts. If Kyle had any knowledge of the ambush, he deserved an Oscar. He looked genuinely surprised and worried.

Moving from boulder to boulder along the bank, he stayed hidden and waved her to stay back. She ignored the unspoken order and followed until they were directly above the cove where they'd anchored. From their vantage point, they could see the houseboat without being visible from the water.

The speedboat had pulled alongside their boat. Two men stayed on the smaller craft while two others searched the houseboat. Rianna recognized Rudy and another of Gregory's employees, by the name of Tabone.

"Nowhere in sight, but they were here." Rudy's voice carried to them. "Search everything, Tabone."

They watched as he moved onto the front deck and did a visual search of the cove. Then he pulled something out of his pocket and waved it in front of him. At first, Rianna thought it might be a gun, but then she thought it looked more like a cell phone. She just couldn't figure why he'd be waving it around.

Kyle touched her arm, urging her to back away from the rock barriers. It wasn't likely that anyone could see them, but they cautiously retraced their steps until they'd returned to the jogging path.

"What did he have?" she finally whispered. Still not sure he could be trusted, she kept the gun leveled at his midsection.

He studied the gun and then her features, his jaw tight and expression grim. "Use it or put it away," he demanded tersely.

Tension quivered between them until she slowly flipped the safety on the gun and tucked it back into her swimsuit.

He grabbed her arm and started pulling her along the path to a clump of trees. "He's got some kind of electronic tracking device."

It made sense, but it didn't make sense. "That would work if he had a signal to follow, but there's no way. How the hell did they find us? Even if they traced our call to Donald, that wouldn't have given our exact location. This place is huge!"

"They have to be honing in on a direct signal."

"That's not possible. I checked everything I brought

out of the estate. Nobody knew where the car was garaged, so they couldn't have bugged it,'' she insisted, thinking aloud. ''I mailed all the jewelry to Maine. Everything else I brought with me is on the boat, so they'd have found the bug when they boarded. It doesn't fit.''

Kyle's expression grew grimmer, his eyes going cold and hard while his jaws clenched. ''Unless it's on you,'' he said.

She didn't like the way he was looking at her, and liked his suggestion even less. ''Where?'' she demanded in a frustrated whisper. ''I'm barely dressed, and I know there's no bug in my gun. I'm not wearing any jewelry, and I haven't even had a cavity filled since I met Gregory.''

''What if it's implanted under your skin?'' he suggested, studying her intently.

Rianna froze, eyes widening in horror. A terrible chill raced over her, freezing, and then numbing her with shock. Her lungs constricted painfully, her throat growing so tight that she could barely whisper the next questions.

''How? Where?''

He pulled her close and spun her around. Then he lifted the hair off the back of her neck and looked at her nape. His voice held a feral snarl when he finally spoke.

''What if your weird accident wasn't an accident at all? What if Haroldson had a device implanted in your neck? It wouldn't have to be very big,'' he added, running a finger lightly over the stitches.

Rianna's stomach roiled. It made sense, and it explained the strange accident. She slapped a hand over her mouth to keep from screaming in outrage and denial. Her body became one giant tremor, shaking her to the very core.

"It's possible," she whispered gruffly. "It sounds like something he'd do. He's fanatic about his possessions and that's what he considered me. He has no morals and no conscience."

Kyle muttered a string of vicious obscenities, and then jerked her around to face him. He gave her a fierce hug that helped soften some of her shock, but it was way too brief. A tracking devise was beyond her worst nightmare, and she was badly shaken.

"We've got to get away from here." His warm breath touched her ear. "Right now, we're shielded by those boulders. The signal probably can't penetrate them, but as soon as they come over that embankment, they'll be able to pinpoint our location."

"What can we do?" she asked, knowing what a wild animal must feel like to be pinned in the headlights of a car.

Kyle was already reaching for the gun at his ankle. He unfastened the strap and then whipped it around her neck, positioning the gun over the scar on her nape.

"We run for it. Hopefully, the metal of the gun will interfere with the signal until we come up with a better solution."

As soon as he'd secured the holster around her neck, he turned to lead the way. Rianna relegated the sick terror of a body invasion to the back of her mind. She couldn't allow herself to dwell on this latest atrocity. Survival came first.

They'd only gone a short distance before she realized an additional handicap. "I'm barefoot," she called softly to Kyle.

He stopped abruptly, turned and stared down at her

bare feet. "You can't run this path like that. There're too many sticks and rocks. You'll have to ride piggy-back."

She stared at him as though he'd lost his mind. He'd already been jogging for an hour. She was way too heavy to carry, and reluctant to be totally dependent on him. Remembering the last time she'd wrapped her legs around him, she panicked briefly, then latched on to the first lame excuse that leapt to mind.

"You smell like dirty socks."

He looked stunned by the inanity of her comment. Then his eyes softened in understanding. "You smell like dead fish," he countered gently. "Now, get on."

She grimaced and conceded, knowing they were wasting precious time. He turned and leaned down so she could hop onto his back. Then he hefted her up until he had a firm grip on her thighs. She wrapped her arms around his upper chest, trying not to strangle him.

He ran deeper into the woods and splashed through a shallow stream of water, then followed it long enough to throw off anyone who tried to track them on foot. After they'd traveled a mile or so, he moved back to-ward the regular path, then stayed parallel with it with-out actually using it.

Rianna ducked her head to avoid low-hanging branches for a while, and then buried her face against his neck. He smelled of sweat and man. The heat of him scorched her inner thighs, belly and chest, making her extremely aware of every hard, muscled inch of his body. His pulse became hers as it pounded rapidly through his veins. It was an experience unlike anything she'd ever known.

"How far do you plan to run?" she whispered in his ear.

"Another few miles."

"You can't carry me that far!"

Kyle slowed, and then stopped just before a clearing with several cabins. He let Rianna slide to the ground. She sat still, watching him closely while he struggled to catch his breath.

"We have two choices," he finally said. "We can try to make it to the marina and hot-wire the car, or we can hide out for a while in one of the deserted cabins around here."

"There's a key to the car hidden under the right front bumper, but we can't risk going after it," she said.

"Why?"

"If Rudy searched the houseboat, he found the marina rental receipt. It has the car's license number. He'll go there next and either have it watched or plant something worse than a bug."

Kyle swore, raking a hand through his hair in frustration. "We can't hitch a ride while that gun's strapped to your neck, so we'll have to hide. I've seen a couple of cabins that don't look inhabited right now."

"You can leave me and hitch a ride to town to find some transportation."

"No!" His response was harsh. He glared at her. "We stay together. Rudy and his men will have to split up if they search the whole area. As long as we're together, one man at a time isn't a threat. We'll go to a cabin and formulate a new plan."

Rianna didn't argue. She didn't want to part ways with him, yet she wondered at his motives. Did he have his own agenda for keeping her safe? Some unknown reason for not wanting her out of his sight? The answers weren't forthcoming, so she nudged the questions to the back of her mind. She'd worked solo for too long and didn't want to go it alone anymore.

"The path goes behind that group of cabins. I didn't see anyone around earlier, but we should try to walk past like we're taking a stroll. Since you're barefoot, we'll go slow."

She nodded and fell into step beside him until they'd covered the short distance across the clearing. Once they were out of sight of the rental cabins, Kyle leaned down and hefted her onto his back once more.

"You're going to owe me a serious rubdown," he insisted, picking up his pace again.

Rianna smiled against his neck, and unconsciously tightened her grip on him. She'd reserve judgment about what she owed him. She still hadn't decided whether it would be a debt of gratitude or slow torture. Come to think of it, a full-body massage might fit the bill in either case.

Kyle left the path and veered deeper into the woods, plunging them from dappled sunlight into near darkness. He slowed down to a walk as they encountered heavier vegetation.

"Are you sure there's a cabin up here? How'd you find this place?"

"I've seen several isolated cabins, and figure they're privately owned. I followed a doe and fawn through the woods here," he explained. "They led me to the cabin with a salt-lick in the yard. Looks deserted."

He breathed deeply from exertion, and she felt every intake of breath like her own. His muscles flexed and her nerves jangled. Never having experienced such an intense physical connection, the feel of it defied description.

The small log cabin stood buried in a cluster of tall evergreens. Covered in ivy, the whole structure was nearly hidden from view. He jogged around the right side to a small back porch, and then stopped to let her slide off his back.

"You're sure nobody's living here?"

"It doesn't look like anyone's been here for a while. Maybe someone only uses it a couple of weeks a year."

"Let's just hope this isn't their week."

"Yeah," Kyle agreed. He searched the door and a small window frame for a spare key, but couldn't find one. "I hate to break in if we don't have to."

She helped to search, overturning rocks and looking under a loose wooden plank in the porch. Kyle reached above them and felt along the rafters of the roof, while she looked in and under a collection of flowerpots.

"Look!" she exclaimed.

# Chapter 7

Rianna held up a key she had found under a dried fern in a clay pot. Kyle took it and ordered her to stay put while he checked the house. She reached for her gun and followed him through the narrow door. It didn't take long to establish that the cabin didn't hold any surprises. There were only two sections, a living room with a small kitchenette and a small bedroom with an even smaller bathroom.

Except for some dust and a cobweb or two, the inside of the cabin appeared neat and well cared for. The furnishings were serviceable rather than fashionable, but with homey touches like dried flower arrangements. A stone fireplace took up one entire end of the living room area.

"Not bad," said Kyle, after checking the kitchen cupboards. "It's stocked with nonperishables."

Rianna headed to the bedroom. "I hope the owners left some clothes here." She opened the closet and found a collection of outerwear that wasn't of much use, but the canvas tennis shoes thrilled her. Her feet hurt.

The dresser drawers offered a change of clothing. "Looks like this place belongs to a married couple. There's a mix of clothing," she told him as he followed her into the room.

"What sizes?"

"Large men's and medium women's. We should be okay. I think our absent host and hostess might be a little heavier than we are, but not so much that we can't borrow a few things."

"It might not hurt to add a little padding around our waists. Any disguise will help."

She agreed. The elastic on the sweatpants would stretch for extra cushioning.

"I think we should shower, eat and head out again," she said. "If we can get a ride to town, we can pick up money at the post office, pay for some transportation, and be miles from here before Rudy spreads out his search."

"You don't think it would be safer to hole up here overnight and head to town tomorrow?"

Rianna thought about spending another night like the last, trying to sleep, yet too achingly aware of her roommate. It wouldn't be wise to invite more intimacy. Besides, neither of them would rest knowing Rudy might find them at any minute.

Then there was the electronic bug buried under her skin. Her teeth clenched in anger at the thought. She wanted it out as soon as possible.

"It'll be a risk to leave, but more of a risk to stay. If you found this cabin, there's a chance Gregory's men will, too. I'd rather take our chances in town. We can appeal to the local sheriff, if necessary.''

''Okay. I'll get the generator running and then get that gun off your neck.''

Rianna touched her nape. The gun felt cold and heavy against her tender skin. ''What can we do?''

''If I cut off the bulk of the holster, the gun can be replaced with a butter knife. It won't be pretty, but it shouldn't attract attention.''

''Chokers are all the rage,'' she muttered grimly, ''but I don't know about knife blades.'' Then another idea had her heading back to the kitchen area.

''We'll have to leave a big tip for our hosts.'' She snatched a little notepad from the refrigerator. ''This is magnetic. A magnet would really scramble the signal, wouldn't it?''

''Good idea,'' agreed Kyle as he followed her. ''We should try to pay for what we take, but all my cash is on the boat. How about you?''

His gaze slid down her body to the juncture of her thighs, making her pulse leap and her flesh tingle. She shifted her legs and responded gruffly.

''Always. I told you I never travel without cash.''

''How much?''

Kyle's voice had dropped an octave. His gaze returned to her face. They stared at each other for a few tense minutes, and then made a concerted effort to shake off the sensual tension caused by his intimate perusal.

''A few hundred. Enough for a couple of days' food and lodging.''

''So we don't need what you mailed to yourself in Somerset?'' he asked.

"It all depends on how long we have to keep running. My stash won't stretch for transportation."

"How much did you leave in Somerset?"

"Several thousand, plus another phony ID."

He sighed. "Okay, I guess we go there next."

Dusk had fallen by the time they'd showered, changed into the borrowed clothing and eaten a cold, canned meal. Rianna had rinsed the lake water from her bikini, but wore the swimsuit under the sweats. She didn't want to be without her special storage pouch, and her hostess's bras were too big.

She'd kept her back to the brick fireplace while Kyle redesigned her leather necklace. It was far from attractive, yet not awful enough to draw unwanted attention. By the time they left the cabin, they looked like an average married couple in slightly creased casual wear and running shoes.

The trek through the woods was slow going—progress was made a few cautious yards at a time. Once they reached the main road, they hailed a teenager in a battered pickup truck. He worked at the marina, but his shift had ended, so he happily accepted twenty dollars to drive them to Somerset.

Rianna spent the ride squeezed between the two of them. The truck's gearshift was on the floor, so she had to lean against Kyle to avoid bumping it with her leg. He slid an arm across the back of the seat to give her room, but that made her feel more trapped. Every curve in the winding road had her pressing into him, and the feel of his hard body kept hers singing with excitement.

They reached the southern edge of town shortly before eleven. Kyle helped her from the truck, but she quickly withdrew her hand from his grasp. They thanked their new friend and bade him farewell, then Kyle reached for her again.

"We'd better keep our hands free for weapons," she insisted, pulling from his grip.

A lift of his brow questioned her response and the evasive action. They'd swapped guns, wrapped them in towels and secured them around their waists. The sweats didn't have pockets, but the belly pouches gave them a place to hide the weapons while adding a few inches to their waistlines. Kyle didn't argue, he just placed his left hand to the back of her waist and guided her into the shadows.

"I've heard of rolling up the sidewalks at dark, but I think this town really does it," said Rianna.

"It's a work night for most people," he added, leading her toward the post office. The occasional streetlight helped illuminate their path, yet left enough shadowy corners to make them wary.

"We'd better not go into the post office together," she said as they drew closer to their destination.

Kyle agreed. "I'll circle around back and come up the alley on the other side."

Rianna watched him disappear, her stomach sinking in an indescribable fashion. She shook her head in amazement. When and how had she let herself get so attached to the man? It was stupid to feel bereft without him by her side.

Surveying the street, she didn't notice anything out of the ordinary, so she made her way to the end of the block. The post office lobby was empty. She collected her package, and then returned the key through the drop slot. Tucking the envelope into her makeshift belly pack, she headed outside again.

After another quick glance up and down the street,

she turned toward the shadowed alley. Suddenly, all the fine hairs on her arms and neck started tingling. Rianna tensed, deciding someone aside from Kyle was causing her alarm.

She didn't react fast enough. A giant arm slammed her body against an equally solid chest. She felt the barrel of a gun pressing against her neck and immediately recognized her captor's voice.

"Well, well, sweet Samantha. Nice to see you again."

Rianna's heart rammed against her ribs, and sweat dampened her skin. She went perfectly still, barely able to breathe as Rudy's arm tightened around her arms and chest. He held her in a bruising grip—evidence that he was furious with her. She'd made a fool of him, and men in his position didn't take that lightly.

Despite his size, he moved with the speed and agility of a martial arts expert. She'd seen him work out in the gym, and knew he wouldn't be easily overpowered or outmaneuvered.

"Where's lover boy, Tony?"

He slowly nudged her forward, and she saw a dark vehicle parked a few yards down the alley.

"We decided to split up."

"Mr. Haroldson will be sorry to hear that. He was hopin' to have you both back home real soon."

An involuntary shiver raced through her at the thought. Rudy must have felt it, and he gave a bark of laughter. "You got that right, honey. You best be shakin' in your shoes. Mr. Haroldson's real upset."

Rianna briefly wondered if Gregory had been arrested. It should have happened today, but they'd had no way to call and check. It didn't seem likely, with Rudy still on the loose.

What could possibly have gone wrong? As far as she knew, Rudy was to be arrested along with several other members of Gregory's staff.

They reached the car, a small Jeep, and he shoved her against the back door on the passenger side. He pressed himself against her in a deliberate attempt to humiliate. His laughter had a lewd edge as he breathed heavily in her ear.

"I sure hope the boss lets me have a go at you, little slut," he said, thrusting his hips against her and grinding them in a disgusting attempt to demean her. "I always thought it was a waste to keep you in that big house with nobody gettin' any of this sweet body."

Another shudder of revulsion coursed through her. The touch of his body sickened her, but she forced herself not to panic. Rudy would never disobey orders, and she was relatively sure Gregory hadn't given him permission to manhandle her.

At least, not yet.

Where the hell was Kyle? Would he be coming to her rescue? He could be trusted, she sincerely believed that, but she wasn't used to depending on anyone. What if he'd been jumped by another of Gregory's men?

"Open the door," Rudy ordered.

He eased his grip on her enough to allow her to reach the handle. Then she heard the unmistakable sound of metal connecting with bone. Rudy grunted, his grip went slack, and she felt him falling to the ground.

"You okay?" asked Kyle.

She was trembling from head to foot, and leaned against the car for support. In the next instant, Kyle's arms were pulling her close. Rianna didn't resist the offer of comfort. She slid her hands around his waist and clung, feeling relieved, yet guilty for having doubted him again.

"Did he hurt you?" His tone sounded low and gruff in her ear.

She shivered again, but with a whole different emotion. Relief surged through her, accompanied by a needy, hopeful feeling that alarmed her. She eased from his grip.

"I'm okay," she insisted, shaking off the momentary weakness. "It sounded like you cracked his skull."

"Not that hard head. He'll be awake and fighting mad in a few minutes. Let's get him tied up."

"With what?"

"Check the car."

While Rianna searched the car, Kyle searched Rudy's pockets. He found the car keys, a cell phone and the electronic tracking device Rudy had used to locate her.

"Nothing in the car."

"He's wearing high-top boots. We'll use his bootlaces."

They each grabbed a foot and began unlacing Rudy's boots. Then they rolled him onto his stomach, tied his hands behind his back and secured his feet. Rudy groaned, prompting Kyle to check his head and his breathing.

"He's not bleeding. He has a goose egg, and his breathing is fine. He'll live."

"What now? Leave him here? Take him to the police? The emergency room?"

"Help me roll him to the side of the alley so he won't get run over," he said. They half lifted, half dragged the big man off the concrete. "We'll leave him and put some distance between us before we call the authorities. Then they can deal with him.''

"Maybe there's a warrant out for his arrest," added Rianna. "If Gregory's been arrested, there should be warrants out for Rudy and Tabone, too.''

They moved back to the car. Kyle automatically headed for the driver's side, so Rianna climbed into the passenger seat.

"Think it's safe to take his car? It could be bugged," she said.

"It's got rental tags," he reassured her as the engine roared to life. "They wouldn't have had a reason to bug it.''

"Probably not." She pulled her seat belt into place. "But Tabone and the others can recognize it, so we'll have to find something else.''

"Later," he insisted. "First thing we have to do is find a hospital and get that metal out of your neck. I've got Rudy's tracking device, but there could be others.''

"There's a regional hospital near here. As anxious as I am to have this thing removed, I'd feel more comfortable if we headed north a while before we stop.''

Kyle glanced toward her, then back to the road. "You're sure?''

"I'm sure I don't want any more confrontations tonight.''

The brief brush with Rudy had made her physically ill. She'd never expected such a violent physical and emotional reaction. It still had her shaken, and that scared her senseless.

How could she bear to go back and face them? Even for a trial? She loathed everything and everybody associated with Gregory Haroldson. The loathing had deepened over the past few months. It wasn't until she'd been free of it that she'd realized how profoundly the assignment had traumatized her.

"Lexington's a couple of hours north," said Kyle, glancing at her again. "You sure you're okay?"

She sensed his concern, but couldn't begin to explain her emotional turmoil. Hugging herself to ward off the deep-seated chill, she answered in what she hoped was a convincing tone.

"I'm fine."

"You cold?"

"A little."

He turned on the heat even though the temperature in the Jeep was plenty warm. The small, sensitive action made Rianna feel weepy and confused. She blinked back tears and stared out the windshield as they left the lights of town behind them.

Darkness settled around them as they hit the open highway. Her thoughts churned along with the echo of tires on the road. Memories of the months spent in Gregory's home kept whirring through her mind like a movie reel, making her more and more agitated.

She'd taken on a phony identity for a noble cause. But no matter how she tried to rationalize her actions, she still felt cheapened by all the pretense and deceit. She'd become someone she neither knew nor liked. Somewhere along the path to justice, she'd lost herself, and it scared the hell out of her.

Despite the warmth of the car, she could quell neither the chills coursing through her nor the sick rolling in her stomach. Each passing mile brought a more frantic need to run and hide. Not just from Gregory, but from life and all the emotional upheaval that went with it.

She'd known going into the assignment that the risks amounted to a lot more than physical danger. She'd been repeatedly lectured by Donald and warned by the psychologists. She'd read all the data and known what to expect.

So why didn't any of it comfort her now? Why were her hands as cold as ice? Why couldn't she steady the shaky, queasy feeling of shock?

They'd been traveling for less than an hour when Kyle slowed the car, pulled to the side of the road and shut off the engine. The unexpected action jarred Rianna out of her silent misery. She glanced around them, seeing nothing but shadows beyond the highway, and then she turned to stare at Kyle.

He took a deep breath, his chest expanding and then relaxing. Next he unclipped his seat belt and hers, reaching to gather her into his arms. The instant she realized he was offering comfort, she launched herself at him. Wrapping her arms tightly around his neck, she clung to him as though her next breath depended on the contact.

His arms tightened in response. He pulled her across his lap as she pressed closer, burying her face in the curve of his shoulder. He felt hard and wonderfully solid, his sweatshirt damp from the excessive heat in the car. He'd sacrificed his comfort to try to soothe her, and that made her feel even more pathetic.

He hugged her tightly, his warmth permeating deep into her bones, chasing away the coldness. A sob clawed at her throat, and a tremor shook her as she battled her personal demons.

"I'm sorry," he said roughly, rubbing his face against her hair. "I should have gotten to you sooner.

I wanted to make sure none of the others were near, but I shouldn't have let Rudy touch you.''

She shook her head in denial. "It's not just Rudy," she said, although his repulsive treatment had triggered her reactions. "It's the whole dirty business."

"Yeah, I know."

His low, soothing tone seeped into her ear and her heart. She realized that he really did understand.

"It's okay," he added, pressing a kiss to her temple. "You're just crashing a little. Don't be scared."

Rianna knew he'd experienced similar situations. Still, she tried to explain. "For a little while, on the boat," she whispered roughly, "I felt so clean and normal."

"I know."

Suddenly, she needed to let it all out, to get the terrible secrets off her mind. "I loved the power and adrenaline of living the lie, but I hate myself for feeling anything but disgust. I want Gregory punished, yet I wonder if I'm any better than him with all the lies and deceit."

"There's no doubt about that," he assured, gently stroking her back. "Bringing him down means avenging a lot of people and saving a lot more."

"I know. I keep telling myself that, over and over again," she whispered. "I know what I did was important, personally and professionally. It just makes me sick. All of it. The games, the deception, the running and hiding. I just want it to be done."

Kyle nuzzled her neck, still speaking quietly and calmly in her ear. "The psychologists warned you, didn't they?"

She nodded, rubbing her head against his, soothed

by the contact. "I know all the psychological explanations. It's just harder to deal with the reality of it."

"Yeah," he gruffly agreed. "It's harder. Especially as deep as you infiltrated."

Rianna felt the increased tension in his body and hugged him even harder. She stopped wallowing in self-pity long enough to wonder what he felt and thought about her assignment. She'd let him believe she'd slept with a murderer and thief.

A heavy dose of guilt assailed her. Kyle had done nothing but help and protect her, yet she'd constantly doubted him and his motives. She'd deceived him by letting him believe a lie, and she'd used that lie to protect her own cowardly fear of involvement. It was past time to level with him, and risk a deeper involvement.

"I was inside the operation, but not as deep as you think," she confessed in a small voice. "Gregory and I were never lovers."

Kyle stiffened, and then eased her away until they could see each other. Moonlight bathed his taut features.

"Explain."

Rianna flattened her hands on his chest and dropped her gaze from the intensity of his. "Gregory's main interest in me was social status. I made it clear from the beginning that I wouldn't have sex until after we were married. He agreed, and kept his end of the bargain."

"He just wanted a pretense of normalcy?"

"Yes."

She dared a glance at him, but he looked even more fierce.

"So you didn't actually prostitute yourself for the

assignment?'' he growled, lifting her off his lap and putting some space between them.

His words stung, and her breathing stilled. Her next words were hard to get past the dryness in her throat. ''That's what you think of me? That I'm some kind of whore who'd use my body to gather evidence?''

''You tell me what to think.''

Rianna felt a small surge of anger, but it was quickly squelched. Sadness and regret followed. As much as she wanted his unconditional respect, she couldn't blame him for thinking the worst. She'd encouraged everyone to believe it.

''Gregory and I had a pact. He wanted a society wife, and I pretended to be penniless. That gained me entrance to his estate.''

Kyle's gaze never wavered. He stared at her with unblinking intensity. ''You're saying you never slept with him?''

''Never.'' The thought nauseated her. ''He has a mistress. She's just not suitable wife material.''

''Damn!''

His curse echoed loud and long as he continued to glare at her. She could almost feel him struggling with the truth. A myriad of expressions crossed his features—first shock and disbelief, then relief, and then renewed anger.

''We've been living in each other's pockets for the past few days, and you knew it bugged the hell out of me,'' he growled. ''Why didn't you tell me the truth?''

She was silent for a minute as she studied his tense expression. Then she warily made another confession. ''I didn't know if I could trust you.''

He rubbed his jaw and stared out the windshield. Rianna held her breath, wondering if she'd completely alienated him with her honesty. When moments passed without any comment, she settled back into her seat and fastened the seat belt.

Kyle fastened his seat belt and reached for Rudy's cell phone. He handed it to her before starting the Jeep and pulling back onto the highway. His attitude didn't invite further confidences.

"Better call directory assistance and get the number for the Somerset police," he said. "Tell them where to find Rudy and that there might be a warrant for his arrest."

"What if he tells them we attacked him and stole the car? They might put out a warrant for us."

"He can't risk involving more law enforcement agencies. His only recourse right now is silence."

Rianna got the number and called the police department. She identified herself as FBI Agent Mary Sullivan, and gave them her shield number. Then she explained her belief that a wanted criminal could be located in the alley near the post office. She added a warning that Rudy was extremely dangerous and might have cohorts in the area.

"Done," she said as she clicked off the connection.

"Did he sound podunk or professional?"

"He sounded skeptical, but intelligent and willing to follow through."

Next, she dialed Sullivan's private number. He answered after the first ring.

"What the hell took you so long to call?"

His impatience brought a smile to Rianna's lips. "We've been a little busy." She briefly outlined their escape from the boat, the electronic bug and the run-in with Rudy.

"He's still tied up in an alley?"

"I just reported him to the Somerset Police Department. You might want to call them and corroborate my story. There is a warrant for his arrest, isn't there?"

"Damn straight. And we have Haroldson behind bars." His tone held deep satisfaction. "He's been denied bail, at least for right now. I'm hoping the bulk of evidence will prevent any judge from releasing him, but you can bet his lawyers are working overtime to get him freed."

"Yes!" she shouted, feeling a rush of triumph. She turned to Kyle and repeated the good news. "He's behind bars and denied bail!" Of Sullivan, she asked, "You found the videotapes?"

"All of them, plus a few more stashed in the hidden safe you told me about. The evidence is damning and indisputable."

"You're being especially careful?"

"I swear on my life. He's not gonna slip through any legal loopholes. We've got him, and he's gonna pay, thanks to you."

"No." Rianna shook her head, thinking about her father and all the others who'd lost their lives. "Not just me. So many people gave so much. They all deserve credit."

"Where are you now?"

She glanced at Kyle, wondering how much to say over the phone. "I'm not on a secure phone. We took this one from Rudy, so I'd better leave details 'til later. When do you need me in D.C.?"

"We'll need depositions as soon as possible. You know the drill. I'd like to get started Monday. Make your way back to the summer place this weekend, and we'll take it from there."

"Okay. I'll see you soon."

"Stay safe," Sullivan insisted, then broke the connection.

Rianna closed the phone and set it on the seat between her and Kyle. She briefly repeated the conversation to him even though he'd heard her end of it.

"Where's the summer place?"

"He has a cabin about an hour from D.C."

"You've been there?"

She shot a glance at him. His expression hadn't softened, and he sounded disgusted again. "I know how to get there." Her answer might not satisfy him, but she didn't want to deal with any more issues tonight.

Realizing she'd gotten really warm, she shut off the heater. "You can open a window if you want. I'm fine now."

"You're sure?"

"I'm sure." She tugged at the strap around her throat. "I'm hot now and this stupid collar is starting to strangle me. Where are we, anyway?"

She desperately wanted to believe they could outrun Gregory's lethal pursuit and make it to somewhere, anywhere safe.

# Chapter 8

The ER doctor in Lexington ordered Kyle out of the room when he got ready to operate on Rianna, but Kyle refused to budge. He wouldn't leave her. Not even for a minute.

The last time he'd let her out of his sight, Rudy had grabbed her. He'd died a thousand deaths while that gun barrel was pressed against her face, and never wanted to feel that kind of fear again. Especially since the short-lived incident had triggered a violent reaction in her. She'd been handling her extraction from the undercover assignment in a safe, gradual manner until that point.

The doctor hadn't put up much of an argument once he'd introduced himself as Rianna's federal bodyguard. Fortunately, the doc had been so appalled by the implant that he'd removed it without asking a lot of questions. They'd gotten by with a minimum of detail.

The procedure only required local anesthetic and a

couple of new stitches. The operation was over in less than an hour with the whole visit charged to the FBI through Rianna's real bureau identification, Mary Sullivan.

"You're sure you feel like leaving the hospital so soon?" Kyle asked, sliding an arm around her back and guiding her out the emergency room doors. They'd decided to leave the Jeep in the hospital parking lot and hire a taxi. Tomorrow, they'd rent a different vehicle.

"I'm sure," she said. "There's no reason for me to stay. It's no different than any other outpatient surgery. Besides, Gregory had the bug implanted while I was in his house." Her tone turned caustic. "He didn't even bother with antibiotics."

Kyle's hands clenched into fists. He hated the idea of that scum touching her or having any control over her, whether they'd been intimate or not.

Endangering her with a less-than-sterile surgery was just one of Haroldson's many crimes. Inserting a foreign body so close to the base of her brain without her consent would be cause for prosecution in most people's eyes. The man had a lifetime of atrocities to atone for.

He couldn't think about it now. He had more immediate worries, like keeping Rianna safe. Just the thought made his gut twist. Somewhere along the line, she'd become more than an assignment; more than his need to avenge a partner's murder; more than just a friend. He hadn't worked it all out in his mind yet, but he was fully committed to protecting her from harm.

The taxi driver took them to a twenty-four-hour shopping mart where they had a bite to eat and bought a few necessities. Then they hired a different cab to take them to a motel on the north side of the city. It was nearing four a.m. by the time they'd registered and settled in to their room.

"Why don't you get cleaned up first," he told her after they'd done a complete security check, double-locking the door and window. The ground-level room was furnished in neutral tones like thousands of others in the chain—generic but clean.

"Suits me fine," said Rianna.

Kyle could see the strain of the day's events etched on her features. The fine skin under her eyes looked bruised and her face creased with worry lines. He had an unexpected urge to smooth away the creases and bring back her confidence.

"You're not supposed to get those stitches wet," he reminded, as she grabbed a shopping bag and walked into the bathroom.

"I know, and my hair's filthy. I'll have to improvise."

"Need help?"

His offer was sincere, yet the vision that popped into his mind was anything but pure. His memory conjured the image of her stretched out on a deck chair, her slim, shapely body glistening in the sun. Then he mentally removed the bikini—and felt a shaft of heat between his legs.

"No, thanks. I'll just be slow and careful."

Her calm rejoinder was further evidence of her exhaustion. She didn't even bother to berate him for the suggestion. Kyle smiled slightly, blocking the mental image and commanding his body to relax.

To pass the time, he sorted through the things he'd bought at the store: jeans, a couple of T-shirts and some underwear. The shoes he'd found at the cabin would be okay until he got home. He'd bought another pair of gym shorts for sleeping.

The only room available so late had been a single with a queen-size bed. That meant they'd have to share, and he'd have to make a strong effort to control his desire. A desire that had been steadily escalating since the first time he held the elusive Phantom in his arms.

Kicking off his shoes, he stretched out on the bed and grabbed the TV remote. The late-night offerings didn't hold much appeal, but he settled on the sports network to pass the time while he waited for his turn in the bathroom.

In less than fifteen minutes, the door reopened, and Rianna came back into the room. His breath stopped at the sight of her, his muscles knotting and slow heat curling in his belly.

The sleepwear she'd picked looked like a man's boxer shorts and a sleeveless white undershirt. It should have been plain, but not with the soft fabric molded to her damp body. She lifted an arm to adjust the towel around her head, and the action brought the shirt tight against the fullness of her breasts. She wore a bra, yet he could still see the outline of hard, round nipples.

Heat poured through him like roiling lava, slow and thick and scalding. A cloud of sweet-smelling steam engulfed him, making his muscles tighten even more, while his heart pumped a little too fast.

It would never do. They were both too tired to deal with sexual complications right now. Their relationship was too fragile, their future too unpredictable. Maybe a really cold shower would help.

Gritting his teeth, he clicked off the TV and rose from the bed. "You done in there?"

"It's all yours, but I could use a little help first, if you don't mind."

Kyle moved closer. Everything about her delighted his senses, so he feasted on the closeness. He wanted to touch and taste and explore. More important, he wanted to do anything he could to help her rest and recuperate from her ordeal.

"What's the problem?"

Her expression, though still weary, was relaxed. The delicate, freshly scrubbed features appealed to him far more than the perfectly made-up socialite demeanor. Everything about her attracted him like a magnet.

"I got my Band-Aid a little damp, so I took it off. Could you please put another one over the stitches?"

She handed him a fresh one and turned her back. His hands trembled as he applied it over the spot on her nape. Just the feel of her skin under his fingers sent erotic messages throughout his body, and had him aching for more. He dragged in a long breath, but that only served to pull her scent more deeply into his system.

"All set." He cleared the gruffness from his throat and grabbed some clean clothes. "I won't be long."

In actuality, it took him fifteen minutes of frigid water to calm his rampaging desire. Then he took his time shaving, brushing his teeth and drying his hair.

He hoped Rianna would be sound asleep by the time he returned to the bedroom, but no such luck. She sat at the top of the bed with her legs curled under her. Her hair framed her face in a perfect oval, the baby-fine tresses looking shiny, clean and soft. Her shorts and top did little to conceal all her tempting curves. The sight of her elevated his temperature again, to dangerous levels.

She gave him a gentle smile that sent his blood pressure soaring with the simple innocence of it. There was nothing sexual or deliberately alluring about her manner, and he didn't know if he liked that or not. He wanted her trust and wanted her to feel safe with him, but he didn't want things to get too platonic between them.

"Watching anything special or ready for some shut-eye?"

"Sleep," Rianna assured him, clicking off the television. She set the remote on the bedside table and switched off the light. Then she slid beneath the sheet.

"Okay if I sleep on the left side?"

"No problem," he said. "I'll leave the bathroom light on and keep the door cracked in case you have to get up during the night."

"Thanks."

Kyle laid the Glock on the table next to his side of the bed. He was certain Rianna had the smaller gun within reach. He didn't expect any trouble, but they couldn't afford to get careless.

He wondered what she'd done about her little security pouch. She obviously wasn't wearing the neon-green bikini anymore or he'd have seen it through her white shorts. Warning himself not to dwell on that area of her body, he switched off his light. Then he stretched out on top of the covers and folded his arms behind his head.

They lay quietly for a while, adjusting to the unfamiliar sounds and shadows. Kyle tried to concentrate on everything but the warm, sexy, sweet-smelling woman at his side and how long it had been since he'd shared a bed with any woman. He thought back to the night Sullivan had called him. He'd been wishing for a woman in his bed. Now he had one, but had to curb his appetite.

He listened to the steady hum of the air conditioner. It drowned out most of the noise beyond the room. He studied the sprinkler system valve on the ceiling, trying to keep his mind occupied until boring details could lull him to sleep.

"Kyle?"

Rianna's soft, hesitant whisper of his name made his nerves go haywire. He dragged in a slow breath.

"Yeah?"

She waited so long to respond that he finally shifted on his side and faced her. She turned toward him, her gaze settling on his face, but she didn't say anything else.

"What's wrong?"

"Would you hold me?"

A wild surge of emotion exploded inside him, so strong that it sent a shudder through his body. He wanted her in every sense of the word, in every way a man could want a woman, but he knew she only needed reassurance. She wasn't asking for sex, just comfort and the intimacy of being close to another human being.

Still, he didn't hesitate. He gathered her, sheet and all, into his arms and pulled her against his chest. She slid one arm around his waist and snuggled her face into the curve of his shoulder. Pressing a light kiss on the silky softness of her hair, he urged her to relax.

"You need to rest."

"I can't seem to shut down my brain."

He slowly rubbed the small of her back, enjoying the contact, even through layers of clothes. "You're not still worried about Haroldson's men?"

"No."

"Then what's bothering you? Something specific or just everything?" he asked, keeping his tone light.

"All of it. The ugliness and deceit and my part in it. Even though I know how important it was to bring him to justice, I wish I'd never heard his name. Never learned all his dirty secrets. Never had to deal with him."

Kyle went still. "Did he hurt you? Does he have some sort of sick or perverted habits?"

"No. I was just another possession."

Anger roared through him, swift and uncontrollable. "How the hell could you stand it? Seeing him every day? Living in his pocket? Letting him believe he had the right to touch you whenever he wanted?"

Rianna stiffened and started to pull from his grip, but Kyle instantly tightened his hold on her. He cursed his own lack of control and willed himself to calm down, willed his muscles to relax until she felt comfortable enough to continue.

"Sorry."

"I understand," she whispered, hugging him briefly. "It makes me sick with anger, too, but I've spent half my lifetime working toward one goal. I want to see him pay for his crimes. Every time I felt sickened by the sight of him, I reminded myself of those long, lonely years."

"Long and lonely?" He didn't understand. "Explain."

When she didn't immediately respond, he tilted her head so that he could look into her eyes. Even in the darkness, he could see the turbulent emotion.

"Why was it so important for you to bring him to

justice? He's just one of a thousand criminals the FBI wants.''

It took a few moments for her to answer, and he had to strain to hear the response.

''He killed my family.''

The cold, hard edge to her voice shook him as much as the bald statement. He knew he wasn't going to like the details, but he wanted her to trust him enough to offer them. Tucking her against his chest again, he murmured in her ear.

''Can you tell me about it?''

''I've never discussed it with anyone but Donald.''

A spike of jealousy caught him unaware, slamming through his body and making his muscles bunch. More slow, deep breaths.

''So tell me.''

A long minute passed. Rianna stroked his back, her hand soft and warm. He didn't know if she was searching for words or refusing to share the story, until she finally responded.

''My dad worked for Gregory a long time ago. As his accountant, Dad was the first to notice the money laundering and other illegal activities. He went to the FBI and agreed to testify, but Gregory managed to lay the blame on one of his bank managers. The charges against him were dropped.''

''Leaving your dad to pay the consequences?'' he put in grimly.

''Our family went into the protection program, but Gregory never stopped searching for us. He had to set an example, he had a reputation to establish, and he wanted revenge. We kept moving, but he kept finding us. When I was sixteen, his men shot both my parents and my baby brother. Then they set our house on fire, and it was all my fault,'' she ended on a sob.

''You can't blame yourself,'' he said gruffly. ''You weren't responsible for his crimes.''

Rianna continued in a strained voice. ''It was my fault he found us again. Dad and Mom were worried and ready to move, but I had a date for the high school prom. I begged them to wait a few more days, and they only stayed because of me,'' she said roughly. ''They'd have been safe if I hadn't been so spoiled and selfish.''

Kyle's heart ached for her. He hugged her closer, wanting to absorb some of her pain. He knew how much it had hurt to lose his dad, then Margie. He could only imagine how Rianna had suffered. She'd lost everyone she loved, and she blamed herself.

''How'd you escape?''

She cleared her throat and continued in a flat tone. ''I was at a neighbor's, but ran home when I heard the sirens. I'd been told to hide and call Donald in an emergency, so that's what I did. He falsified the records to show that I'd died, too, and then put me in protection again.''

She didn't need to say any more. Kyle could figure out what had happened from that point. She'd become obsessed with the need to avenge her family, to see some form of justice done. Then she'd spent more than a decade working toward her most important assignment.

''You've got him now.''

''He needs to pay for destroying my family.''

Her breath caught on a strangled sob that made him ache to ease the pain. How could you comfort someone who'd lost so much? He still hadn't come to terms with the guilt over Margie's death. Rianna had lost her family, plus the innocence of youth. No wonder she was driven.

"Your family would be proud."

"You think?" she asked wistfully. "I wonder sometimes. My parents wanted to see Gregory brought to justice, but I'm not sure they'd approve of my methods. They'd never condone lying and deceit. I just didn't know any other way."

"How could they not be proud of your dedication and determination? You're working on the side of the law. That's the lesson they taught you."

She sighed, snuggling closer. "You're right. I followed in my dad's footsteps when I gave evidence to the FBI. And I'll testify just like he did, but I'm sick and tired of it. Once Gregory is convicted, I never want to hear his name again."

"I'll second that." He swore softly. "I don't care if I never hear the name again, either."

With those words, the conversation ended and the room grew quiet again.

"We'd better get some sleep," he finally murmured.

Rianna made a soft sound that could have been agreement, and then exhaustion took its toll. Her grip on his waist eased, and Kyle knew she'd finally drifted to sleep. He smiled slightly and dropped another kiss on her hair. The soft, silky feel of it soothed him as much as the warmth of her womanly body.

She generated a whole host of feelings he'd never experienced with any other woman, possessiveness being primary. He wanted to lay claim to her in the most elemental fashion, make love to her until she forgot every other man she'd ever known. Until her world revolved around him, not Haroldson, her job or anything else.

It was a selfish desire, but he felt it nonetheless. The admission made him frown. He'd never been the jealous, possessive type, had never wanted a woman to be solely dependent on him.

Rianna was different.

And definitely off-limits right now. He had to be patient. This wasn't the time or place to stake a claim. They both needed sleep. He pressed his cheek against the softness of hers and gradually let his mind and body relax.

Hours later, he awakened as the warmth of Rianna's body left his side. Grumbling in complaint, he reached for her, but she dodged his arms. He struggled with grogginess as she moved to the foot of the bed, pulling the sheet with her.

When she grasped one of his feet in her hands, her touch jarred him awake.

"What?"

He had no concept of the time, though sunshine glistened around the edges of the heavy drapes. The room was still shadowed, but light enough to see his sexy bedmate as she knelt at his feet. Her hair was tousled, her face flushed with sleep, and her expression mysterious.

She took his right foot into her hands and slowly massaged his heel, then his arch and the ball of his foot. Her hands were warm and soft, her thumbs stroking firmly. Heat arrowed up his leg to his groin. By the time she reached for his other foot, his morning arousal had surged to aching fullness.

"I owe you a massage," she said quietly, her gaze locking with his. "Remember?"

His voice came roughly. "You don't owe me anything."

He wanted her more than his next breath. The blood sang through his veins in a heated rush, but he didn't want her offering anything out of gratitude.

"You carried me too far. You'll be stiff and sore this morning." She moved between his legs and began to rub his right calf with long, strong strokes, her fingers working magic on the hard muscles. She gave the same slow, diligent attention to his left leg, and then both knees.

Kyle groaned with pleasure. "Damn, that feels good," he muttered, holding her gaze. They stared into each other's eyes for a long, breathless moment.

"Be warned," he told her softly. "If you keep it up, I'll want a whole lot more than a massage."

"I'll do my best," she promised huskily.

He gave her a fierce frown. "Not from gratitude." He didn't want gratuitous sex. He wanted her as needy as him.

She smiled, a slow, sultry, beautiful smile that turned his insides to mush and made his flesh prickle with anticipation.

"The massage is in appreciation. Anything else will be strictly my pleasure."

She trusted him. He'd finally earned her trust, and he knew it wasn't something she gave lightly. He hadn't realized how badly he wanted it until she offered it. Satisfaction flowed over him like warm honey.

Her palms flattened across the top of his thighs, her fingers still kneading. She spread his legs wider and inched closer. Her touch electrified him, the heat sizzling along his nerves, his muscles clenching with each new stoke.

When she slid her fingers toward the hem of his shorts, he shuddered and reached for her. She countered the move by grabbing his hands, pressing them on the bed and clucking her tongue in rebuke. Then she urged him to roll onto his stomach.

Kyle complied, turning, and muffled a moan against the pillow as she straddled his hips. Her heat seared him, her thighs blanketing him with feminine softness through the thin barrier of clothing. Blood roared in his head.

She worked on the muscles of his back and shoulders, her touch strong and sure. His hands curled into fists at his sides as his body sang with excitement. Next, she slowly slid off his hips and straddled his thighs.

"You're a little tense, Tremont," she teased.

His tone was hoarse with arousal. "No kidding."

Then her hands cupped his buttocks, strong fingers igniting an even stronger reaction from his flesh. His nerves were strung taut, his muscles bunched, his arousal growing thicker and harder with every beat of his heart.

Rianna slid off his legs and urged him to turn onto his back again. This time she straddled his hips, pressing her soft warmth tightly against his straining flesh. He made a sound deep in his throat and reached for her, but she snatched his hands and pressed them down on either side of his head. He tried to steal a kiss while she nibbled on his chin.

Her next caress was a string of wet, open-mouth kisses down his neck and across his chest. She took a long, torturous time to bathe his nipples. Her tongue sent hot, primitive need racing through him. Every nerve ending in his body hummed with tension.

By the time she'd worked her way down to his navel, his breathing had grown ragged and his chest heaved. He broke a sweat as her nimble fingers reached inside his shorts.

"You're killin' me," he groaned.

She cupped him and stroked him until Kyle nearly strangled on his own need. He couldn't let her fondle him much longer. This time when he reached for her, she didn't resist, but slid back up his body and locked her mouth with his.

Their moans mingled as he plunged his tongue through her lips and explored the sweet depths beyond. He wanted to taste every inch of her, eat her up and lose himself in the taste, scent and feel of her.

He cupped her head in his hands, clutching fistfuls of silky hair to guide her closer. Their mouths were pressed tightly together, but he still couldn't get enough of her. He angled his head, then sucked her tongue between his teeth and molded it with his own.

His hunger for her was insatiable. The more she gave, the more he wanted. He'd never wanted anyone so desperately. Even the need for breath annoyed him. After a quick drag of air, he captured her mouth in another deep, drugging kiss.

While he clung to her head, her hands were busy tugging at the waistband of his shorts. He paused long enough to shrug out of his clothes and kick them aside. Then he helped her lift her shirt over her head.

When she unhooked her bra and removed it, he was awed at her beauty. He forced himself to take long, calming breaths while he admired the feel and shape of her. He slid his palms over her rib cage and cupped the soft, firm mounds of her breasts, using his thumbs to bring the tips to rigid attention. She rocked against him in response, and her mewing sounds of pleasure fed his excitement.

''Kyle!''

The sound of his name on her lips had desire coiling even tighter in his groin. He pulled her up his body until he could replace his hand with his lips, and then sucked a nipple deeply into his mouth. He teased the tight bud with the tip of his tongue and felt her body arching against him in feminine demand.

Her throaty sound of hunger made him quiver like a tightly plucked bowstring. Together, they managed to get her out of her shorts and panties. Then they swallowed each other's groans as they savored the feel of bare flesh against bare flesh.

He clutched her thighs and bucked against her as they got lost in another potent, probing kiss. He felt her hands on his cheeks, her grasp tight. Her mouth grew demanding as she rubbed her breasts against his chest, the hard nubs of her nipples spiking the heat in him even higher.

They kissed until neither of them could breathe. Their chests heaved, their bodies straining for more. Then Rianna slid down his body until his straining arousal was trapped at the cradle of her thighs. He gasped for breath, his chest heaving at the exquisite feel of her.

''Protection?'' she insisted throatily.

''In the drawer,'' he muttered.

She took care of that, too, and he almost came apart at her touch. Before he could completely recover, she eased herself onto his straining flesh and enveloped him with her soft, wet warmth.

So tight. So damn hot and tight. And so tense. It

took a minute, but he finally realized that she'd gone really still and tense.

"Rianna?"

"I'm okay," she whispered, but she still didn't move.

"What do you mean, 'okay'?" He didn't like the sound of it or her stillness. "It's been a while for you?" That would explain the incredible tightness.

She mumbled something he couldn't understand, and then an amazing thought struck him. "Please don't tell me this is your first time."

"Okay."

Her lack of denial sent a shudder through him and convinced him that he'd hit on the truth. A deep, possessive thrill coursed through him, quickly followed by a desperate need to be gentle.

He closed his eyes and groaned, but held completely still until she'd had time to adjust to the size and feel of him. She gripped him tightly, sending another quiver of erotic pleasure up his spine. Once she'd accepted him and begun to move, he grasped her hips, arching upward to meet her slow, careful thrusts.

The pressure built too quickly, the need too forceful. He strained to hold back, until Rianna moaned his name. Then he surged against her and felt himself exploding in one long, fierce burst of pleasure.

She collapsed against him, their chests heaving from exertion, the sound of their labored breathing filling the silence. He knew it hadn't been all that great for her, but he silently swore to make it up to her.

For the next few minutes, all they could do was fight for air and hold each other while they recovered from the emotional and physical high.

Kyle hugged her tightly, wanting to prolong the exquisite contact. He closed his eyes, relishing the shared intimacy and the gift she'd given him. Not just her body, but her trust. He knew she didn't give either one too freely. He'd made love to his share of women, but never to one who'd been as generous in her loving. Gut instinct told him what a treasure he'd found. She was his now, and he intended to keep her.

His partner.

His lover.

His woman.

# Chapter 9

"**W**ow." Rianna exclaimed in a soft, sighing whisper. She'd never shared anything so intimate, but she could understand why women enjoyed it so much.

Their chests had stopped heaving, but his vibrated again with triumphant male laughter.

"'Wow' doesn't even come close," he argued gruffly. "It gets a lot better, I promise."

That brought a smile of satisfaction to her lips. She'd wanted their loving to be incredibly special because that's how she felt about him—a special, unique feeling unlike anything she'd ever known with a man.

His response thrilled her and sounded so sincere that she pressed a hard kiss on his chest.

"Control yourself, woman," he teased, running his fingers through her hair.

Then he cupped her head with his palm and lifted her face for a long, sweet kiss. She gently sucked his tongue into her mouth until a low, hungry sound gurgled from his throat.

When their lips parted, their gazes tangled. They stared into each other's eyes, intently searching. Rianna wondered what he hoped to find in hers. The dark, possessive gleam in his sent a tremble over her. Her nipples tightened in reaction. Their bodies were still so closely entwined that she felt his muscles begin to twitch with renewed energy.

"You should have told me," he insisted.

She didn't want to discuss her virginity or make a big deal of it. Nor did she want to tell him that he was the first man who'd ever tempted her to part with it.

"I'm the one who did the seducing," she reminded.

He wasn't satisfied with her response. He started to speak, but she placed a hand over his mouth. "We have to get moving." She wanted nothing more than to spend the day, or several, in bed in his arms. There was so much about him that she still needed to explore.

Kyle lifted his arm to check his watch. "It's after eleven and we have to be out of here by noon."

He didn't mention that Gregory's men might have tracked down Rudy and the rented Jeep by now. Given enough time, they'd eventually find them.

Rianna sighed. "First dibs on the bathroom," she said, wondering how to gracefully extricate herself from their embrace. Even though they'd just shared an incredible intimacy, she suddenly felt shy and awkward. She had no experience to fall back on, and modesty had her searching for something to cover herself.

"How about we share a shower? It'll save time," said Kyle.

She blinked, and then studied his wickedly suggestive expression. His eyes had that hungry look again.

Her stomach muscles clenched, but she had to resist temptation.

"You don't really think that will save time, do you?" she admonished, laughing and wedging some space between their upper bodies.

"It could happen."

When she started to sit up, he cupped her breasts in his hands. The contrast between his deeply tanned skin and her pale flesh gave her a feminine thrill. She watched him watching her as her breasts swelled, the tips budding. He teased them to hardness. When she felt his body hardening within hers, she cried out softly.

"Kyle!"

He held her gaze. "I know, we have to go, and you can't take a shower. You can't get your neck wet. But we could share a quick bath."

So sexy. So much a man. He was so handsome and irresistible that Rianna felt herself melting all over again. She barely recognized her own throaty voice when she finally managed a response.

"A bath sounds nice."

Kyle twisted around until his feet hit the floor, then he grasped her hips, lifting her without withdrawing from her body. She gasped at the exquisite sensation that coursed through her. His strength and obvious desire stirred hers to a frenzy again.

"Gun and condom," he mumbled as he locked his mouth on her neck, sucking strongly, drawing another gurgle of approval from deep in her throat.

Rianna grabbed both from the bedside stand, then wrapped her arms around his shoulders, rubbing her breasts against his chest to ease their tight ache.

She locked the door behind them once they'd entered the bathroom, then scattered kisses over his chest while he reached down to turn on the faucets. They paused for a long kiss as water filled the tub and steam began to fill the room.

Kyle laid the gun on the soap shelf, took care of protection and brought his hands back to her buttocks. He cupped her with his big palms, squeezing gently, then more roughly as sharp, heated passion flared between them again. He clutched her closer. She rocked against him in demand, and then swallowed his low growl.

She felt the heavy thrust of his hips as he began to move deep inside of her with renewed fervor. The fire in her belly flared like a torch to kindling. She wanted him closer, deeper. She wanted him so close that he became an extension of herself.

He turned, pressing her back against the wall so that he could free a hand to grasp her head. Then he plunged his tongue into her mouth, demanding another deep, wet, devouring kiss.

Rianna's thighs clenched convulsively, and she hugged him with arms and legs as he rocked against her. She returned his hungry kisses while meeting him thrust for powerful thrust, until they exploded in another fierce eruption of pleasure.

Guttural sighs of completion mingled in their mouths. When Kyle finally broke the contact, he pressed his forehead against hers. They sagged against the wall, trembling from head to toe, momentarily exhausted. Their breathing was labored again, with each fighting to draw air into depleted lungs.

"Whew!" he exclaimed on a harshly exhaled breath.

Rianna didn't even have the strength to laugh. She gave him a shaky smile, then a light kiss on the nose.

She clung to his sweat-slick body with what little strength she had left in hers.

He tightened his hold on her again, turning toward the tub. After testing the temperature, he shut off the taps and slowly eased her into the water. She tried to tug him in with her, but he resisted.

"Better not," he said, his voice still rough, his eyes glazed with satisfaction. He pressed a hard kiss to her lips, then drew in a rough breath and continued. "We'll have an overflow and end up wasting more time."

Rianna knew he was right. She reluctantly released him, then immediately felt naked and exposed. As soon as he'd moved back a step, she pulled the curtain to block his view.

"Hey!" he complained.

"I'm shy," she responded, grabbing a washcloth and soap.

His sexy laughter echoed in the small room. "You'll get over it," he promised.

She smiled to herself, but wondered at his assurances. Would she get the chance to grow accustomed to Kyle's loving? Would there ever be time and opportunity to make love until they were totally comfortable with each other? She doubted it, and it scared her to want it so badly.

As soon as he was out of sight, doubts started to assail her. For years, the only future she'd considered was the successful completion of this assignment. She hadn't allowed herself to think beyond that goal.

She had never allowed herself to become emotionally involved with a man. Never allowed herself to care so much, so fast. Had she just risked their lives by tempting fate? In her life, caring too much meant inviting pain and heartache.

One thing was certain. They had to concentrate on getting back to D.C. She couldn't fail now. She couldn't worry about relationships or the future or anything other than bringing Gregory Haroldson to justice. Everything else had to be put on hold until she'd accomplished that objective. She needed to stay focused, but it was getting harder and harder to do, with Kyle so near.

He shaved while she finished bathing, then they switched places. By the time he'd finished showering, she'd dressed in jeans and a yellow T-shirt. She was getting really tired of stiff, itchy new clothes, but didn't have much choice. Soon she'd be home and could get comfortable again.

Just a few more hours.

Then what? What would happen when she no longer needed Kyle's protection? When his promise to Donald had been fulfilled and their extraordinary partnership dissolved? Would that be the end of it? Would he go home, get on with his life and chalk up their time together as just one final assignment to be forgotten?

It hurt to even think about the what-ifs.

And that scared her spitless. The hurting part. She'd had more than her fair share of hurting. She'd been so careful not to care too much about anyone, yet Kyle had sneaked past her guard. He'd crept into her wary heart while she'd been too busy staying alive to notice the risk.

She couldn't worry about it now. They had to get back to Virginia. Their best hope was that Donald had all Gregory's men rounded up by now. Rudy should still be in jail, but they couldn't relax until Tabone, Damon and the others were accounted for. Not to mention anyone in the agency who remained on Gregory's payroll.

Rianna sat down on the bed and started pulling on her shoes, but when the bathroom door opened, her gaze flew to it. She caught her breath at the sight of Kyle, still damp from his shower, wearing nothing but a towel hitched around his waist.

Gorgeous didn't even come close to describing him. Extremely sexy. Incredibly virile. Unbearably appealing. His sun-bronzed skin glistened over broad shoulders, a muscled chest and flat stomach. Silvery-blond hair curled between dark nipples and arrowed downward toward the low-slung towel. Her blood began to heat all over again.

He returned her stare with equal intensity until the emotion flowing between them became almost too painful to bear. Panic clutched at her chest and climbed into her throat.

Her brave, sexy lover was also one of the most honorable men she'd ever known. That thought crowded out his physical appeal and reminded her that she'd complicated his life, endangered it, and made him an unwilling accomplice to the nightmare she'd been living for months.

''What's wrong?''

She shook her head and dropped her gaze, then concentrated on tying her shoes.

''Rianna?''

He started toward her, but she rose and put out a hand to halt him.

He frowned. ''You're not sorry...''

''No!''

Her emphatic response seemed to reassure him. He

gave her a smile and she returned it with one of her own.

"You're sure?" he demanded.

"Positive."

He studied her for another few seconds. "Good," he said. "I don't want you to have any regrets."

When she gave her head a vigorous shake, he finally turned away and started pulling clothes out of shopping bags.

She tried to lighten the mood. "I'm just worrying again," she said, moving toward the window to peek out the curtain. "Everything looks quiet, and there's only one car in the parking lot. We're probably the last to leave."

"Yeah, I imagine most of their customers are vacation travelers. Everyone else probably got an early start."

Rianna kept her gaze on the parking lot, but her attention stayed on Kyle. She heard him pulling on his shorts, then jeans, the zipper sounding especially loud in the quiet of the room. When he tugged a white T-shirt over his head, she turned to watch the flex of muscles as he tucked in his shirt and fastened the snap of his jeans.

Everything he did, every move he made, fascinated her. She wanted more time to explore, wanted to sate herself with him and then start all over again. Her heart pounded painfully in her chest at the idea of unrestrained, uninhibited loving.

Until today, she'd never thought of herself as a particularly sensual woman, but he'd changed that image forever. She wanted to smell and taste and feel until she had her fill. Just a pipe dream at this point in her life.

''Rianna? You sure you're okay?''

She realized she was staring at him again, and licked her suddenly dry lips. ''To be honest, I'm having a little withdrawal here. I want to go back to bed with you and stay there for a long, long time.''

She could see the effect her honesty had on him. His eyes darkened, his jaw tightened and his hands clenched into fists at his sides. His whole body went tense, then he took a deep breath and slowly exhaled.

''Someday soon,'' he swore softly.

She forced herself to breathe deeply, too. ''I'm going to hold you to that, Tremont.''

He grinned, a purely male, purely wicked grin that lightened her spirits. ''You won't have to work too hard at it.''

''Promise?''

''On my life.''

She returned his grin, and then crossed the room to collect the small pistol from the nightstand. She stashed it in a leather fanny pack she'd bought at the store last night, added the plastic bag with the disabled electronic bug they'd smashed and bagged, along with the refrigerator magnet. It was further evidence of Gregory's treachery.

Kyle tucked the Glock into the waistband of his jeans and covered it with his shirt. They were ready again.

''What now? Rent a car and drive to D.C.? Or take a cab to the airport?''

''I vote for flying, but the airports would be the most likely place to look for us. Especially Dulles,'' she said.

''We could drive into Ohio and catch a flight to Newark, then rent a car. They can't watch every airport in the region.''

Rianna nodded. "I want to call Donald again and get his input before deciding."

She could tell the idea didn't set well with Kyle. Why? Just a male thing, or a genuine mistrust of the other man? Surely that couldn't be the case. He was here as a favor to Donald.

"The fewer people who know our plans, the safer we'll be," he reminded.

"Donald may have news about Rudy and the others, and I want to make sure Gregory's still behind bars."

Kyle seemed reluctant, but finally nodded. "Okay, we call Sullivan, but not from Rudy's cellular. We'll bag it up with anything else we don't want and toss it in the Dumpster. We can find a pay phone to call Sullivan." He looked around. "Is that it?"

She'd already bagged up what few clothes she wanted to take with her and discarded the others. After surveying the room one last time, she nodded. "I don't think there's anything else."

"No extra underwear?" The frown on his face kicked up in a provocative grin. His blue eyes glittered like sapphires.

Rianna felt her face heat at the suggestion. "A good old safety pin will suffice in the absence of built-in panty pouches."

"Glad to hear it."

She'd forgotten to give him some money in case they got separated. Turning her back, she unfastened her jeans, unclipped the safety pin and pulled out a couple of big bills. When she'd refastened everything, she turned again, slamming into Kyle's chest.

The look on his face was so lascivious that she laughed out loud. "Back off, Tremont. You're altogether too interested in my secret hiding place."

"Damn straight," he growled, stealing a quick kiss.

Rianna returned his kiss with fervor, but they refrained from holding each other. When they broke apart, she handed him some money.

"First time I ever got paid for a kiss." He tucked the bills into his pocket.

"Consider it an advance," she teased.

"On services to be rendered?"

"Sounds good to me."

He made a move to take her into his arms, but quickly backed off. "Damn."

"I know." She felt the same way. She didn't want to leave their little cocoon and face the world again, but they had no real choice. "A cab or a rental company?"

"There's a little restaurant a couple of blocks down the street," he told her. "I noticed it last night. Why don't we walk down there, get something to eat, and see if any of Haroldson's men crawl out of the woodwork. If it looks safe, we can hire a cab to take us to the airport."

Rianna thought about it. Flying would certainly be the fastest way to make the trip. Kyle probably didn't want to waste any more time on the road dodging henchmen. He'd gone above and beyond his duty as a private citizen. He had to be anxious to get rid of her and get back to his normal life.

The idea shouldn't hurt, yet it did.

"Sounds like a plan." She hoped her tone sounded brisk and professional. It was time to start putting some emotional distance between them.

Turning from his probing gaze, she added, "I'm starved."

"Rianna?" He stopped her as she reached for the

doorknob. When she turned, he placed a brief, hard kiss on her lips, and then nudged her aside.

"I'll go first, make a sweep of the parking lot and toss our trash in the Dumpster. Then I'll check the office, and signal from there if it's all clear."

She sighed, but nodded agreement. As he made his way around the motel lot, she watched for any sign of trouble. She'd guarded the backs of other agents in the past, but never one that meant so much to her. She barely breathed until she saw him waving an all-clear from the doorway of the office. Quickly donning a pair of sunglasses, she joined him on the main sidewalk, where he put himself between her and the busy street.

The midday sun was hot, and their walk brisk. The street was lined with cars parked in front of various small shops. Two lanes of traffic moved steadily along, but no one seemed to pay them any undue attention. None of the passing vehicles held familiar faces or any sort of threat to them.

By the time they reached the restaurant, they were ready for the air-conditioning. Kyle settled into a corner booth with a clear view of the entrance and parking lot, while she made use of the pay phone just inside the front door.

She heard a series of clicks as Donald's home answering system forwarded her call. He picked up within a few seconds and didn't bother with polite greetings.

"Where are you?"

"We're in Lexington, and we want to fly back, but I wanted to make one last check with you before leaving here. What's happening?"

"Haroldson is still behind bars, but his lawyer is pulling out all the stops to get him freed. I convinced the police down there to keep Rudy until we can make a prisoner transfer.''

''Good. How about Tabone and the others?''

''I'm trying to verify their whereabouts, but they're still wild cards. Our best guess is they won't do anything too stupid or too public.''

''So you think it's safe for us to fly?''

''I don't advise it,'' he said. ''I don't have enough manpower to patrol the airports and there are too many of Haroldson's men unaccounted for. If you keep driving, you'll be one step ahead of them and leave a cold trail.''

Rianna didn't know how Kyle would take the news of more hours on the road, but she had to agree. She didn't like the odds of a busy airport. If they flew, they wouldn't have the authority to carry their weapons, so they'd be especially vulnerable.

Donald barely paused. ''You know the drill. Make sure you aren't being tailed, and head for the cabin. It's as secure as any safe house and you know the alarm codes. I should be there ahead of you, or as soon as I can get there.''

''It'll take us another eight or ten hours.''

Something in her tone had alerted him to her mood. ''Tremont giving you trouble?''

''No.''

''Your neck all right? You're not hurting?''

''No, I'm fine, really. I'm just ready to be home.''

''Soon,'' he reassured her. ''It's been the longest six months of my life, but I'll have you home soon. Then I'm never letting you out of my sight again.''

The fierceness of his tone made Rianna chuckle. ''Yes, sir,'' she teased. ''Suits me just fine.''

His voice dropped to a low murmur. "You know I love you."

"I know," she whispered. His unfaltering devotion had sustained her through some rough times. "I love you, too."

They said goodbye, and she returned to the booth. Kyle stared at her for a minute, his expression unexpectedly grim, and then he turned his attention to a menu.

She frowned, wondering what had caused his mood to darken, but she didn't ask. Instead, she studied her own menu. Once the waitress had taken their order and they were alone again, she outlined Donald's plan.

"I forgot we'd have to ditch our guns if we flew," he admitted, his brow furrowing. "Does Sullivan think Tabone and the others are still tailing us?"

"He can't be sure. They're unaccounted for, at this point. Damon's a wild card, too. I didn't have any concrete evidence against him, so he's not in custody. There's a warrant for Tabone if Donald finds him before he finds us."

"Let's hope he went into hiding when he heard about the other arrests."

"He's more of a lackey than a thinker, so he and the others might have given up the chase. With Gregory and Rudy in jail, there's no one left to organize the troops. At least, not for a while."

"I'm sure Haroldson has someone on payroll who's doing his bidding and seeing that his orders are obeyed."

"That would be Sanderson, his lawyer and flunky. He'll be the go-between for a while, but Donald is trying to freeze Gregory's assets. In that case, nobody gets paid."

"And a good crook's loyalty has to be bought."

"Right. If we spend another day on the road, all the rats will be abandoning ship."

Kyle gave her a strange look but didn't comment. Their meal arrived, so they were quiet while they ate. Despite being hungry, the food didn't sit well on Rianna's stomach.

Her thoughts churned while she considered the best way to handle the rest of the trip. She knew she needed to give him the opportunity of opting out of the mission, yet she hated to broach the subject. He'd be relieved or offended by her suggestion, and either option made her sick at heart.

When she'd eaten as much as she could manage, she studied Kyle for a minute, until the intensity of her scrutiny caught his attention.

"What's worrying you now?"

Rianna wasn't sure she liked having him read her mind or be so aware of her mood swings. She'd never had a truly intimate, sharing sort of relationship with a man who could sense her thoughts and feelings.

Avoiding the problem wouldn't solve it, so she explained. "I'm thinking it might be safer to go our separate ways now. If Gregory's men are still searching for us, they'll be looking for Tony and Samantha, not a lone woman who doesn't look very glamorous anymore."

Kyle's expression went stone cold. His lips thinned and his eyes glittered. The muscles in his jaw clenched, and she knew she'd really ticked him off. Part of her exalted in the knowledge while part of her cringed.

"Trying to give me my walking papers, Rianna?"

His tone rivaled the air-conditioning for chill factor. She fidgeted with her napkin. Then, annoyed with her uncharacteristic restlessness, she tossed it down and looked him directly in the eyes.

"I don't want you to feel obligated to drive all the way back to D.C. with me. I know you put your own life on hold to help Donald, but you've already done more than you bargained for. I think I'll be safe from here on out."

His expression went blank, his tone bland. "You think?"

She clenched her jaw, wishing she knew what he really wanted. "I'm a highly trained professional, remember?"

"Even the best professional needs backup sometimes." He watched her with unerring intensity. "What about the promise you just made? We have a lot of unfinished business between us."

"I'm not denying that," she said, lowering her lashes to hide how deeply his words touched her. "I'm just suggesting that it might have to wait until this whole case is settled."

"You don't think we make good traveling partners?"

She forced herself to look up at him again. "I'm more like a liability you haven't been able to shake. Not to mention you're risking your own life."

"If this is all about me, then why don't you let me decide if and when I want to be cut free?"

Relief rushed through her. She desperately wanted him to want to stay with her, but not out of some misguided sense of duty and honor. She took a deep breath and forced herself to relax.

"You think we can manage to stay one step ahead of the bad guys without risking life or limb?"

The tension in Kyle's expression eased at her attempt to dispel the dark mood, but his steady gaze didn't waver from her face. His tone was terse when he spoke again, his expression accusing.

"Was that a test, Special Agent Phantom?"

She blinked, disconcerted again by the way he read her thoughts and intentions. When she locked gazes with him again, hers was clear and steady. "Maybe a little one, but please don't be offended. I really want to do what's best for you at this point. You've put your own life on hold for a long time now."

He lifted a brow in arrogant disagreement. "How long have you been working the case?"

Rianna stared at him. She'd been undercover for a good part of the year, but she'd been working the case half her life. She shook her head, unwilling to voice the whole truth.

They were quiet for a minute, and then Kyle broke the silence with a new suggestion. "I think what's best for both of us is a little moving excursion."

She didn't follow his line of thinking. "What do you mean?"

He nodded toward the window facing the intersection. She followed his gaze, but didn't see anything out of the ordinary.

"What?"

"A truck rental company," he explained, pointing across the street. "Nobody's likely to be looking for us in a moving van. What do you say to renting one of those for the trip back east?"

She offered him a genuine grin. "Sounds like a winner. I still have one more phony ID to use."

His eyes darkened and his tone dropped an octave. "In your security pouch?"

She laughed out loud and then rose from the table. "In my jeans pocket, Tremont. My jeans pocket."

His answering grin warmed her heart.

# Chapter 10

They rented a small panel van and Kyle took the first shift of driving. Rianna couldn't believe how exhausted she still felt. She dozed during the next few hours, interspersing her sleep with long conversations about his home in Texas and his woodcraft business.

She learned that after retiring from the agency, he'd worked as a security guard for a fast-growing company. His investment in the company's stock allowed him the financial freedom to work for himself. He'd developed a longtime love of woodworking into a small business that was just starting to earn a profit.

The more she learned about Kyle, the more her admiration for him grew. He knew who he was and what he wanted from life. He had a real home and a plan for his future. In comparison, hers seemed really bleak. She'd never allowed herself to dream of any life beyond her obsessive need to see Gregory Haroldson punished.

Once she'd accomplished that objective, she had no idea what she'd be doing. The future loomed big and empty, all her insecurities threatening to rear their ugly heads. Despite her confidence in her ability to do her job, she had little else to be confident about these days. She had no close friends, no relationship skills or long-term goals.

In other words, not much to offer any man. That depressing thought had alarm bells ringing in her head. She was getting in way over her head with the renegade retiree. He'd never mentioned anything about perma-nency or long-term commitments. They had only known each other a few days, even though it seemed so much longer.

They stopped for dinner in Charleston, West Vir-ginia, and then Rianna took the wheel so that Kyle could get some rest. The freeway driving was monot-onous, but uneventful, as they swapped places every couple of hours. The steady speed allowed them to make good time, and they reached Maryland a little before midnight. It took another hour to get to Donald's cabin.

The natural wood, A-frame house nestled atop a small hill in a copse of evergreen trees. It sat about a hundred yards from the road and was surrounded by aesthetically appealing, high-security fencing. Lights blazed, illuminating the house from several directions.

Rianna's heart skipped a beat as they approached the iron entrance gates. The cabin had become her second home over the past few years, and the thrill of being close delighted her beyond words. She gave Kyle the code, and the heavy gates silently slid apart for them to pass.

As soon as they pulled to a stop near the house, the

front door opened. Donald stepped onto the porch, a tall, distinguished man with thick, graying hair and a smile that lit his craggy, aristocratic features with happiness. Rianna threw open her door, hopping out of the van before Kyle turned off the engine.

In the next instant, she and Donald had narrowed the distance between them, and she threw herself into his waiting arms. He hugged her fiercely, and she returned the embrace with all her strength. Her chest tightened, her throat constricting at the feel of his solid strength. She'd missed him badly.

"Welcome home, baby," he whispered near her ear, tenderly rocking her back and forth.

"You can't imagine how great it is to be here!" she insisted, blinking back tears and fighting a landslide of emotion. It rolled over her with an intensity that had her trembling in his arms.

"It's been too long," he added gruffly, reassuring her. "It's okay now. You're home and you're safe. I can do all the worrying from here on out. You just relax."

"I'll be happy to," she said, easing a little space between them so she could study his familiar, ageless features. "I'm ready to be done with it."

Their quiet conversation was interrupted by Kyle's terse greeting to Donald. "Sullivan."

His cold, hard tone had them slowly pulling apart and turning toward him. He stood in the shadows, but the bright porch light shone on his dark, angry expression. His stance was combative, his hand folded around the Glock. Rianna was taken aback by his belligerent attitude. He looked like an gunfighter itching for a fight.

"Kyle?" Her tone was questioning, but he ignored her and continued to glare at Donald.

"Tremont." Donald returned the greeting. The arm around her waist tightened protectively.

"Rianna's too exposed out here." Kyle ground the words out roughly.

The two men continued to scowl at each other for a few seconds, and then Donald agreed. "You're right." He nudged her toward the doorway. "Let's get inside." To Rianna, he added, "Somebody else is a little anxious to see you."

She shrieked with excitement. "Sophie's here?"

"Against my better judgment, but you know she never listens to anything I say."

They'd barely stepped into the house and closed the door before Rianna was being wrapped tightly in another pair of arms. The women shared cries of joy at seeing each other again. Donald's wife added her enthusiastic welcome with motherly hugs and kisses.

When they'd quieted, Donald made introductions.

"Tremont, this is my wife, Sophie," he said with an amused lift of his brow. "Sophie, this is Kyle Tremont. You've heard me mention him in the past. He used to be one of my agents, but I don't think the two of you ever met."

The slim, attractive redhead freed one hand and reached it to him. He grasped it briefly and nodded in greeting.

"I'll never be able to thank you enough for bringing Mary safely back to us," she insisted.

The Sullivans had always used the abbreviated form of Marianna for security purposes. They'd wanted her to retain part of her identity without putting her at risk, so she'd been Mary to them. Just another of her many names.

"She's the daughter of our hearts, and we've been worried sick about her for months," Sophie explained.

Kyle's thunderous expression lightened, and Rianna belatedly realized he'd been jealous of Donald. Her eyes widened at his misconception. Did he think her that dense and insensitive?

She frowned, flashing him a chastising look.

He returned her glance with an arrogant arch of a brow and without apology.

Donald cleared his throat, and Sophie chuckled softly at the byplay. "Boys," she scolded. "None of that macho posturing. We're all adults here."

Rianna just shook her head in disbelief. She actually felt flattered by Kyle's possessive attitude, and she'd never have believed it possible. Maybe she was getting soft in the head.

Or the heart.

That errant thought made her frown. She'd never aspired to be softheaded or softhearted.

"How's your neck?" asked Donald. "Let me see."

Rianna slid her hand up to touch the tiny row of stitches.

"What's wrong with your neck?" Sophie asked in alarm. "Did somebody try to strangle you?"

"No, no," Rianna insisted, glancing at Donald for guidance. He gave her a subtle shake of his head. She didn't like lying to Sophie, so she kept her explanation to a minimal. "I got hurt and had to have a couple of stitches, but it's fine now."

Sophie frowned, glancing from one of them to the other. Noting their closed expressions, she made a clucking sound of disgust. "Okay, don't tell me. I'm sure it's classified. Just show me and let me decide if it's all right or not."

Rianna turned her back, lifted her hair and tugged the Band-Aid off her neck. Sophie and Donald both shifted closer, studying the sutures. Sophie ran a gentle finger near the slightly raised flesh. Then they both conceded that the wound was healing nicely.

"Does it still hurt?" asked Donald.

"It never hurt very much, but it's starting to itch."

"That's just part of the healing process," chimed Sophie. "Did you need a tetanus shot? Your last one is probably outdated. Are you on antibiotics?"

"The doctor gave me a tetanus booster and a few days' worth of antibiotics," Rianna lied, intent on calming her concern. Sophie worried too much over the small things because she knew she had no control over the life-threatening ones.

"But it's never felt like it might be infected," she added. "It's really just a scratch."

Sophie cleared her throat. "Of course it is. Absolutely nothing to worry about. I promise I'm not going to waste time clucking over you like a mother hen." She quickly changed the subject. "Are you hungry? Donald insists that I can only stay a couple of hours. Safety first and all that, but we have time to share a meal."

"Something smells delicious," said Rianna.

"Your favorite, of course." Sophie hugged her close again. They led the way down the hall to the kitchen with the men following. "Pot roast with new potatoes and baby carrots. I even outdid myself with dessert. Coconut cream pie with lots of tall, fluffy meringue."

Rianna moaned in delight. "You shouldn't have

gone to so much trouble, but I'm glad you did. My mouth's watering already.''

"Consider yourself lucky," Donald teased. "My stomach's been growling loud enough for the neighbors to hear, but Sophie wouldn't give me a scrap of food until you got home."

"My poor darling," Sophie cooed, wrinkling her nose at her husband. "You do have it rough, don't you."

Their good-natured teasing set the tone for the next hour. Everyone seemed determined to enjoy the meal without letting reality intrude. There was no mention of the ongoing case or anything serious until they'd finished eating.

Over coffee, Donald caught them up on the Haroldson matter. The overwhelming evidence against the man prevented him from using his money or power to influence the courts. None of his wealthy associates was willing to risk supporting him at this point. He was still being held without bond, and his lawyer was starting to discuss the possibility of cutting a deal.

"The district attorney has assured me that the state won't accept a plea bargain. Not unless it's from Rudy Barrick. If he wants to turn state's evidence against Haroldson, then they might bargain for reduced sentences, but nobody is walking in this case."

"Is there any way Mary can avoid testifying?" asked Sophie.

"As the agent assigned to the case, her testimony is crucial," Donald explained. "I wish we could get by with a formal deposition, but her eyewitness accounts need to be heard by the judge and jury. We probably have enough evidence to lock Haroldson away for a few years, but her testimony can keep him behind bars with no chance of parole.''

"Couldn't she do one of those video testimonies?'' asked Sophie. ''Aren't they sometimes used to protect an agent's identity or safety?''

"The judge might allow it,'' he replied, his tone noncommittal. ''But it's not nearly as effective as putting her in the courtroom.''

"There could be years of appeals,'' said Kyle.

"I understood all that from the beginning,'' Rianna insisted, her tone firm. ''I'm totally committed to seeing the process to an end, however long it takes. I will not let him win this battle.''

Quiet settled over the room as they all accepted the reiteration of her decision. Then Kyle changed the subject. ''What have you learned about Blaine? How long's he been dirty?''

Before Donald could respond, Rianna added another question. ''Was he the mole who kept selling my family's whereabouts to Gregory?'' She'd vowed to learn who was responsible for the breach in security that had compromised her family's location every few years.

"I don't see how Blaine could have had access to that kind of high-level information,'' said Kyle.

"He didn't,'' explained Donald. ''When we searched Blaine's apartment, we found a ledger that belonged to my predecessor, Bob Mullet. Apparently Bob had been selling information to Haroldson for years.''

"Didn't Mullet die a few months after Margie?'' asked Kyle.

"Yeah, supposedly of natural causes, but we're checking into that a little closer now, too. From what we can determine, Blaine learned about Mullet's involvement though Margie's death and started black-mailing him. When Mullet died, Blaine offered himself as Haroldson's new mole.''

''And now they're both gone.''

Rianna's comment brought silence to the room. The new information went a long way toward answering some unresolved issues regarding her family.

''I'm sure Haroldson is actively recruiting new informants,'' said Donald. ''All we can hope for is to stay one step ahead of him.''

''And we still don't know who actually killed my parents and brother.''

''Mullet's records might give us another lead on that, too,'' added Donald. ''There's a mention of a hired gun. We think it relates to an international hit man, but that's all we have to work with. No name or country of origin.''

''So he could be dead or alive?''

''Anything's possible, but that was a long time ago and it's not a very safe profession. Chances are he's dead or serving time for another murder. Haroldson isn't likely to cough up that kind of information, so we might never know for certain.''

Rianna wished they could be sure. She desperately wanted to put all the questions, all the worrying and wondering behind her. She wanted to be able to remember her family without the pain, guilt and heartache. Thinking about them led to another question.

''Did you get the video I asked you to keep for me? The personal one?'' she asked.

Donald smiled, his eyes lighting with pleasure. ''It's in the living room. We noticed the date on the label, and I can see why it's so important to you.''

She gave him a big smile. ''Thanks a bunch.''

To Kyle, she explained. "When I was searching through Gregory's tapes, I found a series of videos from his annual staff parties. My parents, brother and I are on one of them."

She cleared the thickness from her voice, wondering if she'd ever be able to speak of them without getting weepy. She'd lost everything in that fire, every personal item, photo and small memento of their family life.

"I couldn't risk watching it too much, so I hid it with the evidence tapes."

Their gazes met and held. His reassuring expression eased the tightness in her chest. For so many years, she'd been unable to mention her family to anyone but Donald and Sophie. Discussing them more openly now brought her an unexpected sense of comfort.

"You'll have to introduce me to them later," Kyle told her in quiet understanding.

His sensitivity brought a lump to her throat. She dropped her gaze to her coffee cup, and then took one last sip. Sophie had finished cleaning the kitchen while they talked. Donald shifted back into his deputy director mode.

"Can you stay a while longer, Tremont? At least until I get Sophie back to the city?"

Kyle nodded, and Donald continued. "I'll take the rented truck and follow her back to our apartment. My car's in the garage in case of emergency, along with the pickup truck, but you should be perfectly safe here. I've got several guards posted on the property. The fence is electrified and the house is heavily armored. I can have more men and equipment brought out at the slightest hint of trouble."

"We'll be fine," said Rianna. "I know this place is a fortress. I helped plan the security, remember?"

Donald chuckled, but Sophie added motherly instructions. "I want you to relax, get some rest and remember to eat. You're a little too thin and you've got dark circles under your eyes."

Rianna grinned. "I have a good start on a tan, though."

"You'll have to tell me all about your adventure when we can visit longer," she said. "I know Donald's version is always heavily edited. It's nearly impossible to pry information out of him. He's the most close-mouthed man I've ever met."

Donald rose from the table, interrupting before she could get started on one of her favorite lectures. "Why don't the two of you get showered and settled a little before we leave," he suggested, deftly changing subjects. "I'll show Tremont around the house, introduce him to the agents and find him a change of clothes."

Rianna rose and stretched. She didn't have to be coaxed. She was feeling stuffed with Sophie's wonderful meal, and getting tired again. After excusing herself, she headed to her own room, stripped and climbed in the shower. A fresh Band-Aid protected her stitches while she allowed the water to pelt her with cleansing strength.

By the time she was dressed again, she felt squeaky clean for the first time in months. The soft, yellow cotton nightgown was nearly transparent, but comfortable. It fell to her knees and clung to her damp body. The matching robe buttoned up the front and wasn't much heavier, but she decided it added a respectable layer of clothing.

Within half an hour, she rejoined the others in the

living room. She gave goodbye hugs to Donald and Sophie, saw them to the door, and then watched as they pulled out of the driveway.

"Wonder why Sullivan was in such a hurry to leave?" Kyle reset the security system and followed her back to the living room. "I would have thought it'd be safer to wait until daylight."

"He's pretty fanatic about not letting Sophie get involved in agency business. I'm guessing she promised him she'd leave as soon as she knew I was okay."

"Has he ever used this place for a safe house before?"

"Never. He's always been adamant about security, but also about keeping this little family hideaway private. I'm sorry he's compromising the location now, but I'm sure glad to be here."

"They seem devoted to you."

"They're the best. I don't know what I would have done without them when my folks were killed. They could never legally adopt me since I'd been declared dead, so they had to create a whole new identity for me. They gave me their name along with their unconditional love and support."

"Not to mention risking his career if anyone learned what he'd done."

"That, too," she said.

Kyle moved to the fireplace and leaned an arm across the mantel. "Have you spent a lot of time here with them?"

Rianna perched on the arm of the sofa, near him, yet not touching. "Donald calls it our 'summer place,' but we sometimes spent the holidays here, too."

"They don't have any children of their own?"

"No, Sophie says they were always too wrapped up

in their careers to take the time. She's a university professor and they had decided against having children, until I got dumped on their doorstep. I was a confused, traumatized teenager, so it took more than the usual parenting skills to straighten me out. They're pretty special people."

"They obviously love you."

Rianna nodded, but wasn't sure she wanted to discuss that particular emotion. "I can't believe you were jealous." She dared to tease, grinning at him. "Did you really think I'd have one lover deliver me into the arms of another?"

Kyle held her gaze. "I wasn't thinking with my head," he admitted, giving her a look so hot that it seared her.

She wanted to know if he'd been thinking with his heart or his hormones, but she didn't have the courage to ask. Instead, she rose and moved closer to him. He'd showered, shaved and dressed in a borrowed white T-shirt and black sweatpants.

Donald had never looked so good in either.

The shirt molded to Kyle's well-toned chest and hugged his lean, ridged stomach. The pants hung low on his hips, tightening over his strong, muscled thighs. Just the sight of him excited her, making her body tingle with anticipation.

As she drew closer, his arm snaked out and wrapped around her waist, drawing her against him. She flattened her hands on his chest, and then flexed her fingers, kneading him as a cat would do through the thin cloth.

"I'm starving for a kiss," he drawled, his gaze meeting with hers as his head slowly lowered. "Everybody's been getting them except me." His tongue flicked out, bathing her lips with warmth and eliciting mewing encouragement from Rianna.

"Poor guy," she murmured, her breath mingling with his. He smelled of rich, dark coffee. "I'll have to see what I can do about that."

Next he nibbled at the corner of her mouth, and she slid her arms around his waist, rocking closer. Then his tongue bridged the barrier of her teeth. She moaned, leaning into his strength as her tongue slid against the hot length of his.

He plundered her mouth, making her weak with need. She felt the evidence of his arousal against her stomach and arched into its hard strength. Kyle made a husky noise of approval, so she continued to rub against him with rhythmic, coaxing pressure.

He raked his hands through her hair, clutching her head and tilting her mouth to fit more tightly against his own. Then he kissed her with steadily escalating passion. Deep, wet, drugging kisses that made her bones melt and her body turn liquid with desire. Primitive hunger erupted between them, so hot and fierce that they had to break apart to level some control.

"Damn, all I have to do is kiss you, and I start spiraling out of control," Kyle grumbled against her mouth, his breath coming in harsh pants.

"No complaints from me," she whispered, licking his lips with the tip of her tongue.

He closed his eyes and rested his forehead against hers. "I want to take my time with you tonight."

"I thought we did that last night."

"No," he argued. "You had your way with me last night. Tonight, I plan to have my way with you."

"Mmm...sounds fascinating," she said, bringing her hands up to cup his face. Their gazes locked, and she thrilled at the desire swirling in his eyes. "Couldn't we do both?"

"Both what?"

He seemed momentarily distracted by the curve of her cheek, planting a row of kisses along her jaw until she captured his wandering lips with her own. She couldn't get enough of him. She'd thought the need would abate once they'd become lovers, but it just kept sharpening.

"Couldn't we have it both ways?" she murmured against his mouth. "Hard and fast, then slow and easy?"

Her bold query had Kyle groaning and clutching her tighter. "Careful, beautiful, or you'll throw a monkey wrench into my well thought-out plans," he accused.

Rianna kissed him until they were both breathing faster. Kyle's hands convulsively stroked her back, and then slid to her hips. He grasped her buttocks, gathering handfuls of her gown and pulling her closer.

When they drew apart to gasp for air, he speared her with a dark, turbulent gaze. "Are you wearing anything under this gown?"

"Not a thing," she confessed, clinging to his shoulders. Her breasts were achy, so she rubbed them against his chest while arching her hips against his groin.

Kyle's big hands slid to her thighs, and he lifted her. Rianna wrapped her legs around his waist, straining for closer contact with the part of him that would make them one again.

"Easy." His command was rough with desire. He rocked his hips against the cradle of her body, and then swallowed her moan of pleasure.

Rianna gasped at the exquisite pleasure of being so close to him, his strength and heat. She took his tongue deeply into her mouth and continued to rub herself against him. He was carrying her to her room, but she didn't want to wait. She wanted him right now.

"Hard and fast," she said on her next gasp of air.

"Slow and easy." His mouth found the pulse at her neck. He sucked deeply, making her blood run even hotter.

"I can't stand it," she whimpered, arching her head back as his kisses poured over her neck and chest.

Kyle didn't respond. His mouth was too busy burrowing under the neckline of her robe and gown, suckling and seeking like a baby. Rianna brought one hand to her robe and started unfastening buttons. She wanted his mouth on her breasts.

"Stop," he insisted gruffly. They'd made it to her room where she'd left the bedside lamp burning. Kyle kicked the door shut, and then slowly lowered her to the bed.

She tried to pull him over her, but he resisted.

"I'll take care of these," he said, reaching for the tiny pearl buttons. Then, one by one, he slid them out of the holes.

Rianna decided that there was no sense trying to hurry him. She went still except for the heaving of her chest, and watched, fascinated, as he slowly undid her robe. He pushed the sides open and then watched as her breasts swelled against the thin fabric of the gown.

Her breathing grew more ragged as his eyes dilated with hot desire. Her nipples tightened wantonly, and a low groan rumbled from his chest. He reached out to cup both breasts in his hands, using his thumbs to stimulate them even more. Rianna cried out as tension coiled from her breasts to her womb.

When he leaned down to take a nipple into his

mouth, she arched against him in demand. His caress dampened the thin fabric and heightened her pleasure. Then he grew impatient with the barrier and slowly stripped off her robe and gown. His eyes gleamed with satisfaction when she lay naked before him. The brush of his gaze over her body made her flesh tingle and her pulse race even more.

Rianna reached out and beckoned him back into her arms. He leaned over her, but wouldn't be hurried. Taking one nipple into his mouth, he lapped it with his tongue while fondling the other breast with his palm.

She sunk her fingers into the thickness of his hair and held him close as pleasure coursed through her body. Impatient, she began to writhe against him and coax him with hungry little sounds that expressed her growing need.

"Slow and easy," he mumbled, sliding down her body to press wet kisses across her ribs, then her stomach.

Rianna clung to his hair, her body growing increasingly tense as his caresses dipped lower. Then he was sliding back over her and taking her mouth with a new surge of passion. She held his face in her hands while they shared more long, breathless kisses.

Kyle continued to stroke his hands down her sides to her legs. When one hand strayed to the apex of her thighs, she gasped and stiffened. He drew back slightly and gazed into her eyes.

"Let me love you," he begged huskily.

Rianna could barely nod, but when he touched her again, she felt the caress from head to toe. She began to tremble.

"Kyle!" Her cry was an urgent plea of surprised

need. His fingers were hard and hot, probing sensitive flesh no man had ever touched.

''Feel good?'' he whispered, locking gazes with her and demanding a response.

Feeling raw and exposed, she closed her eyes to keep him from seeing the vulnerability, but she nodded.

Then his mouth fell to her breast again. The combined caresses had her quivering so badly that she craved release. When his loving pushed her higher, she reached out frantically to strip off his shirt. She wanted him as naked and needy as she.

## Chapter 11

Kyle halted the sensual assault long enough to move off the bed, quickly shed his clothes and grab a condom. Rianna opened her eyes and watched him bare his broad chest, then his lower body, exposing a jutting arousal that made her gasp.

She reached for him, but he grabbed her hands and pressed them to the bed on either side of her head. He stole another long kiss and began his loving all over again. All she could do was clutch his head as he alternately licked each of her nipples.

A tremor shot through her when he kissed her stomach, and then he was sliding lower in the bed, moving his hot kisses to even more sensitive areas. At the first touch of his mouth, she cried out again, arching her hips off the bed and pressing herself against his face.

Kyle grasped her thighs and held her close while he slowly explored her most sensitive flesh. The intimacy of his caresses stole her breath and shot fire through her body. A tremor shook her, followed by another and then another, coming harder and faster than she could draw in air and prepare for them.

She cried his name, her fingers digging into his hair in an attempt to stop the onslaught. She wanted him over her and in her, but he would not be hurried. When the climax finally hit her, she screamed his name in a long, low wail as heated pleasure swept her body.

Then it was all she could do to draw in a breath. Her lungs were on fire, her chest rising and falling with the effort to drag in air. Her toes were tightly curled and the rest of her body depleted. She felt limp and washed out, but still Kyle didn't stop his ardent loving.

He began kissing his way back up her body, over her quivering stomach, to each of her breasts, to her throat and finally to her mouth. When he'd moved above her again, she latched on to him, wrapping her arms tightly around his neck and holding him close as she silently, but passionately, thanked him for his loving with hard kisses.

She felt his arousal pressing against her hip and savored a renewed rush of desire. Sliding her hands down his body, she cupped his buttocks in her hands and massaged the tight flesh until he was moaning into her mouth. Then she wiggled beneath him until their bodies were once again aligned.

She could feel him pressing against her and shifted her legs wider to accommodate him. Then she pulled in a breath as he completed the union with one strong, sure stroke. Her body came alive with excitement and renewed desire.

Rianna shifted slightly to accept him more fully, then cupped his face in her hands. She stroked his cheeks, her gaze adoring. They stared into each other's eyes as he began the slow, steady dance of love in an ancient rhythm that would bring them ultimate satisfaction.

Soon they were scaling the heights together, each lost in the other as they shuddered to a climax that went beyond physical satisfaction to something much more intense and soul rending. Their hoarse cries of completion echoed in the silence of the room as Kyle's full weight collapsed on her.

Even though Rianna was struggling for each puff of air, she welcomed his weight, wrapping her arms tightly around him and holding him close. She relished the aftermath of their loving as their chests heaved, their bodies still intimately entangled.

In another minute, Kyle took his weight on his forearms and lifted his chest from hers, allowing them both a little freer breathing. He looked into her eyes again, delving into her soul. She wasn't sure what he hoped to see there.

*I could fall desperately in love with you!*

The words reverberated in her head, but she didn't say them out loud. The thought was still too new and too incredibly frightening. She perversely wanted Kyle to say the words to her, yet feared saying them to him. She waited, wondering if he expected her to proclaim her feelings.

When they could breathe again, she finally broke the silence with a gentle taunt. "If that was slow and easy, why am I sweating?"

His husky male laughter filled the room. Rolling onto his side, he pulled her across his chest. Then he smoothed her damp hair behind her ears, continuing to study her features with his warm gaze.

"You're incredible," he insisted, his voice thick. "And you make me feel incredible. Sweat and all."

"You're the one who's incredible," she teased, stroking his face with gentle fingers. "All I did was enjoy."

Laughter rumbled from his chest again, and she loved the feel of it against her breasts.

"Glad to be of service, ma'am," he replied, brushing a soft kiss across her lips, then pulling her head down to his shoulder. "I didn't mean to exhaust you. I planned to do all the work, but I got a little carried away."

"Okay by me," she mumbled against his damp skin.

"You've had a rough few days, and I haven't been letting you recuperate. Didn't that ER doctor advise against too much strenuous exercise?"

"Hmm…" Rianna practically purred as she snuggled against him. "What's he know? I've never felt better in my life."

She felt the flexing of his chest muscles again, and delighted in the fact that she'd made him feel good, too. Heaven help her, but she was in way over her head. She loved everything about him.

"Are we going to sleep?" he asked once they'd both quieted.

"We're just resting our eyes," she mumbled, her whole body limp and lethargic. She couldn't even lift her lashes.

"Does that mean we can make love again in a little while?" he teased, nibbling on her ear.

"Sure." The word was slurred.

He continued to stroke her hair with one hand while caressing her back with the other. "Good, 'cause I really like making love to you."

Rianna heard him, but couldn't find the strength to

respond. She drifted to sleep, feeling more safe and contented than she could ever remember.

He woke her near dawn, his hands and mouth at her breasts, his teeth and tongue plucking at her nipples. Desire flowed through her like lava, thick and aflame, stirring her senses to a red-hot frenzy of need. He drove her to new heights before they sated themselves once again. Depleted, they fell into a deep, passion-drugged sleep.

The sun had neared its zenith by the time Rianna woke again. Kyle had rolled to one side of the bed. She watched him sleep for a long time, just savoring the sight of him. She felt tempted to wake him the way he'd done her, but decided he needed the rest. He'd had a busy night, and she had to go to the bathroom.

He was still sleeping soundly after she'd showered. She pulled on an old, faded blue T-shirt and matching gym shorts before leaving her room and heading for the kitchen. After making a pot of coffee, she waited for it to perk, and then carried a cupful into the living room.

The room was bathed in sunlight. She pulled back the drapes and opened the window a crack. It had rained sometime during the night, making the air clean and clear. Inhaling deeply, she took a minute to watch the birds at Sophie's feeder and enjoy the uncomplicated normalcy.

Everything seemed quiet, but Rianna knew there was nothing uncomplicated or normal about her life, however much she'd like to wish for it. She needed to talk to Donald and see what was happening in D.C.

Perching on the edge of the sofa, she picked up the

phone and dialed his number. He picked up after the second ring.

"Good morning, Mr. Deputy Director," she teased him, using her private nickname.

"Good morning, Special Agent," he teased back.

Rianna smiled. "Everything all right with you and Sophie?"

"Just fine. She nagged me all the way to the apartment last night, but I stayed tough. I refused to turn around and head back to the cabin, even though she came up with some pretty good reasons why we should."

"She's a woman of many skills."

"You can say that again. After nearly twenty years of marriage, she's pretty adept at using them on me."

"And you love it."

"Damn right."

The deep satisfaction in his voice widened her smile.

"You sound pretty chipper this morning," said Donald. "Get a good night's sleep?"

Rianna was glad he couldn't see the blush that warmed her cheeks. She tried to keep her tone casual. "It was great to be home in my own bed."

"I imagine it was. Kyle up and about yet?"

"He's not up yet, but I just brewed coffee, so the smell will probably lure him out soon."

"I hate to dampen your mood, but I'm afraid I have some disturbing news for him."

Rianna hated it, too, more than he could know. She didn't want the ugliness of law enforcement intruding on her world today. Her heart grew heavy at the thought of Kyle becoming more deeply enmeshed in her problems.

Anytime she dared to take a risk on happiness, something always happened to burst her bubble and threaten those she loved. Hands shaking, she set the cup down in the saucer and tried to mentally prepare herself for the worst.

"What's wrong?"

"Haroldson's lawyer is trying to convince a judge that he's a law-abiding citizen who's been victimized by a con artist. He's claiming Kyle kidnapped you and assaulted his employees."

She swallowed hard, but kept her tone calm. "Is he threatening to file counter charges?"

"I told the assistant U.S. attorney that you'd gone with him of your own free will. I doubt his lawyers will press it any further."

Rianna's chest grew tighter. Kyle could face charges, however flimsy, for coming to her aid. To a man with his deep respect for the law, it would be the ultimate insult. His reputation was being sullied, yet there was nothing he could do. He didn't deserve the grief or the injustice after years of service to his country.

Rianna's feelings of guilt just kept escalating. "I don't want him to face charges because of me."

"Shouldn't be a problem, it's just an unexpected glitch and some extra red tape."

"Gregory is famous for causing glitches," she growled. "I'll tell Kyle you're working to get it straightened out."

"There's more." Donald prefaced his next announcement with a gentle tone he reserved for really bad news.

She tensed, her fingers fisting. "What else?"

"I figured Haroldson's mole in the agency identified Tremont, so I sent some agents to keep an eye on his house. We guessed Haroldson would do the same once he knew the two of you were traveling together.''

Nausea rose in her throat. Why hadn't she considered that angle? Gregory always sought retribution against anyone who crossed him.

She remembered the pride in Kyle's voice when he'd described his home and dreaded hearing the details. ''I'm not going to like it, am I.''

'''Fraid not,'' Donald said on a sigh. ''The agents did a check on his place just in time to keep it from going up in flames. Someone had trashed the house and set the shop on fire. Most of his workshop was destroyed. The house had some smoke damage, but it's still structurally sound and can be remodeled. I've already hired a team to clean and do the interior work.''

Rianna closed her eyes and sank back against the sofa cushions. Her stomach churned, her thoughts filled with anger and shame. Kyle's grandfather's shop had been destroyed, and it was all her fault.

If he hadn't helped her, he wouldn't be involved with the kind of conscienceless people who wreaked havoc for a living. He'd chosen to leave that world, but he'd been tossed back into it on her account. She hated being the cause of so much destruction. She was a jinx to anyone who dared get too close.

''Mary?'' Donald interrupted her black thoughts.

''I'm still here. It makes me sick,'' she said, giving a sad sigh. Then her tone grew stronger and took on a low snarl. ''I want him to pay, Donald. He has so much death and destruction to pay for.''

''He's going to pay dearly,'' he swore. ''We're making sure of that. I can't imagine anything worse for a fastidious control freak that being incarcerated for life. The AUSA will petition for the death penalty, but a lifetime in prison will be Haroldson's ultimate punishment.''

Rianna supposed he was right. She just wanted guarantees, but she knew there were none.

''I think I hear Kyle in the shower now. As soon as he comes out, I'll tell him what's been happening. I just hate it that he's not free to go home and take care of everything himself.''

''Hopefully soon. I'm staying in the city today to try to stay abreast of things.''

''Thanks.'' She tried to sound more upbeat, not wanting to add to his worries. ''Give Sophie a hug for me.''

''You bet.''

Rianna held the phone to her ear for a while after she heard the click of his disconnection and the hum of the dial tone. Then she slowly lowered the receiver back to its base. Her thoughts were whirling and none of them were pleasant.

She'd caused Kyle nothing but trouble, yet she was helpless to halt the chain of events at this point. There had to be a way to make things right. She'd think of something, and soon.

Her legs were a little unsteady when she rose from the sofa, but she mentally scolded herself. She didn't like feeling weak and fearful at the thought of Gregory going after Kyle. The emotional involvement scared her even more than did the threat of violence. She could handle his vengeance if it was directed at her, but not at those she loved.

Kyle joined her shortly after she started cooking breakfast. Freshly shaved and showered, he set her pulse skittering. He looked rested, yet predatory, like a contented, sexy tiger on the prowl. The gleam in his eyes sent heat through her veins.

His hair, on head and chest, glistened with moisture, coiling into tight curls and tempting her to touch. All he wore was a pair of Donald's too-large jeans, with the waist sliding low on his hips. She had a hunch he wasn't wearing anything under them, and that thought made her tingle with anticipation.

He greeted her with a kiss that sent her senses swirling and temporarily blocked all thought from her mind. He tasted of mint and hungry man. She clung to him, savoring his solid warmth and uninhibited loving.

"Good morning," she finally whispered against his lips.

"It's okay now," he told her as he nibbled at her mouth. "But it wasn't so good when I woke up in a cold, empty bed."

Rianna laughed softly. "That is terrible," she teased, running her hands over his shoulders, loving the satin-smooth feel of his skin. "I couldn't stay. Nature called, so I decided I might as well get up and find us something to eat."

Kyle's stomach chose to growl at that very minute, making them both laugh. By mutual agreement, they dished up the scrambled eggs she'd cooked and made some toast. Rianna poured them both some juice, then sat across from him at the table.

They ate in silence because she didn't want to discuss what was on her mind. Kyle gave her a few searching looks, but she couldn't think of anything cheery and casual to say. She wasn't in the mood for small talk. She was busy trying to find a way to tell him what she'd learned this morning.

When they'd finished, Kyle carried their dishes to

the sink and ran some water over them. He poured them each a cup of coffee. Rianna watched his every movement while shredding her paper napkin in nervousness. Her legendary control seemed nonexistent when it came to this man.

She thanked him when he placed the cup in front of her, sipped at her coffee, and stalled for more time.

"Looks like a nice day," he finally said, breaking the silence. "Sullivan said there's a stream out back where we can do some fishing."

She nodded and glanced toward the window. Sunlight streamed through the pane, bathing the room with early afternoon light. She, too, had thought the day perfect, until she'd called Donald.

"It does look like a perfect summer day. I know where he keeps his fishing tackle. Maybe we can catch tonight's dinner."

"Fishing sounds good. What else is on the agenda?"

"Nothing much, I guess. I want to watch the video Donald confiscated from Gregory's estate."

"We'll do that first," he said, taking a long swallow of coffee. Rianna watched his throat work, and hers grew tight.

When he set down the cup, he reached out and grasped her hand. She gave him a wary glance, but didn't resist when he tugged harder. Rising from her chair, she moved close enough for him to wrap his hands around her waist. Then he lifted her until she straddled his lap.

Her bare legs slid over his jeans-covered thighs, the friction sending a sizzle of sensation over her sensitized skin. She splayed her hands on his chest and felt more heat coursing through her.

''Wanna tell me what's worrying you so much this morning?'' he asked gently, his gaze locking with hers.

Rianna dropped her lashes. Emotion clogged her throat, making her reluctant to speak in case she embarrassed herself.

Kyle lifted her chin, stared into her eyes. His voice went low and intimate. ''You're not upset about last night, are you? Did I move too fast? Do something that made you uncomfortable? Cross some invisible boundary?''

''No!'' She cupped his face in her hands, wanting him to know that her mood had nothing to do with the physical side of their relationship. ''Absolutely not. I loved every touch and kiss and caress. I swear it on my life. Last night was incredible,'' she whispered softly.

Some of the tension drained from his features. Before he could comment, Rianna pressed her lips to his. She slid her tongue into his mouth, trying to communicate without words. Trying to show him the emotion she couldn't describe.

The kiss was long and deep and sweet. Kyle's hands slid down her body, pulling her closer. She wrapped her arms around his neck, savoring the taste and feel of him. One kiss led to another and another.

Then guilt had her pulling back. She couldn't keep stalling or pretending everything was all right. He might not even want to touch her when he learned the whole truth. A tremor shook her at the dark thought.

He drew in a deep breath and then sighed heavily. His hands tightened at her hips, fingers massaging.

''Why don't you tell me what's bothering you?''

She dropped her gaze again. ''I talked to Donald this

morning. He had some bad news and some worse news.''

She felt Kyle stiffen. He lifted her chin again and forced her to look at him. His eyes darkened stormily.

"Haroldson's been freed on bond?" he asked tightly.

"No!" Rianna shook her head vigorously. "At least, not yet, but his attorney is trying to sway a judge."

"That's no surprise." Kyle visibly relaxed. "Then, what's the latest development? Let's start with the bad news."

She stroked his face, smoothing his brows, the strong line of his jaw and the curve of his cheek. She loved touching him, and showed it in the tenderness of her caresses.

"Gregory's trying to make you out to be the bad guy."

Kyle's eyes narrowed. After a brief hesitation, he said, "We already assumed that. What's different?"

"He's claiming you assaulted his staff and threatening to file charges. Donald's sure they won't stick, but you should stay put until he gets things straightened out."

He seemed to relax a little more. "That's not so bad," he teased, sliding his hands to the small of her back and rubbing her through the soft fabric. "I like the idea of staying holed up with you for days or maybe even weeks."

Rianna didn't share his smile. "That's not the worst of it," she warned.

"So, what's the worst?"

"Gregory had some men vandalize your house. They destroyed a lot of your personal possessions and set it on fire." Rianna paused, swallowing the tears clogging her throat. "The house can be repaired, but your wood-shop burned to the ground."

Kyle went rigid. For a second, he looked so fierce and angry that her breathing faltered. She would have slid off his lap, but his hands tightened at her hips. She wouldn't blame him if he hated her and rued the day he'd met her, yet the thought of him harboring such feelings brought more tears to her eyes.

"I'm so sorry," she whispered, hating her own shaky voice and emotional upheaval. "I'm so sorry that helping me means losing everything you've worked for, for so long."

"Don't!" he commanded, his voice rough. "Don't start blaming yourself for something totally out of your control."

"I can't help it," she whispered, tears welling in her eyes. She blinked rapidly. "You shouldn't be punished for doing what's right. It just isn't fair."

"It'll be okay," he insisted, visibly forcing himself to relax. "Everything's insured. I don't own anything that can't be replaced. Nothing."

"What about the things that belong to your customers or your grandfather? You said you refinish valuable antiques."

"I cleared all that stuff out of the shop before I left. The rest is just…stuff. Nothing special. Just things."

She gave him a dubious stare.

His features reflected a myriad of emotions, and then his expression went blank. She could tell that he'd deliberately blocked his own feelings to soothe hers. When she continued to stare at him in silence, he rationalized.

"In fact, Haroldson might have done me a favor. I

have replacement insurance. I can get all those old, secondhand tools replaced with brand-new ones.''

His attempt to make her feel better brought another rush of tears to her eyes. Try as she might, she couldn't keep a couple from spilling down her cheek.

Kyle groaned in protest, then flicked out his tongue to capture a teardrop. ''Don't,'' he mumbled against her skin, licking and kissing his way down her cheek. ''Don't cry. I can't stand it. All the bad news isn't worth one of your tears.''

Rianna smothered a soft sob against his mouth. He returned her kiss gently at first, but she didn't want gentle. Badly needing reassurance, she kissed him with a force and hunger that quickly wiped everything but him from her mind. He pulled her tighter against his chest while they devoured each other with lips and tongues and teeth.

She strained to get closer, pressing her breasts against the solid wall of his chest and tightening her grip on his neck. Her thighs clenched around his and their bodies rocked against each other in rhythmic demand.

When they finally drew apart long enough to catch their breath, Kyle nuzzled her neck. He pressed hot kisses on the pulse frantically beating there.

Rianna sighed, wondering at his ability to make her forget everything but the taste and feel of his body. Then the guilt crept back into her thoughts.

''I still wish there was something I could do to make it better,'' she murmured against his cheek.

He deliberately misinterpreted her words. ''There is something,'' he suggested, his breath warm on her ear.

''What?''

''You could take off your shirt.''

Surprised, Rianna leaned back in his arms and stared at him. The gleam in his eyes was totally wicked and just as totally irresistible. It offered not only acceptance, but also the promise of the same sweet satisfaction she always found in his arms. The thought dried her tears, but she smacked him on the arm.

"You're so bad."

"Because you're so good."

Her laugh held a note of surprise, and warmth invaded her cheeks. He was bold and audacious and so impossibly sexy. She wanted to be bold and sexy, but didn't know how to go about it. Then Kyle took hold of her shirttail and slowly pulled it over her head.

She hadn't bothered with a bra.

The sudden darkening of his eyes as he stared at her made her breasts ache for attention.

"So beautiful," he murmured.

She felt the damp heat of his breath an instant before he took her into his mouth. A shiver raced over her as fire spiked from breast to womb. Her muscles clenched in passionate anticipation.

Burying her fingers in his hair, Rianna arched her back to give him better access. His body responded, his arousal swelling and pressing against her.

"There's another way you can make it up to me," he said, while shifting his mouth from one breast to the other.

"How's that?"

"Unsnap these damn jeans."

Rianna laughed softly, thrilled by his impatience and eager to do his bidding. In a matter of minutes, he'd coerced her from guilt ridden to highly aroused. Being with Kyle offered a roller coaster of emotions—one that she wanted to ride as long as possible.

*   *   *

Once they'd sated each other, they took a long, leisurely shower together. They didn't make love again,
but they explored each other with an intimate thor-
oughness that kept their bodies singing with sexual tension.

After dressing, they spent what was left of the afternoon wandering around the grounds. They rechecked the
security system and touched base with the agents posted
at the front entrance and back property line.

The protection team worked eight-hour shifts, changing at eight a.m., four p.m. and midnight. Rianna didn't
know them, but she recognized a couple of names. She
asked that her personal thanks be passed on to all the
team members.

By early evening, they were ready to eat again, and
finished off the leftover pot roast and pie. Then they
settled in the living room to watch the eighteen-year-
old video Donald had confiscated from the Haroldson
estate.

Her family had been caught in the camera's eye at
intervals during one of Gregory's early staff parties.
First they'd been gathered around the buffet table, then
their own table and finally near the dance floor.

Rianna wept quietly as the film progressed.

She'd been about ten at the time, with pigtails, missing front teeth, and a frilly party dress. Jimmy had worn
new clothes, too, but she remembered him complaining
about them being tight and uncomfortable. He'd been
so small that he'd begged their dad to lift him so he
could see everything.

Her mother looked wonderfully alive and heart-
breakingly dear in those years before the lines of strain
marked her lovely skin. Her father had been so young

and handsome and confident, his features free of the constant worry she'd seen in the years after he'd left Gregory's employ.

For just an instant in time, Rianna had them back again and felt whole. Even though the video was of poor quality, she'd treasure it always. It held a rare glimpse of her family when they'd still been normal and happy.

Her heart ached for the decent people she knew them to be and the price they'd paid for their integrity. It pleased her to know she'd brought Gregory a few steps closer to justice. She silently renewed her vow to see him punished.

"You look like your mother," said Kyle, gathering her in his arms and offering comfort, "but you have your dad's nose and you're built more like him."

"Thank you," she said, sniffling but making an effort to control the flow of tears.

Her mother had always cursed her short, round body, while her dad had been on the thin side. Rianna loved knowing she carried physical traits from each of them.

She paused the tape, rewound it, and then hit replay. Kyle never complained, watching the same few minutes of film over and over again.

His sensitivity and compassion touched her more deeply than she'd have thought possible. He just kept giving of himself, and she kept taking. She was so incredibly needy. Their relationship seemed too one-sided to be healthy, but she tried not to dwell on the negative.

When Rianna finally found the strength to shut off the VCR, she turned into Kyle's arms and pressed her mouth to his, trying to convey all the complexity of her feelings in one long, lingering kiss.

He responded, as always, with a need that matched hers. She wanted the sight and scent and feel of him indelibly printed in her memories, so she relished every touch and kiss.

Kyle accepted the intensity of her loving and responded in kind, equally intent on making memories.

## Chapter 12

Later, they cuddled in front of the TV, fed each other popcorn and watched a romantic comedy. Kyle said it gave him naughty ideas. Rianna laughed and agreed that they'd have to experiment a little, but maybe tomorrow.

"Are you telling me you don't want to make love again tonight?" he teased.

"Are you telling me you do?" she asked.

He took his time responding. "The spirit's willing but the flesh is weak," he explained, grinning.

The expression on his face made her laugh harder. "There's nothing weak about your flesh," she chided, knowing he was more worried about her being tender. "I'm willing to vouch for the strength of your body parts any time you like."

That brought back the wicked grin she loved so much.

"I'll remember that."

When they finally went to bed, they held each other close, mingling soft whispers with even softer kisses and caresses. It was another unique and wonderful experience for Rianna. One she knew she'd treasure the rest of her life.

They fell asleep in each other's arms, but her dreams were anything but peaceful. She dreamed of a house on fire, a raging inferno with black, billowing smoke and out-of-control flames licking at a midnight sky. Silent screams tore at her throat as she watched, terrified and helpless, while her family's home burned.

The dream had plagued her in the early years after she'd been orphaned, but now it took on a new and sinister twist. As she watched the house burning, she saw Kyle's face at a window. He stared at her, his expression accusing and filled with hate as the flames engulfed him.

Rianna fought her way out of the nightmare. Tremors shook her body until she could force the terror of her dream out of her mind. Soaked in sweat but chilled to the bone, she felt locked in a time warp. Forcing herself to breathe deeply, she tried to rationalize the horror her mind had conjured, but it didn't help.

Then Kyle's arms enfolded her, drawing her close to his side. He sensed her trauma and mumbled soft, reassuring words of comfort. His hands gently stroked her back and shoulders until some of the tension began to subside.

She finally relaxed, snuggling closer and basking in his tenderness. Her renegade was so incredibly special. She loved him beyond words and reason. She wanted to block out all the ugliness and take comfort in his arms, but she knew she wouldn't get another minute's rest.

When he'd drifted back to sleep, she stayed in his arms until his grip relaxed. Then she carefully slid from his side and climbed out of bed. Dawn was nearing, so she knew it wouldn't be too early to call Donald. She tiptoed into the living room and phoned his apartment.

He answered and they exchanged greetings, but he immediately sensed her tension. "What's wrong?"

"I think it's time for us to get Kyle out of this situation," she told him, her tone clipped and decisive.

There was a pause, and then Donald's response. "I agree, but I got the impression there's something special going on between the two of you."

"There is, but there's no way we can pursue it right now. Kyle's already given up too much. He deserves to have his life back," she insisted. "Have charges been filed against him?"

"No. I took care of it. The AUSA told Haroldson's lawyers the charges wouldn't stick."

"Then there's no reason Kyle can't go home."

"It's for the best. You don't need any distractions right now."

The thought of him leaving made her heart ache, so she suggested a way to make it easier. "I'm not going to give him a choice."

"Maybe you'd better tell me exactly what you are planning."

She could almost hear his frown, but that didn't deter her. "I'm going to be the one who leaves. I'll go on up the coast a ways." Rianna didn't mention her destination over the phone, but Donald would know.

Margaret Wilding had been her foster mother for a short time before the Sullivans had taken her in. Margaret had no blood relatives, but she was a surrogate aunt to many. Her house had always been considered an alternative safe house, since she had no traceable connection to anyone in the agency.

"You're going to drive my car?"

"If you don't mind."

"No problem. Take Special Agent Payne with you. He's young and won't mind being gone a few days. He's also smart and totally trustworthy. I'll let him know about the change of plans."

Now that the decision had his stamp of approval, she felt all sad and weepy again. She wouldn't cry. She was supposed to be a professional and this was a professional decision.

Clearing her throat, she said, "Thanks, Donald. I can't tell you how much it means to me."

"You just take care of yourself and call when you're settled. Don't take any chances, and don't worry about Tremont. I'll deal with him when he calls to raise hell."

"I'm sorry to dump it on you, but I'd rather leave without him knowing. He'll try to talk me out of it and make things even more complicated."

She didn't want to waste time arguing with Kyle. It would be hard enough to leave him. He'd be hurt, angry and probably hate her for taking matters into her own hands, but she could live with that as long as she knew he was safe. He needed time to rebuild his home and his life.

"Leave him a note so he doesn't freak out when he realizes you're gone. I'll explain when I get there."

"He'll be furious."

They both knew that was a gross understatement.

"Yeah. Can't say I blame him, but I've been a casualty of his wrath before and survived. It's part of the job description."

Rianna thanked him again, and then hung up the phone. The weight of her decision lay heavily on her heart, but she knew it was the right thing to do. It was the only solution at this point.

He'd be so disappointed in her, and that saddened her most of all. She'd lose his trust and respect, but he'd be free of the baggage she brought to the relationship. She didn't want him embroiled in months, possibly years, of legal battles to bring Gregory and his men to justice.

She wanted him to have a choice. It was the only thing she could give him, and it was important to her own emotional well-being. She couldn't live in fear of losing him the way she'd lost her family.

After quietly packing a suitcase, she took one precious minute to study his sleeping form. Her heart ached as she slipped out of the house into the darkness.

Kyle woke when sunshine poured into the bedroom. He slowly opened his eyes and blinked at the invading light, dragging himself from the deepest sleep he'd had in months. He stretched, enjoying the pull of his muscles as he worked out the stiffness.

His morning arousal throbbed into life, garnering his full attention. A deep, anticipatory smile creased his face and a deeper yearning settled into his gut at the thought of burying himself in the sweet, passionate woman at the side.

Then he reached for Rianna.

She wasn't in bed, which dampened his spirits considerably. He wanted a kiss and a snuggle and some special loving to start their day. He'd gotten really fond of having her in his arms.

Tossing back the sheet, he climbed from bed and

headed for the bathroom, hoping to find his ladylove close by. He didn't hear the shower running, but she could be naked and need some help getting dry. His smile returned at the thought.

But the bathroom was empty with no evidence that Rianna had recently showered. After brushing his teeth and splashing some water on his face he went back to the bedroom and pulled on a pair of gym shorts. Then he followed the smell of freshly brewed coffee to the kitchen, thinking she must be cooking some breakfast for them.

But the kitchen was empty, too, and the coffeepot had a timer. There was no beautiful woman waiting for him.

Suddenly, all the hair on his body stood on end. He tensed, his body going rigid as he realized how unnaturally quiet the place seemed. There was no sound indicating the presence of anyone else in the house.

"Rianna!"

Fear surged through him as he yelled and tore through the house searching for her.

"Rianna!"

How stupid could he be? He should have realized she wasn't here the instant he woke alone. He continued to yell her name as he did a room by room search, checking closets, the basement and attic until he grew hoarse and there was nowhere else to check.

Retracing his steps, he looked out windows, checking the grounds, trying to convince himself that she'd just slipped outside for a minute. He opened the kitchen door and yelled for her again.

She didn't answer, and the silence caused a new upheaval of panic. Had Haroldson's men gotten past the other agents? Could they have snatched her from the house without him knowing? How could he have been so stupid? He'd relaxed his guard too soon, too much, and had slept like the dead.

He'd failed her again, and his chest constricted at the thought of her being alone or at the mercy of Haroldson's goons. He had to find her.

"Rianna!"

Fear and pain mingled in the frantic repetition of her name. What if the agents outside were unconscious or dead? He reached for the phone, quickly punching in the beeper number for one of the guards. Then he held the receiver to his ear and waited for a response, hoping there would be one.

When the phone rang, he growled his relief at the caller. "This is Tremont. Where the hell is Agent Sullivan?"

The reply came hesitantly. "Would that be the deputy director you're looking for, sir, or Special Agent Sullivan?"

Kyle ground his teeth in frustration at the man's calm question. "Special Agent Sullivan. You're supposed to be guarding her, remember?"

"No, sir," the agent replied quietly. "Special Agent Sullivan left a couple of hours ago with Special Agent Payne."

"What do you mean, left?" he shouted, body shuddering as his temper shot upward. "Where the hell did they go? The grocery store? She's not supposed to leave the house without armed guards. Why the hell would they risk going anywhere?"

"That I don't know, sir. My orders are to stay here and make sure nobody gets close to the house. You'll have to call the deputy director if you want details."

Kyle swore viciously as he jammed the receiver

down and then lifted it again for a dial tone. He punched in Sullivan's private number, then waited the interminable time it took for the other man to answer.

"Sullivan."

He didn't waste time with pleasantries. "Where the hell is Rianna? I can't believe you let her leave this house. Have you lost your mind!" he exploded.

"You're always so cheerful in the morning, Tremont."

Sullivan's attempt at lightness didn't impress him. "Your man outside said she left with Payne. What the hell is going on?" he snapped.

"We decided it was time for her to move to another safe house."

"You *what?*" Kyle knew he was losing it. He was yelling at the top of his lungs because he could barely draw air into them. A suffocating tightness had settled there.

"You moved her without clearing it with me? You let her sneak out of here in the dead of night with one young, inexperienced agent? What the hell is wrong with you?"

"We decided it was best," Sullivan explained patiently.

Kyle heard the sympathy in his voice, and it chilled him to the bone. "Are you saying Rianna agreed without an argument or a word of goodbye?"

"She said she'd leave a note."

That didn't reassure him in the least. "I want to know where she went." His tone went cold and implacable.

"You know I can't tell you that."

"Can't?" Kyle's response was feral, but he knew he was wasting his time. He slammed down the phone and starting prowling the house again, looking for the note Rianna was supposed to have left him.

He found it on the telephone stand in the living room. A plain white envelope bearing his name was propped against a flower vase. Hand trembling, he reached for it and tore the envelope to get to the scrap of paper inside.

Dear Kyle,
I'm sorry to leave so abruptly, but it was time for me to move to another safe house.

Please go home and take care of your house and business. I promise I'll have Donald keep you apprised of the agency's case against Gregory.

Thank you so much for keeping me safe. I'll be forever grateful that you were the one who helped me escape and begin to heal.

Yours, Rianna

*Yours, Rianna?* Kyle raked a hand through his hair, shaking his head in rejection of that. She wasn't his and never had been, except maybe in his mind. If she really cared about him, why wasn't she here?

Why had she slipped away in secret to escape him? Had he gotten too close to her heart or had she just feared he was beginning to care more than she could ever reciprocate?

Gone. He couldn't believe she'd been coldhearted enough to leave with nothing more than a few pathetic words on a slip of paper, to leave knowing there was no way he could follow to her newest hiding place.

Impotent fury raged through him, followed by a pain so excruciating that he began to tremble. He couldn't move, couldn't seem to catch his breath.

Then a sound near the door snapped his head in that direction. He wasn't sure he could trust his eyes. Rianna had entered the house and slowly moved toward him. Her gaze settled on his face. Then she spoke quietly, hesitantly.

"I was hoping I could make it back before you woke up and found that," she said.

Her voice sounded as shaky as he felt. Kyle soaked up the sweetness of it, his eyes feasting on her. She looked so good, so precious, so sweetly repentant. His throat tightened and his body hardened. The violent, involuntary reactions had him grinding his teeth.

He crushed the note in his fist, then wadded it into a tight ball and threw it as hard as he could. It didn't go far, but the action offered minimal relief to the crippling tension of his body.

He turned and headed to the bedroom without a word. Once there, he stripped off his shorts, and pulled on jeans and a T-shirt. His movements were fast and furious, but no amount of activity could calm his seething anger—an anger directed at himself more than Rianna. He should know by now that caring too much always led to heartache and regrets.

He'd just sat on the bed to put on socks, when Rianna appeared in the doorway.

"You'd better keep your distance," he warned as he fought to control his temper. She'd wounded him with her rejection and mistrust. When he hurt, he got angry.

"I don't blame you for being furious—" she started.

"Don't you?" he snapped. "That's generous."

She flinched at his tone, but Kyle was beyond caring. She'd made it clear she wanted him out of her life as painlessly as possible. So be it. He'd leave and never look back. He didn't need the humiliation of being dumped. Didn't need the pain and anger and gnawing need.

"I wish you'd let me explain," she begged.

"Explain!" he shouted, surging to his feet and glaring at her. "Forget the explanations. Actions speak a whole helluva lot louder than words."

"I'm sorry—"

He cut her off with another sharp exclamation, too angry to listen to reason. "Save the sorries. You made your point, and you're right. It's time we parted ways."

"You're going?"

"That's right. I'm going home and wiping my hands of this whole mess."

She flinched and went pale. His chest tightened, and he cursed himself for caring, then funneled the emotion into more anger.

"I'm tired of being jerked around to suit your needs. I'm tired of playing puppet with you and Sullivan controlling the strings. I thought we had something special between us, but that must have been just another attempt to keep me in line so that you could jerk me around some more. Well, I'm not interested in explanations or apologies."

When he'd finished, they stared at each other for a pregnant moment. She waited to make sure he'd finished his tirade. Then she looked him straight in the eyes.

"I hadn't been gone an hour before I realized I had to come back." Her voice quivered, and she swallowed hard. When he didn't interrupt or start yelling again, she continued.

"I've never thought of myself as a coward, but leaving here without a word was a spineless way to handle the situation. I rationalized the decision in all the usual ways, but the truth finally hit me. I was running away again. The same way I've done most of my life, and I'm tired of running.''

Her voice dropped to a shaky whisper. She shifted her gaze so that she wasn't looking directly at him anymore, but Kyle couldn't take his eyes off her. She looked so fragile and weary, so unsure and unlike the lover he knew.

He needed to stroke his anger and pretend he didn't care, yet he couldn't bear seeing her so shaken.

''I got scared, really, truly scared, and I hate being scared,'' she confessed raggedly.

When her lips quivered, his gut tightened. Her admission cracked through some of his newly polished armor. A good part of his remaining anger stemmed from the scare she'd given him, but they needed to hash this out.

''I thought you were fearless,'' he taunted.

''I thought so, too,'' she said, searching his face with eyes that made his skin prickle with awareness. ''After my family was murdered, I couldn't shake the guilt of surviving. No amount of counseling can completely wipe that out of a person's system. Donald accused me of having a death wish, and maybe he was right.''

''You have a death wish?'' The question seemed ripped from his soul.

''Not anymore,'' she swore. ''That's what frightens me so much. I didn't used to care if I lived or died. I only cared about vengeance and seeing Gregory brought to justice. Nothing and nobody ever tempted me to veer from a path of self-destruction.''

Kyle finally realized what she was telling him. ''Until me,'' he injected gruffly.

''Until you,'' she answered softly, her gaze locking

again with his. "You made me care again. You made me start thinking of a future and the possibility of a real, normal life. You made me feel things I didn't want to feel. It…scares me."

Her honesty and vulnerability stole the rest of the anger from Kyle, leaving him just as vulnerable. He unclenched his fists and took the steps that brought her within reach. Then he cupped her head in his hands, tilting it upward and forcing her to lock gazes with him.

"Do you care? Really care about more than the great sex?" he asked, his thumbs stroking the softness of her cheeks.

"Yes," she whispered softly.

He closed his eyes, and then reopened them. He wasn't ready to proclaim his everlasting love, nor was he ready to let her go. "I think we've got something special going, and we should give it a chance."

Rianna's expression went from vulnerable to incredibly sad. "I don't see how," she insisted. "I've been on this crusade to punish Gregory for too long to let it go now. My life can never be my own. Even if he's found guilty and put behind bars, there will be years and years of appeals."

He could feel her pain and disillusionment as she continued to bare her heart.

"He'll still want me dead, and he'll still have the wealth and power to have me hunted. I'll never be completely safe, and I'd never ask anyone I care about to live that kind of life. I saw what it did to my parents. I couldn't bear having it happen all over again."

Kyle finally cut off the flow of words with a kiss. He hadn't planned to kiss her, but he didn't know any other way to stop the outpouring of worry and fear. He understood her concerns now, but they'd find a way.

"If we let him destroy our relationship, then he wins," he told her, nibbling on her lips. He felt her sharp intake of breath and knew she understood. "He's been controlling your life for too long," he added. "It stops here. You're not the only one who wants him to pay for his crimes. It's us against him."

With that, he dipped his head.

Rianna wrapped her arms around him and leaned into his kiss. Their mouths locked, tongues searching, soothing, and then demanding. In a matter of seconds, heat exploded between them, but she suddenly pulled away.

"There's something else."

Kyle knew by her tone and expression that he wasn't going to like it.

"I was wrong to run today, but I'm right about you going home. You need to take care of things in Texas, or Gregory will have succeeded in destroying that, too."

"The insurance company can handle the details," he argued, not voicing his own concerns.

"We need some distance between us for a while."

He wanted to argue, but she pressed a finger against his lips. "Please," she coaxed.

Kyle nodded, and she continued.

"The psychologists warned me about becoming too dependent on anyone who helped me escape the undercover work. I know what we have is much stronger than that, but I'll never be sure unless we give it some time and distance."

"That's bull," he grumbled. "How we met isn't what counts. It's how we feel now."

"I know, but I'm going to be trapped in a safe house

with round-the-clock guards for the next few weeks. I don't want you to be forced to live that way.''

''You think I'll resent having to spend time with you? That makes me pretty shallow, doesn't it? Sounds like you just want to be rid of me while you reevaluate our relationship.''

''I didn't mean it that way,'' she said on a sigh. ''It's just not practical for you to go into hiding when you could be taking care of things at home. The agency will give you protection if you want, but Donald doesn't want me that far from D.C.''

''You've talked to him and he's suggesting we don't see each other again until after Haroldson's trial?''

''He thinks it's the safest thing to do at this point.''

Her lips found the pulse at his throat. When she sucked at his flesh, he drew in a breath and his body started to sing with anticipation. A rush of possessiveness nearly brought him to his knees. No other woman had ever given him so much or claimed so much of his soul. Her virginal innocence combined with her innate sensuality made him feel humble and needy.

''Maybe we can manage to rendezvous every once in a while, providing you're interested,'' she whispered.

Interested? He'd have to be dead not to be interested, but he had a feeling it wasn't going to happen.

Swinging her into his arms, he carried her to the bed, and then fell on it with her. He locked his arms around her and moaned with delight as she held on just as tightly. Everything else could wait until he'd found a physical release for all the pent-up emotion.

Then they could talk logistics.

# Chapter 13

*Paris, France*

Steven studied his image in the mirror. Short, thin, balding and nondescript. That was the real Steven Partoll's reflection, but he never left France without a disguise. In all the years he'd traveled the world, he'd always presented a different, unmemorable facade. Interpol had a photo of him on file, as did the United States Federal Bureau of Investigation, but those images were just two of the many faces he'd used and discarded.

They called him Le Ferret, but he despised the appellation. It sounded more like a rodent than the powerful beast of prey he epitomized. He'd privately called himself Le Parisian, a proud, suitable nickname for a national treasure, he thought, his laughter echoing through the spartan apartment.

This would be his last job, and he'd decided to be himself. The idea was so ingenious that he laughed out loud. Who would ever suspect a mild-mannered, small-time tabloid editor of being a hired murderer? Who'd ever guess he topped Interpol's list of most wanted international hit men?

He planned to retire on the five million Haroldson had promised. The first million had already been deposited in his Swiss account. The rest would be transferred once the hit had been confirmed.

He'd considered taking the million and disappearing. Haroldson was in no position to come after him, he thought smugly, but even professional criminals had reputations to uphold. He planned to retire in a blaze of glory that no one would ever duplicate.

Besides, this would be the ultimate test, a challenge unlike any other. The hit would go down in a U.S. federal courthouse, with metal detectors, armed guards and FBI's finest agents. The job would be his swan song, his pièce de résistance. Others might view it as a suicide mission, but they didn't have his skill and daring.

He was the best, and this job would prove it. He intended to live a long and pampered life with the earnings from this final paycheck. He already had his sights set on a lush plantation in South America. He planned a complete physical transformation with the best plastic surgery money could buy. He'd grow a little opium for pleasure, buy the favors of some beautiful mademoiselles, and thumb his nose at international extradition treaties.

The woman.

He should have killed her years ago outside her family's burning home. He'd recognized her among the horrified bystanders, but it had been too late. He hadn't dared to draw attention to himself at that point, so he'd let her live.

It had been his first job, and he'd done it for a mere pittance. His brow creased at the memory. Haroldson had put a price on each family member's head, so he'd lied and sworn they were all dead.

She'd been a dent in his pride for years, but he'd been given a chance to restore his self-image. This job would prove, once and for all, that no man could match him in courage and cunning.

Viva le Parisian.

## Chapter 14

Margaret Wilding owned an elegant old Victorian home along the craggy shoreline of northern Maine. At seventy years old, she was as weathered as the rocks along the waterfront, but still as strong and sure as the tides. She welcomed Rianna and Special Agent Payne with open arms and a minimum of questions.

After Rianna introduced her bodyguard and briefly outlined the situation, the older woman made them comfortable in her home and treated them like long-lost relatives.

For the next few weeks, the bodyguards came and went in a regular rotation, while the women developed even deeper bonds. Margaret's old house was in serious need of repair that she couldn't afford on her social security income. Rianna sold the jewelry she'd mailed from Somerset to fund a renovation. Then she threw herself into the project, desperate to fill the long hours of waiting and isolation.

When she wasn't working on the house, she spent a lot of time watching the water beat against the rocks and wondering about the purpose of life. She risked an occasional call to Kyle, but their conversations were brief and strained.

Tabone had never been apprehended, so her security was too tight to allow for a romantic rendezvous. She wondered if Kyle had some other less-complicated woman who was willing to warm his bed, but she couldn't find the courage to ask him.

While alone at Margaret's, she kept asking herself what she wanted from life. The answer remained the same.

Kyle Tremont.

She loved him, missed him unbearably, and badly wanted a chance for a normal relationship.

The blistering heat of the Texas sun had faded a bit as autumn progressed, but it still beat down on Kyle's head as he hammered another nail into the roofing shingle. His muscles strained and sweat glistened over his bare torso, but the hot, physically taxing work gave him a satisfaction that little else had these past few weeks.

It had taken a while to get all the insurance claims settled and even longer to get his house back to normal. He'd decided to rebuild it himself, and now the woodshop was nearing completion.

He'd thought the hours of backbreaking work would help keep his mind off Rianna, but he'd been wrong. Images of her filled his thoughts daily, sometimes hourly—her sweet, tantalizing smile, her sexy confidence and her iron determination to see justice served.

His isolated lifestyle no longer appealed. He ate because he needed strength, but he didn't enjoy much of anything. His sleep was restless, at best. His body yearned for its mate. The occasional phone calls just intensified his need for a more permanent arrangement.

The damage to his personal property hadn't been that devastating. Things just weren't important. He couldn't work up much enthusiasm for his business, though he'd tried to bully himself into caring.

He missed her more than he'd ever thought possible. He loved her, and it was his first experience with the deathless, aching kind of love he suffered. He'd cared deeply for Margie, but even those emotions seemed mild compared to the depth of feeling he had for Rianna.

He wasn't coping very well, and he wondered how she was dealing with the situation. Had she decided they had something worth fighting for or that he was just a means to an end? Now that her quest for justice would soon be complete, would she want independence more than commitment?

After weeks of slow, painstaking construction, he should be excited about the progress of his new workshop, but he couldn't think much beyond the progress of Haroldson's legal case. It was nearing time for the case to go to trial.

He still hadn't told her how much he loved her. Kyle asked himself why, as he lay in bed and ached for her. He'd been slow to recognize the emotion, slow to put a name to the feelings he experienced every time she smiled or spoke or made love to her.

He was in regular contact with the assistant U.S. attorney in charge of the case, availing himself for interviews and volunteering to back up Rianna's testimony. He'd submitted a detailed case report and undergone a lie-detector test.

She might not want him involved, but he was already in, heart-and-soul deep. He didn't trust Uncle Sam's best to protect her once she appeared in court. Her identity and location would be compromised by then, her every move monitored.

Kyle planned to do some monitoring of his own.

National and international news had been slow, so the media created a circus around the Haroldson case. Reporters for every major news operation had probed for details on the affluent banker and the undercover operative who'd posed as his fiancée. Rumors were rampant, though most remained unsubstantiated.

It was the stuff of TV movies and best-selling novels, so everyone and his brother wanted a piece of the action. Sullivan managed to get background checks on each reporter and photographer that was granted access to the courtroom. Security was especially tight, but Kyle had no trouble getting preferential clearance.

As the courtroom started filling for the first day of the trial, Kyle, Sullivan and a team of other agents watched each attendee as he or she passed through the door. They made sure every face was recorded on camera and mentally cataloged every man and woman who entered the room.

When the judge took his seat behind the bench, Kyle took his a row behind the railing that separated the galley from the prosecution table.

Rianna wasn't let into the room until everyone else had been seated. She'd reverted to her undercover disguise with platinum blond hair and blue eyes. She wore a demure blue suit with a plain white blouse, and looked like one classy lady.

Kyle feasted on the sight of her, absorbing every

nuance of her voice and re-exploring every beloved feature. She only allowed her gaze to meet his once, albeit briefly, but the awareness of each other's presence throbbed strongly between them. It was an emotional connection that he couldn't have described if his life depended on it.

His presence symbolized his support. He wanted her to be one hundred percent sure of him. He nearly burst with pride as she took the stand, and then answered hour after hour of questions in a calm, professional manner.

Her voice remained clear and firm as she related the personal tragedy she'd experienced and then the aspects of the case she'd been professionally assigned. For every accusation she made, the AUSA presented evidence to back it up. There were computer files, ledgers, videos and tape-recorded conversations between Haroldson and his staff. There were bank records, and evidence of money laundering in a six-state radius.

It didn't take a genius to realize she had the jury in the palm of her hand by the end of the morning session. A couple of jurors blinked tears from their eyes, while other expressions ranged from shock to outright horror. The looks they sent Haroldson were telling.

As much as he preferred to keep his attention on the government's primary witness, Kyle couldn't afford to watch her for very long. He listened intently, but kept his gaze roaming the room, searching each face and then searching his memory for any connection with Haroldson.

Despite Sullivan's efforts to minimize the risks, there were still too many strangers in the courtroom with too many cameras and too much high-tech equipment.

During the break for lunch, he and Sullivan compared notes. "Are you having the courtroom checked?" he asked Sullivan when the two of them met in the outer hallway.

"We're running metal detectors over every inch of it, every time we get the chance."

"Someone could use a plastic explosive."

"Which would kill Haroldson, too, and have a whole host of law enforcement agencies out for vengeance. Not to mention the media."

"You don't think Haroldson has associates who'd like to see him dead?" asked Kyle, his gaze perusing the throngs milling in the hallway.

"I'm sure there are plenty, but probably none stupid enough to pull off a hit in a federal courtroom. Still, we have dogs searching for anything out of the ordinary."

"Good," said Kyle. Then he changed the subject. "How's Rianna?"

"You mean our Mary?" asked Sullivan.

"I mean your star witness," came his terse reply. "I want to talk to her."

Sullivan raised his brows and stared at him for a minute. "I'll see what I can do, but only if she agrees."

"After court today?"

The deputy director hedged. "That might not be a good idea. Everybody who makes contact with her increases the danger. You know that."

Kyle would protect her with his life. He wouldn't let anyone hurt her, but he needed to see her and get close to her. Then he'd know if her feelings had changed.

"How long do you expect the trial to last?"

"At first, Haroldson's lawyers were in a big rush to go to trial in hopes of having the charges dropped or the case dismissed. Our case is too airtight for that.

Next, they'll try to discredit Rianna. Failing that, my guess is they'll try to lay the blame on one of Haroldson's other employees.''

Another agent poked his head out the door and gave them the all-clear to return to the courtroom. They had repeated their scrutiny of everybody that entered with each new session.

''By the way,'' Sullivan mumbled to him. ''The code word is *dive*. If you see anything out of the ordinary, yell the word *dive* and Rianna knows to duck for cover.''

''Will do.''


''Tremont wants to see you,'' Donald told Rianna later that evening.

She'd moved from Maine to a safe house in D.C. for the duration of the trial, and he shared dinner with her.

Her breath faltered at the mention of Kyle's name. Seeing him in the courtroom had stirred a longing in her that wouldn't be appeased. Just one look at him had nearly been her undoing. She ached to talk to him, touch him and feel his arms around her. It had been weeks since they'd been together, but it felt like an eternity.

''I was a little surprised to see him there. He never told me he planned to attend.''

She felt Donald's gaze on her face, but couldn't quite meet his eyes. Her emotions were too raw where Kyle was concerned, so she continued to pick at her food.

''He's not the sort of man you can easily dismiss. Nor is he one to wimp out of a difficult situation. He cares a great deal for you.''

She hoped so. Dear heaven, she hoped he cared enough to wait for her and accept whatever lifestyle she might be forced to endure. His presence in the courtroom had given her spirits a much-needed lift. His silent offer of support had boosted her courage. She desperately wanted him in her future, but he'd never mentioned marriage. Maybe he wasn't sure enough of his feelings for her. The idea scared her almost as badly as did loving him.

"Did he say how long he was staying? Where? Or how he thought the trial went today?"

"He's staying as long as it takes, and I think he's bunking down at Special Agent Payne's apartment. The two of them have gotten chummy since they met at the cabin."

Rianna smiled faintly. The young agent had probably kept him apprised of the activity at Margaret's house. Payne wouldn't have given away any secrets, but he still could have shared information.

"I told him he could come here for a few minutes when Payne goes off duty."

Her heart raced at the suggestion, but she quickly controlled the excitement. As badly as she wanted to see him, she couldn't risk having her concentration shattered right now. She didn't dare give Gregory and his high-priced vultures an edge. His defense team would be after blood.

Their discussion was interrupted when the doorbell rang, followed by a knock. Donald told her to sit tight while he coordinated the changing of guard shifts. She heard the door opening and the hum of male conversation.

Restless and on edge, she cleared the table and filled the dishwasher. With her back turned to the kitchen door, she felt him before she saw him. The fine hairs on her neck tingled with awareness.

"Rianna."

Kyle's deep voice washed over her like the warmest of caresses. She closed her eyes and let the pleasure seep into her body. Nothing would please her more than to succumb to the comfort she knew she could find in his arms, but she forced herself to stay calm and controlled.

Turning, she gave him a smile, but she didn't cross the room to greet him or throw herself into his arms the way she wanted to do. A table and chairs, plus a whole lot of insecurity separated them.

"It's good to see you, Tremont."

His eyes narrowed and his jaw went taut. Rianna knew her lack of enthusiasm probably confused him, but she couldn't let her personal emotions distract her right now.

"Seems our relationship has seriously deteriorated if I'm back to being Tremont," he said.

"Do we still have a relationship?" she asked.

"I'm here, aren't I?"

"Yes, but we've been apart a long time." She nervously twisted a dishcloth in her hands. "I thought you might have someone else in your life now."

"There's no one else in my life or my bed, if that's what you really want to know. I'm not that superficial, and we have unfinished business between us."

Relief rushed through Rianna. She'd secretly feared he would tell her he wasn't interested anymore.

"We need privacy and some uninterrupted time to work things out. I just want to keep our relationship totally separate from all the ugliness of the trial. Does that make any sense?"

She watched some of the tension drain from Kyle. He nodded in acceptance. "We've waited a long time to put an end to Haroldson's reign of terror. It'll be over soon, and then we can discuss the future."

Neither his expression nor his tone gave her a hint at what he was feeling, but she was content to know he didn't plan to disappear once Haroldson had been convicted.

"Sullivan says we can get you out of the courtroom as soon as you're done testifying."

"No." She shook her head. "I don't want to miss any of it. I need to hear what the other witnesses have to say."

"You can always read the court transcripts. I'm not sure it's safe for you to be there unless you're testifying."

"What can possibly go wrong in a federal courthouse?" she asked. "I know you and Donald are doing everything humanly possible to keep it safe, and I can't think of anyone I'd rather have on my side. I'm not afraid." Her tone was more dismissive than she intended.

"Good." Kyle studied her for another long moment and then turned to go. "I'll see you in court."

It was hard to watch him leave, but Rianna knew it was for the best. At least, for now.

Kyle's skin crawled the next day as the judge pounded the gavel on his bench and started the proceedings. He had that prickly feeling he always got when something was dangerously wrong. Adrenaline surged through him as he scoured the courtroom for anything or anyone that seemed out of place.

He hadn't slept much last night. Seeing Rianna, yet

not being able to touch her had kept him too keyed up to rest. She hadn't given him much of a clue about her feelings, but at least she hadn't sent him packing. That meant there was hope. He just had to be patient until this damnable trial was over.

Most of the faces in the courtroom were the same as yesterday with a few variations of paparazzi. He knew Sullivan had checked and rechecked every person, but he couldn't shake the feeling that something sinister was present today.

Rianna took the stand again in the morning session for the cross-examination. Today, she wore a simple black dress that made her look cool and elegant. Coupled with the blond hair, she looked fragile, yet she continued to impress him and everyone else with her professionalism.

Haroldson's high-priced legal team was good, but they couldn't shake her unfaltering conviction that he was guilty on all charges. The only time her control wavered was when the lead defense attorney, Robert Fenton, started to badger her about her family.

"You were very young when your father worked for Mr. Haroldson, isn't that correct?"

"I was ten when my dad went to work for Haroldson, and he worked for him nearly two years."

Fenton, a distinguished, silver-haired man of sixty, continued in a pleasant, noncombative tone. "How would you describe your life during those two years? Pleasant? Your family prosperous?"

A small frown creased Rianna's brow. Kyle knew she was wondering where the questioning might lead. So was everyone else in the courtroom.

"I'm not sure what you mean," she replied. "I always thought we were a normal family. My father went to work on weekdays. My mother worked part-time at a grocery store. My brother and I went to school.''

"Would you say that your quality of life continually improved while your father was in Mr. Haroldson's employ?''

"Improved how?'' asked Rianna.

"Isn't it true that you moved into a nice new home, that your dad bought a new car, you got to buy a lot of pretty new clothes, and your family was generally more prosperous?''

"I think my dad was pleased with his salary, if that's what you mean.''

"What I mean is that your dad was spending more money than could be justified by his salary,'' said Fenton.

The AUSA protested. "Objection, Your Honor. I don't see the relevance.''

The judge looked pointedly at Fenton.

"We intend to prove that Ms. Sullivan's testimony is tainted by her personal vendetta against my client.''

"That's a lie!'' insisted Rianna.

Fenton didn't hesitate, but turned his attention to the jurors. "In order to defend my client, I have to prove that Ms. Sullivan's testimony is prejudiced. My client terminated her father's employment rather than file criminal charges against him, but she was too young to understand.''

"Objection, Your Honor!'' said the AUSA. "Mr. Winthrop is not on trial here.''

"That's a twisted pack of lies.'' Rianna's heated accusation had the courtroom stirring with whispers and the judge pounding his gavel for quiet.

Kyle wanted to rip Fenton's throat out for deliberately baiting Rianna, jabbing at her tender recollections of her family, and attacking her where she was most vulnerable. He didn't like seeing her upset, and he wanted to strangle the arrogant defense lawyer. He willed her strength, and noticed that her spine stiffened and her chin hiked higher.

The ploy to rattle her backfired. When he glanced at the jury, he noticed that most of the jurors were glaring angrily at Fenton. Chalk one up for the good guys. If the legal eagles were smart, they'd get her off the stand instead of trying to discredit her.

Fenton and the AUSA spent a minute arguing with the judge, but then Fenton was allowed to continue.

He spoke directly to the jurors, his tone sympathetic. "Ms. Sullivan was only a youngster at the time. She can't be faulted for seeing Mr. Haroldson as the villain."

"The authorities brought charges against him," Rianna interjected in a tight voice.

Fenton turned back to her. "They were dropped as soon as another employee confessed."

"Which would have cleared my father, as well."

"We have no way of proving his innocence. This court, on the other hand, has the trusted word of an honorable man and a highly respected citizen."

Kyle glanced at Haroldson. His demeanor throughout the trial had remained cool and confident, but his eyes narrowed slightly when Rianna turned to stare at him. It was the first time she'd made eye contact with anyone other than the attorneys, so all eyes were on her. No man is his right mind could misunderstand the warning glint. She was getting more furious by the minute, so much so that Haroldson actually frowned.

"I wouldn't rely too heavily on your client's honor," she insisted, her voice holding a veiled threat.

"There was more than financial misconduct that sent my dad to the authorities."

"Don't believe a word she says!" shouted Haroldson. He shocked the courtroom by jumping to his feet and waving a threatening hand toward Rianna. "She'll do or say anything to protect her father's name."

The judge pounded his gavel again, quieting the stir of sensation caused by the unexpected outburst. Fenton moved swiftly to his client's side and urged him to sit down. They exchanged fierce whispers, and Fenton requested an extra few minutes to confer with his client.

Kyle had never seen Haroldson sweat, but he was sweating now. His expression was tight, his demeanor visibly agitated as he exchanged heated whispers with his attorney.

What did Rianna know that could shatter his smooth, practiced calm? It had to be something deeply personal, something that would permanently mar his public image, something that Haroldson feared even worse than the criminal charges against him.

While the defense team huddled around their client, Kyle took another slow look around the courtroom. The faces were mostly the same as yesterday, with a couple of exceptions. Sullivan had identified one of the new faces as Haroldson's sister. She sat on the defense side of the aisle. He knew she'd been subpoenaed to testify.

Another unfamiliar face was that of a tabloid editor from France. He was seated a couple of rows behind the defense table. As Kyle watched, the pale, thin man took a camera out of his case and began fiddling with the dials on it.

Something about the way the man handled the camera made Kyle tense. He watched as a small zoom lens began to protrude from the casing. The shape reminded him too much of a gun barrel.

At first, the editor had the lens pointed straight at Haroldson, but then he slowly angled it above his head and directed it toward the witness seat. All the fine hairs on Kyle's body stood on end.

Everything seemed to move in slow motion after that. Fenton declared his cross-examination finished, shocking everyone in the courtroom. The judge excused Rianna, but she was still bent on vengeance.

"What's the matter, Gregory?" she taunted. "Are you afraid I might mention the main reason my dad left your employ? That he caught you trying to molest his daughter?"

"You lying bitch!" Haroldson yelled, charging to his feet again.

Kyle watched in shock as Haroldson's head seemed to explode and his body crumpled.

"Dive!" he shouted, leaping to his feet and over the railing. He saw a second bullet shatter the wood of the witness seat, missing Rianna's head by inches as she dropped to the floor. Panic that he couldn't reach her in time had his heart pounding riotously.

All hell broke loose as he dove to cover her body with his own. He draped his arms over her head and buried his face in her hair, shielding her as much as possible as he dragged her under the prosecution table.

The courtroom erupted into pandemonium. Screams split the air along with loud shouts and a roar of mass confusion. Bodies were thudding against bodies in the rush to get out of the way. Kyle knew the guards at the door would be no match for the stampeding mob.

People fell to the floor all around them, some crouching under the same table. He stayed put, reas-

sured by the feel of Rianna beneath him. Her heart
pounded against his, the warmth of her permeating his
clothes.

"Clear the room, but nobody leaves the building!"
Sullivan's voice rose above the din. "I want all exits
locked and guarded. Find a short bald guy with a dark
gray suit."

Good, thought Kyle. They had an ID on the shooter.
He'd made his getaway, but he'd never get out of the
building. Sullivan's team had planned for every eventuality, and men were posted throughout the courthouse.

"Get the paramedics in here, and a forensic team."
Sullivan continued to issue orders, and they could hear
men scrambling to obey them.

Kyle listened, his heart racing, his body folded
around Rianna's, until some sounds of normalcy returned. He didn't start to relax until the AUSA and his
assistant rose from the floor. Once the room had been
cleared, he finally moved his arms and spoke softly to
Rianna.

"You okay?"

Her voice came in a puff of breathlessness. "You're
squishing me."

Relief rolled over him like an avalanche, making his
limbs tremble. Her gentle complaint was music to his
ears. He propped his weight on his forearms, and slid
lower until they were face to face, nose to nose. Then
he just stared at her for a minute, savoring every feature.

"Sorry." He hadn't meant to crush her.

"No," Rianna said swiftly. She wiggled until she
freed her hands, and brought them up to his face. "No,
I'm the one who's sorry," she whispered, her heart in

her eyes. "I'm so sorry I dragged you into this ugly mess."

Her touch sent heat coursing through him. Her words brought an ache to his chest. She shouldn't be apologizing for circumstances she had no way of controlling.

Right now there were more important personal things to deal with. He had so much emotion to express. There was so much to say, there were so many things crowding his mind. Things he should have said, but hadn't. Important things, life-altering things, all cluttering his thinking, quivering through his limbs and clogging his throat.

"I love you" was the only part of the turmoil he could verbalize.

He watched her beautiful eyes fill with tears, but the moisture didn't blur the love shining through. He felt it to the depth of his soul. Her response was little more than a whisper.

"I love you more."

"Impossible," he insisted huskily. "Kiss me." He needed the contact, the reassurance and the intimacy.

Their mouths met in a slow, sweet coupling that expressed hearts full of yearning. Kyle didn't want it to end. He wanted to keep her locked to him for all time, to feel her warmth and femininity, her generous heart beating against his own.

But they were rudely interrupted. "Hey, you two okay?"

They broke off the kiss and turned toward the voice. Sullivan had crouched beside the table. His grim expression softened a little when he saw them.

"We're fine." Rianna's reply was soft but sure.

Kyle cleared his throat. "I guess it's safe to surface?"

"Yeah, but it's not pretty."

The deputy director shifted out of sight again. Kyle reluctantly rolled off Rianna, then helped her crawl from beneath the table and stand. As soon as he saw what was left of Haroldson, he took her in his arms and pressed her face to his chest.

"What the hell happened?" he asked Sullivan.

"Apparently it was a hired hit man, and a damn good one. I don't know how the hell he got a gun in here, but I plan to get some answers if I have to personally beat 'em out of that lowlife."

"I saw the Frenchman pull out a camera. The gun must have been modified to fit in the casing."

"Well, it didn't impair the accuracy. If Haroldson hadn't lunged to his feet, the first bullet would have taken out Mary. Your warning and her quick reflexes saved her from the second one."

Rianna made a soft sound, and Kyle tightened his arms around her, folding her closer.

"Did you get the shooter?"

"Yeah, I just got word that he's in custody. He ditched the camera, but we'll find it."

"You need help?"

"We'll be fine. Why don't you two head to my apartment? I'll be there as soon as I have some answers."

## Chapter 15

As soon as Kyle and Rianna closed the apartment door behind them, he ordered her to stay put and began a thorough check of the premises.

By the time he returned to the dimly lit foyer, she'd kicked off her shoes and tossed aside the blond wig. Her own hair felt limp. She fluffed it with her fingers, and then reached for the buttons of her dress.

Kyle approached slowly, his gaze raking her from head to toe, his expression going so dark and hungry that it made her heart pound. She loved him so much that she ached with it.

"Oh, no you don't, beautiful," he scolded, grabbing her hands to halt her stripping. He brought her fingers to his mouth and kissed them gently. "We're not rushing. As bad as I need you, we're not making love here. I want you naked in bed, where I can feel every inch of you against every inch of me."

Rianna had her own ideas about which of them

should be in control. The look in his eyes made her
shiver with excitement. The touch of his lips spread
warmth throughout her body. She wanted him, here and
now.

Wrapping her arms around his neck, she drew him
close. Then she looped a nylon-clad leg around his
thigh and pulled him even closer. Their bodies pressed
together in one slow, fluid move, every male angle burrowing into every feminine curve. Her blood heated at
the feel of his hard, hot body.

Kyle slapped his hands against the door on either
side of her head and leaned down to steal a kiss. But
one was never enough between them. Each long,
searching kiss slipped into another, and another, until
they were moaning and writhing against each other.

"Bed," he insisted, dragging his mouth from hers.
He crushed her against the door while his hands cupped
her face. His eyes were turbulent with emotion—love,
desire, and a need so fierce that it wiped all thought of
resistance from Rianna's mind.

"My room's the one on the other side of the
kitchen," she whispered, nibbling on the strong line of
his jaw.

He swept her into his arms. "I know," he admitted
gruffly. "I smelled you there."

Rianna trembled and held him tighter. She could
never get enough of him. She loved his sensitivity, the
sound of his voice, the strength and feel of his body,
even his macho protectiveness. She loved the intensity
of his desire for her. In that, they were well matched.
She needed him just as desperately.

Kyle laid her on the bed and followed her down,
pressing his body against hers while he cradled her
head in his palms. His kiss was slow and deep and

sweet. Rianna understood his need for reassurance. As badly as they wanted to make love, they didn't want to be parted long enough to rid themselves of clothes. They'd already spent too much time in forced separation.

When he finally ended the kiss, he leaned back far enough for their gazes to meet. The naked vulnerability in his eyes made her muscles turn to mush.

"Say the words again," he coaxed gruffly.

She knew what he wanted to hear. "I love you," she whispered, her throat going tight as she saw the way her admission affected him. He closed his eyes, but not before she saw the depth of his response.

"I love you," she repeated, feathering kisses over his face. "Now and forever. More than I ever thought it was possible to love anyone. More than I thought I had the courage to give."

"I love you that way, too," he declared in a voice rough with emotion. "I want you to be my wife. I want a lifetime to explore this love. What do you think?"

"Marriage—" Rianna faltered over the word. As much as she loved him, she hadn't dared to dream about marriage. He'd never so much as hinted at that type of permanency.

"When? Where? How? What about the case? Even though Gregory is dead, Donald will still need me to testify against the others."

"We can be married whenever and wherever you want. I'd rather it be soon, but we can work around the trials. Your life shouldn't be in jeopardy, so you don't have to be a slave to the system. Marry me," he reiterated.

Rianna badly wanted to believe. "You're sure? I

don't know anything about sustaining long-term relationships. What if I'm a terrible failure at it?''

Kyle's slow smile helped to ease her small spurt of panic. The confidence in his expression boosted hers.

''I don't have any experience, either,'' he confessed, sliding his hands down her throat to the open neck of her dress. He caressed the tender flesh, but his gaze stayed riveted to hers. ''My folks were far from role models when it came to marriage, and I never put much effort into other relationships. But if you love me half as much as I love you, we can make it work. Nothing is impossible if we're together.''

Rianna went limp under his caressing hands. ''We're a helluva team, aren't we?'' she whispered, her eyes filling with tears of joy.

''Perfect partners,'' he murmured as he slid down her body and began to re-acquaint himself with much-adored territory. ''How about it? Willing to trust me with your future?''

''With my life,'' she returned softly. ''My life, my heart, my soul.''

''Your body?'' Kyle teased, nuzzling her breasts.

Rianna laughed, tugged at his hair, and then set about convincing him just how much she trusted him.

Six hours and a lot of loving later, they were cuddled on the Sullivans' living room sofa. Donald had just stunned them with the news that the state had accepted Rudy's plea bargain. Tabone had been arrested and was expected to plea, as well.

The hit man refused to say anything, but the evidence against him was damning.

''You took a huge risk with that accusation you hurled at Haroldson,'' chided Donald.

"I know, but he made me furious. I would have kept his dirty little secret if he hadn't tried to save himself by tarnishing my dad's name."

"Apparently, Haroldson didn't care that the world might think him a murderer and a thief, but he couldn't bear the thought of being considered a sexual pervert," said Kyle.

"In his twisted mind, murder and fraud were all a part of a successful man's rise to power," said Donald. "Anything was acceptable when it came to prestige, but he knew that a child molester is considered the lowest form of life, even in prison. Whatever his psychological hang-ups, I'm glad the man's gone. All his army of thugs will run like rats."

"It's finally over," whispered Rianna. A chill raced down her spine, but the warmth of Kyle's embrace swiftly comforted her.

"For the most part," Donald agreed. "You may still be called to testify, but your safety shouldn't be an issue."

"It's time to put it behind me and get on with my life."

"Amen," said Donald. "Have any idea what that means in terms of your job?"

"She'll be moving to Texas," said Kyle.

Donald frowned. "What do you mean, moving?"

Rianna laughed softly. "He's not suggesting anything immoral," she teased. "He's asked me to be his wife, and I've agreed. I'll need someone to give me away and some help organizing a small wedding."

"A small wedding that can be organized in a couple of weeks," added Kyle.

"Sophie'll have heart failure," said Donald, grinning widely. "She'll want the whole shebang with bridesmaids and tuxedos and towering wedding cakes. I think she's already made some plans.''

Rianna and Kyle both shook their heads, then looked into each other's eyes for a minute that stretched into two and then longer.

Donald finally cleared his throat to regain their attention. ''I'll let you work out the details. If you want to get married right away, we can pull it off somehow.''

''Do you think you could check about getting me a position in the El Paso field office?''

''I think that can probably be arranged, but it might take some time.''

''Good,'' said Kyle. ''We're thinking about a very long honeymoon.''

Donald chuckled and bade them a good night.

Rianna turned into Kyle's arms and snuggled closer. She loved the warm, solid feel of him. She couldn't get enough of him. He seemed to feel the same way, and she couldn't remember ever being happier.

It had taken her more than a decade, but she'd finally accomplished two very important objectives in life. She'd revealed Gregory Haroldson for the murderous criminal she knew him to be, finishing the job her dad had started. And as a bonus, she'd found Kyle, her protector, lover and soul mate.

''What's on your mind?'' asked Kyle. ''You've gotten awful quiet.''

He used his nose to stroke the sensitive underside of her chin, and Rianna arched her neck, granting him better access.

''I was just thinking about how lucky I am,'' she said. Then she murmured her approval of his caresses. Goose bumps shivered down her back as he nibbled at her throat. All he had to do was touch her, and she quivered with need.

"Luck had nothing to do with it," he argued. "Years of hard work and dedication are what got the job done."

Rianna smiled and slid her mouth over his jaw. "I wasn't talking about Gregory. He's out of my life forever. He's part of my past, and I refuse to allow him to clutter my thoughts anymore."

"Sounds good to me," he agreed, his tongue flicking out to bathe her lips. "I wouldn't care if I never heard his name again, either. He's history."

"Right," she mumbled, all thoughts of anyone but Kyle sliding from her mind.

She wanted more kisses. He tasted so good, and felt so hot. Her endless need for him would have been worrisome if it weren't being totally reciprocated. She no longer harbored any doubts about that fact. What Kyle couldn't put into words, he'd expressed with his touch. She'd never felt so loved.

He shifted until he lay flat on the sofa with her on top of him. His hands roamed slowly along her back and thighs. Their bodies were perfectly aligned, perfectly attuned.

"So why are you feeling lucky?" he asked.

"You," she murmured against his mouth. "Just you."

\*   \*   \*   \*   \*

# *Intimate*®

6 Brand New Stories Each Month

*Adventure, suspense, melodrama, glamour*

Harlequin Mills & Boon®

# LUNA

# The new face of fantasy

Powerful women. Captivating worlds. Magical Journeys.
*A world you can only imagine…*

# COMING JUNE 2004

# Send in for a
# FREE BOOK
## today!

How would you like to escape into a world of romance and excitement? A world in which you can experience all the glamour and allure of romance and seduction?

## No purchase necessary - now or ever!

To receive your FREE Harlequin Mills & Boon romance novel simply fill in the coupon and send it to the address below, together with $1.00 worth of loose postage stamps (80 cents in NZ) to cover postage and handling (please do not send money orders or cheques). There is never any obligation to buy!

**Send to: HARLEQUIN MILLS & BOON FREE BOOK OFFER**
**Aust: Locked Bag 2, Chatswood, NSW, 2067**
**NZ: Private Bag 92122, Auckland, 1020**

Harlequin
Mills & Boon
*Direct to you*

✂ — — — — — — — — — — — — — — — —

Please send me my FREE Harlequin Mills & Boon Sexy romance valued at $5.75 (NZ$6.95). I have included $1.00 worth of loose postage stamps (80 cents in NZ). Please do not stick them to anything.

Name: Mrs / Ms / Miss / Mr: _____

Address: _____

_____ P/Code _____

Daytime Tel. No.: (_____) _____

FBBP03/ZFBBP

This offer is restricted to one free book per coupon. Only original coupons with $1.00 worth of loose postage stamps (80 cents in NZ) will be accepted. Your book may differ from those shown. Offer expires 31st December, 2004 or while stocks last. Offer only available to Australian and NZ residents over 18 years. You may also receive offers from other reputable companies as a result of this application. If you do not wish to share in this opportunity please tick the box. ☐